W9-AGT-189

RANDOM HOUSE

LARGE PRINT

The Man from Beijing

HENNING MANKELL

Translated from the Swedish by Laurie Thompson

RANDOM HOUSE
LARGE PRINT

This is a work of fiction. Names,
characters, places, and incidents either are
the product of the author's imagination or are
used fictitiously. Any resemblance to actual
persons living or dead, events, or locales
is entirely coincidental.

Translation copyright © 2010 by Laurie Thompson

All rights reserved.
Published in the United States of America by
Random House Large Print in association with
Alfred A. Knopf, New York.
Distributed by Random House, Inc., New York.

Cover photograph by Lonny Kalfus/Getty Images
Cover design by John Gall

Originally published in Sweden in slightly different form
as Kinesen by Leopard förlag, Stockholm, in 2008.
Copyright © 2008 by Henning Mankell.
Portions of this work originally appeared in slightly different form
in Asia Literary Review.

The Library of Congress has established a
cataloging-in-publication record for this title.

ISBN: 978-0-7393-7758-1

www.randomhouse.com/largeprint

FIRST LARGE PRINT EDITION

Printed in the United States of America

10 9 8 7 6 5 4 3 2 1

This Large Print Edition published in accord with the standards
of the N.A.V.H.

Contents

CONTENTS

Part 4

PART 1

The Silence (2006)

I, Birgitta Roslin, do solemnly declare that I shall endeavor to the best of my knowledge and in accordance with my conscience to pass judgment without fear or favor, be the accused rich or poor, and according to the laws and statutes of Sweden; never to pervert the law nor to promote wrongdoing on grounds of family connections, friendship, jealousy, malevolence, or fear, nor in response to bribes or gifts or for any other reason of no matter what nature; never to impute guilt where there is innocence, nor innocence where there is guilt. I shall never reveal to those who appear in court, neither before nor after judgment is passed, deliberations that have taken place behind closed doors. As an honest and sincere judge I shall endeavor always to adhere to this solemn oath.

Code of Judicial Procedure, Ch. 4, §11,
Judicial Oath

The Epitaph

1

Frozen snow, severe frost. Midwinter.

Early in January 2006 a lone wolf crosses the unmarked border and enters Sweden from Vauldalen in Norway. A man on a snowmobile thinks he might have glimpsed it just outside Fjällnäs, but the wolf vanishes into the trees heading east before he is able to pinpoint it. In the remote Norwegian Österdalarna Mountains it had discovered a lump of frozen moose carcass, with remnants of meat still clinging to the bones. But that was more than two days ago. It is beginning to feel the pain of hunger and is desperately searching for food.

The wolf is a young male that has set out to find a territory of his own. He continues his way eastward. At Nävjarna, north of Linsell, he finds another moose carcass. For a whole day he stays and eats his fill before resuming his trek east. When he comes to Kårböle he trots over the frozen Ljusnan and then follows the river along its winding route toward the sea. One moonless night he lopes silently over the bridge at Järvsö, then heads into the vast forests that stretch to the coast.

In the early morning of January 13 the wolf reaches Hesjövallen, a tiny village south of Hansesjön Lake in Hälsingland. He pauses and sniffs the air. He detects the smell of blood. He looks around. There are people living in the houses but no smoke rising from the chimneys. His sharp ears can't detect the slightest sound.

But the wolf is in no doubt about the blood. He skulks at the edge of the forest, nose in the air. Then he moves forward, silently, through the snow. The smell comes from one of the houses at the far end of the hamlet. He is vigilant now—with humans around it's essential to be both careful and patient. He pauses again. The smell originates from the back of the house. He waits. Then eventually starts moving once more. When he gets there he finds another carcass. He drags his large meal back to the trees. He has not been discovered, not even the village dogs have stirred. The silence is total this freezing-cold morning.

The wolf starts eating when he comes to the edge of the trees. It is easy, as the flesh has not yet frozen. He is very hungry now. Having pulled off a leather shoe, he starts gnawing away at an ankle.

It snowed during the night but stopped before dawn. As the wolf eats his fill, snowflakes once again start dancing down toward the frozen ground.

2

When Karsten Höglin woke up he remembered dreaming about a photograph. He lay motionless in bed and felt the image returning slowly, as if the negative of his dream were sending a copy into his conscious mind. He recognized the picture. It was black-and-white and depicted a man sitting on an old iron bed, with a hunting rifle hanging on the wall and a chamber pot at his feet. When he saw it for the first time, he had been gripped by the old man's wistful smile. There was something timorous and evasive about him. Much later Karsten had discovered the background. A few years earlier the man had accidentally shot and killed his only son while hunting seabirds. From then on the rifle had never come down from the wall, and the man had become a hermit.

Höglin thought that of all the thousands of photographs and negatives he had seen, this was the one he would never forget. He wished he had taken it himself.

The clock on his bedside table read half past seven. Höglin usually woke up very early, but he had slept badly that night, the bed and its mattress were uncomfortable. He made up his mind to complain about them when he checked out of the hotel.

It was the ninth and final day of his journey. It had been made possible by a scholarship enabling him to study deserted villages and other small settlements that were being depopulated. He had come as far as Hudiksvall and had one hamlet left to photograph. He had chosen this particular one because an old man who lived there had read about his project and sent him a letter. Höglin had been impressed by the letter and decided that this was the place for him to conclude his study.

He got up and opened the curtains. It had snowed during the night and was still gray, the sun not yet risen. A bundled-up woman was cycling past in the street below. Karsten considered her and wondered how cold it was. Negative five degrees Celsius, possibly negative seven.

He dressed and took the slow-moving elevator down to reception. He had parked his car in the enclosed courtyard behind the hotel. It was safe there. Even so, he had taken all his photographic equipment up to his room, as was his practice. His worst nightmare was to come to his car one day and find that all his cameras had vanished.

The receptionist was a young girl, barely out of her teens. He noticed that her makeup was slapdash and gave up on the idea of complaining about the bed. After all, he had no intention of ever returning to the hotel.

In the breakfast room a few guests were absorbed in their morning papers. For a fleeting moment he was tempted to get a camera and take a shot. It gave him the feeling that Sweden had always been exactly like this. Silent people, poring over their newspapers with a cup of coffee, absorbed in their own thoughts, their own fates.

But he resisted the temptation, served himself coffee, buttered two slices of bread, and tucked into a soft-boiled egg. Without a newspaper, he ate quickly. He hated being at a meal on his own without anything to read.

It was colder than he expected when he emerged from the hotel. He stood on tiptoe to read the thermometer in the reception window. Negative eleven degrees. And falling, he suspected. This winter has been far too warm. Here comes the cold spell we've been expecting. He put his cases on the backseat, started the engine, and began scraping ice off the windshield. There was a map on the passenger seat. The previous day, after taking pictures of a village not far from Lake Hassela, he had worked out how to get to his final port of call: take the main road southward, turn off toward Sörforsa near Iggesund, then follow either the east or the west shore of the lake called Storsjön in some parts and Långsjön in others. The guy at the gas station on the way into Hudiksvall had warned him that the east road was bad, but he decided to take it anyway. It would be quicker. And the light was so lovely this winter morning. He could already envisage the smoke rising straight up to the sky from the chimneys.

It took him forty minutes to get there. By then he had already made a wrong turn, a road leading southward to Näcksjö.

Hesjövallen was situated in a little valley by a lake whose name he couldn't recall. Hesjön, maybe? The dense forests extended all the way to the hamlet, on both sides of the narrow road leading up toward Härjedalen.

Karsten stopped at the edge of the tiny village and got out of the car. There were breaks in the clouds now. The light would become more difficult to capture, perhaps not so expressive. He looked around. Everything was very still. The houses gave the impression of having been there since time immemorial. In the distance he could hear the faint noise of traffic on the main road.

He suddenly felt uneasy. He held his breath, as he always did when confronted with something he didn't really understand.

Then it dawned on him—the chimneys, they were cold. There was no sign of smoke, which would have been an effective feature of the photographs he hoped to take. His gaze moved slowly from house to house. Somebody's cleared the snow already, he thought. But not lit a single fire? He remembered the letter he'd received from the man who had told him about the village. He had referred to the chimneys and how the houses seemed, in a childish sort of way, to be sending smoke signals to one another.

He sighed. People don't write the truth, but what

they think you want to read. Now should I take pictures with cold chimneys or abandon the whole business? Nobody was forcing him to take photographs of Hesjövallen and its inhabitants. He already had plenty of pictures of the Sweden that was fading away: the derelict farms, the remote villages whose only hope of survival was that Danes and Germans would buy up the houses and turn them into summer cottages. He decided to leave and returned to his car. But he didn't start the engine. He had come this far; the least he could do was to try to create some portrait of the local inhabitants—he wanted faces. As the years passed, Karsten Höglin had become increasingly fascinated by elderly people. He wanted to compile an album: pictures that would describe the beauty found only in the faces of very old women, their lives and hardships etched into their skin like the sediment in a cliff wall.

He got out of his car again, pulled his fur hat down over his ears, picked out a Leica M6 he'd been using for the past ten years, and made for the nearest of the group of houses. There were ten in all, most of them timber and painted red, some with added stoops. He could see only one modern house. If it could still be called modern, that is—a 1950s detached house. When he came to the gate, he paused and raised his camera. The nameplate indicated that the Andrén family lived there. He took a few shots, varying the aperture setting and exposure time, trying out several angles, though it was clear that there wasn't enough light yet and he would get only an indistinct blur. But you never know. Photographers sometimes expose unexpected secrets.

Höglin was intuitive with his work. Not that he didn't bother to measure light levels when required, but sometimes he'd pull off surprising results without paying attention to carefully calculated exposure times. Improvisation went with the territory.

The gate was stiff. He had to push hard in order to open it. There were no footprints in the newly fallen snow. Still not a sound, not even a dog. It's deserted, he thought. This isn't a village; it's a Flying Dutchman.

He knocked on the front door, waited, then knocked again. Nothing. He began to wonder what was going on. Something was amiss. He knocked again, harder and longer. Then he tried the door handle. Locked. Old people scare easily, he thought. They lock their doors and worry that all the things they read about in the papers are going to happen to them.

He banged on the door. Nothing. He concluded there must not be anybody at home.

He went back through the gate and moved on to the next house. It was starting to get lighter now. The house was painted yellow. The putty around the windows was coming off—it must be very drafty inside. Before knocking he tried the door handle. Locked again. He knocked hard, then began banging away even before anybody could possibly have had time to answer. Once again, empty.

If he went back to his car now, he would be at home in Piteå by early afternoon. That would please his wife. She was convinced that he was too old to be embarking on all these trips, despite the fact that he was only sixty-three. But he had been diagnosed with symptoms of imminent angina. The doctor had advised him to watch what he ate and try to get as much exercise as possible.

One last try. He went around to the back of the house and tried a door that seemed to lead to a utility room behind the kitchen. That was also locked. He went to the nearest window, stood on tiptoe, and looked in. He could see through a gap in the curtains into a room with a television set. He continued to the next window. It was the same room, and he could still see the TV. A tapestry hanging on the wall informed him that JESUS IS YOUR BEST FRIEND. He was about to move on to the next window when something on the floor attracted his attention. At first he thought it was a ball of wool just lying there. Then he saw that it was a woolly sock, and that the sock was on a foot. He stepped back from the window. His heart was pounding. Was that really a foot? He went back to the first window, but he couldn't see as far into the room from there. He went on to the second window. Now he was certain. It really was a foot. A motionless foot. He couldn't be sure if it was a man's or a woman's. The owner of the foot might be sitting in a chair. It was hard to make out—but if so why hadn't the person stirred?

He knocked on the window as hard as he dared, but there was no response. He took out his cell phone and dialed the emergency number. No signal. He ran to the third house and banged on the door. Nothing. He felt like he was in the middle of a nightmare. He picked up a foot scraper, smashed the door lock, and forced his way in. He had to find a telephone. There was an old woman lying on the kitchen floor. Her head was almost totally severed from her neck. Beside her lay the carcass of a dog, cut in two.

Höglin screamed and turned to flee. As he ran through the hall he saw the body of a man sprawled on the floor of the living room, between the table and a red sofa with a white throw. The old man was naked. His back was covered in blood.

Höglin raced out of the house. He couldn't get away fast enough. He dropped his camera when he reached the road but didn't stop to pick it up. He was convinced that somebody or something he couldn't see was about to stab him in the back. He turned his car and sped away.

He stopped when he reached the main road, then dialed the emergency number, his hands shaking uncontrollably. As he raised the phone to his ear, he felt a sharp pain in his chest. It was as if somebody had caught up with him and stabbed him.

He could hear someone speaking to him on the phone, but he was incapable of answering. The pain was so intense that all he could manage was a faint hiss.

"I can't hear you," said a woman's voice.

He tried again. Once more nothing but a faint hiss. He was dying.

"Can you speak a bit louder?" asked the woman. "I don't understand what you're saying."

He made a supreme effort and produced a few words.

"I'm dying," he gasped. "For God's sake, I'm dying. Help me."

"Where are you?"

But the woman received no reply. Karsten Höglin was on his way into the endless darkness. In a desperate attempt to escape from the excruciating pain, like a drowning man trying in vain to rise to the surface, he stepped on the gas. The car shot over to the wrong side of the road. A truck on the way to Hudiksvall carrying office furniture had no chance to avoid a head-on collision. The truck driver jumped down from his cab to check on the driver of the car he had crashed into. Höglin was prostrate over the steering wheel.

The truck driver, from Bosnia, spoke little Swedish.

"How is you?" he asked.

"The village," mumbled Karsten Höglin. "Hesjövallen."

Those were his final words. By the time the police and the ambulance arrived, Karsten Höglin had succumbed to a massive heart attack.

It was not at all clear what had happened. Nobody could possibly have guessed the reason for the sudden heart attack suffered by the man behind the wheel of the dark blue Volvo. It wasn't until Karsten Höglin's body had been taken away and tow trucks were trying to extricate the badly damaged furniture van that a police officer bothered to listen to the Bosnian driver. The officer's name was Erik Huddén, and he didn't like talking to people who spoke bad Swedish unless he was forced to. It was as if their stories were less important if they were unable to articulate them properly. Naturally, the officer began with a Breathalyzer. But the driver was sober, and his driver's license seemed to be in order.

"He tried saying something," said the truck driver.

"What?" Huddén asked dismissively.

"Something about Herö. A place, perhaps?"

Huddén was a local, and shook his head impatiently.

"There's nowhere around here called Herö."

"Maybe I hear wrong? Maybe it was something with an **s**? Maybe Hersjö?"

"Hesjövallen?"

The driver nodded. "Yes, he said that."

"And what did he mean?"

"I don't know. He died."

Huddén put his notebook away. He hadn't written down what the driver said. Half an hour later, when the tow trucks had driven off and another police car had taken the Bosnian driver to the station for more questioning, Huddén got into his car, ready to return to Hudiksvall. He was accompanied by his colleague Leif Ytterström, who was driving.

"Let's go via Hesjövallen," said Huddén out of the blue.

"Why? Has there been an emergency call?"

"I just want to check up on something."

Erik Huddén was the older of the two officers. He was known for being both uncommunicative and stubborn. Ytterström turned off onto the road to Sörforsa. When they came to Hesjövallen Huddén asked him to drive slowly through the village. He still hadn't explained to his colleague why they had made this detour.

"It looks deserted," said Ytterström as they slowly passed house after house.

"Hang on. Go back," said Huddén. "Slowly."

Then he told Ytterström to stop. Something lying in the snow by one of the houses had attracted his attention. He got out of the car and went to investigate. He suddenly stopped dead and drew his gun. Ytterström leaped out of the car and drew his own gun.

"What's going on?"

Huddén didn't reply. He moved cautiously forward. Then he paused again and bent over as if he had suddenly been afflicted by chest pains. When he came back to the car Erik Huddén was white in the face.

"There's a dead man lying there," he said. "He's been beaten to death. And there's something missing."

"What do you mean?"

"One of his legs."

They stood staring at each other without speaking. Then Huddén got into the car and picked up the radio and asked for Vivi Sundberg, who he knew was on duty that day. She responded immediately.

"Erik here. I'm out at Hesjövallen."

"What's happened?"

"I don't know. But there's a man lying dead in the snow."

"Say that again."

"A dead man. In the snow. It looks as if he's been beaten to death. One of his legs is missing."

They knew each other well. Sundberg knew that Erik Huddén would never exaggerate, no matter how incredible what he said seemed to be.

"We'll be there," said Sundberg.

"Get the forensic guys from Gävle."

"Who's with you?"

"Ytterström."

She thought for a moment.

"Is there any plausible explanation for what's happened?"

"I've never seen anything like this before."

He knew she would understand. He had been a police officer for so long that there was no real limit to the suffering and violence he was forced to face up to.

It was thirty-five minutes before they heard sirens approaching in the distance. Huddén had tried to persuade Ytterström to accompany him to the nearest house so that they could talk to the neighbors, but his colleague refused to move until reinforcements arrived. As Huddén was reluctant to enter the house alone, they stayed by the car. They said nothing while they waited.

Vivi Sundberg got out of the first car to pull up beside them. She was a powerfully built woman in her fifties. Those who knew her were well aware that despite her cumbersome body, she was very mobile and possessed considerable stamina. Only a few months earlier she had chased and caught two burglars in their twenties. They had laughed at her as they started to run off. They were no longer laughing when she arrested the pair of them after a chase of a few hundred yards.

Vivi Sundberg had red hair. Four times a year she visited her daughter's hair salon and had the redness reinforced.

She was born on a farm just outside of Harmånger and had looked after her parents until they grew old and eventually died. Then she began educating herself, and after a few years applied to the police college. She was amazed to be accepted. Nobody could explain why she had got in, given the size of her body; but nobody asked any questions, and she said nothing.

Vivi Sundberg was a diligent, hardworking police officer. She was persistent, and outstanding when it came to analyzing and following up on the slightest lead.

She ran a hand through her hair and looked hard at Erik Huddén.

"Well, are you going to show me?"

They walked over to the dead body. Sundberg pulled a face and squatted down. "Has the doctor arrived?"

"She's on her way."

"She?"

"Hugo has a sub. He's going to be operated on. A tumor."

Vivi Sundberg momentarily lost interest in the body lying in the snow. "Is he ill?"

"He has cancer. Didn't you know?"

"No. Where?"

"In his stomach. Apparently it hasn't spread. Anyway, he has a sub from Uppsala. Valentina Miir's her name. If I've pronounced it right."

Huddén shouted to Ytterström, who was drinking coffee by one of the cars. He confirmed that the police doctor would be here at any moment.

Sundberg started examining the body closely. Every time she was confronted by a corpse, she was overcome by the same feeling of pointlessness. She was unable to awaken the dead, the best she could do was to expose the reasons for the crime and send the killer to a prison cell or to an asylum for the mentally ill.

"Somebody has gone berserk," she said. "With a long knife. Or a bayonet. Possibly a sword. I can see at least ten wounds, nearly all of them potentially fatal. But I don't understand the missing leg. Do we know who the man is?"

"Not yet. All the houses appear to be empty."

Sundberg stood up and looked around the village. The houses seemed to return her attentive gaze.

"Have you been knocking on doors?"

"I thought I should wait. Whoever did this might still be around."

"You're right."

She beckoned to Ytterström, who threw his empty cardboard mug into the snow.

"Let's go in," she said. "There must be people around. This isn't a ghost town."

"There's been no sign of anybody."

Sundberg looked again at the houses, the snowed-over gardens, the road. She drew her pistol and set off toward the nearest house; the two men followed. It was a few minutes past eleven.

What the three police officers discovered was unprecedented in the annals of Swedish crime and would become a part of Swedish legal history. There were bodies in every house. Dogs and cats had been stabbed to death, even a parrot had had its head cut off. They found a total of nineteen dead people, all of them elderly except for a boy who must have been about twelve. Some had been killed while asleep in bed; others were lying on the floor or sitting on chairs at the kitchen table. An old woman had died with a comb in her hand, a man by a stove with an over-turned coffee-pot by his side. In one house they found two people locked in an embrace and tied together. All had been subjected to frenzied violence. It was as if a blood-laden hurricane had stormed through the village just as the old people who lived there were getting up. As the elderly in the country tend to rise early, Sundberg assumed the murders had taken place close to sunrise.

Vivi Sundberg felt as if her whole head were being submerged in blood. She shook off her outrage, but felt very cold. It was as if she were viewing the dead disfigured bodies through a telescope, which meant that she didn't need to approach too closely.

And then there was the smell. Although the bodies had barely turned cold, they were already giving off a smell that was both sweet and sour. While inside the houses, Sundberg tried to breathe through her mouth. The moment she stepped outside, she filled her lungs with fresh air. Crossing the threshold of the next house was like preparing to face something almost unbearable.

Everything she saw, one body after another, bore witness to the same frenzy and the same wounds caused by a very sharp weapon. The list she made later that day, which she never revealed to anybody, comprised brief notes on exactly what she had seen:

House number one. Dead elderly man, half naked, ragged pajamas, slippers, half lying on the staircase. Head almost severed from body, the thumb of the left hand three feet away. Dead elderly woman, nightgown, stomach split open, intestines hanging out, false teeth smashed to pieces.

House number two. Dead man and dead woman, both at least eighty. Bodies found in a double bed on the first floor. The woman might have been killed in her sleep with a slash from her left shoulder and through her breast toward her right hip. The man tried to defend himself with a hammer, but one arm severed, throat cut. Remarkably, the bodies have been tied together. Gives the impression that the man was alive when bound but the woman dead. No proof, of course, just an immediate reaction. Young boy dead in a small bedroom. Might have been asleep when killed.

House number three. Lone woman, dead on the kitchen floor. A dog of unknown pedigree stabbed to death by her side. The woman's spine appears to be broken in more than one place.

House number four. Man dead in the hall. Wearing pants, shirt; barefoot. Probably tried to resist. Body almost cut in two through the stomach. Elderly woman sitting dead in the kitchen. Two, possibly three wounds in the top of her head.

House number seven. Two elderly women and an elderly man dead in their beds upstairs. Impression: they were awake, conscious, but had no time to react. Cat stabbed to death in the kitchen.

House number eight. Elderly man lying dead outside, one leg missing. Two dogs beheaded. Woman dead on the stairs, hacked to pieces.

House number nine. Four people dead in the living room on the first floor. Half dressed, with cups of coffee, radio on, station one. Three elderly women, an elderly man. All with their heads on their knees.

House number ten. Two very old people, a man

and a woman, dead in their beds. Impossible to say if they were aware of what was happening.

Toward the end of her list she no longer had the mental strength to record all the details. Nevertheless, what she had seen was unforgettable, a vision of hell itself.

She numbered the houses according to the discovery of the bodies. That was not the same order as their locations along the road. When they came to the fifth house during their macabre inspection, they found signs of life. They could hear music coming from inside the house. Ytterström thought it sounded like Jimi Hendrix.

Before going inside they called in two other officers as backup. They approached the front door—pistols drawn. Huddén banged hard on it. It was opened by a half-naked, long-haired man. He drew back in horror on seeing all the guns. Vivi Sundberg lowered her pistol when she saw he was unarmed.

"Are you alone in the house?"

"My wife's here as well," said the man, his voice shaking.

"Nobody else?"

"No. What's going on?"

Sundberg holstered her pistol and gestured to the others to do the same.

"Let's go inside," she said to the half-naked man, who was shivering with cold. "What's your name?"

"Tom."

"Anything else?"

"Hansson."

"Come on, Tom Hansson, let's go inside. Out of the cold."

The music was at full volume. Sundberg had the impression there were speakers in every room. She followed the man into a cluttered living room, where a woman in a nightdress was curled up on a sofa. He turned down the music and put on a pair of pants that had been hanging over a chair back. Hansson and the woman on the sofa were about sixty.

"What's happened?" asked the woman, who, clearly scared, spoke with a broad Stockholm accent. Probably they were hippies left over from the sixties. Sundberg decided not to beat about the bush; there was no time to waste—it was possible that whoever had been responsible for this outrage might be on the way to carry out another massacre.

"Many of your neighbors are dead," Sundberg said. "Horrendous crimes have taken place in this little village overnight. It's important that you answer our questions. What's your name?"

"Ninni," said the woman. "Are Herman and Hilda dead?"

"Where do they live?"

"In the house to the left."

Sundberg nodded.

"Yes, I'm afraid so. They've been murdered. But they're not the only ones."

"If this is your idea of a joke, it's not a very good one," said Tom Hansson.

Sundberg lost her composure briefly.

"I'm sorry, but we only have time for you to answer my questions. I can understand that you think what I'm telling you seems incredible, but it's true— horrific, but true. Did you hear anything last night?"

The man sat down on the sofa beside the woman.

"We were asleep."

"Did you hear anything this morning?"

They both shook their heads.

"Haven't you even noticed that the place is crawling with police officers?"

"When we play music loudly, we don't hear anything."

"When did you last see your neighbors?"

"If you mean Herman and Hilda, yesterday," said Ninni. "We usually run into each other when we go out with the dogs."

"Do you have a dog?"

Tom Hansson nodded in the direction of the kitchen.

"He's pretty old and lazy. He doesn't even bother to get up when we have visitors."

"Didn't he bark during the night?"

"He never barks."

"What time did you see your neighbors?"

"At about three o'clock yesterday afternoon. But only Hilda."

"Did everything seem to be as usual?"

"She had back pains. Herman was probably in the kitchen, solving crosswords. I didn't see him."

"What about the rest of the people in the village?"

"Everything was the same as it always is. Only old people live here. They stay indoors when it's cold. We see them more often in spring and summer."

"There aren't any children here, then?"

"None at all."

Sundberg paused, thinking about the dead boy.

"Is it really true?" asked the woman on the sofa. She was frightened.

"Yes," Sundberg said. "It could well be that everybody in this village is dead. Apart from you."

Huddén was standing by the window.

"Not quite everybody," he said slowly.

"What do you mean?"

"Not quite everybody's dead. There's somebody out there on the road."

Sundberg hurried over to the window and saw a woman standing in the road outside. She was old, wearing a bathrobe and black rubber boots. Her hands were clasped in prayer.

Sundberg held her breath. The woman was motionless.

3

Tom Hansson came up to the window and stood beside Vivi Sundberg.

"It's only Julia," he said. "We sometimes find her outside in the cold without a coat on. Hilda and Herman usually keep an eye on her when the home help isn't here."

"Where does she live?" asked Sundberg.

He pointed at the house next to the last one at the edge of the village.

"When we moved here," he said, "Julia was married. Her husband, Rune, used to drive forestry vehicles, until he burst an artery and died in the cab of his truck. She went a bit odd after that—wandering around with her hands clenched in her pockets, if you see what I mean. I suppose we've always thought she should be able to die here. She has two children who come to see her once a year. They're just waiting for their little inheritance and couldn't care less about her."

Sundberg and Huddén went outside. The woman looked up when Sundberg paused in front of her, but she said nothing. Nor did she protest when Huddén helped to lead her back home. The house was neat and tidy. On one wall were photographs of her dead husband and the two children who didn't care about her.

Sundberg took out her notebook for the first time. Huddén examined a document with official stamps that was lying on the kitchen table.

"Julia Holmgren," he said. "She's eighty-seven."

"Make sure somebody phones the home help service. I don't care what time they normally come to see to her, get them here right now."

The old woman sat at the kitchen table, looking out of the window. Clouds were hanging heavily over the landscape.

"Should we try asking her a few questions?"

Sundberg shook her head.

"There's no point. What could she possibly tell us?"

She nodded at Huddén, indicating that he should leave them alone. He went out to the yard. Sundberg went into the living room, stood in the middle of the floor, and closed her eyes. She tried to come to terms with what had happened.

There was something about the old woman that set bells ringing faintly in the back of Sundberg's mind. But she was unable to pin the thought down. She continued standing there, opened her eyes, and tried to think. What had actually happened that January morning? A number of people murdered in a tiny remote village. Plus several dead pets. Everything pointed toward a wild frenzy. Could a single attacker really have done all this? Had several killers turned up in the middle of the night, then disappeared again after carrying out their brutal massacre? It was too soon to say. Sundberg had no answers, only a set of circumstances and many dead bodies. She had a couple still alive who had withdrawn to this place in the middle of nowhere from Stockholm, years ago. And a senile old woman in the habit of standing in the road wearing only a nightdress.

But there was a starting point, it seemed. Not

everybody in the village was dead. At least three people had survived. Why? Coincidence, or did it have some meaning?

Sundberg stood motionless for a few more minutes. She could see through the window that the forensic team from Gävle had arrived, along with a woman she assumed was the police doctor. She took a deep breath. She was still the one in charge—for the time being, at any rate, but she needed help from Stockholm today.

She pulled out her cell phone and called Robertsson, the district prosecutor, to explain the situation.

Sundberg wondered how he would react. None of us has ever seen anything like this before, she thought.

She went outside, where the two forensic officers and the police doctor were waiting.

"You need to see this for yourselves. We'll start with the man lying outside in the snow. Then we'll go through the houses one by one. You can decide if you'll need extra assistance. It's a very big crime scene."

Sundberg parried their questions. They had to see it all with their own eyes. She led the procession from one macabre scene to the next. When they came to the third house, Lönngren, the senior forensic officer, said he needed to call for reinforcements right now. At the fourth house, the police doctor said the same thing. Calls were made. They continued through the remaining houses and gathered once more on the road. By then the first journalist had arrived. Sundberg told Ytterström to make sure nobody spoke to him. She would do it herself as soon as she had time.

The people standing around her on the snow-covered road were pale and silent. None of them could grasp the implications of what they had just seen.

"Well, that's the way it is," said Sundberg. "Our collective experience and abilities are going to be put to the test. This investigation is going to dominate the mass media, and not only in Sweden. We're going to be under enormous pressure to produce results by tomorrow. At the latest. Let's hope that whoever is responsible for all this has left traces that we can follow to catch him or them pronto. We need to try to remain calm and get help whenever necessary. District Prosecutor Robertsson is on his way here. I want him to see everything for himself, and to take charge of the investigation. Any questions? If not, we need to get down to work."

"I think I have a question," said Lönngren.

He was a short, thin guy. Sundberg considered him a very efficient technician. But his weakness was that he tended to work too slowly for those desperate for answers by yesterday.

"Shoot."

"Is there a risk that this maniac, if that's what he is, might strike again?"

"Yes," said Sundberg. "As we know nothing at all, we have to assume that anything might happen."

"There's going to be panic out there," said Lönn-gren. "For once I'm relieved to live in town."

The group split up just as Sten Robertsson arrived. The reporter who'd been hovering outside the taped-off area immediately closed in on Robertsson as he got out of his car.

"Not now," shouted Sundberg. "You'll have to wait."

"Oh, come on, Vivi! Can't you say anything at all? You're not usually impossible."

"Right now I am."

She disliked the reporter, who worked for **Hudiksvalls Tidning**. He often wrote articles criticizing the way the police worked. What probably irritated her most was that he was often right to criticize.

Robertsson was feeling the cold—his jacket was far too thin. He's vain, was Sundberg's immediate thought.

"So, let's hear all about it," said Robertsson.

"No. Come with me."

For the third time that morning Vivi Sundberg went through the entire crime scene. On two occasions Robertsson was forced to go outside, on the point of throwing up. She waited patiently for him. She wasn't sure he was up to the task. But she also knew that he was the best of the prosecutors currently available.

When they finally arrived back at the road, she suggested that they sit in her car. She had managed to grab a thermos of coffee before leaving the police station.

Robertsson was rattled. His hand holding the mug of coffee was shaking noticeably.

"Have you ever seen anything like that before?" he asked.

"Never."

"Surely nobody but a lunatic could have done this?"

"Who knows? I've asked the forensic guys to call up whatever extra resources they think are appropriate. And the doctor as well."

"Who's she?"

"A sub. This is probably her first crime scene. She's called for help."

"And what about you?"

"What do you mean?"

"What do you need?"

"First and foremost an indication from you if there's anything in particular we should concentrate on. And then we have to bring in the National Investigation Department, of course."

"What should we be concentrating on?"

"You're the one in charge of the investigation, not me."

"All that matters is that we find the bastard who's responsible for this."

"Or bastards. We can't exclude the possibility that there's more than one of them."

"Lunatics don't usually work in teams."

"But we can't exclude the possibility."

"Is there anything we can exclude?"

"No. Nothing. Not even the possibility of it happening again."

Robertsson nodded. They sat lost in thought. People were moving on the road and between the houses. There was an occasional flash from a camera. A tent had been raised over the body discovered in the snow. Several photographers and reporters had arrived. And the first television crew.

"I want you to participate in the first press conference," she said. "I can't cope on my own. And we'll have to hold it today. Later this afternoon."

"Have you spoken with Ludde?"

Tobias Ludwig was the chief of police in Hudiksvall. He was young and had never been a beat cop. He'd studied law, then followed that with a course for future chiefs of police. Neither Sten Robertsson nor Vivi Sundberg liked him. He had little idea of what practical police work entailed and spent most of his time worrying about internal police administration.

"No, I haven't spoken with him," she said. "All he'll do is urge us to be extra careful filling out the paperwork."

"He's not that bad," said Robertsson.

"No, he's worse," said Sundberg. "But I'll call him."

"Do it now."

She called the police station in Hudiksvall, but Tobias Ludwig was on official business in Stockholm.

She asked the switchboard to contact him on his cell phone.

Robertsson was busy talking to the newly arrived forensic officers from Gävle. Sundberg was left standing beside Tom and Ninni Hansson in their yard. The Hanssons had donned their army-issue fur coats and were observing what was happening with interest. Start with those still alive, Vivi Sundberg thought. Tom and Ninni Hansson might have seen something without realizing it.

A killer who decides to eliminate a whole village must have some kind of plan for how to go about it, even if he's totally crazy.

She walked over to the road and looked around. The frozen lake, the forest, the distant mountains with all their peaks and valleys. Where had he come from? she asked herself. I think I can be certain that whoever did this was not a woman. But he, or they, must have come from somewhere, and they must have gone somewhere.

She was just about to go back in through the gate when a car pulled up with one of the dog patrols they had sent for.

"Only one?" she asked, without trying to conceal her irritation.

"Bonzo's not feeling well," said the officer.

"Are you telling me that police dogs can be out sick?"

"Evidently. Where do you want me to start? What's happened?"

"Talk to Huddén."

The officer was about to ask her something else, but she turned her back on him and took Tom and Ninni Hansson back into their house. As they sat down, her cell phone rang.

"I hear you've been trying to contact me," said Tobias Ludwig. "You know I don't like being disturbed when I'm at meetings of the National Police Board."

"I'm afraid that can't be helped on this occasion."

"What's happened?"

"We have several dead bodies in Hesjövallen."

She described the situation briefly. Ludwig didn't say a word. She waited.

"I understand. I'll set off as soon as I can."

Vivi Sundberg glanced at her watch.

"We need to call a press conference," she said. "We'll time it for six o'clock. Until then I'll just say that there's been a murder. I won't reveal how many victims. Come as fast as you can. But don't crash the car."

"I'll see if I can get an emergency car to take me."

"Preferably a helicopter. We're talking about nineteen murdered people, Tobias."

They hung up. The Hanssons had heard every word she said. She could see the disbelief in their faces.

The nightmare was expanding all the time. Reality was a long way off.

She sat down in a chair, having shooed away a sleeping cat.

"Everybody in the village is dead. You two and Julia are the only ones still alive. Even people's pets have been killed. I can understand that you are shocked. We all are. But I have to ask you some questions. Please try to answer as accurately as possible. I also want you to try and think of things I don't ask you about. Even the smallest thing you can remember might be important. Do you understand?"

The response was silent, worried-looking nods. Sundberg decided to tread carefully. She started talking about that morning. When had they woken up? Had they heard anything? What about during the night? Had anything happened? Had anything been different from usual? She asked them to ransack their memories.

They took turns replying. One filled in when the other broke off. It was obvious that they were doing their very best to be helpful.

She went backward, a sort of wintry retracing of steps through an unknown landscape. Had anything special happened the previous evening? Nothing. "Everything was the same as usual" were the words recurring in almost every answer they gave her.

They were interrupted by Erik Huddén. What should he do with the journalists? More kept arriving, and they were getting restless.

"Hang on a bit longer," she said. "I'll be with you shortly. Tell them there'll be a press conference in Hudiksvall at six o'clock this evening."

"Will we be ready in time?"

"We have to be."

Huddén left. Sundberg resumed her questioning. Another step backward, to yesterday morning and afternoon. This time it was Ninni who answered.

"Everything was as usual yesterday," said Ninni. "I had a bit of a cold. Tom spent all day chopping wood."

"Did you speak to any of your neighbors?"

"Tom exchanged a few words with Hilda, but we've already told you that."

"Did you see any of the others?"

"Yes, I suppose I must have. It was snowing. People always come out to shovel and keep the paths clear. Yes, I saw several of them without really noticing."

"Did you see anybody else?"

"What do you mean, 'anybody else'?"

"Somebody who doesn't live here? Or maybe a car you didn't recognize?"

"No, nobody at all."

"What about the previous day?"

"I suppose it was more or less the same. Nothing much ever happens here."

"Nothing unusual?"

"Nothing at all."

Vivi took out her notebook and a pencil.

"Now I'm afraid I have to ask you something difficult," she said. "I must ask you for the names of all your neighbors."

She ripped out a sheet of paper and placed it on the table.

"Draw a map of the village," she said. "Your house and all the rest. Then we'll give each one a number. Your house is number one. I want to know the names of everybody who lived in each of the houses."

The woman stood up and fetched a bigger sheet of paper. She sketched out the village. Sundberg could see that she was used to drawing.

"How do you earn your living?" Sundberg asked.

"We're day traders—stocks and shares."

It occurred to Vivi Sundberg that nothing ought to surprise her anymore. Why shouldn't a pair of aging hippies in a village in Hälsingland deal in stocks and shares?

"And we talk a lot," Ninni added. "We tell each other stories. People don't usually do that nowadays."

Sundberg felt the conversation was drifting away from the point.

"The names, please," she said. "Preferably ages as well. Take your time so that you get it right."

She watched the pair of them huddled over the piece of paper, muttering to each other. The thought crossed her mind—maybe one of the villagers was responsible for the massacre.

Fifteen minutes later, she had the list in her hand. The number didn't tally. They were a name short. That must be the boy. She stood by the window and read through the list. There seemed to be basically three families in the village: the Anderssons, the Andréns, and two people by the name of Magnusson. As she stood there with the list in her hand, she considered all the children and grandchildren who had moved away, who a few hours from now would be hit by this terrible news. Many, many people would be affected, and the resources required would be considerable.

All the first names flitted through her mind: Elna, Sara, Brita, August, Herman, Hilda, Johannes, Erik, Gertrud, Vendela. . . . She tried to picture their faces in her mind's eye, but they were blurred.

Then a thought suddenly struck her, something she had overlooked entirely. She went outside and shouted for Erik Huddén, who was talking to one of the forensic officers.

"Erik, who was it that discovered all this?"

"Some guy called us—had a heart attack and crashed into a truck with a Bosnian driver."

"Could he be the one responsible for all this?"

"Maybe. His car was full of cameras. Probably a photographer."

"Find out what you can about him. Then we need to set up some kind of HQ in that house over there. We have to go through the list of names and find their next of kin. What happened to the truck driver?"

"He was Breathalyzed, but he was sober. He spoke such poor Swedish they took him to Hudiksvall instead of interrogating him in the middle of the road. But he didn't seem to know anything."

Huddén left. As she was going back indoors she noticed a police officer running along the road toward the village. She went to the gate and waited for him.

"We've found the leg," he said, clearly shaken. "The dog uncovered it about fifteen yards in among the trees."

He pointed toward the edge of the forest. There was more, judging from his expression.

"Was that all?"

"I think it's best if you take a look yourself," he said.

Then he turned away and threw up. She left him to it and hurried toward the trees. She slipped and fell twice.

When she arrived she could see what had upset the officer. In places the flesh had been gnawed off the leg to the bone. The foot had been bitten off completely.

She looked at Ytterström and the dog handler, who were standing next to the find.

"A cannibal," said Ytterström. "Is that what we're looking for? Did we arrive and spoil his meal?"

Something touched Sundberg's hand. She gave a start. But it was only a snowflake, which soon melted.

"A tent," she said. "We need a tent here. I don't want the footprints obliterated."

She closed her eyes and suddenly saw a blue sea and white houses climbing up a warm hillside. Then she went back to the day traders' house and sat down in their kitchen with the list of names.

There must be something somewhere I haven't noticed, she thought.

She started to work her way slowly through the list. It was like walking through a minefield.

4

Vivi Sundberg had the feeling that she was studying a memorial to the victims of a major catastrophe, a plane crash or a sunken ship. But who would raise a memorial for the people of Hesjövallen who had been murdered one night in January 2006?

She slid the list of names to one side and stared at her trembling hands. She was unable to keep them still.

She shuddered, and picked up the list once again.

> Erik August Andersson
> Vendela Andersson
> Hans-Evert Andersson
> Elsa Andersson
> Gertrud Andersson
> Viktoria Andersson
> Hans Andrén
> Lars Andrén
> Klara Andrén
> Sara Andrén
> Elna Andrén
> Brita Andrén

August Andrén
Herman Andrén
Hilda Andrén
Johannes Andrén
Tora Magnusson
Regina Magnusson

Eighteen names, three families. She stood up and went into the room where the Hanssons were sitting on the sofa, whispering to each other. They stopped when she entered.

"You said there weren't any children in this village? Is that right?"

They both nodded.

"And you haven't seen any children during the last few days?"

"When sons or daughters of the old folk come to visit, they sometimes bring their own children with them. But that doesn't happen often."

Sundberg hesitated before continuing.

"Unfortunately there is a young boy among the dead," she said.

She pointed at one of the houses. The woman stared at her, eyes wide open.

"You mean he's dead as well?"

"Yes, he's dead. If what you've written is accurate, he was in the house with Hans-Evert and Elsa Andersson. Are you sure you don't know who he is?"

They turned to look at each other, then shook their heads. Sundberg went back to the kitchen. He's the odd one out, she thought. Him and the couple living in this house, and Julia who suffers from dementia and has no conception of this catastrophe. But somehow or other, it's the boy that doesn't fit in.

She folded up the sheet of paper, put it in her pocket, and went out. A few snowflakes were drifting down. All around her was silence. Disturbed only by an occasional voice, a door being closed, the clicking of a forensic tool. Erik Huddén came toward her. He was very pale. Everybody was pale.

"Where's the doctor?" she asked.

"Examining the leg."

"How's she doing?"

"She's shocked. The first thing she did was to disappear into a restroom. Then she burst out crying. But there are more doctors on the way. What shall we do about the reporters?"

"I'll speak to them."

She took the list of names from her pocket.

"The boy doesn't have a name. We must find out who he is. Make sure this list is copied, but don't hand it out."

"This is beyond belief," said Huddén. "Eighteen people."

"Nineteen. The boy's not on there."

She produced a pen and added "unidentified boy" to the bottom of the list.

Then she gathered the freezing-cold and mystified reporters into a semicircle on the road.

"I'll give you a brief statement," she said. "You can

ask questions, but we don't have any answers at the moment. There'll be a press conference later today in Hudiksvall. Provisionally at six o'clock. All I can say for now is that several very serious crimes were committed here during the night. I can't give you any more details."

A young girl, her face covered in freckles, held up her hand.

"But surely you can tell us a bit more? It's obvious that something terrible has happened when you cordon off the whole village."

Sundberg didn't recognize the girl, but the logo on her jacket was the name of a big national newspaper.

"You can ask as many questions as you like, but I'm afraid that for technical reasons connected with the investigation, I can't tell you any more for the moment."

One of the television reporters thrust a microphone under her nose. She had met him many times before.

"Can you repeat what you've just said?"

She did so, but when he tried to ask a follow-up question she turned her back on him and left. She didn't stop walking until she came to the last of the tents that had been pitched. She suddenly felt very ill. She stepped to one side and took a few deep breaths, and only when she no longer felt the need to throw up did she approach the tent.

Once, during one of her first years as a police officer, she had fainted when she and a colleague had entered a house and found a man hanging there. She would prefer not to have that happen again.

The woman squatting down at the side of the leg looked up when Sundberg entered. A powerful spotlight made it very warm inside the tent. Sundberg introduced herself.

"What can you tell me?"

Valentina Miir, probably in her forties, spoke with a pronounced foreign accent. "I've never seen anything like this before," she said. "You come across limbs that have been pulled off or severed, but this one . . ."

"Has somebody been trying to eat it?"

"The probability is that it's an animal, of course. But there are aspects that worry me."

"Such as?"

"Animals eat and gnaw at bones in a particular way. You can usually be more or less sure which particular animal has been involved. I suspect it was a wolf in this case. But there's something else you ought to see."

She reached for a transparent plastic bag. It contained a leather boot.

"We can assume that it was on the foot," she said. "Obviously, an animal can have pulled it off in order to get at the foot itself. But what worries me is that the shoelaces were undone."

Sundberg recalled that the other boot was tightly tied and on the man's other foot. The leg belonged to Lars Andrén.

"Is there anything else you've established?"

"Not yet, it's too soon."

"Can you come with me? I need your help."

They left the tent and went to the house where the unknown boy was lying with two other persons who were probably Hans-Evert and Elsa Andersson. The silence inside was deafening.

The boy was lying in bed, on his stomach. The room was small, with a sloping roof. Sundberg gritted her teeth in order not to burst out crying. His life had barely begun, but before he could take another breath it had ended.

They stood there in silence.

"I don't understand how anybody can commit such a horrendous attack on a small child," said Valentina eventually.

"Can you see how many stab wounds he has?" said Sundberg.

The doctor leaned forward and directed the bedside lamp at the body. It was several minutes before she answered.

"It seems that he has only one wound. And it killed him instantly."

"Can you explain further?"

"It would have been quick. His spine has been cut in two."

"Have you had time to examine the other bodies?"

"As I've said, I'm waiting for backup."

"But can you say off the top of your head how many of the other victims died from a single blow?"

At first Valentina didn't seem to understand the question. Then she tried to recall what she had seen.

"None of them, I think," she said slowly. "Unless I'm much mistaken, all the others were stabbed repeatedly."

"And no single wound would have been fatal?"

"It's too soon to say for sure, but probably not."

"Many thanks."

The doctor left. Sundberg searched through the room and the boy's clothes in the hope of finding something to indicate who he was. But found nothing, not even a bus pass. She went downstairs and out into the yard to the rear of the house overlooking the frozen lake. She tried to work out the significance of what she had discovered. The boy had died from a single blow, but all the rest had been subjected to more systematic violence. What could that mean? She could think of only one plausible explanation: whoever killed the boy hadn't wanted him to suffer. Everyone else had been subjected to violence that was a sort of extended torture.

She gazed at the distant mountains, which were veiled in mist beyond the lake. He wanted to torture them, she thought. Whoever wielded that sword or knife wanted them to know that they were going to die.

Why? She had no idea. She was distracted by the sound of rotor blades approaching and went to the front of the house. A helicopter was descending over the wooded hillsides and soon landed in a field, whipping up a cloud of snow. Tobias Ludwig jumped out, and the helicopter set off again immediately, heading south.

Sundberg went to meet him. Ludwig was wearing city shoes, and as he trudged through the snow it came well over his ankles. He looked to Vivi like a confused insect stuck in the snow and flapping violently with its wings.

They met on the road as Ludwig was brushing himself down.

"I'm trying to get my head around it," he said. "What you told me, that is."

"You have to see them. Sten Robertsson is here. I've done as much as I can in the way of resources. But now it's up to you to make sure we get all the help we need."

"I still can't get my head around it. Lots of dead old people?"

"There's a boy who's the odd one out. He's young."

She went through the houses for the fourth time that day. Ludwig kept groaning as he accompanied her from crime scene to crime scene and came to the tent where the leg was. The doctor was nowhere to be seen. Ludwig shook his head helplessly.

"What on earth has happened? Surely only a madman could have done anything like this."

"We don't know if it was just one. There could have been several of them."

"Madmen?"

"Nobody knows."

He looked hard at her.

"Do we know anything at all?"

"Not really."

"This is too big for us. We need help."

Robertsson came walking along the road toward them.

"This is horrendous, horrific," said Ludwig. "I doubt anything like this has ever happened before in Sweden."

Robertsson shook his head. Sundberg eyed the two men. The feeling that this was urgent, that something even worse might happen if they didn't act quickly enough, became even stronger.

"Get going on those names," she said to Tobias Ludwig. "I really need your help."

Then she took Robertsson by the arm and led him off along the road.

"What do you think?"

"I'm scared. Aren't you?"

"I don't have time to think about it."

Sten Robertsson screwed up his eyes.

"But you're onto something, aren't you? You always are."

"Not this time. There could have been ten of them, we just don't know at the moment. We have absolutely nothing to go on. You'll have to be present at the press conference, by the way."

"I hate talking to journalists."

"Too bad."

Robertsson left. She was about to go and sit down

in her car when she noticed that Huddén was waving to her. He was approaching and had something in his hand. He must have found the murder weapon, she thought. That would be a stroke of luck.

But Huddén was not carrying a weapon. He handed over a plastic bag. Inside it was a thin red ribbon.

"The dog found it. In the forest. About thirty yards from the leg."

"Any footprints?"

"They're looking—but when the dog found the ribbon, he showed no sign of wanting to follow a trail."

She lifted the bag and peered closely at it.

"It's thin," she said. "It seems to be silk. Did you find anything else?"

"No, that's all. It seemed to sparkle in the snow."

She handed back the bag.

"Well, we have something at least," she said. "At the press conference we can announce that we have nineteen dead bodies and a clue in the form of a red silk ribbon."

"Maybe we'll find something else."

When Huddén had left she sat in her car to think. Through the windshield she could see Julia being led away by a woman from the home help service. Ignorance is bliss, thought Sundberg.

She closed her eyes and let the list of names scroll through her mind. She still couldn't connect the various names to the faces she had now seen on four different occasions. Where did it start? she wondered. One house must have been the first, another one the last. The killer, whether or not he was alone, must have known what he was doing. He didn't pick the houses haphazardly, he made no attempt to break into the day traders' house, or that of the senile woman.

She opened her eyes and gazed out through the windshield. It was planned, she thought. It must have been. But can a madman really prepare for that kind of deed? Surely it doesn't add up.

She poured out the last few drops of coffee from her thermos. The motive, she thought. Even a lunatic must have a motive. Perhaps inner voices urge him to kill everybody who crosses his path. But would those voices point him to Hesjövallen of all places? If so, why? How big a role was played by coincidence in this drama?

The boy may be the key, she thought. He doesn't live in the village. But he dies even so. Two people who have lived here for twenty years are still alive. Then it dawned on her—something Erik Huddén had said. Did she remember correctly? What was Julia's surname?

Julia's house wasn't locked. She went in and read the document that Huddén had found on the kitchen table. The answer she found to her question made her heart start beating faster. She sat down and tried to marshal her thoughts.

The conclusion she reached was improbable, but it

might be correct anyway. She dialed Huddén's number. He answered immediately.

"I'm sitting in Julia's kitchen. The woman standing on the road in her nightdress. Come here right away."

"Will do."

Huddén sat opposite her at the table. Then stood up again and looked down at the chair seat. Sniffed at it, then changed to another chair. She stared at him in bafflement.

"Urine," he said. "The old lady must have peed herself. What did you want to say?"

"I want to try out a thought on you. It seems implausible but is somehow logical nevertheless. I have the feeling that there's a sort of underlying logic to what happened here last night. I want you to listen, and then tell me if I've got the wrong end of the stick.

"It's to do with names," she began. "We still don't know the boy's name, but if I remember rightly he's related to the Andersson family who lived and died in the house where we found them. A key to everything that happened here last night is the names. Families. People in this village seem to have been called Andersson, Andrén, or Magnusson. Julia's surname is Holmgren. Julia Holmgren. She's still alive. And then we have Tom and Ninni Hansson. They're also still alive, and have a different surname. It should be possible to draw a conclusion from that."

"That whoever did this, for some reason or other, was out to get people with those names," said Huddén.

"Think another step ahead! This is a tiny little hamlet. People probably haven't moved. Most likely there has been intermarriage between the families. I'm not talking about incest, just that there is good reason to believe that we're not looking at three families, but perhaps two. Or maybe even only one. That may explain why Julia Holmgren and the Hanssons are still alive."

Sundberg paused for Huddén's reaction. She didn't consider him particularly intelligent, but she respected his ability to use his intuition.

"If that is true, it must mean that whoever did this knew these people very well. Who would do that?"

"Possibly a relative?"

"A **mad** relative? Why would he want to do anything like this?"

"We don't know."

"How do you explain the severed leg?"

"I can't. But I think we have a start. That and a red silk ribbon are all we have.

"I want you to go back to Hudiksvall," she said. "Tobias is supposed to be delegating officers to search for next of kin. Make sure that happens. And look for links between these three families. But keep it between you and me for the time being."

Shortly before half past five, some of the senior police officers gathered in Tobias Ludwig's office to discuss the press conference. It was decided to not issue a list of names of the dead, but they would say how many people had been killed and admit that, so far, the police had no clues. Any information the general public could supply would be appreciated.

Ludwig would give preliminary details, and then Sundberg would take over.

Before entering the room crammed full of reporters, she shut herself away in a restroom. She examined her face in a mirror. If only I could wake up, she thought. And find that this whole business had gone away.

She went out, slammed her fist hard into the corridor wall several times, then went into the room chock-full of people and far too hot. She walked up to the little podium and sat down next to Tobias Ludwig.

He looked at her. She nodded. He could begin.

The Judge

5

A moth detached itself from the darkness and fluttered restlessly around the desk lamp. Birgitta Roslin put down her pen, leaned back in her chair, and watched the moth's vain attempt to force its way through the porcelain shade. The noise of its fluttering wings reminded her of something from her childhood, but she couldn't pin it down.

Her memory was always especially creative when she was tired, as she was now. Just as when she was asleep, inaccessible memories from long ago might crop up out of nowhere.

Like the moth.

She closed her eyes and massaged her temples with her fingertips. It was a few minutes past midnight. She had heard the night security officers passing through the echoing halls of the court building as they made their rounds twice. She liked working late at night, when the place was empty. Years ago, when she had been an associate in a law office in Värnamo, she had often gone into the empty courtroom late in the evening, switched on a few lights, sat down, and listened to the silence. She would imagine she was in an empty theater. There were echoes in the walls, whispering voices still living on after all the drama of past trials. Murderers had been sentenced there, violent criminals, thieves. And men had sworn their innocence in a never-ending stream of depressing paternity cases. Others had been declared innocent and reinstated as honorable men.

When Birgitta Roslin had completed her probationary period and been offered the post in Värnamo, her intention had been to become a prosecuting counsel. But during her clerkship she changed course and began to specialize in what was to become her eventual career. To a large extent this was due to Anker, the old district judge, who made an indelible impression on her. He displayed exactly the same patience as he listened to young men who told obvious lie after lie in an attempt to avoid responsibility in paternity cases as he did when faced with hard-boiled men of violence who showed no remorse for their brutal misdeeds. It was as if the old judge had instilled in her a new degree of respect for the judicial system she had previously taken for granted. Now she actually experienced it, not just in word, but in deed. Justice meant action. By the time she left Värnamo, she had made up her mind to become a judge.

She stood up and walked over to the window. Down below in the street a man was peeing against the wall. It had been snowing in Helsingborg during the day, and a thin layer of powdery snow was now whirling along the street. As she watched the man nonchalantly, her mind was working overtime on the judgment she was busy preparing. She had allowed herself until the following day, but it had to be ready by then.

The man down below moved on. Roslin returned to her desk and picked up her pencil. She always worked with pencil until she'd finalized her work.

She leaned over the messy pages with all their alterations and additions. It was a simple case and the evidence against the accused was overwhelming; nevertheless, she was having problems making her judgment.

She wanted to impose sanctions, but was unable to.

A man and a woman had met in one of Helsingborg's dance restaurants. The woman was young, barely twenty, and had drunk too much. The man was in his forties and had volunteered to see her home, then was invited into the apartment for a glass of water. The woman had fallen asleep on the sofa. The man had raped her, without waking her up, then left. The next morning the woman had only a vague memory of what had happened on the sofa. She contacted the hospital, where she was examined and it was established that she had had intercourse. The man was charged. The case came to court a full year after the incident had taken place. Birgitta Roslin had presided over the trial and observed the young woman. She had read in the preliminary case notes that the woman earned her living by working as a temporary cashier in various food stores. It was clear from a personal statement that the woman was in the habit of drinking too much. She had also been found guilty of petty theft and was once fired for neglecting her duties.

In many respects the accused was her opposite. He worked as a real estate agent, specializing in commercial properties. Everyone gave him good references. He was unmarried and earned a high salary. He did not appear in police records, but Birgitta Roslin felt that she could see through him, as he sat before her in his expensive and well-pressed suit. She had no doubt that he had raped the woman as she lay asleep on the sofa. DNA tests had established beyond doubt that intercourse had taken place, but he denied rape. She had been a willing partner, he maintained, as did his counsel, a lawyer from Malmö whom Roslin had come across before. It was one person's word against another's, an irreproachable property broker versus a drunken checkout girl who had invited him into her apartment in the middle of the night.

Roslin was upset about not being able to convict him. She couldn't shake the feeling that on this occasion a guilty man would go free. There was nothing to be done.

What would that wise old bird Anker have done? What advice would he have given her? He would certainly have shared my concern, Roslin thought. A guilty man is going to be set free. Old Anker would have been just as upset as I am. And he would have had as little to say as I do. There's the rub as far as judges are concerned: we have to obey the law in the knowledge that we are releasing a criminal without punishment. The woman may not have been an angel, but she would have to live with that outrageous injustice for the rest of her life.

She left her desk chair and went to lie down on the sofa. She had paid for it herself and put it in her office instead of the uncomfortable armchair provided by the National Courts Administration. She had learned from Anker to hold a bunch of keys in her hand and close her eyes. When she dropped the keys, it was time to wake up. But she needed a short rest. Then she would finish writing her judgment, go home to bed, and produce a clean copy the next day. She had worked through everything there was to work through and confirmed that there was no question of a guilty verdict.

She dozed off and dreamed about her father, of whom she had no personal memories. He had been a ship's engineeer. During a severe storm in the middle of January 1949 the steamship **Runskär** had sunk in the Gävlebukten, with all hands on board. His body had never been found. Birgitta Roslin had been four months old at the time. The image she had of her father came from the photographs in her home. The picture she remembered best was of him standing by the rail of a ship, smiling, his hair ruffled and his shirtsleeves rolled up. Her mother had told her it was a ship's mate holding the camera, but Birgitta Roslin had always imagined that he was actually smiling at her, despite the fact that the photograph was taken before she was born. He kept reappearing in her dreams. Now he was smiling at her, just as he did in the photograph, but then he vanished as if swallowed up by fog.

She woke with a start. She realized immediately that she had slept for far too long. The key-ring trick hadn't worked. She had dropped it without noticing. She sat up and checked the clock: it was already six. She had slept for more than five hours. I'm shattered, she thought. Like most other people, I don't get enough sleep. There's too much going on in my life that worries me.

She called her husband, who had begun to wonder where she was. It was not unusual for her to spend the night on the sofa in her office after they'd quarreled, but this was not the case now.

Staffan Roslin had been a year ahead of her at Lund, where they both studied law. Their first meeting was at a party given by mutual friends. Immediately Birgitta knew he was the man for her, swept off her feet by his eyes, his height, his large hands, and his inability to stop blushing.

But, after completing his studies, Staffan did not take to the law. He decided to retrain as a railroad conductor, and one morning he appeared in the living room dressed in a blue-and-red uniform and announced that at 12:19, he would be responsible for departure 212 from Malmö to Alvesta, and then on to Växjö and Kalmar.

He became a much happier person. By the time he chose to abandon his legal career, they already had four children: first a son, then a daughter, and finally twins, both girls. The children had arrived in rapid succession, and she was amazed when she thought back to those days. How had they managed it? Four children within six years. They had left Malmö and moved to Helsingborg, where she was appointed a district judge.

The children were grown up now. The twins had flown the nest the previous year, to Lund, where they shared an apartment. But she was pleased that they were not studying the same subject and that neither of them had ambitions to become a lawyer. Siv, who was nineteen minutes older than her sister Louise, had eventually decided, after much hesitation, to become a veterinarian. Louise, who had a more impetuous temperament than her twin sister, had tried her hand at several things, sold clothes in a men's store, and in the end decided to major in political science and religious studies in college. Birgitta had often tried to coax out of her what she wanted to do with her life, but she was the most withdrawn of the four children and rarely said anything about her innermost thoughts. Her mother suspected that Louise was the daughter most like herself. Her son, David, who worked for a big pharmaceutical company, was like his father in almost every way. The eldest daughter, Anna, had astonished her parents by embarking on long journeys in Asia, about which they knew very little.

My family, Birgitta thought. Big worries but a lot of pleasure. Without it, most of my life would have been wasted.

There was a large mirror in the corridor outside her office. She examined her face and her body. Her close-clipped dark hair had started to grow gray at the temples. Her habit of pursing her lips tended to give her face a negative expression. But what really worried her was the fact that she had put on weight over the last few years. Three, four kilos, no more. But enough to be noticeable.

She didn't like what she saw. She knew she was basically an attractive woman. But she was beginning to lose her charm. And she was not making any attempt to resist.

She left a note on her secretary's desk, saying that she would be in later in the day. It had become a little warmer, and the snow had already started to melt. She started walking to her car, which was parked on a side street.

But then she changed her mind. What she really needed above all else was not sleep. It was more important to give her mind a rest and think about something else. She turned and headed for the harbor. There was not a breath of wind. The overcast sky from the previous day had begun to open up. She went to the quay where the ferries departed for Elsinore. The crossing took only a few minutes. But she liked to sit on board with a cup of coffee or a glass of wine, watching her fellow passengers going through the bags of cheap spirits they had bought in Denmark. She sat down at a corner table that was very sticky. Annoyance flared up inside her, and she shouted to the girl who was clearing the tables.

"I really have to complain," she said. "This table has been cleared, but it hasn't been wiped. It's very sticky."

The girl shrugged and wiped it clean. Birgitta Roslin gazed in disgust at the filthy rag the girl had used, but she didn't say anything. Somehow the girl reminded her of the young woman who had been raped. She didn't know why. Perhaps it was her lack of enthusiasm for her work? Or maybe it was a kind of helplessness she couldn't put a finger on?

The ferry started to vibrate. It gave her a feeling of well-being. She remembered the first time she had gone abroad. She had been nineteen. She had traveled to England with a friend to take a language course. The trip had started on a ferry, from Gothenburg to London. Birgitta Roslin would never forget the feeling of standing on deck, knowing she was on her way to somewhere liberating and unknown.

That same feeling of freedom would often come over her when she sailed back and forth over the narrow strait between Sweden and Denmark. Today, all thoughts about the unfortunate judgment she would have to make disappeared from her mind.

I'm no longer even in the middle of my life, she thought. I've passed the point that one doesn't even realize is being passed. There won't be that many difficult decisions left for me to make. But I shall remain a judge until I retire. With luck I should be able to enjoy my grandchildren before it's all over.

Her thoughts drifted to her husband, and her mood changed. Her marriage was beginning to shrivel and die. They were still good friends and could give each other the necessary feeling of security. But love, the sensual pleasure of being in each other's vicinity, had completely vanished.

Four days from now it would be a whole year since they had last caressed each other and made love before going to sleep. The closer that anniversary came, the more impotent she felt. And now it was almost upon her. Over and over again she had tried to speak to Staffan about how lonely she was. But he wasn't prepared to talk, withdrew into his shell, tried to postpone the discussion he nevertheless knew was important. He insisted that he was not attracted to anybody else, they were just missing a particular feeling that would no doubt soon return. All they needed to do was be patient.

She regretted losing the feeling of togetherness she had shared with her husband, the imposing-looking chief conductor with the big hands and the propensity for blushing. But she had no intention of giving up. She didn't yet want their relationship to be an intimate friendship and nothing more.

She went to the counter to refill her cup and moved to another, less sticky table. A group of young men who were already noticeably drunk despite the early hour were discussing whether it was Hamlet or Macbeth who had been imprisoned in Kronborg Castle, which skulked on its cliff just outside Elsinore. She listened to the discussion with amused interest and felt tempted to join in.

A group of boys was sitting at another table. They couldn't have been older than fourteen or fifteen and were probably playing hooky. And why not, when nobody seemed to care whether or not they showed up at school? She had absolutely no nostalgic feelings about the authoritarian school she had attended. But she recalled an incident from the previous year. Something that had driven her crazy about the state of Swedish justice and made her long more than ever for the advice of her mentor Judge Anker, who had now been dead for thirty years.

In a housing estate outside Helsingborg an old woman just short of her eightieth birthday had suffered an acute heart attack and collapsed on a public footpath. A couple of young boys, one of them aged thirteen, the other fourteen, had come by. Instead of helping the old woman, without a second thought they had first stolen her purse and then tried to rape her. If it hadn't been for a man walking his dog, they would probably have succeeded in their attempt. The police traced and arrested the two boys, but as they were underage, they were allowed to go free.

Birgitta Roslin heard about the incident from a public prosecutor, who had in turn been informed by a police officer. She had been furious and tried to find out why the crime hadn't been reported to social services. It then dawned on her that maybe a hundred or so underage children committed crimes in the Helsingborg area every year with absolutely no follow-up. Nobody told their parents, nobody informed social services. It was not merely the occasional case of petty pilfering but also robbery and grievous bodily harm, which could easily have ended up as murder.

She began to despair over the Swedish judicial system. Whose servant was she, in fact? Was she a servant of the law, or of indifference? And what would the consequences be if more and more children were allowed to commit crimes without anybody bothering to react? How had things been allowed to lapse to such an extent that the very basis of democracy was being threatened by a lame judicial system?

She drank her coffee and contemplated the fact that she would probably need to work for another ten years. Would she have the strength? Was it possible to be a good and fair judge if you began to doubt the country's legal structure?

In order to shake off questions she couldn't answer, she went back over the strait one more time. When she disembarked on the Swedish side, it was nine o'clock. She crossed the wide main street that carved its way through the center of Helsingborg. As she turned off, she happened to notice a billboard with headlines from one of the national evening newspapers: they were just being posted. The large letters in bold print caught her attention. She paused and read: MASS MURDER IN HÄLSINGLAND. HORRIFIC CRIME. NO LEADS FOR POLICE. NUMBER OF DEAD UNKNOWN. MASS MURDER.

She continued walking to her car. She seldom if ever bought the evening papers. She was put off, and sometimes offended, by the papers' frequent attacks on the police. Even if she agreed with quite a lot of what was alleged, she had little sympathy with the sensationalizing. What reporters wrote often harmed genuine criticism, even if the intentions were honorable.

Birgitta Roslin lived in Kjellstorp, an upmarket residential area on the northern edge of Helsingborg. On the way home she stopped at a little store. It was owned by a Pakistani immigrant who always greeted her with a broad smile. He knew she was a district judge and was very respectful toward her. She wondered if there were any female judges in Pakistan, but she had never gotten around to asking him.

When she arrived home she took a bath before going to bed. She woke up at one o'clock and at last felt fully rested. After a couple of sandwiches and a cup of coffee, she returned to her work. A few hours later she printed out her judgment that acquitted the guilty man, drove back to court, and left it on her secretary's desk. Her secretary was evidently attending some kind of in-service training course: Birgitta Roslin hadn't been informed or, more likely, had forgotten all about it. When she arrived back home she heated up some leftover chicken stew from yesterday's dinner and left the rest in the fridge for Staffan.

She settled down on the sofa with a cup of coffee and switched on teletext. She was reminded of the headlines she had seen earlier in the day. The police had no clues to follow up and declined to reveal how many people had been killed or their names, since the next of kin had not yet been contacted.

A madman, she concluded, who either had a persecution complex or considered himself to have been badly treated by the world.

Her years as a judge had taught her that there were many different forms of madness that could drive people to commit horrendous crimes. But she had also learned that forensic psychiatrists did not always succeed in exposing criminals who merely pretended to be mentally ill.

She switched off the television and went down to the basement, where she had created a little cellar of red wines complete with several wine lists and order forms from a number of importers. Only a few years ago it had dawned on her that thanks to her children moving out, the family finances had changed fundamentally. She now felt she could afford to spend money on something special and had decided to buy a few bottles of red wine every month. She enjoyed studying the lists and picking out new wines to try.

Paying five hundred kronor or so for a bottle seemed to her an almost forbidden pleasure.

It was cool in the cellar. She checked that the temperature was fourteen degrees Celsius, then sat down on a stool between the racks. Down there, among all the bottles, she could feel at peace with the world. Given the alternative of soaking in a warm pool, she would have preferred to sit in her cellar surrounded on this particular day by one hundred fourteen bottles lying in their racks.

But then again, was the peace she could experience in her cellar really genuine? When she was a young woman, if anybody had suggested to her that one day she would become a wine collector, she would never have believed her ears. She wouldn't merely have denied any such possibility, she would have been upset. As a student in Lund she had been in sympathy with the left-wing radicals who, in the late 1960s, had questioned the validity of university education and the very foundations of the society in which she would eventually work. In those days, collecting wine would have been regarded as a waste of time and effort, a typically middle-class and hence objectionable hobby.

She was still sitting there lost in thought when she heard Staffan moving around on the floor above. She put the wine lists away and went back upstairs. He had just taken the chicken stew out of the refrigerator. On the table were a couple of evening newspapers he had brought with him from the train.

"Have you seen this?"

"I gather something awful's happened in Hälsing-land."

"Nineteen people have been killed."

"Teletext said that the number of dead wasn't yet known."

"These are the latest editions. They've killed practically the whole population of a hamlet up there. It's incredible. How did it go with the judgment you were working on?"

"It's finished. I acquitted him. I didn't have any choice."

"The papers are all abuzz."

"Thank God for that."

"You're going to come in for some stick."

"No doubt. But I can suggest that the reporters might like to check what the law says, and then decide if they'd prefer us to go over to lynch law in Sweden."

"These mass murders are going to detract attention from your case."

"Of course. What's a petty little rape compared with a brutal mass murder?"

They went to bed early that night. He would be in charge of an early train the following morning, and she had failed to find anything of interest on television. She had also decided which wine she was going to buy. A case of Barolo Arione 2002, at 252 kronor per bottle.

She woke up with a start at midnight. Staffan was

sleeping soundly by her side. She was fairly frequently woken up by pangs of hunger in the middle of the night. She put on her robe, went downstairs to the kitchen, made herself a cup of weak tea and a couple of sandwiches.

The evening papers were still lying on the kitchen table. She leafed absentmindedly through one of them—it was hard to form a clear picture of what had happened in that little village in Hälsingland. But there was no doubt that a large number of people had been brutally murdered.

She was just going to put the paper to one side when she gave a start. Among the dead were several people called Andrén. She read the text carefully, then checked in the other paper. The same there.

She stared hard at the page in front of her. Could this really be true? Or did she remember wrongly? She went to her study and took out from a desk cupboard a folder of documents wrapped in a red ribbon. She switched on the desk lamp and opened the folder. As she hadn't brought her glasses down with her, she borrowed a pair of Staffan's. They were not as strong as hers, but they were usable.

The folder contained all the documents connected with her parents. Her mother had been dead for more than fifteen years. She had been diagnosed with cancer of the pancreas and died within three months.

She eventually found the photograph she had been looking for in a brown envelope. She took out her magnifying glass and examined the picture. It depicted a group of people in old-fashioned clothes standing in front of a house.

She took the photograph with her to the kitchen. In one of the newspapers there was a general view of the village where this major tragedy had taken place. She examined the picture carefully through her magnifying glass. She paused at the third house and began comparing the two photographs.

She had remembered rightly. This hamlet that had been struck down by unannounced evil was not just any old place. It was the village in which her mother had grown up. Everything fit—it was true that her mother's surname had been Lööf as a child, but as her parents had both been alcoholics, she had been placed with a family called Andrén. Birgitta's mother had rarely mentioned those days. She had been well looked after, but had always longed to be acquainted with her real parents. However, they had both died before she was fifteen, and so she had to stay in the village until she was considered old enough to find work and look after herself. When she met Birgitta's father, the names Lööf and Andrén disappeared from the scene. But now one of them had returned with a bang.

The photograph lying among her mother's papers had been taken in front of one of the houses in the village where the mass murders had been perpetrated. The façade of the house, the ornamental carving around the windows, was exactly the same in the old photograph as in the newspaper.

There was no doubt about it. A few nights previously, people had been murdered in the house where her mother grew up. Could it be her mother's foster parents who had been killed? The newspapers wrote that most of the dead were old people.

Her mother's foster parents would be more than ninety years of age now. Perhaps.

She shuddered at the thought. She seldom if ever thought about her parents. She even found it difficult to recall what her mother looked like. But now the past came unexpectedly rushing toward her.

Staffan entered the kitchen. As always, he made hardly a sound.

"You make me jump when I don't know you're coming," she said.

"Why are you up?"

"I felt hungry."

He looked at the papers lying on the table. She told him about the conclusion she'd reached and that she was becoming more and more convinced that what she suspected was in fact the truth.

"But it's pretty remote," he said when she'd finished. "It's a very thin thread connecting you to that little village."

"Thin, but remarkable. You have to admit that."

"Maybe. But you have to get some sleep."

She lay awake for ages before dozing off. That thin thread became stretched almost to the breaking point. She slept fitfully, and her sleep was broken by thoughts about her mother. She still found it hard to see traces of herself in her mother.

She dropped off to sleep eventually and woke up to find Staffan standing at the foot of the bed, hair damp from the shower, putting on his uniform. I'm your general, he used to tell her. Without a weapon in my hand, only a pen to cancel tickets.

She pretended to be still asleep and waited until the door closed behind him. Then she jumped up and switched on the computer in her study. She went through several search engines, looking for as much information as she could find. The events that had taken place in Hälsingland still seemed to be shrouded in uncertainty. The only thing that appeared clear was that the weapon used was probably a large knife or something similar.

I want to know more about this, she thought. At least I want to know if my mother's foster parents were among those murdered the other night. She searched until eight o'clock, when she put all thoughts about the mass murders aside to consider the day's trial concerning two Iraqi citizens accused of smuggling people.

It was a further two hours before she had gathered together her papers, glanced through the preliminary investigation notes, and taken her seat in court. Help me now, dear old Anker, to get through this day as well, she pleaded. Then she tapped her gavel lightly on the desk in front of her and asked the prosecuting counsel to open the proceedings.

There were high windows behind her back.

Just before she sat down, she had noticed that the

sun was beginning to break through the thick clouds that had moved in over Sweden during the night.

6

By the time the trial was over two days later, Birgitta Roslin knew what her verdict would be. They were guilty, and the elder of the two men, Abdul ibn Yamed, who was the ringleader, would be sentenced to three years and two months in prison. His assistant, the younger Yassir al-Habi, would get one year. Both men would be deported on release.

The sentences given were similar to what had gone before. Many of the individuals smuggled into Sweden had been threatened and assaulted when it transpired that they were unable to pay what they owed for the forged immigration papers and the long journey. She had taken a particular dislike to the elder of the two men. He had appealed to her and the prosecutor with sentimental arguments, claiming that he never retained any of the money paid by the refugees but donated it all to charities in his homeland. During a break in proceedings the prosecuting counsel had stopped by for a cup of coffee and mentioned in passing that Abdul ibn Yamed drove around in a Mercedes worth almost a million kronor.

The trial had been strenuous. The days had been

long, and she had no time to do more than eat and sleep and study her notes prior to returning to the bench. Her twin daughters phoned and invited her to Lund, but she didn't have time. As soon as the case was over, she was faced with a complicated one involving Romanian credit card swindlers.

She had no time to keep abreast of what was happening in the little village in Hälsingland, missing the morning newspapers and the evening TV news bulletins.

The morning Roslin was due to start preparing for the trial of the swindlers from Romania, she discovered that she had a note in her diary about an appointment with her doctor for a routine annual checkup. She considered postponing it for a few weeks. Apart from feeling tired, being out of shape, and occasionally suffering anxiety attacks, she couldn't imagine there being anything wrong with her. She was a healthy person who led an unadventurous life and hardly ever even had a cold. But she didn't cancel the appointment.

The doctor's office was not far from the municipal theater. She left her car on the side street where it was parked and walked to the office from the court. It was cold, fine weather with no wind at all. The snow that had fallen a few days earlier had melted away. She stopped by a shopwindow and contemplated a dress. But the price tag gave her a shock, and she moved on.

In the waiting room was a newspaper whose front

page was laden with news about the mass murder in Hälsingland. She had barely got as far as picking it up when she was summoned by the doctor. He was an elderly man who reminded her of Judge Anker. Roslin had been his patient for ten years. He had been recommended by one of her legal colleagues. He asked her how she felt, if she'd had any pains, and having noted her responses he passed her on to a nurse, who took a blood sample from one of Roslin's fingertips. She then sat in the waiting room. Another patient had claimed the newspaper. Roslin closed her eyes and waited. She thought about her family, what each of them was doing, or at least where they were, at that very moment. Staffan was on a train heading for Hallsberg; he wouldn't be home until late. David was working in AstraZeneca's laboratory just outside Gothenburg. It was less certain where Anna was: the last time she had been in touch was a month ago, from Nepal. The twins were in Lund and wanted their mother to visit them. She dozed off and was woken up by the nurse shaking her by the shoulder.

"You can go in to the doctor now."

Surely I'm not so exhausted that I need to drop off in a doctor's waiting room, Roslin thought as she returned to the doctor's office and sat down.

Ten minutes later Birgitta Roslin was standing on the street outside, trying to come to terms with the fact that she wouldn't be working for the next two weeks. The doctor had introduced sudden and unex-pected disorder into her life. Her blood pressure was far too high, and coupled with her anxiety attacks caused the doctor to insist on two weeks' leave from work.

She walked back to the court and spoke to Hans Mattsson, a chief judge and her immediate superior. They managed to work out between them a way of dealing with the two cases she was currently embroiled in. She spoke to her secretary, mailed a few letters she had written, called at the pharmacy to pick up her new medication, then drove home. The lack of anything to do was paralyzing.

She made lunch, then flopped down on the sofa with the newspaper. Not all the bodies in Hesjövallen had been named publicly. A detective by the name of Sundberg made a statement and urged the general public to contact the police with any information. There were still no leads, but the police were sure, no matter how hard it might be to believe, that they were looking for only the one killer.

On another page a public prosecutor called Robertsson claimed that the investigation was progressing on a very large scale totally without prejudice. The police in Hudiksvall had received the assistance that they had requested from the central authorities.

Robertsson seemed to be confident of success: "We shall catch whoever did this deed. We shall not give up."

An article on the next page was about the unrest that had spread throughout the Hälsingland forests.

Many villages in the area had few inhabitants. There was talk of people acquiring guns, of dogs, alarms, and barricaded doors.

Birgitta Roslin slid the newspaper to one side. The house was empty, silent. Her sudden and unwanted free time had come out of the blue. She went down to the basement and fetched one of the wine lists. She decided to order the case of Barolo Arione online. It was really too expensive, but she felt the urge to treat herself. She thought about doing some cleaning, an activity that was almost always neglected in her household. But she changed her mind just as she was about to bring out the vacuum cleaner. She sat down at the kitchen table and tried to assess her situation. She was on sick leave, although she wasn't really ill. Is having high blood pressure really being ill? Maybe she really was close to burning herself out, and perhaps it could affect her judgment in court?

She looked at the newspaper in front of her on the table and thought again about her mother and her childhood in Hälsingland. An idea struck her. She picked up the telephone, rang the local police station, and asked to speak to Detective Chief Inspector Hugo Malmberg. They had known each other for many years. At one time he had tried to teach her and Staffan to play bridge, without arousing much enthusiasm.

She heard Malmberg's gentle voice at the other end of the line. Most people imagine police officers sound gruff; Hugo would convince them otherwise.

He sounded more like a cuddly pensioner sitting on a park bench feeding the birds.

She asked how he was and wondered if he had time to see her. He did. She'd walk.

An hour later, Birgitta Roslin entered Hugo Malmberg's office with its neat and tidy desk. Malmberg was on the phone, but he gestured, inviting her to sit down. The call concerned an assault that had happened the previous day.

Malmberg hung up and smiled at her. "Would you like a cup of coffee?"

"I'd rather not, thank you."

"Meaning what?"

"The police station's coffee is just as bad as the brew they serve up in the district court."

He stood.

"Let's go to the conference room," he said. "This telephone rings nonstop. It's a feeling I share with every other decent Swedish police officer—that I'm the only one who's really working hard."

They sat down at the oval table, cluttered with empty coffee mugs and water bottles. Malmberg shook his head disapprovingly.

"People never clean up after themselves. They have their meetings, and when they've finished they disappear and leave all their rubbish behind. How can I help? Have you changed your mind about those bridge lessons?"

She told him about what she'd discovered, about her connection to the mass murders.

"I'm curious," she said. "All I can gather from what's in the papers and the news bulletins is that many people are dead, and the police don't have any leads."

"I don't mind admitting that I'm glad I don't work in that district right now. They must be going through sheer hell. I've never heard of anything like it. In its way it's just as sensational as the Palme murder."

"What do you know that isn't in the newspapers?"

"There isn't a single police officer the length and breadth of the country who isn't wondering what happened. Everybody has a theory. It's a myth that police officers are rational and lack imagination. We start speculating about what might have happened right away."

"What do you think happened?"

He shrugged and thought for a moment before answering.

"I know no more than you do. There are a lot of bodies, and it was brutal. But nothing was stolen, if I understand things correctly. The probability is that some sick individual was responsible. What lies behind it, goodness only knows. I assume the police up there are lining up known violent criminals with psychological problems. They've doubtless been in touch already with Interpol and Europol in the hope of finding a clue that way, but such things take time. That's all I know."

"You know police officers all over Sweden. Do you

have a contact up in Hälsingland? Somebody I could perhaps phone?"

"I've met their chief of police," said Malmberg. "A man by the name of Ludwig. To tell you the truth, I wasn't all that impressed by him. As you know, I don't have much time for police officers who've never been out in the real world. But I can call him and see what he has to say."

"I promise not to disturb them unnecessarily. I just want to know if it was my mother's foster parents who died. Or if it was their children. Or if I've got the wrong end of the stick altogether."

"That's a fair-enough reason for calling them. I'll see what I can do. But I'm afraid you'll have to excuse me now. I have an unpleasant interview with a very nasty violent man coming up."

That evening she told Staffan what had happened. His immediate reaction was that the doctor had done the right thing, and he suggested that she should take a trip to the south and the sun. His lack of interest irritated her. But she didn't say anything.

Shortly before lunch the following day, when she was sitting in front of her computer and surveying holiday offers, her telephone rang.

"I've got a name for you," said Hugo Malmberg. "There's a woman police officer called Sundberg."

"I've seen that name in the papers, but I didn't know it was a woman."

"Her first name's Vivian, but she's known as Vivi. Ludwig will pass your name on to her, so that she knows who you are when you call her. I've got a phone number."

"Thanks for your help. Incidentally, I might go south for a few days. Have you ever been to Tenerife?"

"Never. Good luck."

Roslin immediately dialed the number she'd been given. An answering machine invited her to leave a message.

Once again she took out the vacuum cleaner, but couldn't bring herself to use it. Instead she returned to the computer and within an hour or so had decided on a trip to Tenerife departing from Copenhagen two days later. She dug out an old school atlas and began dreaming of warm water and Spanish wines.

Maybe it's just what I need, she thought. A week without Staffan, without trials, without the daily grind. I'm not exactly experienced in confronting my emotions or indeed my life. But at my age I ought to be able to look at myself objectively and face up to my weaknesses and to change things if necessary. Once upon a time, when I was young, I used to dream of becoming the first woman to sail around the world single-handed. It never happened. But nevertheless, maybe I could do with a few days sailing out to Denmark, or strolling along a beach in Tenerife. Either will work out if old age is already catching up with me, or if I can scramble out of the hole I'm sinking into. I managed menopause pretty well, but

I'm not really sure what's happening to me now. What I must establish first of all is whether my high blood pressure and panic attacks have anything to do with Staffan. I must understand that we will never feel content unless we lift ourselves out of our current dispirited state.

She started planning her trip without further ado. There was a glitch that prevented her from finalizing her booking online, so she e-mailed her name and telephone number, and specified the package she was interested in. She had an immediate reply, saying she would be contacted within an hour.

Almost an hour later the telephone rang. But it wasn't the travel agency.

"Vivi Sundberg here. I'd like to speak to Birgitta Roslin."

"Speaking."

"Ah. I've been informed who you are, but I'm not sure what you want. As you can probably understand, we're under a lot of pressure right now. Am I right in thinking that you are a judge?"

"Yes, I am. I don't want to make too much of a fuss about this, but my mother—who died several years ago—was adopted by a family called Andrén. I've seen photographs that suggest she lived in one of the houses in Hesjövallen."

"Contacting the next of kin is not my responsibility. I suggest you speak to Erik Huddén."

"But am I right in thinking that some of the victims were in fact called Andrén?"

"Since you ask I can tell you that the Andrén family was the largest one in the village."

"And are all of them dead?"

"I can't tell you that. Do you have the first names of your mother's foster parents?"

She had the file on the desk in front of her; she untied the ribbon and leafed through the papers.

"I'm afraid I don't have time to wait," said Vivi Sundberg. "Call me when you've found the names."

"I have them here. Brita and August Andrén. They must be over ninety, possibly even ninety-five."

There was a pause before Sundberg responded. Roslin could hear the sound of papers rustling. Then Sundberg picked up the phone again.

"They are on the list. I'm afraid they are both dead, and the oldest was ninety-six. Please don't pass that information on to any newspaper."

"Why in God's name would I want to do that?"

"You're a judge. I'm sure you know what can happen, and why I'm asking you to keep the details to yourself."

Birgitta Roslin knew exactly what was meant, although she had occasionally discussed with her colleagues how they were seldom if ever buttonholed by journalists—reporters hardly thought that judges would release information that ought to be kept secret.

"I'm obviously interested in how the investigation is going."

"Neither I nor any of my colleagues has time to

release specific information. We are besieged by the mass media here. I recommend that you talk to Erik Huddén if you phone Hudiksvall."

Vivi Sundberg sounded impatient and irritated.

"Many thanks for calling. I won't disturb you any longer."

Birgitta Roslin hung up and thought over what had been said. At least she was now quite certain that her mother's foster parents were among the dead. Like everybody else, she would have to remain patient while the police went about their work.

She considered phoning police HQ in Hudiksvall and talking to this Erik Huddén. But what would he be able to add? She decided not to. Instead, she started reading more carefully the papers inside the file devoted to her parents. It was many years since she had last opened it. She realized that, in fact, she had never read some of the documents before.

She sorted the contents of the thick file into three piles. The first one comprised the life history of her father, whose body was lying on the seabed in Gävle-bukten. The water in the Baltic Sea was so salty that skeletons did not corrode especially quickly. Some-where in the silt were his bones and cranium. The second pile dealt with the shared life of her mother and father, and she featured in there herself, both before and after she was born. The third pile was the largest and contained papers relevant to Gerda Lööf, her mother, who became an Andrén. She read slowly through everything, especially when she came to the documents referring to the time when her mother had been fostered and adopted by the Andrén family. Many of them were faded and difficult to read, despite the fact that she used a magnifying glass.

She slid over a notepad and wrote down names and ages. She herself had been born in the spring of 1949. Her mother was then seventeen, having been born in 1931. She also found the birth dates of August and Brita Andrén: she was born in August 1909, and he in December 1910. So they had been twenty-two and twenty-one respectively when Gerda was born, and under thirty when she came to join them in Hesjövallen.

She found nothing to indicate that Hesjövallen was the place where they lived, but the photograph that she now checked again with the picture in the newspaper convinced her. There could be no mistake.

She started to examine the people standing upright and stiff in the ancient photograph. There were two younger people in it, a man and a woman standing a little to one side of the elderly couple at the center of the picture. Could they be Brita and August? There was no date, nothing written on the back of the picture. She tried to work out when it might have been taken. What did the clothes indicate? The people in the photograph had obviously dressed up for it, but they were rural people for whom a suit could last for a whole lifetime.

She pushed the photos to one side and turned to

the other documents and letters. In 1942 Brita had suffered from some stomach problem and been treated in the hospital in Hudiksvall. Gerda writes her a card and hopes she will soon be better. She is eleven at the time, and her handwriting is awkward. Some words are misspelled, and she has drawn a flower with irregular petals on one side of the card.

Birgitta was quite touched on reading this card and surprised that she hadn't noticed it before. It had been lying inside another letter. But why had she never opened it? Was it because of the pain she felt when Gerda died, which meant that she didn't want to touch anything that would remind her of her mother?

She leaned back in her chair and closed her eyes. She had her mother to thank for everything. Gerda didn't even finish school, but she had always urged her daughter to continue her studies. It's our turn now, she'd said. Now it's time for daughters of the working classes to get themselves an education. And that is precisely what Birgitta Roslin had done. During the 1960s, when no longer only middle-class children flocked to universities, it had been only natural for her to join radical left-wing groups. Life was not just a matter of understanding, but also of bringing about change.

She continued working her way methodically through the documents. She discovered another letter. The envelope was pale blue, and postmarked from America. The thin paper was filled with tiny handwriting. She focused the light from her desk lamp and with the aid of a magnifying glass tried to make out what the letter said. It was written in Swedish but contained a lot of English words. Somebody called Gustaf is describing his work as a pig farmer. A child called Emily has just died, and there is "stor sorrow" in the household. He wonders how things are back home in Hälsingland, how the family's doing, and the harvests and the animals. The letter was dated June 19, 1896. The address on the envelope was August Andrén, Hesjövallen, Sweden. But my maternal grandfather wasn't even born then, she thought. Presumably the letter must have been addressed to her great-grandfather, since it had been kept by Gerda's family. But why had it been passed down to her?

Right at the bottom, under the signature, was an address: **Mr. Gustaf Andrén, Minneapolis Post Office, Minnesota, United States of America.**

She checked her old school atlas again. Minnesota is farming country. So one of the Andrén family in Hesjövallen had emigrated there more than a century ago.

But she found another letter that showed another member of the Andrén family had ended up in different parts of the United States. His name was Jan August, and he evidently worked on the railroad that linked the East and West Coasts. His letter asked about relatives, living and dead, though large parts of the letter were illegible. The writing had become blurred.

Jan August's address was Reno Post Office, Nevada, United States of America.

She continued reading, but found nothing else in the piles that related to her mother's connection with the Andrén family.

She put the documents back in the file, returned to the Internet, and, without much hope of success, tried to find the postal address in Minneapolis that Gustaf Andrén had given. As expected, she came to a dead end. She tried the address in Nevada and was referred to a link to a newspaper called the **Reno Gazette-Journal.** Just then the phone rang: it was the travel agency. A friendly young man with a Danish accent ran through all the details of the package holiday with her and described the hotel. She didn't hesitate. She made a preliminary booking and promised to confirm it the following morning at the latest.

She returned to the computer and called up the **Reno Gazette-Journal** again. She was just about to move on to another page when she recalled that her search was for Andrén, not merely the postal address. So there must be some reference to that name in a recent issue of the **Reno Gazette-Journal.** She started reading through the list of articles and subjects, clicking her way from one page to the next.

She gave a start when the relevant page eventually appeared. At first she read it without really grasping its implications. Then she read it again, more slowly, and began to wonder if she could believe her eyes.

She stood up and backed away from the computer. But the text and the pictures didn't disappear.

She printed them out and took them with her to the kitchen. She read everything once more, very slowly.

On January fourth a brutal murder took place in the little town of Ankersville, northeast of Reno. The proprietor of an engineering workshop and his whole family were found dead that morning by a neighbor, who had become suspicious when the workshop didn't open as usual. The police have no leads as yet. But it is clear that the whole Andrén family—Jack, his wife, Connie, and their two children, Steven and Laura—had been murdered with some kind of knife or sword. There was nothing to indicate robbery or burglary. No obvious motive; the Andrén family was well liked and had no enemies. The police are now looking for a mentally unbalanced perpetrator, or perhaps a desperate drug addict, in connection with these horrific murders.

She sat there motionless. The sound of a garbage truck drifted up from the street below.

For the first time, she felt fear creeping up on her. As if she were being observed unawares.

She went to check that the front door was locked. Then she returned to the computer and started to work her way backward through the articles in the **Reno Gazette-Journal.**

The garbage truck had moved on. It was starting to get dark.

7

Long afterward, when the memory of everything that had taken place began to grow dim, she sometimes wondered what would have happened if she had in fact gone on that holiday to Tenerife, then come home and returned to work with her blood pressure lowered and her tiredness banished. But reality turned out differently. Early the next morning she called the travel agency and canceled her holiday. As she had been sensible enough to take out an insurance policy, the cancellation cost her only a few hundred kronor.

Staffan came home late that evening, as the train he was working on had been stranded, thanks to an engine failure. He had been forced to spend two hours consoling disgruntled passengers, including an elderly lady who had taken ill. By the time he got home he was tired and irritated. She let him eat his evening meal in peace. But when he'd finished she told him about her discovery of what had happened in distant Nevada, and how in all probability it was linked to the mass murders in Hälsingland. She could see he was doubtful, but she didn't know if that was because he was tired or because he didn't believe her theory. When he went to bed she returned to the computer and kept alternating between Hälsingland and Nevada. At midnight she made a few notes in a pad, just as she did when she was preparing a judgment. No matter how unlikely it might seem, she was convinced that there must be a connection between the two incidents. She was also well aware that, in a way, she was an Andrén too, even if her name was now Roslin.

Was she in danger? She sat for hours, hunched over her notepad. Then she went out into the clear January night and looked up at the stars. Her mother had once told her that her father had been a passionate stargazer. With long intervals in between, she used to receive letters from him describing how he would stand on deck at night in faraway places. Studying the stars and their various constellations. He had a strange belief that the dead were transformed into stars. Birgitta Roslin wondered what he had been thinking when the **Runskär** sank in Gävlebukten. The heavily laden ship had keeled over in the severe storm and sunk in less than a minute. Only one SOS signal had been sent out before the radio fell silent. Had he had time to realize that he was about to die? Or had the freezing water taken him so much by surprise that he had no time to think? Just sudden terror, then an icy chill, and death.

The sky seemed close; the stars shone brightly that night. I can see the surface, she thought. There is a connection, thin threads intertwining with one another. But what lay behind it all? What was the motive for killing nineteen people in a small village in the north of Sweden, and also putting an end to a family in the Nevada desert? Probably no more than the usual: revenge, greed, jealousy. But what injustice could require such drastic revenge? Who could gain financially by murdering a number of pensioners in a northern hamlet who were already well on their way to death? Who could possibly be jealous of them?

She went back indoors when she began to feel cold. She usually went to bed early because she always felt tired in the evening and hated to go to work the following morning without having had a good night's sleep, especially when a trial was taking place. She lay down on the sofa and switched on some music, quite softly so as not to disturb Staffan. It was a cavalcade of modern Swedish ballads. Birgitta Roslin had secretly dreamed of writing a pop song that would be chosen to represent Sweden in the Eurovision Song Contest. She was embarrassed about this desire but at the same time felt very positive about it. She even had several preliminary versions of songs locked away in her desk. Perhaps it was inappropriate for a practicing judge to write pop songs; but as far as she knew there was no rule against it.

It was three o'clock by the time she went to bed, and she gave Staffan a shake, as he was snoring. When he had turned over and fallen silent, she fell asleep herself.

The following morning she recalled a dream she'd had during the night. She had seen her mother, who spoke to her without Birgitta being able to grasp what she'd said. It was like being behind a pane of glass. It seemed to go on forever, the mother becoming more and more upset because her daughter didn't understand what she was saying, the daughter wondering what was keeping them apart.

Memory is like glass, she thought. A person who has died is still visible, very close. But we can no longer contact each other. Death is mute; it excludes conversations, only allows silence.

Birgitta Roslin got up. A thought was beginning to form inside her head. She fetched a road map of Sweden. When the children were small, every summer the family used to drive to various cottages they had rented, usually for a month. Very occasionally, such as the two summers they had spent on the island of Gotland, they had flown there. But they had never taken the train, and in those days it had never occurred to Staffan that one day he would exchange his lawyer's existence for that of a train conductor.

She turned to a general map of Sweden. Hälsingland was farther north than she had imagined. She couldn't find Hesjövallen. It was such an insignificant little hamlet that it wasn't even marked.

When she put the map down, she had made up her mind. She would take the car and drive up to Hudiksvall. Not primarily because she wanted to visit the crime scene, but in order to see the little village where her mother had grown up.

When she was younger she had dreamed of one day making a grand tour of Sweden. "The Journey Home," she used to call it. She would go to Treriksröset in the far north, where the borders of Sweden,

Norway, and Finland converged, and then back
south to the coast of Skåne, where she would be close
to the Continent, with the rest of Sweden behind her
back. On the way north she would follow the coast,
but on the way back south she would take the inland
route. However, that journey had never taken place.
Whenever she had mentioned it to Staffan, he had
displayed no interest. And it had not been possible
when the children were at home.

But now she had the opportunity to make at least
part of that journey.

When Staffan had finished his breakfast and was
preparing to join the train to Alvesta, the last one
before he was due for several days off, she told him her
plan. He didn't object, merely asked how long she
would be away and if her doctor would be happy about
the strain that such a long drive was bound to impose.

It was only when he was in the hall with his hand
on the front-door handle that she became upset.
They had said good-bye in the kitchen, but now she
followed him and threw the morning paper angrily
at him.

"What on earth are you doing?"

"Have you no interest at all in why I want to take
this trip?"

"But you've told me why."

"Doesn't it occur to you that I might also need
some time to think about our relationship?"

"We can't start in on that now. I'll miss my train."

"There's never a good time as far as you're concerned!

It's no good in the evening, no good in the morning. Don't you ever want to talk to me about our life?"

"You know that I'm not as perturbed about it as you are."

"Perturbed? You call it being perturbed when I wonder why we haven't made love for over a year?"

"We can't talk about that now. I don't have time."

"You'll soon have plenty of time."

"Meaning what?"

"Perhaps I've run out of patience."

"Is that a threat?"

"All I know is that we can't keep going on like this. Go away, go to your damned train."

She turned on her heel, headed for the kitchen, and heard the front door slam. She felt relieved at having said at last what she'd been wanting to say for ages, but she was also anxious about how he would react.

He phoned that evening. Neither of them mentioned what had happened in the hall that morning. But she could tell by his voice that he was shaken. Perhaps it would be possible now, and not a moment too soon, for them to talk about what could no longer be suppressed?

The following day, early in the morning, she got into the car, ready to drive north from Helsingborg. Staffan, who had arrived home in the middle of the night, carried her bag out to the car and put it on the backseat.

"Where are you going to stay?"

"There's a little hotel in Lindesberg. I'll spend the night there. I promise to call you. Then I suppose I'll find somewhere in Hudiksvall."

He stroked her cheek gently and waved as she drove off.

A day later she found herself six or seven miles from Hudiksvall. If she turned off inland a bit farther north, she would pass through Hesjövallen. She hesitated a moment, felt a bit like a hyena, but banished the thought. She had a good reason for going there, after all.

When she reached Iggesund she took a left, and went left again when she came to a fork in the road at Ölsund. She passed a police car traveling in the opposite direction, and then another. The trees suddenly gave way to a lake. A row of houses lined the road, all of them cut off by red-and- white police tape. Police officers were walking along the road.

She could see a tent erected at the edge of the trees, and a second one in the nearest yard. She scanned the village slowly through a pair of binoculars she'd brought with her. People in uniform or overalls were moving between the houses, smoking by the gates in groups. She sometimes visited crime scenes as part of her work and was familiar with the setup—though not on such a scale. She knew that prosecuting counsels and other officers of the law were not especially welcome, as the police were often wary of criticism.

A uniformed police officer tapped on her windshield and interrupted her thoughts.

"What are you doing here?"

"I didn't realize that I'd strayed inside the cordoned-off area."

"You haven't. But we keep an eye on everybody who comes here. Especially if they have binoculars. We hold our press conferences in Hudiksvall, in case you didn't know."

"I'm not a reporter."

The young police officer eyed her suspiciously.

"What are you, then? A crime-scene junkie?"

"Actually I'm a relative."

The officer took out his notebook.

"Of whom?"

"Brita and August Andrén. I'm on my way to Hudiksvall, but I can't remember the name of the person I'm supposed to see."

"Erik Huddén. He's the one responsible for contacting relatives. Please accept my condolences."

"Thank you."

The officer saluted; she felt like an idiot, turned around, and drove off. When she came to Hudiksvall she realized that it wasn't only the battalions of reporters that made finding a vacant hotel room impossible. A friendly receptionist at the First Hotel Statt told her that there was also a conference taking place that involved delegates from all over Sweden, "discussing forests." She parked her car and wandered around the little town. She tried two hotels and a guesthouse, but everything was full.

She looked for somewhere to have lunch and found a little Chinese restaurant. It was quite full, but she got a small table next to a window. The room seemed to be exactly like every other Chinese restaurant she'd been to. The same vases, porcelain lions, and lamps with colored ribbons serving as shades.

A Chinese woman came with the menu. Birgitta Roslin ordered with difficulty; the young woman could speak practically no Swedish at all.

After her hasty lunch, she tried to book a room and eventually got one at the Andbacken Hotel in Delsbo. There was a conference going on there as well, this one for an advertising company. Everyone in Sweden appeared to be tied up traveling between hotels and conference venues.

Andbacken turned out to be a large white building on the shore of a snow-covered lake. As she waited in line at reception, she read that the advertising folk would be busy that afternoon with group work. In the evening there would be a gala dinner, at which prizes would be distributed. Please God, don't let this be a noisy night with drunks running up and down the corridors and slamming doors, she thought.

Her room looked out over the frozen lake and the wooded hills. She lay down on the bed and closed her eyes for a short while, then got up, put on her jacket, and drove to Hudiksvall. Reporters and TV crews thronged the police station. Eventually she found herself face-to-face with a young, exhausted receptionist and explained what she wanted.

"Vivi Sundberg doesn't have time."

The dismissive response surprised her.

"Aren't you even going to ask me what I want to see her about?"

"I take it you want to ask her questions, like everybody else. You'll have to wait until the next press conference."

"I'm not a journalist. I'm a relative of one of the families in Hesjövallen."

The woman behind the counter changed her attitude immediately.

"I apologize. You need to speak to Eric Huddén."

She dialed a number and told Eric that he had a visitor. It was evidently not necessary to say any more. "Visitor" was a code word for "relative."

"He'll come down and collect you. Wait over there by the glass doors."

She found a young man standing by her side.

"Unless I'm much mistaken, I think I heard you say that you were a relative of one of the murder victims. Can I ask you a few questions?"

Birgitta Roslin usually kept her claws tucked into her paws. But not now.

"No. I've no idea who you are."

"I write."

"For whom?"

"For everybody who's interested."

She shook her head. "I've nothing to say to you."

"Obviously, I'm very sorry about your sad loss."

"No," she said. "You're not sorry at all. You are speaking softly in order not to attract attention—so others don't realize you've found a relative."

The glass doors were opened by a man with a badge informing the world that he was Erik Huddén. They shook hands. A photographer's flash was reflected in the glass doors as they closed again.

There were people everywhere. The tempo here was radically different from that in Hesjövallen. They went into a conference room where a table was covered in files and lists. This is where the dead are gathered together, Roslin thought. Huddén invited her to sit down and took a seat opposite her. She told the full story from the beginning, the two different name changes, and how she discovered that she was related to the victims. She could see that Huddén was disappointed when he realized that her presence was not going to help.

"I realize that you no doubt need other information," she said. "I work in the law, and I'm not totally unaware of the procedures involved."

"Obviously, I'm grateful that you've come to see us."

He put down his pen and squinted at her.

"But have you really come all the way from Skåne to tell us this? You could have phoned."

"I have something to say that is relevant to the investigation. I'd like to speak to Vivi Sundberg."

"Can't you tell me? She's extremely busy."

"I've already started talking to her, and it would be useful to continue where we left off."

He went out into the corridor and closed the door behind him. Roslin slid the file labeled BRITA AND AUGUST ANDRÉN toward her. What she saw horrified her. There were photographs, taken inside the house. It was only now that she realized the scale of the bloodbath. She stared at the pictures of the sliced and diced bodies. The woman was almost impossible to identify, as she had been slashed by a blow that almost cut her face in two. One of the man's arms was hanging from just a couple of thin sinews.

She closed the file and pushed it away. But the images were still there; she wouldn't be able to forget them. During her years in court she had often been forced to look at photographs of sadistic violence, but she had never seen anything to compare with what Erik Huddén had in his files.

He came back and beckoned her to follow him.

Vivi Sundberg was sitting at a desk laden with documents. Her pistol and cell phone were lying on top of a file filled almost to the bursting point. She indicated a visitor's chair.

"You wanted to speak to me," said Sundberg. "If I understand it rightly, you've traveled all the way from Helsingborg. You must feel what you have to say is important."

Her cell phone rang. She switched it off and looked expectantly at her visitor.

Roslin told her story without getting bogged down

in details. She had often sat on the bench and thought about how a prosecuting or defending counsel, an accused or a witness, ought to have expressed themselves. She was an expert in that particular skill.

"Perhaps you already know about the Nevada incident," she said when she had finished.

"It hasn't come up at our briefings yet."

"What do you think?"

"I don't think anything."

"It could mean that the murderer you are looking for is not a madman."

"I shall evaluate your information the same way I do every tip and suggestion. And believe me—there are masses of them here, phone calls, letters, e-mails. You name it, we got it. Who knows, something may turn up."

She reached for a notepad and asked Birgitta Roslin to repeat her story. When she had finished making notes she stood up and escorted her visitor to the exit.

Just before they came to the glass doors, she paused.

"Do you want to see the house where your mother grew up? Is that why you've come here?"

"Is it possible?"

"The bodies are gone. I can let you in, if you'd like to. I'll be going there in half an hour. But you must promise me not to take anything away from the house. There are people who'd be only too pleased to rip up the cork tiles on which a murdered person has been lying."

"I'm not like that."

"If you wait in your car, you can follow me."

Vivi Sundberg pressed a button, and the glass doors slid open. Birgitta Roslin hurried out into the street before any of the reporters who were still gathered in reception could get hold of her.

As she sat with her hand on the ignition key, it struck her that she had failed. Sundberg hadn't taken her seriously. It was unlikely they'd look into the Nevada lead, and if they did it would be without much enthusiasm.

Who could blame them—the leap between Hesjövallen and Nevada was too great.

A black car with no police markings drew up beside her. Vivi Sundberg waved.

When they reached the village, Sundberg led her to the house.

"I'll leave you here, so that you can be alone for a while."

Birgitta Roslin took a deep breath and stepped inside. All the lights were on.

It was like stepping from the wings onto a floodlit stage. And she was the only person in the play.

8

Birgitta Roslin stood in the hall and listened. There is a silence in empty houses that is unique, she thought. People have left and taken all the noise with them. There isn't even a clock ticking anywhere.

She went into the living room. Old-fashioned smells abounded, from furniture, tapestries, and pale porcelain vases crammed onto shelves and in between potted plants. She felt with a finger in one of the pots, then went to the kitchen, found a watering can, and watered all the plants she could find. She sat down on a chair and looked around her. How much of all this had been here when her mother lived in this house? Most of it, she suspected. Everything here is old; furniture grows old with the people who use it.

The floor, where the bodies had been lying, was still covered in plastic sheeting. She went up the stairs. The bed in the master bedroom was unmade. There was a slipper lying halfway under the bed. She couldn't find its mate. There were two other rooms on this upper floor. In the one facing west, the wallpaper was covered in childish images of animals. She had a vague memory of her mother having mentioned that wallpaper once. There was a bed, a wardrobe, a chest of drawers, a chair, and a heap of rag-rugs piled up against one of the walls. She opened the wardrobe: the shelves were lined with newspaper pages. One was dated 1969. By then her mother had been gone for more than twenty years.

She sat in the chair in front of the window. It was dark now, the wooded ridges on the other side of the lake were no longer visible. A police officer was moving around at the edge of the trees, lit up by a colleague's flashlight. He kept stopping and bending down to examine the ground, as if he were looking for something.

Birgitta Roslin had the feeling that her mother was near. Her mother had sat in this very place long before Birgitta had ever been thought of. Here, in the same room at a different time. Somebody had carved squiggles into the white-painted window frame. Perhaps her mother. Perhaps every mark was an expression of a longing to get away, to find a new dawn.

She stood up and went back downstairs. Off the kitchen was a room with a bed, some crutches leaning against a wall, and an old-fashioned wheelchair. On the floor next to the bedside table was an enamel chamber pot. The room gave the impression of not having been used for a very long time.

She returned to the living room, tiptoeing around as if afraid of disturbing somebody. The drawers in a writing desk were half open. One was full of tablecloths and napkins, another of dark-colored balls of wool. In the third drawer, the bottom one, were some bundles of letters and notebooks with brown covers. She took out one of the notebooks and opened it. There was no name in it. It was completely filled with tiny handwriting. She took out her glasses and tried to make sense of what looked to be a diary. The spelling was distinctly old-fashioned. The notes were about locomotives, coaches, railroad tracks.

Then she noticed a word that gave her a start: Nevada. She stood stock-still and held her breath. Something had suddenly begun to change. This mute, empty house had sent her a message. She tried to decipher what followed, but she heard the front door opening. She replaced the diary and closed the drawer. Vivi Sundberg came into the room.

"No doubt you've seen where the bodies were lying," she said. "I don't need to show you."

Birgitta Roslin nodded.

"We lock the houses at night. You ought to leave now."

"Have you found any next of kin of the couple who lived here?"

"That's exactly what I came to tell you. It doesn't seem like Brita and August had any children of their own, nor any other relatives apart from the ones living in the village who are also dead. The list of victims will be made public tomorrow."

"And then what will happen to them?"

"Maybe that's something you ought to think about, as you are related to them."

"I'm not actually related to them. But I care about them in any case."

They left the house. Sundberg locked the door and hung the key on a nail.

"We don't expect anybody to break in," she said. "Just now this village is as well guarded as the Swedish royal family."

They said their good-byes on the road. Powerful searchlights illuminated some of the houses. Once again, Birgitta Roslin had the feeling of being on a stage in a theater.

"Will you be going back home tomorrow?" asked Vivi Sundberg.

"I suppose so. Have you thought any more about what I told you?"

"I shall pass on your information tomorrow when we have our morning meeting."

"But you must agree that it seems possible, not to say probable, that there is a connection."

"It's too early to answer that question. But I think the best thing you can do now is to let it drop."

Birgitta Roslin watched Vivi Sundberg get into her car and drive away. She doesn't believe me, she said aloud to herself in the darkness. She doesn't believe me—and, of course, I can understand that.

But then again, it annoyed her. If she had been a police officer, she would have given priority to information that suggested a link with a similar incident, even though it had taken place on another continent.

She decided to speak to the prosecutor who was in charge of the preliminary investigation.

She drove far too quickly to Delsbo and was still upset when she came to her hotel. The advertising executives' ceremonial dinner was in full swing in the dining room, and she had to eat in the deserted bar. She ordered a glass of wine to accompany her meal. It was an Australian Shiraz, very tasty, but she couldn't make up her mind if it had overtones of chocolate or licorice, or perhaps both.

After her meal she went up to her room. Her indignation had subsided. She took one of her iron tablets and thought about the diary she had glanced at. She ought to have told Vivi Sundberg what she had discovered. But for whatever reason, she hadn't. There was a risk that the diary would become yet another insignificant detail in a wide-ranging investigation overflowing with evidence.

Good police officers had a special gift for weeding out links in a mass of evidence that to others might seem haphazard and chaotic. What type of police officer was Vivi Sundberg? An overweight middle-aged woman who didn't give the impression of being all that quick-witted.

She immediately withdrew that judgment. It was unfair. She knew nothing about Vivi Sundberg.

She lay down on the bed, switched on the television, and heard the vibrations from the double basses in the dining room.

Birgitta's cell phone rang and woke her up. She glanced at the clock and saw that she had been asleep for more than an hour. It was Staffan.

"Where in the world are you? Where am I calling?"

"Delsbo."

"I barely know where that is."

"Hudiksvall, just to the west. If my memory isn't playing tricks on me, people in the old days used to talk about brutal knife fights featuring farmhands in Delsbo."

She told him about her visit to Hesjövallen. She could hear jazz playing in the background. He most likely thinks it's good to be on his own, she thought.

He can listen as much as he wants to the jazz I don't like at all.

"What happens next?" he asked when she had finished.

"I'll decide that tomorrow. You can go back to your music now."

"It's Charlie Mingus."

"Who?"

"You mean you've forgotten who Charlie Mingus is?"

"I sometimes think all your jazz musicians have the same name."

"Now you're offending me."

"I didn't mean to."

"Are you absolutely sure about that?"

"Meaning what?"

"All I mean is that you have nothing but contempt for the music I like so much."

"Why should I?"

"That's a question only you can answer."

The conversation came to an abrupt end. He slammed the phone down. That made her furious, so she rang him back, but he didn't answer. She gave up. I'm not the only one who's weary, she thought. He no doubt thinks I'm as cold and distant as I think he is.

She got ready for bed. It was some time before she could fall asleep. Early in the morning, while it was still dark, she was woken up by a door slamming somewhere. She remained lying there in the dark, recalling what she had dreamed. She'd been in Brita and August's house. They had been talking to her, both of them sitting on the dark red sofa, while she was standing on the floor in front of them. She had suddenly noticed that she was naked. She tried to cover herself up and leave, but couldn't. Her legs seemed to be paralyzed. When she looked down she saw that her feet were enclosed by the floorboards.

That was the moment she had woken up. She listened to the darkness. Loud, drunken voices approached and faded away. She glanced at her watch. A quarter to five. Still a long time to go before dawn. She settled down to try to go back to sleep, but a thought struck her.

The key was hanging from a nail. She sat up in bed. Obviously, it was forbidden and preposterous. Going to get what was in the chest of drawers. Not waiting until some police officer might just possibly happen to take an interest in what was there.

She got out of bed and stood by the window. Still, deserted. I can do it, she thought. If I'm lucky I might be able to ensure that this investigation doesn't get stuck in the mud like the worst case I've ever come across, the murder of our prime minister. But I'd be taking the law into my own hands, some zealous prosecutor might be able to convince a stupid judge that I was interfering in a criminal investigation.

Even worse was the wine she had drunk. It would be disastrous to be arrested for drunk driving. She worked out how many hours it was since she had dinner. The alcohol should be out of her system by now. But she wasn't sure.

I shouldn't do this, she thought. Even if the police on duty there are asleep. I can't do it.

Then she dressed and left her room. The corridor was empty. She could hear noises from various rooms where afterparties were still carrying on. She even thought she could hear a couple making love.

Reception was clear. She caught a glimpse of the back of a light-haired woman in the room behind the counter.

The cold hit her as she left the hotel. There was no wind; the sky was clear; it was much colder than the previous night.

Birgitta Roslin began to have second thoughts in the car. But the temptation was simply too great. She wanted to read more of that diary.

There was no other traffic on the road. At one point she braked hard when she thought she saw a moose by the piled-up snow at the side of the road, but it was only a tree stump.

When she came to the final hill before the descent into the village, she stopped and switched off the lights. She kept a flashlight in the glove compartment. She started walking carefully along the road. She kept stopping to listen. A slight breeze rustled through the invisible treetops. When she reached the crest of the hill, she saw that two searchlights were still shining, and there was a police car parked outside the house closest to the trees. She would be able to approach Brita and August's house without being seen. She cupped her hand around the flashlight, went through the gate into the yard of the neighboring house, then crept up to the front door from behind. Still no sign of life from the police car. She fumbled around until she found the key.

Once inside the house, Birgitta Roslin shuddered. She took a plastic carrier bag from her jacket pocket and cautiously opened the drawer.

The flashlight went out. She shook it, but couldn't bring it back to life. Even so, she started to fill the bag with the letters and diaries. One of the bundles of letters slipped out of her hand, and she spent ages fumbling around on the cold floor until she found it.

Then she hurried away, back to her car. The receptionist stared at her in astonishment when she got back to the hotel.

She was tempted to start reading right away, but decided it would be best to get an hour or two of sleep. At nine o'clock she borrowed a magnifying glass from the front desk and sat down at the table, which she had moved to the window. The advertising crowd was saying its good-byes before tumbling into cars and minibuses. She hung the DO NOT DISTURB sign on her door handle, then turned her attention to the diary she had started reading. It was slow work—some words, and even some sentences, she couldn't work out.

The author gave no name, only the initials JA. For some reason he never used the first person when referring to himself, but always the initials **JA.** She remembered the second letter she had found among her mother's papers. Jan August Andrén. That must be him. A foreman on the railroad construction moving slowly eastward through the Nevada desert, who described in great and meticulous detail his role in the venture. How he readily submitted to those above him in the hierarchy, who impressed him with the power they wielded. His illnesses, including a persistent fever that prevented him from working for a long time.

In places his handwriting would become shaky. JA described "a high temperature, and blood in the frequent and painful vomiting that afflicts me." Birgitta Roslin could almost feel the fear of death that radiated from the pages of the diary. As JA didn't date most of his entries, she was unable to judge how long he was ill. On one of the subsequent pages he wrote his last will and testament: "To my friend Herbert my best jackboots and other clothing, and to Mr. Harrison my rifle and my revolver, and I beg him to inform my relatives in Sweden that I have passed on. Give money to the railroad priest in order to enable him to arrange a decent burial with at least two hymns. I had not suspected that my life would be over so soon. May God help me."

But JA didn't die. Abruptly, with no evident transitional stage, he is fit and well again.

So JA appears to have been a foreman with the Central Pacific Company, which was building a railroad from the Pacific Ocean to a point in the middle of the continent where it would meet up with the line from the East Coast. He sometimes complains that the workers "are exceeding lazy" if he doesn't keep a close watch over them. The ones who annoy him most are the Irish, because they drink heavily and are late starting work in the mornings. He calculates that he will be forced to dismiss one out of every four Irish laborers, which will create major problems. It is impossible to employ American Indians, as they refuse to work in the required way. Negroes are easier, but former slaves who have either been liberated or run away are unwilling to obey his orders. JA writes that "a workforce of decent Swedish peasants would have been much preferable to all the unreliable Chinese laborers and drunken Irishmen."

Birgitta Roslin was finding that interpreting the text was straining her eyes, and she frequently needed to lie down on her bed, close her eyes, and rest. She turned to one of the three bundles of letters instead. Once again, it is JA. The same, barely legible handwriting. He writes to his parents and tells them how he's getting on. There is a glaring difference between what JA notes down in his diary and what he writes in his letters home. If what's in his diary is the truth, the letters are full of lies. He wrote in the diary that his monthly wage was eleven dollars. In one of the first letters he writes home, he says that his "bosses are so pleased with me that I'm now earning 25 dollars a month, which is about what an inspector of taxes earns back home." He's boasting, she thought.

Birgitta Roslin read more letters and discovered more lies, each one more astonishing than the last. He suddenly acquires a fiancée, a cook named Laura who comes from "a family well placed in high society in New York." Judging from the date of the letter, this was when he was close to death and wrote his last will and testament. Perhaps Laura appeared in one of his delirious dreams.

The man Birgitta Roslin was trying to pin down was slippery, somebody who always managed to wriggle away. She started leafing through the letters and diaries all the more impatiently.

Between the diaries she found a document she assumed was a pay slip. In April 1864 Jan August Andrén had been paid eleven dollars for his labors. Now she was certain that this was the same man who had written the letter she found among her mother's papers.

She looked out the window. A lone man was shoveling snow. Once upon a time a lone man named Jan August Andrén emigrated from Hesjövallen, she thought. He ended up in Nevada, working on the railroad. He became a foreman and didn't seem to have been too fond of those in his charge. The fiancée he invented might just have been one of the "loose women who gravitate towards the railroad construction sites," as one entry detailed. Venereal disease was rife among the workforce. Whores who followed the railroad were disruptive. It wasn't just that VD-infected workers had to be fired: violent fights over women were a constant source of delay.

In one instance, JA describes how an Irishman named O'Connor had been sentenced to death for murdering a Scottish laborer. They had been drunk and ended up fighting over a woman. O'Connor was now due to be hanged, and the judge who traveled to the camp in order to preside over the trial had agreed that the hanging didn't need to take place in the nearest town, but could be carried out on a hill close to the point the railroad track had reached. Jan August Andrén writes, "I like the idea of everybody being able to see what drunkenness and violence can lead to."

He describes the Irishman as young, with "barely more than down on his chin."

The execution will take place early, just before the morning shift begins. Not even a hanging can result in a single sleeper car or even a single coach bolt being fitted behind schedule. The foreman has been instructed to make sure that everybody attends the execution. A strong wind is blowing. Jan August Andrén ties a bandanna over his nose and mouth as he goes around checking that his team has left its tents for the hill where the hanging will take place. The gallows is on a platform made of newly tarred sleepers. The moment O'Connor is dead the gallows will be dismantled and the sleepers carried back down to where the track is being laid. The condemned man arrives, surrounded by armed guards. There is also a priest present. Andrén describes the scene: "A growling dissent could be heard from the assembled men. For a moment one might suppose the grumbling was directed at the hangman, but then one realized that all present were relieved not to be the one about to have his neck broken. I could well imagine that many of them who hated the daily toil were now feeling blissful delight at the prospect of being able to carry iron rails, shovel gravel, and lay sleepers today."

Andrén writes like an early crime reporter, Birgitta Roslin thought. But was he writing for himself, or possibly for some unknown reader in the future? Otherwise why use terms like "blissful delight"?

O'Connor trudges along in his chains as if in a trance, but suddenly comes to life at the foot of the gallows and starts shouting and fighting for his life. The unease among the assembled men increases in volume, and Andrén writes that it is "terrible to watch this young man fighting for the life he knows he will soon lose. He is led kicking and screaming to the rope, and continues bellowing until the trapdoor opens and his neck is broken." At that moment the growling ceases, and according to Andrén it becomes "totally silent, as if all those present have been struck dumb, and felt their own necks breaking."

He expresses himself well, Roslin thought. A man with emotions, who can write.

The gallows is dismantled, the body and the sleepers carried off in different directions. There is a fight between several Chinese who want the rope used to hang O'Connor.

The telephone rang. It was Sundberg.

"Did I wake you up?"

"No."

"Can you come down? I'm in reception."

"What's it about?"

"Come down and I'll tell you."

Vivi Sundberg was waiting by the open fire.

"Let's sit down," she said, pointing to some chairs and a sofa around a table in the corner.

"How did you know I was staying here?"

"I made inquiries."

Roslin began to suspect the worst. Sundberg was reserved, cool. She came straight to the point.

"We are not entirely without eyes and ears, you know," she began. "Even if we are only provincial police officers. No doubt you know what I'm talking about."

"No."

"We are missing the contents of a chest of drawers in the house I was kind enough to let you into. I asked you not to touch anything. But you did. You must have gone back there at some time during the night. In the drawer you emptied were diaries and letters. I'll wait here while you get them. Were there five or six diaries? How many bundles of letters? Bring them all down. When you do, I shall be kind enough to forget all about this. You can also be grateful that I went to the trouble of coming here."

Birgitta Roslin could feel that she was blushing. She had been caught in flagrante, with her fingers in the jam jar. There was nothing she could do. The judge had been found out.

She stood up and went to her room. For a brief moment she was tempted to keep the diary she was reading just then, but she had no idea exactly how much Sundberg knew. Her seeming uncertainty about how many diaries there were was not necessarily significant—she could have been testing Roslin's honesty. She carried everything she had taken down to reception. Vivi Sundberg had a paper bag into which she put all the diaries and letters.

"Why did you do it?" she asked.

"I was curious. I can only apologize."

"Is there anything you haven't told me?"

"I have no hidden motives."

Sundberg eyed her critically. Roslin could feel she was blushing again. Sundberg stood up. Despite being powerfully built and overweight, she moved daintily.

"Let the police take care of this business," she said. "I won't make a song and dance about you entering the house during the night. We'll forget it. Go home now, and I'll carry on working."

"I apologize."

"You have already."

Sundberg left the hotel and got into the police car waiting outside. Birgitta Roslin watched it drive away in a cloud of snow. She went up to her room, fetched a jacket, and went for a walk along the shore of the ice-covered lake. The wind came and went in chilly gusts. She bowed her head. She felt slightly ashamed.

She walked all the way around the lake and was warm and sweaty when she returned to the hotel. After a shower and a change of clothes, she thought about what had happened.

She had now seen her mother's room and knew

that it was her mother's foster parents who had been killed. It was time to go home.

She went down to reception and asked to keep the room for one more night. Then she drove into Hudiksvall, found a bookshop, and bought a book about wines. She wondered whether to eat again at the Chinese restaurant she'd visited the previous day, but chose an Italian place instead. She lingered over her meal and read the newspapers without bothering to see what had been written about Hesjövallen.

She drove back to the hotel, read some pages of the book she had bought, went to bed early.

She was woken up by her phone ringing. It was pitch-dark. When she answered nobody was there. There was no number on the display.

She suddenly felt uncomfortable. Who had called?

Before going back to sleep she checked to make sure the door was locked. Then she looked out the window. There was no sign of anybody on the road to the hotel. She went back to bed, thinking that the next day she would do the only sensible thing.

She would go home.

9

She was in the breakfast room by seven o'clock. The windows looked out over the lake, and she could see that it had become windy. A man approached, pulling a sled with two well-bundled children as passengers. She recalled the days when she had spent so much time and effort dragging her own children up slopes that they could sled down. That had been one of the most remarkable periods of her life—playing with her children in the snow, and at the same time worrying about what judgment to pass in a complicated lawsuit. The children's shouts and laughter contrasting with the frightening crime scenes.

She had once worked out that during the course of her career, she had sent three murderers and seven people guilty of manslaughter to prison. Not to mention several more sentenced for grievous bodily harm, who could count themselves lucky that their crimes had not resulted in murder.

The thought worried her. Measuring her activities and her best efforts in terms of people she had sent to prison—was that really the sum of her life's work?

As she ate she avoided looking at the newspapers, which were naturally wallowing in the events at Hesjövallen. Instead she selected a business supplement and leafed through the stock-market listings and discussons about the percentage of women represented on the boards of Swedish companies. There were not many people at breakfast. She refilled her coffee cup and wondered if it might be a good idea to take a different route home. A touch farther west, perhaps, through the Värmland forests?

She was interrupted in her thoughts by somebody addressing her. A man sitting alone at a table several feet away.

"Are you talking to me?"

"I just wondered what Vivi Sundberg wanted."

She didn't recognize the man and didn't really understand what he was asking about. Before she had a chance to reply, he stood up and walked over to her table. Pulled out a chair and sat down.

He was in his sixties, red-faced and overweight, and his breath was foul.

"I'd like to eat my breakfast in peace."

"You've finished eating. I just want to ask you a few questions."

"I don't even know who you are."

"Lars Emanuelsson. Freelance journalist. Not a reporter. I'm better than that lot. I'm not a hack. I do my homework, and what I write is thoroughly researched and stylishly written."

"That doesn't give you the right to prevent me from eating my breakfast in peace."

Lars Emanuelsson stood up, and sat down on a chair at the next table.

"Is that better?"

"A bit. Whom do you write for?"

"I haven't made up my mind yet. First I need to get the story, then I'll decide where to offer it. I don't sell my work to just anybody."

She was irritated by his self-importance. She was also repulsed by his smell—it must have been a very long time since he had last taken a shower. He came off as a caricature of an intrusive reporter.

"I noticed that you had a chat with Vivi Sundberg yesterday. Not an especially cordial exchange of views, I would say. More like two cockerels, marking their territory. Am I right?"

"You are wrong. I have nothing to say to you."

"But you can't deny that you spoke with her?"

"Of course I can't."

"I wonder what a judge from another town is doing up here. You must have something to do with this investigation. Horrible things happen in a little hamlet up north, and Birgitta Roslin comes rushing up from Helsingborg."

She became even more cautious.

"What do you want? How do you know who I am?"

"It all boils down to methods. We spend our whole lives searching for the best way of getting results. I take it that applies to judges as well. You have rules and regulations. But you choose your own methods. I don't know how many criminal investigations I've reported on. I spent a full year—or, to be more precise, three hundred sixty-six days—following the Palme investigation. I realized early on that the murderer would never be caught because the investigation ran aground before it had even been launched. It was obvious that the guilty party would never appear in court because the police and the prosecutors were not trying to solve the murder; they were more interested in appearing on prime-time television. Many people assumed then that the culprit was Christer Pettersson. Apart from some sane and sensible investigators who realized that this accusation was wrong, completely wrong. But nobody paid any attention to them. Me, I prefer to hover around the periphery, see things from the outside. That way I notice things that the others miss. For instance, a judge being visited by an investigating officer who can't possibly have time for anything else but the case she's busy with from morning till night. What was it that you handed over to her?"

"I'm not going to answer that question."

"So I interpret that as meaning you are deeply involved in what has happened. I can see the headline now: 'Scanian Judge Involved in the Hesjövallen Drama.' "

She drank the rest of her coffee and stood up. He followed her into reception.

"If you give me a tip, I can repay you in spades."

"I have absolutely nothing to say to you. Not because I have any secrets, but because I know nothing that could possibly be of any interest to a reporter."

Lars Emanuelsson looked depressed. "Not a reporter, a freelance journalist. Let's face it, I don't call you a shyster."

"Was it you who called me last night?"

"Eh?"

"So it was. At least I know."

"You mean to say that your cell phone rang? In the middle of the night? When you were asleep? Is that something I ought to follow up?"

She didn't answer but pressed the button to summon the elevator.

"There's one thing you ought to know," said Lars Emanuelsson. "The police are suppressing an important detail. If you can call a person a detail."

The elevator doors opened; she stepped in.

"It wasn't only old people who died. There was a young boy in one of the houses."

The doors closed. When she came to her floor, she pressed the down button again. He was waiting for her, hadn't moved an inch. They sat down. Lars Emanuelsson lit a cigarette.

"You're not allowed to smoke in here."

"Tell me something else that I couldn't care less about."

There was a potted plant on the table that he used as an ashtray.

"You always need to look for what the police don't tell you. What they conceal can reveal the way they are thinking, where they think they might be able to pin down their perpetrator. In among all those dead people was a twelve-year-old boy. They know who his next of kin are, and why he was there in the village. But they aren't telling the general public."

"How do you know this?"

"That's my secret. In an investigation like this there's always a potential leak. It's a question of identifying it, and then listening carefully."

"Who is this boy?"

"At the moment he's an unknown factor. I know his name, but I'm not going to say. He was visiting relatives. He really ought to have been at school, but he was convalescing after an eye operation. The poor kid had a lazy eye. But now his eye was in the right place, back in its slot, you might say. And then he was killed. Like the old folks he was staying with. But not quite the same."

"What was different?"

Emanuelsson leaned back in his chair. His stomach overflowed his waistband. Roslin found him totally repulsive. He was aware of that, but didn't care.

"Now it's your turn. Vivi Sundberg, the books, and letters."

"I'm a distant relative of some of the people who've been murdered. I gave Sundberg some material she'd asked for."

He screwed up his eyes and peered at her. "Do you expect me to believe that?"

"You can believe whatever you like."

"What books? What letters?"

"They were about family circumstances."

"What family?"

"Brita and August Andrén."

He nodded thoughtfully, then stubbed out his cigarette with unexpected energy.

"House number two or seven. The police have given every house a code. House number two is called two slash three—which obviously means that they found three dead bodies there."

He continued watching her closely as he took a half-smoked cigarette from a crumpled pack.

"That doesn't explain why your exchanges were so cold in tone."

"She was in a hurry. What was different about the death of the boy?"

"I haven't managed to find out every detail. I have to admit that the Hudiksvall police and the ones they've called in from the CID in Stockholm are keeping their cards unusually close to their chest. But I think I'm right in saying that the boy wasn't exposed to unwarranted violence."

"What do you mean by that?"

"What can it mean but that he was killed without first having to experience unnecessary suffering, torture, and fear? You can draw various conclusions from that, each one more likely but probably more false than the next. But I'll let you do that yourself. If you're interested."

He stood up, having first once again stubbed out his cigarette in the plant pot.

"I'd better get back to circulating," he said. "Maybe we'll bump into each other again. Who knows?"

She watched him go out through the door. A receptionist came past and paused when she smelled the smoke.

"It wasn't me," said Birgitta Roslin. "I smoked my last cigarette when I was thirty-two years old, which must be around about the time you were born."

She went up to her room to pack her bag. But she

paused by the window, watching the persistent father with his sled and his children. What exactly had that unpleasant man said? And was he really as unpleasant as she thought? No doubt he was only doing his job. She hadn't been particularly cooperative. If she'd treated him differently, he might have had more to tell her.

She sat down at the little desk and began making notes. As usual, she could think more clearly when she had a pen in her hand. She hadn't read anywhere that a young boy had been murdered. He was the only young person to be killed, unless there were other victims the general public didn't know about. What Lars Emanuelsson had said about excessive violence could only mean that the others in the house had been badly beaten, perhaps even tortured, before they were killed. Why had the boy been spared that? Could it simply be that he was young and the murderer had somehow taken that into account? Or was there some other reason?

There were no obvious answers. And anyway, it wasn't her problem. She still felt ashamed of what had happened the previous day. Her conduct had been indefensible. She didn't dare think about what would have happened if some journalist had found her out. Her return back home to Skåne would have been humiliating, to say the least.

She packed her bag and prepared to leave her room. But first she switched on the television to catch the weather forecast, which would help her make up her mind about which route to take. She stumbled on the broadcast of a press conference at police HQ in Hudiksvall. There were three people sitting on a little dais, and the only woman was Vivi Sundberg. Her heart skipped a beat—what if Sundberg was about to announce that a judge from Helsingborg had been exposed as a petty thief? She sat down on the edge of the bed and turned up the sound. The man in the middle, Tobias Ludwig, was speaking.

She gathered it was a live broadcast. When Tobias Ludwig had finished what he had to say, the third person—public prosecutor Robertsson—pulled the microphone toward him and said that the police badly needed any relevant information they could get from the general public. Nonlocal cars, strangers who had been noticed in the vicinity, anything that seemed unusual.

When the prosecutor had finished, it was Vivi Sundberg's turn. She held up a plastic bag. The camera zoomed in on it. There was a red ribbon inside. Sundberg said the police would like to hear from anybody who recognized the ribbon.

Birgitta Roslin leaned towards the screen. Hadn't she seen a silk ribbon like the one in the plastic bag? She knelt down in order to get a better view. The ribbon certainly reminded her of something. She racked her brains, but couldn't place it.

The press conference proceeded to the stage where journalists started asking questions. The picture vanished from the screen. The room in police HQ was replaced by a weather map. Snow showers would drift into the east coast from the Gulf of Finland.

Birgitta Roslin decided to take the inland route. She paid at the front desk and told the girl on duty that she had enjoyed her stay. There was a bitterly cold wind as she made her way to the car. She placed her bag on the backseat, studied the map, and decided to drive through the forest to Järvsö and continue south from there.

When she came out onto the main road, she pulled into the first parking bay. She couldn't stop thinking about that red ribbon she had seen on television. She remembered having seen an identical ribbon, but couldn't put her finger on when or where. She could almost identify it but couldn't take that final step. If I've come this far, surely I'll be able to find out, she thought, and phoned police HQ. Timber trucks kept rumbling past, whipping up heavy clouds of snow that restricted her view. It was quite some time before the phone was answered. The operator who responded sounded harried. Roslin asked to speak to Erik Huddén.

"It's related to the investigation," she explained. "Hesjövallen."

"I think he's busy. I'll give him a buzz."

By the time he came to the telephone, she was starting to have second thoughts. He also sounded impatient and under pressure.

"Huddén."

"I don't know if you remember me," she said. "I'm that judge who insisted on speaking to Vivi Sundberg."

"I remember."

She wondered if Sundberg had said anything about what had happened that night. But she had the distinct impression that Huddén knew nothing about it. Perhaps Sundberg had in fact kept it to herself, as she'd promised? Perhaps I'm helped by the fact that she broke the rules by letting me into the house in the first place?

"It's about that red ribbon you showed on TV," she said.

"Hmm, I'm afraid it seems to have been a big mistake to do that," said Huddén.

"Why?"

"Our switchboard has practically gone up in smoke thanks to all the people who claim to have seen it. Usually wrapped round Christmas presents."

"My memory tells me something quite different. I think I've seen it."

"Where?"

"I don't know. But it has nothing to do with Christmas presents."

He was breathing heavily at the other end of the line, and seemed to have trouble making up his mind.

"I can show you the ribbon," he said eventually. "If you come right away."

"Within half an hour?"

"You can have two minutes, no longer."

He met her in reception, coughing and sneezing. The plastic bag with the red ribbon was on the desk in his office. He took it out of the bag and laid it on a piece of white paper.

"It's exactly seven and a half inches long," he said. "Just under half an inch wide. There's a hole at one end suggesting that it's been fastened to something. It's made of cotton and polyester, but gives the impression of being made of silk. We found it in the snow. One of the dogs sniffed it out."

She was certain she recognized it, but still couldn't remember where from.

"I've seen it," she said. "I can swear to that. Maybe not this particular one, but something identical."

"Where?"

"I can't remember."

"If you've seen a similar one in Skåne, that's hardly going to help us."

"No," she said seriously. "It was somewhere up here."

She stared at the ribbon while Erik Huddén leaned against the wall, waiting.

"Still can't place it?"

"No, I'm afraid not."

He put the ribbon back into the plastic bag and accompanied her down to reception.

"If your memory returns, you can call us," he said. "But if it turns out to be a ribbon around a Christmas present, don't bother."

THE MAN FROM BEIJING

Lars Emanuelsson was standing outside, waiting for her. He was wearing a threadbare fur hat pulled down over his forehead. He was annoyed when he realized she had unmasked him.

"Why are you following me?"

"I'm not. I'm circulating, as I said. I just happened to see you going into police HQ, and I thought I'd wait to see what developed. Right now I'm wondering what your very brief visit entailed."

"That's something you'll never know. Now leave me alone, before I get really annoyed."

She turned on her heel and walked away, but heard him say behind her: "Don't forget that I can write."

She turned back angrily.

"Are you threatening me?"

"Not at all."

"I've told you why I'm here. There's absolutely no reason whatsoever to embroil me in what's going on."

"The public reads what is written, whether it's true or not."

Now it was Lars Emanuelsson who turned on his heel and walked away. She looked on in disgust, and hoped she would never meet him again.

Birgitta Roslin returned to her car. She had only just settled down behind the wheel when the penny dropped, and she remembered where she had seen that red ribbon. It came out of the blue, without warning. Could she be mistaken? No, she could see everything in her mind's eye, as clear as day.

She waited for two hours, as the place she wanted

to visit was closed. She killed time by wandering aimlessly around town, impatient because she couldn't ascertain immediately what she thought she had discovered.

It was eleven o'clock when the Chinese restaurant opened. Birgitta Roslin went in and sat down in the same place as last time. She studied the lamps hanging over the tables. They were made of transparent material, thin plastic designed to give the impression of paper-covered lanterns. They were long and thin, cylinder-shaped. Four red ribbons hung down from the bottom.

After her visit to police HQ she knew that each of the ribbons was exactly seven and a half inches long. They were attached to the lampshade by a little hook that threaded in through a hole at the top of the ribbon.

The young woman who spoke bad Swedish came with the menu. She smiled when she recognized Birgitta Roslin. Roslin chose the buffet, despite the fact that she was not very hungry. The dishes laid out for her to choose from gave her the opportunity to scan the dining room. She soon found what she was looking for at a table for two in a corner at the back. The lamp hanging over the table was missing one of the red ribbons.

She stopped short and held her breath.

Somebody had been sitting there, she thought. At the back in the darkest corner. Then he had stood up, left the premises, and made his way to Hesjövallen.

She looked around the restaurant. The young woman smiled. She could hear voices coming from the kitchen, speaking Chinese.

It struck her that neither she nor the police had the slightest idea what had happened. It was all much bigger, deeper, and more mysterious than any of them could have imagined.

They knew absolutely nothing.

PART 2

The Railroad (1863)

LOUSHAN PASS

The westerly wind whines sharp,
wild geese cry in the sky, the frosty morning's
    moon.
Frosty the morning's moon,
horses' hooves clatter hard,
stifled the sound of the trumpet . . .

Mao Zedong, 1935

The Way to Canton

10

It was during the hottest part of the year, 1863. The second day of San's and his two brothers' long trek to the coast and the town of Canton. Early in the morning they came to a crossroads where three human heads were mounted on bamboo poles that had been driven into the ground. They couldn't work out how long the heads had been there. Wu, the youngest of the brothers, thought at least a week because the eyes and parts of the cheeks had already been hacked to pieces by crows. Guo Si, the eldest, maintained the heads had been cut off only a couple of days before. He thought the contorted mouths still retained traces of horror at what was about to happen.

San said nothing. They had fled from a remote village in Guangxi Province. The severed heads were like a warning that their lives would continue to be in danger.

They left what San called Three Heads Crossroads. While Guo Si and Wu argued about whether the heads had belonged to executed bandits or peasants who had displeased a powerful landowner, San thought about the events that had driven them onto the road. Every step they took carried them farther away from their former lives. Deep down, his brothers probably hoped that one day they would be able to return to Wei Hei, the village where they had grown up. He wasn't at all sure what he hoped himself. Perhaps poor peasants such as themselves could never tear themselves away from the misery that tainted their lives. What lay in store for them in Canton, where they were headed? It was said that you could smuggle yourself aboard a ship and be carried eastward over the ocean to a country where there were rivers filled with glittering gold nuggets the size of hens' eggs. Rumors had even reached as far as the remote village of Wei Hei, telling of a land populated by a strange white people, a land so rich that even simple people from China could work their way up out of squalor to unimaginable power and wealth.

San didn't know what to think. Poor people always dreamed of a life with no landowner pestering them. He himself had thought along those lines since he was a small boy, having to stand at the roadside with his head bowed while some overlord passed by in his covered sedan chair. He had always wondered how it was possible for people to lead such different lives.

He had once asked his father about it and received a box on the ears in reply. One didn't ask unnecessary questions. The gods in the trees and the streams and the mountains had created the world we humans lived in. In order for this mysterious universe to attain a divine balance, there must be rich and poor, peasants guiding their plows pulled by water buffalo and overlords who hardly ever set foot on the ground that had given birth to them as well.

He had never again asked his parents what they dreamed about as they knelt before their idols. They lived their lives in a state of unrelieved servitude. Were there people who worked harder and received so little in return for their labor? He had never found anybody he could ask, since everybody in the village was just as poor and just as afraid of the invisible landowner whose stewards, armed with whips, forced the peasants to carry out their daily tasks. He had watched people go from cradle to grave constantly weighed down by the burden that was their daily grind. It was as if children's backs became hunched even before they learned how to walk. The people in the village slept on mats that were rolled out every evening on the cold earth floors. They rested their heads on bundles of hard bamboo poles. Days followed the monotonous rhythm dictated by the seasons. They plowed the soil behind their phlegmatic water buffalo, planted their rice. They hoped that the coming year, the coming harvest, would be sufficient to feed them. When the harvest failed, there was almost nothing to live on. When there was no rice left, they were forced to eat leaves.

Or to lie down and die. There was no alternative.

He was roused from his thoughts. Dusk had started to fall. He looked around for a suitable place where they could sleep. There was a clump of trees by the side of the road, next to some boulders that seemed to have been ripped out of the mountain range that loomed on the western horizon. They rolled out their mattresses filled with dried grass and divided up the rice they had left, which would have to last until they reached Canton. San glanced furtively at his brothers. Would they be able to make it? What would he do if one of them fell ill? He himself still felt strong. But he wouldn't be able to carry one of his brothers unaided, if that became necessary.

They didn't talk much to one another. San had said they shouldn't waste what little strength they had left on arguing and quarreling.

"Every word you shout robs you of one footstep. It's not words that are important, but the steps you need to take to get to Canton."

Neither of his brothers objected. San knew they trusted him. Now that their parents were no longer alive and they had taken flight, they had to believe that San was making the right decisions.

They curled up on their mattresses, adjusted their pigtails down their backs, and closed their eyes. San could hear how first Guo Si and then Wu fell asleep. Though both are now twenty, less than a year apart, they are still like little children, he thought. I am all they have.

All around him was a smell of mud and fear. He lay on his back and gazed up at the stars.

His mother had often taken him out after dark and shown him the sky. On such occasions her weary face would break into a smile. The stars provided some consolation for the hard life she led. She normally lived with her face pointed down to the ground, which embraced her rice plants as if it were waiting for her to join them there one of these days. When she gazed up at the stars, just for a brief while, she didn't need to look at the brown earth beneath her.

He allowed his eyes to wander over the night sky. His mother had named some stars. One especially bright star in a constellation that looked a bit like a dragon she had called San.

"That's you," she said. "That's where you come from, and that's where you'll return to someday."

The idea of having come from a star had scared him. But he said nothing, as the idea gave his mother so much pleasure.

Then he thought about the violent incidents that had forced him and his brothers to run away. One of the landowner's new stewards, a man by the name of Fang, with a big gap between his front teeth, had come to complain that his parents had failed to do their day's work properly. San knew that his father had been suffering severe back pains and was unable to cope with the heavy work. His mother helped out, but they had fallen behind even so. Now Fang was standing outside their mud hut, his tongue gliding in and out of the gap between his teeth like a threatening snake's. Fang was young, about the same age as San, but they came from different worlds. Fang glared at San's parents squatting in front of him, heads bowed and straw hats in their hands; he seemed to think they were insects that he could squash underfoot whenever he pleased. If they didn't do their work, they would be thrown out of their home and forced to become beggars.

During the night San had heard his parents whispering together. As it was very rare for them not to go to sleep the moment they lay down, he listened—but he'd been unable to grasp what they were saying.

The next morning the woven mat on which his parents slept was empty. His immediate reaction was fear. Everybody in that cramped little hut would rise at the same time. His parents must have snuck out quietly in order not to wake their sons. He stood up cautiously, put on his ragged trousers and the only shirt he owned.

When he emerged from the hut, the sun still hadn't risen. The horizon was bathed in pink light. A cockerel crowed from somewhere nearby. The inhabitants of the village were just waking up. Everybody apart from his parents. They were hanging from the tree that provided shade at the hottest part of the year. Their bodies swayed slowly in the morning breeze.

He had only a vague memory of what happened next. He didn't want his brothers to have to see their parents hanging from a rope with their mouths open. He cut them down with the sickle his father used out in the fields. They fell heavily on top of him, as if they were trying to take him with them into death.

The village elder, old Bao, who was half blind and shook so much that he could barely stand up, was summoned by the neighbors. Bao took San aside and told him it would be best for the brothers to run away. Fang would be bound to take his revenge, throw them into the prison cages by his house. Or he would execute them. There was no judge in the village; the only law that applied was that of the landowner, and Fang spoke and acted in his name.

They had set off immediately after their parents' funeral. Now he was lying here under the stars, with his brothers asleep by his side. He didn't know what lay in store for them. Old Bao had said they should head for the coast, to the city of Canton, where they'd be able to look for work. San had tried asking Bao what kind of work might be available, but the old man was unable to say. He simply pointed eastward with his trembling hand.

They had walked until their feet were raw and bleeding, and their mouths parched with thirst. The brothers had wept over the death of their parents, and also in view of the unknown fate that awaited them. San had tried to console them, but also urged them not to walk too slowly. Fang was dangerous. He had horses and men with lances and sharp swords who might still be able to catch up with them.

San continued to gaze up at the stars. He thought about the landowner, who lived in an entirely different world, one where the poor were not allowed to set foot. He never appeared in the village, but was merely a threatening shadow, indistinguishable from the darkness.

San eventually fell asleep. In his dreams the three severed heads came racing toward him. He could feel the sharp edge of the sword against his own neck. His brothers were already dead, their heads had rolled away into the sand, blood pouring out of the stumps that had been their necks. Over and over again he woke up to free himself from that dream, but it returned every time he drifted back into sleep.

They set off early in the morning, after drinking what remained of the water in the flask hanging from a strap around Guo Si's neck. They had to find clean water as soon as possible. They walked fast along the stony road. They occasionally met people making their way to the fields or carrying heavy burdens on their heads and shoulders. San began to wonder if this road would ever end. Perhaps there wasn't an ocean at the end of it. Perhaps there was no city by the name of Canton. But he said nothing to Guo Si or Wu. That would make it too difficult for them to keep going.

A little black dog with a white patch on its chest joined the trio. San had no idea where it came from; it simply appeared out of the blue. He tried to shoo it away, but it kept coming back. They tried throwing stones at it. But still it persisted in following them.

"Let's name the dog Dayang Bi An De Dacheng-shi, 'the big city on the other side of the ocean,' " said San. "We can call it Dayang for short."

At noon, when the heat was most unbearable, they rested under a tree in a little village. They were given water by the villagers and were able to fill their flask. The dog lay at San's feet, panting.

He observed it carefully. There was something special about the dog. Could it have been sent by his mother as a messenger from the kingdom of the dead? San didn't know. He'd always found it difficult to believe in all the gods his parents and the other villagers believed in. How could one pray to a tree that was unable to answer, that had no ears and no mouth? Or to a dog without an owner? But if the gods did exist, now was the time he and his brothers needed their help.

They continued their trek in the afternoon. The road meandered ahead of them, seemingly without end.

After another three days they started coming across more and more people. Carts would clatter past laden with reeds and sacks of corn, while empty carts headed in the opposite direction. San plucked up his courage and shouted to a man sitting in one of the empty carts.

"How far is it to the sea?"

"Two days. No more. Tomorrow you'll start to smell Canton. You won't be able to miss it."

He laughed and drove on. San watched him dwindling into the distance. What had he meant, suggesting that they would be able to smell the city?

That same afternoon they suddenly hit upon a dense cloud of butterflies. The insects were transparent and yellow, and their flapping wings sounded like rustling paper. San paused in the middle of the swarm, entranced. It felt like he'd entered a house with walls made of wings. I'd love to stay here, he thought. I wish this house didn't have any doors. I could stay here, listening to the butterflies' wings until the day I fall down dead.

But his brothers were out there. He couldn't abandon them. He used his hands to create an opening in the wall of butterflies and smiled at his brothers. He wouldn't let them down.

They spent another night under a tree after eating a little of the rice they had left. They were all hungry when they curled up for the night.

The following day they came to Canton. The dog was still with them. San was becoming more and more convinced that his mother had sent it from the kingdom of death to keep an eye on them and protect them. He had never been able to believe in all that nonsense. But now, as he stood outside the city gates, he began to wonder if that was really the way things were.

They entered the teeming city that had announced its imminent presence with no end of unpleasant smells, as they had been warned it would. San was afraid he might lose contact with his brothers in the mass of unknown people thronging the streets. He tied a long rope around his waist and attached it in similar fashion to his brothers. Now they couldn't possibly get lost, unless somebody cut through the rope. They slowly made their way forward through the mass of people, amazed by all the enormous houses, temples, and goods offered for sale.

The rope linking them together suddenly tightened. Wu pointed. San saw what had brought his brother to a halt.

A man was sitting in a sedan chair. Curtains usually hid whoever was being carried, but in this case they were opened. Nobody could doubt that the man was dying. He was white, as if somebody had drenched his cheeks in a white powder. Or perhaps he was evil? The devil always sent demons with white faces to terrorize the earth. Besides, he didn't have a pigtail and had a long, ugly face with a big, crooked nose.

Wu and Guo Si elbowed their way closer to San and asked if it was a man or a devil. San didn't know. He'd never seen anything like it, not even in his worst nightmares.

Suddenly the curtains were drawn, and the sedan chair was carried away. A man standing next to San spat after the chair.

"Who was that?" San asked.

The man looked disparagingly at him and asked him to repeat the question. San could hear that their dialects were very different.

"The man in the sedan chair. Who is he?"

"A white man who owns many of the ships that visit our harbor."

"Is he ill?"

The man laughed.

"They all look like that. As white as corpses that ought to have been buried ages ago."

The brothers continued through the dirty, foul-smelling city. San observed the people all around him. Many were well dressed. They weren't wearing ragged clothes like he was. He began to suspect that the world was not quite what he had imagined.

After wandering through the city for many hours, they glimpsed water at the end of the alleys. Wu broke loose and raced toward it. He plunged in and started drinking—but stopped and spat it all out when he realized that it was brine. The bloated body of a cat floated past. San observed all the filth, not just the dead body but also both human and animal feces. He felt sick. Back home they had used their feces to fertilize the small patches of land where they grew their vegetables. Here, it seemed that people simply emptied their shit into the water, despite the fact that nothing grew there.

He gazed out over the water without being able to see the other side. What they call the sea or the ocean must be a very wide river indeed, he thought.

They sat down on a seesawing wooden jetty surrounded by so many boats that it wasn't possible to count them all. Everywhere they could hear people shouting and screaming. That was another thing that distinguished life in the city from life in the village. Here people seemed unable to shut up, always having something to say or complain about. Nowhere could San detect the silence he had been so used to.

They ate the very last of the rice and shared the remains of the water in the flask. Wu and Guo Si eyed him hopefully. He would have to live up to their expectations. But how would he find work for them in this deafening, chaotic maelstrom of humanity? Where would they find food? Where would they sleep? He looked at the dog, which was lying with one paw over its nose. What do I do now?

He could feel that he needed to be alone in order to assess their situation. He stood up and asked his brothers to wait where they were, together with the dog. In order to put their minds at rest, and convince them that he wasn't going to disappear into the mass of people and never return, he said, "Just think about that invisible rope that binds us together. I'll be back soon. If anybody speaks to you while I'm away, answer them politely, but don't go away from here. If you do, I'll never be able to find you again."

He explored all the alleys, but kept turning back in order to remember the way he'd come from. One of the narrow streets suddenly opened out into a square with a temple. People were genuflecting and walking with bowed heads toward an altar laden with offerings and incense.

My mother would have run forward to the altar and bowed down there, he thought. My father would also have approached the altar, but somewhat more hesitantly. I can't remember him ever setting one foot before the other without hesitating.

But now he was the one who had to make up his mind what to do.

There were a few stones scattered around that had fallen from the temple wall. He sat down on one, feeling somewhat confused, thanks to the heat, the mass of people, and the hunger he had tried to ignore for as long as possible.

When he had rested sufficiently, he returned to the Pearl River and all the quays that lined its banks. Men bowed down by heavy burdens were staggering along rickety-looking gangways. Farther upriver he could see big ships with lowered masts being towed by tugs under bridges.

He paused and scrutinized all these men carrying burdens, each one bigger than the last. Foremen stood by the gangways, ticking off all the loads being carried aboard or ashore. They slipped a few coins to the porters, who then vanished into the alleys.

An idea hit him. In order to survive, they would have to carry. We can do that, he thought. My brothers and I, we are porters. There are no meadows here, no paddies. But we can carry things. We're strong.

He returned to Wu and Guo Si, who were huddled up on the jetty. He stood there for a while, observing how they were clinging to each other.

We are like dogs, he thought. Everybody kicks us, we have to live on what others throw away.

The dog noticed his arrival and ran up to greet him.

San didn't kick it.

11

They spent the night on the jetty, as San couldn't think of anywhere better to go. The dog watched over them, growling at any silent, tiptoeing feet that came too close. But when they woke up the next morning they found that somebody had succeeded in stealing their water flask. San was furious as he looked around. The poor steal from the poor, he thought. Even an empty water flask is desirable to somebody who has nothing.

"He's a nice dog, but he's not much good as a watchdog," said San.

"What shall we do now?" asked Wu.

"We shall try to find work," said San.

"I'm hungry," said Guo Si.

San shook his head. Guo Si knew just as well as he did that they didn't have any food.

"We can't steal," said San. "If we did, we might end up like the trio whose heads are on those poles at the crossroads. We must find work, and then we'll be able to buy something to eat."

He led his brothers to the place where men were running back and forth carrying their burdens. The dog was still with them. San stood there for a long time, watching the men on the ships' gangways giving the orders. He eventually decided to approach a short, stocky man who didn't beat the porters, even if they were moving slowly.

"We are three brothers," he said. "We're good at carrying."

The man glanced angrily at him but continued checking the porters emerging from the hold with heavy loads on their shoulders.

"What are all these yokels doing in Canton?" he shouted. "Why do you come here? There are thousands of peasants looking for work. I already have more than enough. Go away. Stop bothering me."

They continued asking at wharf after wharf, but the response was always the same. Nobody wanted them. They were of no use to anybody here in Canton.

That day they ate nothing apart from the filthy remains of vegetables trampled underfoot in a street next to a market. They drank water from a pump surrounded by starving people. They spent another night curled up on the jetty. San couldn't sleep. He pressed his fists hard against his stomach in an attempt to suppress the pangs of hunger. He thought of the swarm of butterflies he'd entered. It was as if all the butterflies had entered his body and were scratching against his intestines with their sharp wings.

Two more days passed without their finding anybody on any of the wharves who nodded and said that their backs would be useful. As the second day drew toward its close, San knew that they wouldn't be able to last much longer. They hadn't eaten anything at all since they'd found the trampled vegetables. Now they were living on water alone. Wu had a fever, and was lying in the shadow of a pile of barrels, shaking.

San made up his mind as the sun began to set. They must have food, or they would die. He took his brothers and the dog to an open square where poor people were sitting around fires, eating whatever they had managed to find.

Now he understood why his mother had sent the dog to them. He picked up a rock and smashed the dog's skull. People from one of the nearby fires came to investigate, their skin was stretched tightly over their emaciated faces. San borrowed a knife off one of the men, butchered the dog, and placed the pieces in a pot. They were so hungry that they couldn't wait until the meat was properly cooked. San cut up the pieces so that everybody around the fire had the same amount.

After the meal they all lay down on the ground and closed their eyes. San was the only one still sitting, staring at the flames. The next day they wouldn't even have a dog to eat.

He could see his parents in his mind's eye, hanging from the tree that awful morning. How far away from his own neck were the branch and the rope now? He didn't know.

He suddenly had the feeling that he was being watched. He squinted out into the night. There really was somebody there, the whites of his eyes gleaming in the darkness. The man approached the fire. He was older than San, but not especially old. He smiled. San thought he must be one of those lucky people who didn't always have to walk around feeling hungry.

"I'm Zi. I saw you eating a dog."

San didn't answer. He waited to see what would come next. Something about this stranger made him feel insecure.

"I'm Zi Quan Zhao. Who are you?"

San looked around uneasily.

"Have I trespassed on your territory?"

Zi laughed.

"Not at all. I just wonder who you are. Curiosity is a human virtue. Anybody who doesn't have an inquiring mind is unlikely to live a satisfying life."

"My name's Wang San."

"Where do you come from?"

San was not used to being asked questions. He started to be suspicious. Perhaps the man calling himself Zi was one of the chosen few who had the right to interrogate and punish? Perhaps he and his brothers had transgressed one of those invisible laws and regulations that surround the poverty stricken?

San gestured vaguely into the darkness.

"From over there. My brothers and I have been walking for many days. We crossed two big rivers."

"It's great to have brothers. What are you doing here?"

"We're looking for work, but we can't find any."

"It's hard. Very hard. Lots of people are drawn to the city like flies to a honey pot. It's not easy to make a living."

San had a question on the tip of his tongue, but decided to swallow it. Zi seemed to be able to see through him.

"Do you wonder what I do for a living, as I'm not dressed in rags?"

"I don't want to be inquisitive about my superiors."

"That doesn't bother me in the least," said Zi, sitting down. "My father used to own sampans, and he would sail his little merchant fleet up and down the river here. When he died, my brother and I took over the business. My third and fourth brothers immigrated to the land on the far side of the ocean, to America. They have made their fortune by washing the dirty clothes of white men. America is a very strange land. Where else can you get rich from other men's dirt?"

"I've thought about that," said San. "Going to that country."

Zi looked him up and down.

"You need money for that. Nobody sails over a great ocean for nothing. Anyway, I wish you good night. I hope you manage to find work."

Zi stood up, bowed, and disappeared into the darkness. San lay down and wondered if he had imagined that short conversation. Perhaps he had been talking to his own shadow? Dreaming of being somebody else?

The brothers continued their vain search for work and food, walking for hours on end through the teeming city. San had decided to rope himself to his two brothers, and it struck him that he was like an animal with two youngsters that kept pressing up against him within the large flock. They looked for work on the wharves and in the alleys overflowing with people. San urged his brothers to stand up straight when they stood in front of some authoritative person who might be able to offer them work.

"We must look strong," he said. "Nobody gives work to men with no strength in their arms and legs. Even if you are tired and hungry, you must give the impression of being very strong."

Any food they ate was what other people had thrown away. When they found themselves fighting with dogs over a discarded bone, it struck San that they were on their way to becoming animals. His mother had told him a story about a man who turned into an animal, with a tail and four legs but no arms, because he was lazy and didn't want to work. But the reason that they were not working was not that they were lazy.

They continued to sleep on the jetty in the damp heat. Sometimes heavy rainfall would drift over the city from the sea during the night. They sheltered underneath the jetty, creeping in among the wet timbers, but they were soaked through even so. San noticed that Guo Si and Wu were beginning to lose heart. Their lust for life shrank with every day that passed, every day of hunger, torrential rain, and the feeling that nobody noticed them and nobody needed them.

One evening San noticed Wu hunched up, mumbling confused prayers to gods his parents used to pray to. That worried him for a moment. His parents' gods had never been of any help. But then, if Wu found consolation in his prayers, San had no right to rob him of that feeling.

San was increasingly convinced that Canton was a city of horror. Every morning, when they set out on their endless search for work, they noticed more and more people lying dead in the gutters. Sometimes the rats or dogs had been chewing the faces of the corpses. Every morning he had the nasty feeling that he would end his life in the gutter of one of Canton's many alleys.

After yet another day in the damp heat, San also found himself losing hope. He was so hungry, he felt dizzy and was incapable of thinking straight. As he lay on the jetty alongside his sleeping brothers, he thought for the first time that perhaps he might just as well fall asleep and never wake up.

There was nothing to wake up for.

During the night he dreamed yet again of the three

severed heads. They suddenly started talking to him, but he couldn't understand what they said.

When he woke up as dawn was beginning to break, he saw Zi sitting on a post, smoking a pipe. He smiled when he saw that San was awake.

"You were not sleeping soundly," he said. "I could see that you were dreaming about something you wanted to get away from."

"I was dreaming about severed heads," said San. "Maybe one of them was mine."

Zi eyed him pensively before responding.

"Those who have a choice choose. Neither you nor your brothers look especially strong. It's obvious that you are starving. Nobody who needs workers to carry or drag or pull chooses anybody who's starving. At least, not as long as there are newcomers who still have some strength left and food in their rucksacks."

Zi emptied his pipe before continuing.

"Every morning there are dead bodies floating down the river. People who don't have the strength to try anymore. People who can't see the point of living any longer. They fill their shirts with stones or tie sinkers to their legs. Canton has become a city full of restless ghosts, the souls of people who have taken their own lives."

"Why are you telling me this? I have enough pain to bear already."

Zi raised his hand dismissively.

"I'm not saying it to worry you. I wouldn't have said anything if I didn't have something else to add.

My cousin owns a factory, and many of his workers are ill just now. I might be able to help you and your brothers."

San had difficulty believing what he had just heard. But Zi said it again. He didn't want to make any promises, but he might be able to find them work.

"Why are you singling us out?"

Zi shrugged.

"Why does anybody do anything? Or not do anything? Perhaps I just thought that you deserved help."

Zi stood up.

"I'll come back when I know," he said.

He placed a few fruits on the ground in front of San, then walked away. San watched him walk along the jetty and disappear into the crowds of people.

True to his word, Zi returned that evening.

"Wake your brothers," said Zi. "We have to go. I have work for you."

"Wu is ill. Can't it wait until tomorrow?"

"Somebody else will have taken the work by then. Either we go now, or we don't go at all."

San hastened to wake up Guo Si and Wu.

"We have to go," he said. "Tomorrow, we'll have work at last."

Zi led them through the dark alleys. San noticed that he was trampling on people sleeping on the sidewalks. San was holding Guo Si's hand, and in turn he had his arm around Wu.

Soon San noticed from the smell that they were close to the water. Everything seemed easier now.

Then everything happened very fast. Strangers emerged from the shadows, grabbed them by the arms, and started to pull sacks over their heads. San caught a punch that felled him, but he continued to struggle. When he was pressed down to the ground again, he bit an arm as hard as he could and managed to wriggle free. But he was caught again immediately.

San heard Wu screaming in terror not far away. In the light from a dangling lantern he could see his brother lying on his back. A man pulled a knife out of his chest, then threw the body into the water. Wu was carried slowly away by the current.

The shattering truth struck home: Wu was dead, and San had failed to protect him.

Then he received a heavy blow on the back of his head. He was unconscious when he and Guo Si were carried onto a rowboat that took them to a ship anchored offshore.

All this happened in the summer of 1863. A year when thousands of Chinese peasants were abducted and taken across the seas to America, which gobbled them up into its insatiable jaws. What was in store for them was the same drudgery they had once dreamed of escaping.

They were transported over a wide ocean. But poverty accompanied them all the way.

12

On March 9, 1864, Guo Si and San started hacking away the mountain blocking the railroad line that would eventually span the whole American continent.

It was one of the severest winters in living memory in Nevada, with days so cold each breath felt like ice crystals rather than air.

Previous to this, San and Guo Si had been working farther west, where it was easier to prepare the ground and lay the rails. They had been taken there at the end of October, directly from the ship. Together with many of the others who had been transported in chains from Canton, they had been received by Chinese men who had cut off their pigtails, wore Western clothes, and had watch chains across their chests. The brothers had been met by a man with the same surname as their own, Wang. To San's horror, Guo Si—who normally said nothing at all—had begun to protest.

"We were attacked, tied up, and bundled on board. We didn't ask to come here."

San thought this would be the end of their long journey. The man in front of them would never accept being spoken to in such a way. He would draw the pistol he had stuck into his belt and shoot them.

But San was wrong. Wang burst out laughing, as if Guo Si had just told him a joke.

"You are no more than dogs," said Wang. "Zi has sent me some talking dogs. I own you until you have paid me for the crossing, and your food, and the journey here from San Francisco. You will pay me by working for me. Three years from now, you can do whatever you like, but until then you belong to me. Out here in the desert you can't run away. There are wolves, bears, and Indians who will slit your throats, smash your skulls, and eat your brains as if they were eggs. If you try to escape even so, I have dogs that will track you down. Then my whip will perform a merry dance, and you will have to work an extra year for me. So, now you know the score."

San eyed the men standing behind Wang. They had dogs on leads and rifles in their hands. San was surprised that these white men with long beards were prepared to obey orders given them by a Chinaman. They had come to a country that was very different from China.

They were placed in a tented camp at the bottom of a deep ravine, with a stream running through it. On one side of the creek were the Chinese laborers, and on the other side a mixture of Irishmen, Germans, and other Europeans. There was high tension between the two camps. The stream was a border that none of the Chinese passed unnecessarily. The Irishmen, who were often drunk, would yell abuse and throw stones at the Chinese side. San and Guo Si couldn't understand what they were saying, but the stones flying through the air were hard; there was no reason to suppose that the words were any softer.

They found themselves living alongside twelve other Chinese. None of the others had been with them on the ship. San assumed Wang preferred to mix the newly arrived laborers with those who had been working on the railway for some time and would be able to tell the newcomers about the rules and routines. The single tent was small; when everyone had gone to bed they were squashed up against one another. That helped them to keep warm, but it also created a distressing feeling of not being able to move, of being tied up.

The man in charge of the tent was Xu. He was thin and had bad teeth but was regarded with great respect. Xu showed San and Guo Si where they could sleep. He asked where they came from, which ship they had sailed on, but he said nothing about himself. Sleeping next to San was Hao, who told him that Xu had been involved in building the railway from the very start. He had come to America at the beginning of the 1850s and started working in gold mines. According to rumor he had failed to pan gold in the rivers, but he had bought a decrepit old wooden hut where several successful gold prospectors had lived. Nobody could understand how Xu could be so stupid as to pay twenty-five dollars for a shack that nobody could live in now. But Xu carefully swept up all the dirt lying on the floor; then he removed the rotten floorboards and swept up all the dust and dirt underneath. In the end he filtered out so much gold dust that he was able to return to San Francisco with a small fortune. He decided to go back to Canton and even bought a ticket for the journey. But while he was waiting for his ship to sail, he visited one of the gambling dens where the Chinese spent so much of their time. He gambled and lost. He even ended up gambling away his ticket. That was when he contacted Central Pacific and became one of the first Chinese to be employed.

How Hao had found out all this without Xu himself ever having said anything about his past, San could never work out. But Hao insisted that every word was true.

Xu could speak English. Through him the brothers discovered what was being shouted over the stream separating the two camps. Xu spoke contemptuously of the men on the other side.

"They call us Chinks," he said. "That is a very disparaging term for us. When the Irishmen are drunk, they sometimes call us pigs, which means that we are **gau**."

"Why don't they like us?" wondered San.

"We are better workers," said Xu. "We work harder, we don't drink, we don't dodge and shirk. And we look different—our skin and eyes. They don't like people who don't look like they do."

Every morning San and Guo Si clambered up the steep path leading out of the ravine, each carrying a lantern. It sometimes happened that one of the gang would slip on the icy surface and tumble all the way down to the bottom. Two men whose legs had been broken helped to prepare the food the brothers ate when they came back after their long working day. The Chinese and the laborers living on the other side of the stream worked a long way apart. Each group had its own path up to the top of the ravine and its own workplace. Foremen were constantly on the lookout to make sure they didn't come too close. Sometimes fights would break out in the middle of the stream between Chinese with cudgels and Irishmen with knives. When that happened, the bearded guards would come racing up on horseback and separate them. Occasionally somebody would be so badly injured that he died. A Chinese who smashed the skull of an Irishman was shot; an Irishman who stabbed a Chinese was dragged away in chains. Xu urged everybody in his tent not to become involved in fights or stone throwing. He kept reminding them that they were guests in this foreign country.

"We must wait," said Xu. "One of these days they'll realize that there will never be a railroad if we Chinese don't build it. One day everything will change."

Later that evening, when they were lying in the tent, Guo Si whispered to his brother and asked what Xu had meant, but San had no satisfactory answer to give him.

They had traveled from the coast inland toward

the desert where the sun became colder and colder. When they were woken up by Xu's loud shouts, they had to hurry in order to make sure the foremen wouldn't be annoyed and force them to work longer than the usual twelve hours. The cold was bitter. It snowed almost every day.

They occasionally caught sight of the feared Wang, who had said that he owned them. He would suddenly appear out of nowhere, then vanish again just as quickly.

The brothers' job was to prepare the embankment on which the rails and sleepers would be fastened down. There were fires burning everywhere, partly to enable them to see what they were doing but also to thaw out the frozen ground. They were constantly watched over by foremen on horseback, white men carrying rifles and wearing wolf-skin coats with scarves tied over their hats to keep the cold at bay. Xu had taught them always to say "Yes, boss" when they were spoken to, even if they didn't understand what had been said.

Fires could be seen burning several miles away. That was where the Irish were fixing sleepers and rails. They could sometimes hear the hooting of locomotives releasing steam. San and Guo Si regarded these enormous black beasts of burden as dragons. Even if the fire-breathing monsters their mother had told them about were colorful, these black, glittering monsters must have been what she was referring to.

Their toil was never-ending. When the long days

were over they had barely enough strength left to drag themselves back to the bottom of the ravine, eat their food, and then collapse in their tent. Over and over again San tried to make Guo Si wash in the cold water. San felt disgusted by his own body when he was dirty. To his surprise he was almost always on his own by the stream, half naked and shivering. The only others who washed regularly were the new arrivals. The will to keep himself clean was worn down by the heavy work. The day eventually came when he too collapsed into bed without washing. San lay in the tent amid the stench from their filthy bodies. It was as if he were slowly being transformed into a being without dignity, without dreams or longings. He could picture his mother and father as he dozed off, and he had the feeling that he had swapped the hell that had been his home for a hell that was different but even worse. They were now forced to work as slaves, in conditions worse than anything their mother and father had endured. Was this what they had hoped to achieve when they had run away and headed for Canton? Was there no way out for the poverty-stricken?

That evening, just before he fell asleep, San made up his mind that their only chance of surviving was to escape. Every day he saw one of the undernourished workers collapse and be carried away.

The following day he discussed his plans with Hao, who lay beside him listening attentively to what San had to say.

"America is a big country," said Hao, "but not so big that a Chinese like you or your brother could simply disappear. If you really mean what you say, you must flee all the way back to China. Otherwise they'll catch up with you sooner or later. I don't need to tell you what will happen then."

San thought long and hard about what Hao said. The time was not yet ripe for running away, nor even for telling Guo Si about his plan.

Late in March a violent snowstorm covered the Nevada desert. More than three feet of snow fell in less than twelve hours. When the storm had passed over, the temperature dropped. The next morning they had to dig themselves out of their tent. The Irishmen on the other side of the frozen stream had fared better, as their tent had been on the lee side of the storm. Now they stood there laughing at the Chinese as they struggled to dig away the snow from the tents and paths leading up to the top of the ravine.

We get nothing for free, San thought. Not even the snow is shared fairly.

He could see that Guo Si was very tired. At times he barely had the strength to lift his spade. But San had made up his mind. Until the white man's New Year came around again, they would keep each other alive.

At the end of March the first black men arrived in the railroad village in the ravine. They pitched their tents on the same side of the stream as the Chinese. Neither of the brothers had ever seen a black man before. They were wearing ragged clothes and were suffering from the cold worse than San had ever seen a person suffer. Many of them died during their first few days in the ravine and on the railroad. They were so weak that they would fall down in the darkness and not be discovered until much later, when the snow had started to melt in the spring. The black men were treated even worse than the Chinese, and "niggers" was pronounced with an intonation that was even worse than that used for "Chinks." Even Xu, who always preached that one should be restrained when talking about other people working on the railroad, made no secret of his contempt for the blacks.

"The whites call them fallen angels," said Xu. "Niggers are animals with no soul, and nobody misses them when they die. Instead of brains they have lumps of rotting flesh."

The unusually severe cold lay over the ravine and the building site like a blanket of iron. One evening, when they were sitting with their evening meal around a small, ineffectual fire, Xu announced that the following day they would be moving to a new camp and a new workplace next to the mountain they would now start digging and blasting their way through.

They set off early. San couldn't remember ever having experienced anything as cold at it was that day. He told Guo Si to go in front of him, as he wanted to make sure his brother didn't fall down and get left behind. They followed the railroad track until they came to the point where the rails ended and then, a few hundred yards farther on, the roadbed itself. But Xu urged them to keep going. The flickering light from the lanterns ate into the darkness. San knew they were now very close to the mountains the whites called the Sierra Nevada. That was where they would have to start making cuttings and tunnels so that the railroad could continue.

Xu stopped when they came to the lowest ridge. There were tents pitched and fires burning. The men who had walked all the way from the ravine flopped down beside the warm flames. San knelt down and held out his frozen hands, which were wrapped up in rags. At that very moment he heard a voice behind him. He turned around and saw a white man standing there, with shoulder-length hair and a scarf wrapped around his face, making him look like a masked bandit. He was holding a rifle. He was wearing a fur coat and had a fox's tail hanging from his hat, which was fur lined. His eyes reminded San of those Zi had focused on them that time in the past.

The white man suddenly raised his rifle and fired a shot into the darkness. The men warming themselves in front of the fire curled into the fetal position.

"Stand up!" yelled Xu. "Take off whatever you have on your heads!"

San stared at him in surprise. Were they expected to take off the hats they'd stuffed full of dry grass and bits of cloth?

"Off with 'em," yelled Xu, who seemed scared of the man with the rifle. "No head wear."

San took off his hat and gestured to Guo Si to do the same. The man with the rifle pulled down the scarf to reveal his face. He had a bristling mustache. Although he was standing several yards away, San could smell strong drink. He was on his guard immediately. White men smelling of spirits were always more unpredictable than sober ones.

The man started speaking in a shrill voice. San thought he sounded like an angry woman. Xu made a big effort to translate what the man said.

"You had to take off your hats so that you could hear better," he said.

His voice was almost as shrill as the voice of the man with the rifle.

"Your ears are so full of shit that you wouldn't be able to hear me if you didn't" was Xu's version of what the man said. "I'm known as JA, but you must simply call me Boss. When I speak to you, you take off your hats. You answer my questions, but you never ask any of your own. Understood?"

San mumbled along with the others. It was obvious that the man in front of them didn't like Chinese.

The man known as JA continued yelling and shouting.

"You have in front of you a wall of stone. Your job is to cleave this mountain in two, wide enough for the railroad to get through. You've been chosen because you've shown that you can work hard. We don't want any of those fucking niggers or those drunken Irishmen. This is a mountain fit for China- men. That's why you're here. And I'm here to make sure you do what you're supposed to do. Anybody who doesn't use every last bit of strength he has, who shows me that he's lazy, will wish he'd never been born. Understood? I want a response from every sin- gle one of you. Then you can put your hats on again. You can collect your pickaxes from Brown—he's mad as a hatter every full moon. He likes to eat Chinamen raw. At other times he's meek as a lamb."

They all responded, each of them mumbling.

The sky was beginning to lighten when they found themselves standing with pickaxes in their hands in front of the cliff, which loomed almost perpendicular in front of them. Steam was coming from their mouths. JA handed his rifle over to Brown for a moment, grabbed hold of a pickax, and hacked two markers into the bottom part of the rock. San could see that the width of the hole they were expected to create was more than eight yards.

There was no sign of any fallen blocks of stone, no piles of gravel. The mountain was going to offer extremely hard resistance. Every fragment of stone they levered loose would need exertions of a kind that couldn't possibly be compared with anything they had done so far.

Somehow or other they had challenged the gods, who had sent them the tests they were now faced with. They would have to cut their way through the mountain in order to become free men, no longer the despised "Chinks" in the American wilderness.

San was overcome by a feeling of utter despair. The only thing that kept him going was the thought that one day he and Guo Si would run away.

He tried to imagine that the mountain in front of him was in fact a wall separating him from China. Only a couple of yards in, the cold would vanish; plum trees would be in blossom.

That morning they started work on the rock face. Their new foreman kept watch over them like a hawk. Even when he turned his back on them, he seemed to be able to see if anybody lowered their pickax just for a moment. He had wrapped strips of leather around his fists that peeled away the skin on the faces of any poor soul who offended. It was not long before everybody hated this man with a rifle. They dreamed of killing him. San wondered about the relationship between JA and Wang. Was it Wang who owned JA, or vice versa?

JA seemed to be in league with the mountain, which was extremely reluctant to let go the tiniest splinter of granite, not even a tear or a strand of hair. It took them almost a month to hack out an opening of the required size. By then, one of them had already died. During the night he had crept silently out of bed and crawled out through the tent door. He had stripped off his clothes and lain down in the snow in order to die. When JA discovered the dead Chinese, he was furious.

"You have no reason to mourn the suicide," he screeched in his shrill voice. "What you should regret is that now it's you who have to hack away the stone that he ought to have shifted."

When they came back from the mountain, the body had disappeared.

When they started to attack the mountain with nitroglycerin, men began to die, and San realized it was time to run. No matter what would be in store for them in the wilderness, it couldn't possibly be worse than what they were going through just now. They would run away, and not stop until they were back in China.

They fled four weeks later. They left the tent silently in the middle of the night, followed the railroad track, stole two horses from a rail depot, and then headed west. Only when they felt they had traveled far enough away from the Sierra Nevada did they pause and rest by a fire; and then they resumed their flight. They came to a river and rode through the shallows in order to mask their tracks.

They frequently stopped and looked around. But there was nothing to be seen; nobody was following them.

San gradually began to think that they might manage to find their way back home after all. But his hopes were fragile.

13

San dreamed that every sleeper lying on the roadbed under the rails was a human rib, perhaps his own. He could feel his chest deflating and was unable to breath air into his lungs. He tried to kick himself free from the weight pressing down and squashing his body, but he failed.

San opened his eyes. Guo Si had rolled over on top of him in order to keep warm. San pushed him gently to one side and covered his body with the blanket. He sat up, rubbed his stiff joints, then put more wood on the fire burning inside a circle of stones they had gathered.

He held his hands out toward the flames. It was now the third night since they had fled the mountain. San had not forgotten what Wang said would happen to anybody silly enough to run away. They would be condemned to work on the mountain for so long that it would barely be possible to survive.

They still hadn't spotted anybody chasing them. San suspected the foremen would assume the brothers were too stupid to use horses when they escaped. It sometimes happened that wandering bands of robbers stole horses from the depot, and if they were lucky the search would still be concentrated in the vicinity of the camp.

But then one of the horses died. San's little Indian pony seemed to be just as strong as the dappled horse Guo Si was clinging to. But suddenly it stumbled and fell over. It was dead by the time it hit the ground. San knew nothing about horses and assumed the horse's heart had simply stopped beating, the way human hearts sometimes do.

They had left the horse after first cutting a large lump of meat from its back. To confuse any possible pursuers they had changed direction rather more to the south than before. For several hundred yards San had walked behind Guo Si, dragging some branches behind him to cover their trail.

He was woken up by a bang that almost made his head explode. When he opened his eyes, his left ear throbbing with pain, he found himself looking into the face he feared most. It was still dark, even if a faint pink glow could be seen over the distant Sierra Nevada. JA was standing there, with a smoking rifle in his hand. He had fired it next to San's ear.

JA was not alone. At his side were Brown and several Indians with bloodhounds on leads. JA handed his rifle to Brown and drew his revolver. He pointed it at San's head. Then he aimed it sideways and fired a shot next to San's right ear. When San stood up, he could see that JA was yelling something, but he couldn't hear a word the foreman said. His head was filled with a thunderous roar. JA then pointed his revolver at Guo Si's head. San could see the terror in his brother's face but could do nothing to help. JA fired two shots, one next to each ear. San could see the tears in Guo Si's eyes caused by the pain.

Their flight was over. Brown tied the brothers' hands behind their backs and placed nooses around their necks, and they started the trek back east.

When they arrived at the mountain, JA paraded the escapees in front of the rest of the workers, their hands still tied behind their backs and nooses around their necks. San looked for Wang, but couldn't see him. As neither of the brothers had recovered his hearing, they could only guess what JA had to say, perched on the back of his horse. When he had finished talking, he dismounted, and in front of the assembled workers he punched each of the brothers hard in the face. San fell over. For a brief moment he had the feeling that he would never be able to stand up again.

But in the end he did. Once more.

After the failed escape, what San expected to happen did in fact happen. They were not hanged, but every time nitroglycerin was used to blast open reluctant chunks of the mountain, it was San and Guo Si who were hoisted up in the baskets of death, as the Chinese workers called them. Even after a month, the brothers were still mostly deaf. San began to think that he would have to spend the rest of his life with the roaring noise filling his head.

Summer, which was long and hot, had reached

them. At enormous physical cost they penetrated farther and farther into the mountain, carved their way
into the mass of stone that yielded not even a single
inch without demanding maximum effort. Every
morning San felt that he couldn't possibly last one
more day.

San hated JA. A hatred that grew as time passed. It
was not the physical brutality, nor even being hoisted
up over and over again in the potentially fatal baskets. It was that when they'd been forced to stand in
front of the other railroad workers with nooses
around their necks, they were put on display like animals.

"I'm going to kill that man," said San to Guo Si.
"I'm not going to leave this mountain without first
having killed him. I shall kill him."

"That means we will also die," said Guo Si.

San was insistent.

"I shall kill that man when the time is right. Not
before. But then."

The summer seemed to get hotter and hotter.
They were working in broiling sunshine from early
morning until distant dusk. Their working hours
increased as the days became longer. Several of the
workers were stricken by sunstroke; others died of
exhaustion. But there always seemed to be more Chinese who could take the places of the dead.

They came in endless processions of wagons. Every
time a newcomer arrived at the door of their tent, he
was bombarded with questions. Where did he come

from, what ship had transported him over the ocean? There was an insatiable hunger for news from China.

During these summer months, as the brothers' hearing returned, JA was struck down by a fever and didn't appear. One morning Brown came to say that as long as the foreman was indisposed, the two brothers would not be the only ones hoisted up in the baskets of death. He made no attempt to explain why he was excusing them from this dangerous work. Perhaps it was because the foreman often treated Brown just as badly as any of the Chinese. San cautiously attempted to get to know Brown better.

San often wondered about the reddish-brown people with long, black hair, which they often adorned with feathers: their facial features reminded him of his own.

One evening he asked Brown, who knew a little Chinese, about them.

"The Red Indians hate us," said Brown. "Just as much as you do. That's the only similarity I can see."

"But even so, they are the ones standing guard over us."

"We feed them. We give them rifles. We let them be one step above you. And two steps above the niggers. They think they have power. But in fact they are slaves like everybody else."

"Everybody?"

Brown shook his head. San was not going to receive an answer to his last question.

They sat in the darkness. Now and then the glow

from their pipes lit up their faces. Brown had given San one of his old pipes and also some tobacco. San was constantly on his guard. He still didn't know what Brown wanted in return. Perhaps he just wanted company, to break the boundless solitariness of the desert, now that the foreman was ill.

Eventually San dared to ask about JA.

Who was this man who never gave up until he had tracked down San and his brother and ruined their hearing? Who was this man who derived pleasure from torturing other people?

"I've heard things," said Brown, biting hard on the stem of his pipe. "The story is the rich men in San Francisco who invested money in this railroad gave him a job as a guard. He was good—chased after escapees and was clever enough to use both dogs and Indians. And so they made him a foreman. But sometimes, as in your case, he reverts to chasing escapees. They say that nobody has ever got away from him, unless you count the ones who died out there in the desert. In such cases he cut off their hands and scalped them, just like the Indians do, to demonstrate that he'd tracked them down despite everything. A lot of people think he's superhuman. The Indians say he can see in the dark. That's why they call him Long Beard Who Sees in the Night."

San thought over what Brown had said.

"He doesn't speak like you do. What he says sounds different. Where does he come from?"

"I don't know for sure. Somewhere in Europe.

From a country in the far north, somebody said, but I'm not sure."

"Does he ever say anything about that himself?"

"Never. That stuff about a country in the far north might not be true."

"Is he an Englishman?"

Brown shook his head. "That man comes from hell. And that's where he'll go back to one of these days."

San wanted to ask more questions, but Brown was reluctant.

"No more about him. He'll soon be back. His fever is dying away, and water doesn't run straight through his stomach anymore. When he's back here there's nothing I'll be able to do to save you from dancing with death in the baskets."

A few days later JA was back on duty. He was paler and thinner than before, but more brutal. The very first day he knocked out two Chinese who worked alongside San and Guo Si simply because he thought they didn't greet him politely enough when he came riding up on horseback. He was not pleased with the progress made while he had been sick.

The brothers were sent back up in the baskets again. They could no longer count on any support from Brown.

They burrowed their way deeper into the mountain, blasting and hacking, shifting boulders and molding hard-packed sand to form the roadbed on which the rails would be laid. With superhuman efforts they conquered the mountain, yard after yard. In the distance they could see the locomotives delivering rails and sleepers and gangs of laborers.

As the nights grew colder and the fall advanced, Guo Si fell ill. He woke up one morning with bad stomach pains. He ran out of the tent and only just managed to pull down his pants before his insides exploded.

His fellow workers were afraid that they might all be infected and so left him alone in the tent. San brought him water, and an old black man by the name of Hoss kept moistening his brow and wiping away the watery mess that leaked out of his body. Hoss had spent so much time tending the sick that nothing seemed to threaten him any longer. He had only one arm; he had lost the other in a landslide.

JA was impatient. He looked down in disgust at the man lying in his own feces.

"Are you going to die, or aren't you?" he asked.

Guo Si tried to sit up but didn't have the strength.

"I need this tent," said JA. "Why do you Chinese always take so long to die?"

The days grew shorter, and as fall gave way to winter, miraculously, Guo Si began to get better.

After four years, they had served their time and could leave the railroad as free men. San heard about a white man named Samuel Acheson who was planning to lead a wagon trek eastward. He needed somebody to prepare his food and wash his clothes and promised to pay for the work. He had made a fortune panning for gold in the Yukon River. Now he was going to traverse the continent in order to visit his sister, his only living relative, who lived in New York.

Acheson agreed to employ both San and Guo Si. Neither of them would regret joining his trek. Samuel Acheson treated people well, irrespective of the color of their skin.

Crossing the whole continent, the endless plains, took much longer than San could ever have predicted. On two occasions Acheson fell ill and was confined to bed for several months. He didn't seem to be plagued by physical illness; it was his mind that descended into gloom so murky that he hid himself away in his tent and didn't emerge until the depression had passed. Twice every day San would serve him food and see Acheson lying at the back of his tent, his face averted from the world.

But both times he recovered, his depression faded away, and they could continue their long journey. He could have afforded to travel by rail, but Acheson preferred his phlegmatic oxen and the uncomfortable covered wagons.

Out in the vast prairies, San would often lie awake in the evenings, gazing up at the endless skies. He was looking for his mother and father and Wu, but he never found them.

They eventually reached New York, Acheson was reunited with his sister, and San and Guo Si were paid and began looking for a ship that would take them to England. San knew that was the only possible route for them to take, since there were no ships sailing directly to Canton or Shanghai from New York. They managed to find places on deck on a ship bound for Liverpool.

That was in March 1867. The morning they left New York, the harbor was shrouded in thick fog. Eerie foghorns wailed on all sides. San and Guo Si were standing by the rail.

"We're going home," said Guo Si.

"Yes," said San. "We're on our way home now."

The Feather and the Stone

14

On July 5, 1867, the two brothers left Liverpool on a ship called **Nellie.**

San soon discovered that he and Guo Si were the only Chinese on board. They had been allocated sleeping places at the very front of the bow in the old ship, which smelled of rot. On board the **Nellie** the same kind of rules applied as in Canton: there were no walls, but every passenger recognized his own or others' private space.

Even before the ship left port San had noticed two unobtrusive passengers with fair hair who frequently knelt down on deck to pray. They seemed unaffected by everything going on around them—sailors pushing and pulling, officers urging them on and barking orders. The two men were totally immersed in their prayers until they quietly stood up again.

The two men turned to face San and bowed. San took a step back, as if he had been threatened. A white man had never bowed to him before. White men didn't bow to Chinese; they kicked them. He hurried back to the place where he and Guo Si were going to sleep and wondered who these two men could be.

Late in the afternoon the moorings were cast off, the ship was towed out of the harbor, and the sails were hoisted. A fresh northerly breeze was blowing. The ship set off in an easterly direction at a brisk pace.

San held on to the rail and let the cool wind blow in his face. The two brothers were now on their way home at last, to complete their voyage around the world. It was essential to stay healthy on the voyage. San had no idea what would happen when they arrived back in China, but he was determined that they would not sink into poverty once more.

A few days after they had left port and reached the open sea, the two fair-haired men came up to San. They had with them an elderly member of the crew who spoke Chinese. San was afraid that he and Guo Si had done something wrong, but the crewman, Mr. Mott, explained that the two men were Swedish missionaries on their way to China. He introduced them as Mr. Elgstrand and Mr. Lodin.

Mr. Mott's Chinese pronunciation was difficult to understand, but San and Guo Si understood enough to discover that the two young men were priests who had dedicated their lives to work in the Christian mission to China. Now they were on their way to Fuzhou in order to build up a community in which they could begin to convert the Chinese to the true religion. They would fight against paganism and show the way to God's kingdom, which was the ultimate destination for all human beings.

Would San and Guo Si consider helping these gentlemen to improve their fluency in Chinese, which was such a difficult language? They had a smattering already but wanted to work hard during the voyage so that they would be well prepared when they disembarked on the Chinese coast.

San thought for a moment. He saw no reason that they should not accept the remuneration the fair-haired men were prepared to pay. It would make their own return to China easier.

He bowed.

"It will give Guo Si and me great pleasure to help these gentlemen become better acquainted with the Chinese language."

They started work the very next day. Elgstrand and Lodin wanted to invite San and Guo Si to their part of the ship, but San said no. He preferred to remain in the bow.

It was San who became the missionaries' teacher. Guo Si spent most of the time sitting to one side, listening.

The two Swedish missionaries treated the brothers like equals. San was surprised that they were not undertaking this voyage in order to find work, or because they had been forced to leave. What drove these young men was a genuine desire and determination to save souls from eternal damnation. Elgstrand and Lodin were prepared to sacrifice their lives for their faith. Elgstrand came from a simple farming family, while Lodin's father had been a rural minister. They pointed out on a map where they came from. They spoke openly, making no attempt to hide their simple origins.

When San saw the map of the world, he realized the full extent of their journey.

Elgstrand and Lodin were keen students. They worked hard and learned quickly. By the time the ship passed through the Bay of Biscay, they had established a routine involving lessons in the morning and in the late afternoon. San started asking questions about their faith and their God. He wanted to understand things about his mother that had been beyond his comprehension. She had known nothing about the Christian God, but she had prayed to other invisible higher powers. How could a person be prepared to sacrifice his life in order to make other people believe in the God that person worshipped himself?

Elgstrand spoke more often, reinforcing the message that all men are sinners but could be saved and after death could enter paradise.

San thought about the hatred he felt for Zi, for Wang (who was probably dead), and for JA. Elgstrand maintained that the Christian God taught that the worst crime a man could commit was to kill a fellow human being.

San didn't like that idea at all; his common sense told him that Elgstrand and Lodin couldn't be right. All the time they talked about what was in store after death, but never about how a human life could be changed while it was being lived.

Elgstrand often came back to the idea that all human beings were equal. In the eyes of God everybody was a poor sinner. But San could not understand how, when the Day of Judgment dawned, he and Zi and JA could be assessed equally.

He was extremely doubtful. But at the same time he was pleasantly surprised by the kindness and apparently boundless patience the two young men from Sweden displayed toward him and Guo Si. He could also see that his brother, who often had private conversations with Lodin, seemed to be impressed by what he heard. As a result, San never initiated any discussions with Guo Si about his opinion of the white God.

Elgstrand and Lodin shared their food with San and Guo Si. San couldn't know what was true and what wasn't true when it came to their God, but he had no doubt that the two men lived in accordance with what they preached.

After thirty-two days at sea the **Nellie** called at Cape Town to replenish stores and rode at anchor in the shadow of Table Mountain before continuing southward. As they came to the Cape of Good Hope, they were hit by a severe southerly storm. The **Nellie** drifted for four days with sails taken in, riding the waves. San was terrified by the thought that the ship might sink, and he could see that the crew was scared as well. The only people on board who were completely calm were Elgstrand and Lodin. Or perhaps they concealed their fear well.

If San was scared, his brother was panic-stricken. Lodin sat with Guo Si throughout the whole of the raging storm. When it was over, Guo Si went down on bended knee and said he wanted to declare his belief in the God the white men were going to introduce to his Chinese brothers.

San was filled with even more admiration for the missionaries who had been so calm while the storm raged. But he couldn't bring himself to do what Guo Si had done and kneel down to pray to a God that for him was still too mysterious and evasive.

They rounded the Cape of Good Hope, and favorable winds assisted their passage over the Indian Ocean. The weather became warmer, easier to cope with. San continued with his teaching, and every day Guo Si would go off with Lodin for their intimate, mumbled conversations.

But San knew nothing of what the future held. One day Guo Si suddenly fell ill. He woke San up during the night and whispered that he had started to cough up blood. Guo Si was deathly pale and shivering. San asked one of the sailors on night watch to fetch the missionaries. The man, who came from America and had a black mother but a white father, looked down at Guo Si.

"Are you suggesting that I should wake up one of the gentlemen just because a coolie is lying here and bleeding?"

"If you don't, they will punish you tomorrow."

The sailor frowned. He fetched Elgstrand and Lodin. They carried Guo Si to their cabin and laid him on one of the bunks. Lodin seemed to be the one who knew more about patient care and gave him several different medicines. San squatted back against the wall in the cramped cabin. The flickering light from the lantern cast shadows onto the walls. The ship progressed slowly through the swell.

The end came very quickly. Guo Si died as dawn broke. Before he breathed his last, Elgstrand and Lodin promised that he would be delivered unto God if he confessed his sins and affirmed his belief. They held his hands and prayed together. San sat by himself in the corner of the room. There was nothing he could do. His second brother had left him. But he couldn't help but notice that the missionaries gave Guo Si a feeling of peace and assurance that he had never experienced before in his life.

San had difficulty understanding the last words Guo Si said to him. But he had the feeling Guo Si wasn't afraid of death.

"I'm leaving you now," said Guo Si. "I'm walking on water, like the man they call Jesus. I'm on my way to a different and a better world. Wu is waiting for me there. And you will come to join us one day."

When Guo Si died, San sat with his head on his

knees and his hands over his ears. He shook his head when Elgstrand tried to talk to him. Nobody could help him with the feeling of solitary impotence that overwhelmed him.

He returned to his place at the very front of the ship. Two members of the crew sewed Guo Si's body into an old sail, together with some rusty iron nails as weights.

Elgstrand told San that the captain would conduct a sea burial two hours later.

"I want to be together with my brother," said San. "I don't want him to lie out there on deck before they drop him into the sea."

Elgstrand and Lodin carried the body in its shroud of sailcloth into their cabin and left San alone with his brother. Guo Si would never return to China, but traditional beliefs made it essential for a part of his body to be buried there. San took a knife from the little table and carefully opened up the bottom of the package. He cut off Guo Si's left foot. He was careful to make sure that no blood dripped onto the floor, tied a piece of cloth around the stump, then tied another piece of cloth around the foot, and put it inside his shirt. Then he repaired the hole in the sail. Nobody would be able to tell that it had been opened.

The captain and crew assembled by the ship's rail. The sailcloth containing Guo Si's body was placed on a plank resting on trestles. The captain took off his cap. He read from the Bible, then launched into a hymn. Elgstrand and Lodin joined in with powerful voices. Just as the captain was about to give the signal for the sailors to tip the body overboard, Elgstrand lifted his hand.

"This simple Chinese man, Wang Guo Si, saw the light before he died. Even if his body will soon be on its way to the bottom of the ocean, his soul is free and already soaring over our heads. Let us pray to the God who looks after the dead and liberates their souls. Amen."

When the captain gave the signal, San closed his eyes. He heard a distant splash as the body hit the water.

San returned to the place he and his brother had occupied during the voyage. He still couldn't register that Guo Si was dead. Just when he'd thought that his brother's will to live had been boosted, not least by the meeting with the two missionaries, Guo Si had been whisked away by an unknown illness.

The night after the sea burial San began the unpleasant task of cutting away skin and sinews and muscles from Guo Si's foot. The only tool he had was an iron screw he'd found on deck. He threw the bits of flesh overboard. When the bones were clean, he rubbed them with a rag to dry them and hid them in his kit bag.

He spent the following week in solitary mourning. There were times when he thought the best thing he could do was to climb silently over the rail under cover of darkness and sink into the sea. But he had to take the bones of his dead brother back home.

When he started his lessons with the missionaries again, he could never stop thinking about how much they had meant to Guo Si. He hadn't screamed his way into death; he had been calm. Elgstrand and Lodin had given Guo Si the most elusive thing of all: the courage to die.

During the rest of the voyage, first to Java, where the ship replenished stores again, and then the final stretch to Canton, San asked a lot of questions about the God who could bring comfort to the dying, and who offered paradise to all, irrespective of whether they were rich or poor.

But the key question was why this God had allowed Guo Si to die just when he and San were on their way back home after all the hardship they had undergone. Neither Elgstrand nor Lodin could give him a satisfactory answer. The ways of the Christian God were inscrutable, Elgstrand said. What did that mean? That life was nothing more than waiting for what came next? That faith was in fact a riddle?

San was brooding as the ship approached Canton. He would never forget any of what he had been through. Now he wanted to learn to write, so that he could record what had happened in his life alongside his dead brothers, from the morning when he'd discovered his parents hanging from a tree.

A few days before they expected to see the Chinese coast, Elgstrand and Lodin came to sit down beside him on deck, wishing to know of his plans on arriving in Canton.

He had no answer.

"We don't want to lose touch with you," said Elgstrand. "We've become close during this voyage. Without you, our knowledge of Chinese would have been even more sketchy than it is. We'd like you to join us. We shall pay you a wage, and you will help us to build up the big Christian community we dream about."

San sat in silence for quite a while before responding. When he'd made up his mind, he stood up and bowed twice to the missionaries.

He would go with them. Perhaps one day he would achieve the insight that had gilded Guo Si's final days.

On September 12, 1867, San stepped ashore in Canton. In his kit bag were the bones from his dead brother's foot. That was all he had to show for his long journey.

He looked around the quay. Was he searching for Zi or for Wu? He didn't know.

A few days later San accompanied the two Swedish missionaries on a riverboat to the town of Fuzhou. He contemplated the countryside drifting slowly by. He was looking for somewhere to bury the remains of Guo Si.

It was something he wanted to do alone. It was a matter between him, his parents, and the spirits of his ancestors.

The riverboat sailed slowly northward. Frogs were singing on the banks.

San had come home.

15

In the fall of 1868, San began with considerable effort to chronicle his story and that of his two dead brothers. Five years had passed since he and Guo Si had been abducted by Zi, and it was now a year since San had returned to Canton with Guo Si's foot in a bag. During that year he had accompanied Elgstrand and Lodin to Fuzhou, had been in attendance as their personal servant, and, thanks to a teacher arranged for him by Lodin, had learned to write.

The night San sat down and began writing his life story, a strong wind was rattling the windows of the house in which he had a room. He sat with his pencil in his hand, listening to the sounds and imagining himself back at sea.

It was only now that he was starting to grasp the significance of everything he'd been through. He made up his mind to recall and record every detail, skipping nothing.

Though who would read his story?

He had nobody to write for. And yet he wanted to do it. If there really was a Creator who ruled over the living and the dead, he would no doubt see to it that whatever San wrote would end up in the hands of somebody who wanted to read it.

San started writing, slowly and laboriously, while

the winds made the walls creak. He swayed slowly back and forth on the stool he was sitting on. The room had soon turned into a ship, and the floor was moving under his feet.

He had placed several piles of paper on the table in front of him. Just like crayfish in the riverbed, he intended to work his way backward to the point where he had seen his parents dangling on the end of ropes, swaying in the wind. But he wanted to start with the journey to the place where he was right now. That was the one most vivid in his memory.

Elgstrand and Lodin had been both exhilarated and nervous when they disembarked in Canton. The chaotic mass of people, strange smells, and their inability to understand the special Hakka dialect spoken in the city made them insecure. They were expected—a Swedish missionary by the name of Tomas Hamberg was there to greet them: he worked for a German Bible society devoted to spreading Chinese translations of biblical texts. Hamberg was very hospitable and let them stay in the house in the German legation where he had his office and his apartment. San played the role of the silent servant he had decided to assume. He took charge of the Chinese delegated to carry the missionaries' baggage, washed his employers' clothes, and saw to their needs at all hours of the day and night. Although he said nothing and kept in the background, he listened carefully to everything that was said. Hamberg spoke better Chinese than Elgstrand and Lodin and often spoke with them in order to help improve their fluency. Through a door standing ajar, San heard Hamberg asking Lodin about how they had come into contact with him. San was surprised to hear that Hamberg warned Lodin not to place too much trust in a Chinese servant.

It was the first time San had heard any of the missionaries say anything negative about a Chinese. But he was confident that neither Elgstrand nor Lodin would think the way Hamberg did.

After a few days of intensive preparation they left Canton and sailed along the coast and then up the Min Jiang River to Fuzhou, the City of the Black and White Pagodas. Hamberg had arranged for them to receive a letter of introduction to the chief mandarin of the city, who had previously shown himself to be well disposed to Christian missionaries. To his astonishment, San watched as Elgstrand and Lodin didn't hesitate to kneel down and touch the ground with their foreheads before the mandarin. He gave them permission to work in the town, and after a thorough search they found a base suitable for their purposes. It was a gated compound containing several houses.

The day they moved in Elgstrand and Lodin knelt down and blessed the compound, which would be their future home. San also bent his knee, but uttered no benediction. It occurred to him that he still hadn't found a suitable place in which to bury Guo Si's foot.

It was several months before he found a place near the river where the evening sun shone over the treetops until the ground was slowly swallowed up by shade. San visited the spot many times and always felt very much at peace as he sat there, his back leaning against a boulder. The river flowed slowly past at the bottom of the gentle slope before him. Even now, although the fall had already set in, there were flowers blooming on the riverbank.

Here he would be able to sit and talk to his brothers. This was where they could come to be with him. They could be together. The dividing line between life and death would disappear.

He dug a deep hole in the ground and buried his brother's foot bones. He filled in the hole meticulously, removed all traces, and on the spot placed a stone that he had brought back from the American desert.

San thought that perhaps he ought to recite one of the prayers he had learned from the missionaries; but since Wu, who was also there in a way, had not become acquainted with the God to whom the prayers would be addressed, he merely mentioned their names. He attached wings to their souls and empowered them to fly away.

Elgstrand and Lodin generated amazing energy. San had more and more respect for their unrelenting efforts to lower all barriers and persuade people to help them build up their mission. They also had money, of course. They needed money to carry out their work. Elgstrand had an arrangement with an English shipping company that regularly visited

Fuzhou and brought deliveries of money from Sweden. San was surprised to note that the missionaries never seemed to worry about the possibility of thieves, who wouldn't hesitate to kill them in order to gain access to their riches. Elgstrand kept the money and bills of exchange under his pillow. When neither he nor Lodin was around, San was responsible.

On one occasion San secretly counted the money, which was kept in a little leather bag. He was surprised by how much there was. For a brief moment he was tempted to take the money and run away. There was enough for him to travel to Beijing and live as a rich man on the interest his fortune earned.

But the temptation was overcome when he thought about Guo Si and the kindness and care the missionaries had shown him during his final days on this earth.

San was leading a life he could never have imagined. He had a room of his own with a bed, clean clothes, plenty of food. From being at the very bottom of the ladder, he was now in charge of all the servants in the house. He was strict and decisive, but never resorted to physical punishment when anybody made a mistake.

Only a few weeks after they arrived in Fuzhou, Elgstrand and Lodin opened their doors to one and all. The courtyard was crammed full. San remained in the background and listened to Elgstrand explaining, in his faltering Chinese, about the remarkable God who had sent his only Begotten Son to be crucified. Lodin handed out colored pictures, which the congregation passed around to one another.

When Elgstrand had finished, the courtyard emptied rapidly. But the following day the same thing happened, and people came again, some of them bringing friends and acquaintances. The whole town began talking about these remarkable white men who had come to live among them. The most difficult thing for the Chinese to understand was that Elgstrand and Lodin were not running a business. They had nothing to sell, and there was nothing they wanted to buy. They simply stood there and spoke in bad Chinese about a God who treated all human beings as equals.

In these early days there was no limit to the missionaries' efforts. They nailed Chinese characters to the arch over the entrance to the courtyard, declaring that this was the Temple of the One True God. The two men never seemed to sleep but were constantly active. San sometimes heard them using a Chinese expression meaning "degrading idolatry," declaring that it must be resisted. He wondered how the missionaries dared to believe that they could persuade ordinary Chinese people to abandon ideas and beliefs they had lived with for generations. How could a God who allowed his only son to be nailed to a cross be able to give a Chinese peasant spiritual comfort or the will to live?

A few weeks after they'd arrived in Fuzhou, early in the morning San drew the bolts and opened the heavy wooden front door to be confronted by a young woman who bowed her head and announced that her name was Lou Qi. She came from a little village up the Min River, not far from Shuikou. Her parents were poor peasants, and she had fled her village when her father decreed that she should be sold as a concubine to a seventy-year-old man in Nanchang. She had begged her father to release her from that obligation, since rumor had it that several of the man's previous concubines had been killed when he had grown tired of them. But her father had refused to listen to her protests, and so she had run away. A German missionary based in the outpost of Gou Sihan had told her that there was a mission in Fuzhou where Christian charity was available to anybody who sought it.

San looked her up and down when she had finished her story. He asked a few questions about what she was capable of doing, then let her in. She would be allowed to see if she could assist the women and the chef who were responsible for feeding the residents of the mission. If things turned out well, he might be able to offer her a job on the household staff.

He was touched by the joy that lit up her face.

Qi did a good job, and San extended her contract. She lived with the other female servants and was liked because she was always unruffled and never tried to avoid tasks allocated to her. San used to watch her as she worked in the kitchen or hurried across the courtyard on some errand or other. Their eyes occasionally met, but he never treated her any differently from the other servants.

One day shortly before Christmas, Elgstrand asked him to hire a boat and appoint some oarsmen. They were going to travel downriver to visit an English ship that had just arrived from London. The British consul in Fuzhou had informed Elgstrand that there was a parcel for the mission station.

"You'd better come with us," said Elgstrand with a smile. "I need my best man when I'm going to collect a bagful of money."

San found a team of oarsmen in the harbor who accepted the assignment. The following day Elgstrand and San clambered down into the boat. Just before, San had whispered to his boss that it was probably best not to say anything about the contents of the parcel they were collecting from the English ship.

Elgstrand smiled.

"I'm no doubt gullible," he said, "but not quite as naïve as you think."

It took the oarsmen three hours to reach the ship and pull up alongside. Elgstrand climbed the ladder with San. A bald captain by the name of John Dunn received them. He eyed the oarsmen with extreme mistrust. Then he gave San a similar look and made a comment that San didn't understand. Elgstrand shook his head and explained to San that Captain Dunn didn't have much time for Chinamen.

"He thinks you are all thieves and confidence

tricksters," said Elgstrand with a laugh. "One of these days he'll realize how wrong he is."

Dunn and Elgstrand disappeared into the captain's cabin. After a short while Elgstrand emerged with a leather briefcase, which he ostentatiously handed to San.

"Captain Dunn thinks I'm crazy for trusting you. Sad to say, Captain Dunn is an extremely vulgar person who doubtless knows a lot about ships and winds and oceans, but nothing at all about people."

They climbed back down to the rowboat and returned to the mission station. It was dark by the time they arrived. San paid the leader of the oarsmen. As they walked through the dark alleys, San began to feel uneasy. He couldn't help thinking about that evening in Canton when Zi had lured him and his brothers into the trap. But nothing happened this time. Elgstrand went to his office with the case while San bolted the door and woke up the night watchman, who had fallen asleep with his back to the outside wall.

"You get paid for being on guard," said San, "not for sleeping."

He said it in a friendly tone of voice even though he knew the watchman was lazy and would soon drop off to sleep again. But the man had a lot of children to look after, and a wife who had been badly scalded by boiling water and had been confined to bed for many years, often screaming out in pain.

I'm a foreman with both feet on the ground, San

thought. I don't sit on horseback like JA. And I sleep like a guard dog, with one eye open.

He went to his room. On the way he noticed that there was a light in the room where the female servants slept. He frowned. It was forbidden to have candles burning at night, as the risk of starting a fire was too great. He went to the window and peeped cautiously through a gap in the thin curtains. There were three women in the room. One of them, the oldest of the servants, was asleep, but Qi and another young woman called Na were sitting up in the bed they shared, talking. There was a lantern on their bedside table. As it was a warm night, Qi had unbuttoned the top of her nightdress, exposing her breasts. San stared spellbound at her body. He couldn't hear their voices and guessed they were whispering so as not to wake up the older woman.

Qi suddenly turned and looked at the window. San shrank back. Had she seen him? He withdrew into the shadows and waited. But Qi didn't adjust the curtains. San returned to the window and stood watching until Na blew out the candle, leaving the room in darkness.

San didn't move. One of the dogs that ran loose in the compound during the night to frighten away thieves came and sniffed at his hands.

"I'm not a thief," whispered San. "I'm an ordinary man lusting after a woman who might one day be mine."

From that moment on, San set his heart on Qi. He

was careful about it, not wanting to scare her. Nor did he want his interest to be too obvious to the other servants. Jealousy was always liable to spread quickly.

It was a long time before Qi understood the cautious signals he kept sending her. They started meeting in the dark outside her room, after Na had promised not to gossip about it. In return for that Na received a pair of new shoes. In the end, after almost half a year, Qi started to spend part of every night in San's room. When they made love San experienced a feeling of joy that banished all the painful shadows and memories that usually surrounded him.

San and Qi had no doubt that they wanted to spend the rest of their lives together.

San decided to speak to Elgstrand and Lodin and ask their permission to get married. San went to visit the two missionaries one morning after they had finished breakfast but before they turned their attention to the tasks that filled their days. He explained what he wanted. Lodin said nothing; Elgstrand did the talking.

"Why do you want to marry her?"

"She is nice and considerate. She works hard."

"She's a very simple woman who can't do nearly as much as you've learned. And she shows no interest in our Christian message."

"She's still very young."

"There are those who say she was a thief."

"The servants are always gossiping. Nobody escapes their attention. Everybody accuses everybody else of anything at all. I know what's true and what isn't. Qi has never been a thief."

Elgstrand turned to Lodin. San had no idea what they said in a language he didn't understand.

"We think you should wait," said Elgstrand. "If you are going to get married, we want it to be a Christian wedding. The first one we've performed here at the mission station. But neither of you is mature enough yet. We want you to wait."

San bowed and left the room. He was extremely disappointed. But Elgstrand had not given him a definite no. One day he and Qi would become a couple.

A few months later Qi told San that she was pregnant. San was overjoyed and decided immediately that if it was a boy, he would be called Guo Si. But at the same time he realized this news would cause problems—the Christian religion insisted that couples had to be married before they had children. Having sexual intercourse before marriage was considered a major sin. San couldn't think of a solution. The growing stomach could be concealed for some time yet, but San would be forced to say something before the truth was revealed.

One day San was informed that Lodin would need a team of oarsmen for a journey several miles upriver to a German-run mission station. As always with these boat trips, San would go as well. The evening before the journey he said good-bye to Qi and promised that he would solve everything upon his return.

When he and Lodin returned four days later, San was summoned to Elgstrand, who wanted to speak to him. The missionary was sitting at his desk in his office. He usually invited San to sit down, but this time he didn't. San suspected that something had happened.

Elgstrand's voice was milder than usual when he spoke.

"How did the trip go?"

"Everything went as expected."

Elgstrand nodded thoughtfully and gave San a searching look.

"I'm disappointed," he said. "I hoped till the very last that the rumor that had reached my ears was not true. But in the end I was forced to act. Do you understand what I'm talking about?"

San knew, but said no even so.

"That makes me even more disappointed," said Elgstrand. "When a person tells a lie, the devil has found its way into the man's mind. I'm referring, of course, to the fact that the woman you wanted to marry is pregnant. I'll give you another opportunity to tell me the truth."

San bowed his head but said nothing. He could feel his heart racing.

"For the first time since we met on the ship bringing us here, you have disappointed me," Elgstrand went on. "You have been one of the people who have given me and Brother Lodin the feeling that even the Chinese can be raised up to a higher spiritual level.

The last few days have been very difficult. I have prayed for you and decided that I can allow you to stay. But you must devote even more time and effort to progress to the moment when you can declare your allegiance to the God we share."

San stood there, head bowed, waiting for what came next. Nothing did.

"That's all," said Elgstrand. "Go back to your duties."

As he reached the door, he heard Elgstrand's voice behind his back.

"You understand, of course, that Qi couldn't possibly stay on here. She has left us."

San was devastated when he emerged into the courtyard. He felt the same as he did when his brother died. Now he was floored once again. He found Na, grabbed her by the hair, and dragged her out of the kitchen. It was the first time San had ever been violent to one of the servants. Na screamed and threw herself onto the ground. San soon realized that she was not the one who had gossiped, but that the old woman had heard Qi confessing the situation to Na. San managed to prevent himself from attacking her as well. That would have meant he would have to leave the mission station. He took Na to his room and sat her down on a stool.

"Where is Qi?"

"She left two days ago."

"Where did she go?"

"I don't know. She was very upset. She ran."

"She must have said something about where she was going."

"I don't think she knew. But she might have gone to the river to wait for you there."

San stood up like a shot, raced out of the room, through the main gate and down to the harbor. But he couldn't find her. He spent most of the day looking for her, asking everybody he came across, but nobody had seen her. He spoke to the oarsmen, and they promised to let him know if Qi showed up.

When he got back to the mission station and met Elgstrand again, it was as if the Swede had already forgotten about what had happened. He was preparing for the service that was to be held the following day.

"Don't you think the courtyard ought to be swept?" Elgstrand asked in a friendly tone.

"I'll make sure that's done first thing tomorrow morning, before the visitors arrive."

Elgstrand nodded, and San bowed. Elgstrand obviously considered Qi's sin so serious that there was no redemption possible for her.

San simply could not understand that there were people who could never be granted the grace of God because they had committed the sin of loving another human being.

He watched Elgstrand and Lodin talking on the veranda outside the mission station's office.

It was as if he were seeing them for the first time in their true light.

Two days later San received a message from one of

his friends at the harbor. He hurried there. He had to elbow his way through a large crowd. Qi was lying on a plank. Despite the heavy iron chain around her waist, she had risen from the depths. The chain had become entangled with a rudder that raised the body to the surface. Her skin was bluish white, her eyes closed. San was the only one able to make out that her stomach contained a child.

Once again San was alone.

San gave money to the man who had sent the message to inform him of what had happened. It would be sufficient to have the body cremated. Two days later he buried the ashes in the same place Guo Si was already resting.

So this is what I've achieved in my life, he thought. I create and then fill my own cemetery. The spirits of four people are resting here already, one of whom was never even born.

He knelt down and hit his head over and over again on the ground. Sorrow swelled up inside him. He was unable to resist it. He howled like an animal. He had never felt as helpless as he did at this moment. He once felt capable of looking after his brothers: now he was a mere shadow of a man, crumbling away.

When he returned to the mission station late that evening he was told by the night watchman that Elgstrand had been looking for him. San knocked on the door of Elgstrand's office, where the missionary was sitting at his desk, writing by lamplight.

"I've missed you," said Elgstrand. "You've been away all day. I prayed to God and hoped that nothing had happened to you."

"Nothing has happened," said San, bowing. "It's just that I had a bit of a toothache, which I cured with the aid of some herbs."

"That's good. We can't manage without you. Go and get some sleep."

San never told Elgstrand or Lodin that Qi had taken her own life. A new girl was appointed. San buttoned up the pain inside himself and continued for many months to be the missionaries' irreplaceable servant. He never said anything about what he was thinking, nor how he now listened to the sermons with a different attitude than before.

It was around this time that San felt he had mastered writing well enough to begin the story of himself and his brothers. He still didn't know for whom he was writing it. Perhaps just for the wind. But if that was the case, he would force the wind to listen.

He wrote late at night, slept less and less but without letting that affect his duties. He was always friendly, ready to help, make decisions, manage the servants, and make it easier for Elgstrand and Lodin to convert the Chinese.

Nearly a year had passed since he had arrived in Fuzhou. San was well aware that it would take a very long time to create the kingdom of God that the missionaries dreamed about. After twelve months, nineteen people had converted and accepted the Christian faith.

He kept writing all the time, thinking back to the reasons that he left his home village in the first place.

One of San's duties was to tidy up in Elgstrand's office. Nobody else was allowed in there. One day when San was carefully dusting the desk and straightening the papers on it, he noticed a letter Elgstrand had written in Chinese. It was written to one of his missionary friends in Canton—they tried to practice their language skills together.

Elgstrand confided in his friend as follows: "As you know, the Chinese are incredibly hardworking and can endure poverty the same way that mules and asses can endure being kicked and whipped. But one mustn't forget that the Chinese are also base and cunning liars and swindlers; they are arrogant and greedy and have a bestial sensuality that sometimes disgusts me. On the whole, they are worthless people. One can only hope that one day, the love of God will be able to penetrate their horrific harshness and cruelty."

San read the letter a second time. Then he finished cleaning and left the room.

He continued working as if nothing had happened, wrote every night, and listened to the missionaries' sermons during the day.

One evening in the fall of 1868 he left the missionary station without anybody noticing. He had packed all his belongings in a simple cloth bag. It was windy and raining when he left. The night watchman was asleep by the gate and didn't hear San climbing over it. As he perched on top, he wrenched off the sign announcing that this was the gateway to the Temple of the One True God. He threw it down into the mud.

The street was deserted. It was pouring down.

San was swallowed up by the darkness, and vanished.

16

Ya Ru liked to sit alone in his office in the evenings. The skyscraper in central Beijing, where he occupied the entire penthouse with floor-to-ceiling windows overlooking the city, was almost empty by then. Only the security guards on the ground floor and the cleaning crew were still around. His secretary, Mrs. Shen, was on call in an anteroom: she always stayed for as long as he thought he might need her—sometimes until dawn.

This day in December 2005 was Ya Ru's thirty-eighth birthday. He agreed with the Western philosopher who had once written that at that age a man was in the middle of his life. He had a lot of friends who, as they approached their forties, felt old age like a faint but cold breeze on the back of their necks. Ya Ru had no such worries; he had made up his mind as a student never to waste time and energy worrying about things he couldn't do anything about. The passage of time was relentless and capricious, and one would lose the battle with it in the end. The only resistance a man could offer was to make the most of time, exploit it without trying to prevent its progress.

Ya Ru pressed his nose up against the cold windowpane. He always kept the temperature low in his vast suite of offices, in which all the furniture was in tasteful shades of black and blood red. The temperature was a constant seventeen degrees Celsius, both during the cold season and in the summer when sandstorms and hot winds blew over Beijing. It suited him. He had always been in favor of cold reflection. Doing business and making political decisions were a sort of warfare, and all that mattered was cool, rational calculation. Not for nothing was he known as Tou Nao Leng—"the Cool One."

No doubt there were some who thought he was dangerous. It was true that several times, earlier in his life, he had lost his temper and physically harmed people, but that no longer happened. He didn't mind that many were frightened of him. More important was not to lose control over the anger that sometimes surged through him.

Occasionally, very early in the morning, Ya Ru would leave his apartment through a secret back door. He would go to a nearby park and perform the concentrated gymnastic exercises known as tai chi. It made him feel like a small, insignificant part of the great, anonymous mass of Chinese people. Nobody knew who he was or what he was called. He sometimes thought it was like giving himself a thorough wash. When he returned to his apartment afterward and resumed his identity, he always felt stronger.

Midnight was approaching. He was expecting two visits that night. It amused him to hold meetings in the middle of the night or as dawn was breaking. Having control of the time gave him an advantage: in a cold room in the pale light of dawn, it was easier for him to get what he wanted.

He gazed out over the city. In 1967, when the Cultural Revolution was stormier than ever, he had been born in a hospital somewhere down there among those glittering lights. His father had not been present; as a university professor, he had been caught up in the frenzied purges of the Red Guard and banished to the country to tend peasants' pigs. Ya Ru had never met him. He had vanished and was never heard from again. Later in life Ya Ru had sent some of his closest colleagues to the place where it was thought his father had been exiled, but without success. Nobody remembered his father. Nor was there any trace in the chaotic archives of that period. Ya Ru's father had drowned in the big political tidal wave that Mao had set in motion.

It had been a difficult time for his mother, alone with her son and her older daughter, Hong Qiu. His first memory was of his mother crying. It was rather blurred, but he had never forgotten it. Later, at the beginning of the 1980s, when their situation had improved and his mother had gotten her job back as a lecturer in theoretical physics at one of the universities in Beijing, he had a better understanding of the chaos that had reigned when he was born. Mao had tried to create a new universe. In the same way as the universe had been created, a new China would emerge from the mass tumult Mao had brought about.

Ya Ru realized early on that the only guarantee to success was to learn where the center of power was at any given time. An appreciation of the various trends in political and economic life was essential to climb to the level at which he now found himself.

When the markets loosened up here in China, I was ready, Ya Ru thought. I was one of those cats Deng spoke about—the ones that didn't need to be black or gray as long as they hunted mice. Now I'm one of the richest men of my generation. I have secured my position thanks to contacts deep in the new age's Forbidden City, where the innermost power circles of the Communist Party rule. I pay for their foreign trips; I fly in dress designers for their wives. I arrange places at top U.S. universities for their children and build houses for their parents. In return, I have my freedom.

He interrupted his train of thought and checked the clock. Nearly midnight. He went to his desk and pressed an intercom button. Mrs. Shen answered immediately.

"I'm expecting a visitor," he said, "in about ten minutes. Make her wait for half an hour. Then I'll buzz her in."

Ya Ru sat down at his desk. It was always bare when he left in the evening. Every new day should be greeted by a clean slate on which new challenges could be spread out.

Lying on it at the moment was a well-thumbed old book whose covers were worn. Ya Ru sometimes thought he ought to engage a skilled craftsman to rebind the book before it fell to pieces. But he had decided to leave it as it was; the contents were still intact after all the years that had passed since it was written.

He placed it carefully to one side and pressed a button under the desk, and a computer screen rose up effortlessly. He typed in a few characters, and his family tree appeared on the glowing screen. It had taken him a lot of time and money to put together this chart, or at least the parts he could be certain about. During the violent and bloodstained history of China, it was not only cultural treasures that had been lost; many archives had been destroyed. There were gaps in the tree that Ya Ru was looking at, gaps that he would never be able to fill in.

Even so, the key names were there. Including, most important, that of the man who had written the diary lying on his desk.

Ya Ru had searched for the house where his ancestor had sat writing in the light from a tallow candle.

But there was nothing of it left. Where Wang San had lived was now covered in a network of highways.

San had written in his diary that his words were meant for the wind and his children. Ya Ru had never understood what was meant by the wind reading the book. Presumably San had been a romantic deep down in his heart, despite the brutal life he had been forced to live and the need for revenge that never left him. But the children were there, above all a son named Guo Si. Guo Si was born in 1882. He had been one of the first leaders of the Communist Party and had been killed by the Japanese in their war with China.

Ya Ru often thought that the diary San had written was meant just for him. Although there was more than a century between its creation and the evening when he had sat reading it, it was as if San were speaking to him directly. The hatred his ancestor had felt all that time ago was still alive inside Ya Ru. First San, then Guo Si, and eventually himself.

There was a photograph of San's son Guo Si from the beginning of the 1930s, posing with several other men in a mountainous landscape. Ya Ru had scanned it into his computer. Whenever he looked at the picture, it seemed to him that he was very close to Guo Si, who was standing just behind the man with a smile on his face and a wart on his cheek. He was so close to absolute power, Ya Ru thought. And I, too, his kinsman, have come that close to power in my life.

There was a soft buzz from the intercom. His first visitor had arrived, but he intended to make her wait. A long time ago he had read about a political leader who had reduced to a fine art the classification of his political friends or enemies according to the length of time they had to wait before getting to see him. They could then compare their times with one another and work out how far they were from the leader's inner circle.

Ya Ru switched off the computer, and it disappeared under the desktop with the same faint humming noise as when it had appeared. He poured himself a glass of water from a carafe on the desk. The water came from Italy and was produced especially for him by a company partly owned by one of his own enterprises.

Water and oil, he thought. I surround myself with liquids. Today oil, tomorrow perhaps the right to extract water from various rivers and lakes.

He went over to the window again and looked toward the district where the Forbidden City lay. He liked to go there, visiting his friends whose money he looked after and increased for them. Today the emperor's throne was empty. But power was still concentrated inside the walls of the ancient imperial city. Deng had once said that the old imperial dynasty would have envied the Communist Party its power. There was no other land in the world with a power base to match it. At this moment in time, every fifth person on earth who breathed was dependent on what the party's emperor-like leader decided.

Ya Ru knew he was a lucky man. He never forgot that. The moment he took it for granted, he would soon lose his influence and his prosperity. He was the éminence grise among this elite in possession of power. He was a member of the Communist Party; he had solid connections in the very center of the inner circles where all the most important decisions were made. He was also a party adviser, and at all times he felt his way forward with his antennae to avoid the traps, and seek out the safe channels.

Today, on his birthday, he knew that he was in the middle of the most significant period China had been through since the Cultural Revolution. Having been preoccupied with itself for centuries, China was in the process of looking out toward the rest of the world. Even if there was a dramatic struggle taking place in the politburo about which direction to choose, Ya Ru had no doubt about the outcome. It was impossible to change the route that China had already embarked upon. For every day that passed, more of his fellow countrymen found themselves slightly better off than before. Even as the gap between urban dwellers and peasants grew wider, a small portion of the new prosperity trickled out to the most poverty-stricken regions. It would be sheer madness to attempt to divert this development in a way that was reminiscent of the past. And so the hunt for foreign markets and raw materials must become more and more intense.

He caught sight of his face reflected in the big picture window. Wang San might well have looked just like that.

More than 135 years have passed, Ya Ru thought. San could never have imagined the life I lead today. But I can picture to myself the life he led, and I can understand his anger. The whole of China was overshadowed by the injustice of the past.

Ya Ru checked the time again; though half an hour had not yet passed, he was ready to receive the first of his visitors.

A hidden door in the wall slid open, and his sister Hong Qiu came in. A vision, she radiated beauty.

They met in the middle of the room.

"Now then, my little brother," she said. "You're a bit older than you were yesterday. One of these days you'll catch up with me."

"No," said Ya Ru. "I won't. But neither of us knows which will bury the other."

"Why mention that now? It's your birthday, after all!"

"If you have any sense, you always know that death is just around the corner."

He escorted her to a group of easy chairs at the far end of the room. As she didn't drink alcohol he served her tea from a gold-plated pot. He continued drinking water.

Hong Qiu smiled at him. Then she suddenly turned serious.

"I have a present for you. But first, I want to know if the rumor I've heard is true."

Ya Ru flung his arms out wide.

"I'm constantly surrounded by rumors. Like all other prominent men, not to mention prominent women. Such as you, my dear sister."

"I want to know if it's true that bribery was involved in order to land the Olympics construction contract." Hong Qiu slammed her teacup down hard on the table. "Do you understand the implications? Bribery and corruption?"

Ya Ru lost his patience. He often found their conversations entertaining, as she was intelligent and caustic in the way she expressed herself. He also welcomed the opportunity to sharpen his own arguments by discussing things with her. She stood for an old-fashioned approach based on ideals that no longer meant anything. Solidarity was a commodity like any other. Classical communism had failed to survive the strains imposed upon it by a reality the old theorists had never really come to grips with. The fact that Karl Marx had been right about many fundamentals concerning an economy for politics, or that Mao had demonstrated that even poor peasants could rise out of their wretchedness, did not mean that the great challenges now confronting China could be overcome by referring back to classical methods.

Hong Qiu was sitting backward on her horse as it trotted into the future. Ya Ru knew that she would fail.

"We will never become enemies," he said. "The

members of our family were pioneers when they first set out to escape decadence and decay. It's just that we have different views on the methods that should be used. But of course I don't bribe anyone, just as I don't allow anyone to buy favors from me."

"All you think about is yourself. Nobody else. I find it hard to believe that you're telling me the truth."

Ya Ru was angry. "What were you thinking sixteen years ago when you applauded the old men leading the party who ordered the tanks to crush the protesters in Tiananmen Square? What were your thoughts then? Did it occur to you that I might well have been one of them? I was twenty-two at the time."

"It was necessary to take action. The stability of the whole country was threatened."

"By a thousand students? Come off it, Hong Qiu. You were afraid of something quite different."

"What?"

Ya Ru leaned forward and whispered to his sister. "The peasants. You were afraid they would turn out in favor of the students. Instead of starting to think about new ways forward for our country, you turned to weapons. Instead of solving a problem, you tried to conceal it."

Hong Qiu didn't answer. She looked her brother unblinkingly in the eye. It occurred to Ya Ru that they both came from a family that only a couple of generations ago would never have dared to look a mandarin in the eye.

"You should never smile at a wolf," said Hong Qiu. "If you do, the wolf thinks you mean to attack."

She stood up and placed a parcel tied with a red ribbon on the table.

"I'm worried about where you're headed, my little brother. I shall do all I can to make sure our country is not transformed in a way that will shame us. The big class struggle will return. Whose side are you on? Your own, not the people's."

"What I'm wondering at the moment is which of us is the wolf," said Ya Ru.

He started toward his sister, but she turned away and left. She stopped in front of the blank wall. Ya Ru walked over to his desk and pressed the button that opened the hidden door.

He returned to the table and unwrapped the parcel Hong Qiu had given him. It contained a little box made of jade. Inside the box was a white feather and a stone.

It was not unusual for him and Hong Qiu to exchange gifts incorporating private riddles or messages. He understood instantly what her gift meant. It referred to a poem by Mao. The feather symbolized a life thrown away, the stone a life—and a death— that had significance.

My sister is warning me, Ya Ru thought. Or perhaps challenging me. Which path shall I choose to follow for the rest of my life?

He smiled at her present and decided that for her next birthday he would commission a handsome wolf carved from ivory.

He respected her stubbornness. She really was his sister, as far as strength of character and willpower were concerned. She would continue to oppose him and those in the government who followed the same path. But she was wrong to condemn the developments he supported, which would once again transform China into the most powerful country in the world.

Ya Ru sat down at his desk and switched on the lamp. He slid a pair of white cotton gloves onto his hands very carefully. Then he began once more leafing through the book Wang San had written and that had been passed down through the family from generation to generation. Hong Qiu had also read it, but had not been gripped by it in the same way as her brother.

Ya Ru turned to the final page of the diary. Wang San was eighty-three years old by then, very ill, and he would soon die. His last words expressed his worry about dying without having done all the things he had promised his brothers.

I'm dying too soon. But even if I lived to be a thousand, I would still die too soon as I would not have succeeded in restoring our family's honor. I did what I could, but it was not enough.

Ya Ru closed the diary and put it away in a drawer, which he locked. He took off the gloves. He opened another desk drawer and produced a thick envelope. Then he pressed the intercom button. Mrs. Shen answered immediately.

"Has my guest arrived?"

"Yes, he's here."

"Ask him to come in."

The door in the wall slid open. The man who entered the room was tall and thin. He moved smoothly and nimbly over the thick carpet. He bowed to Ya Ru.

"It's time for you to leave, Liu Xin," said Ya Ru. "The beginning of the Western New Year is the most appropriate time for you to carry out your task. All you need is in this envelope. I want you back here in February, for our New Year."

Ya Ru handed over the envelope. The man took it and bowed.

"Liu Xin," said Ya Ru. "The task I have given you is more important than anything I've ever asked you to do. It has to do with my own life, my own family."

"I shall do what you ask."

"I know you will. But if you fail, I beg you not to return here. If you did, I would have to kill you."

"I shall not fail."

Ya Ru nodded. The conversation was over. Liu Xin left, and the door closed silently. For the last time that evening Ya Ru spoke to Mrs. Shen.

"A man has just left my office," said Ya Ru.

"He was very taciturn but friendly."

"But he has not been here to see me this evening."

"Of course not."

"Only my sister, Hong Qiu, has been here."

"I haven't seen anyone else. Nor have I noted down any name other than Hong Qiu in the diary."

"You may go home now. I'll stay for a few more hours."

The conversation was over. Ya Ru knew that Mrs. Shen would stay until he had left. She had no family, no life apart from the work she carried out for him. She was his demon guarding his door.

Ya Ru returned to the window and gazed out over the sleeping city. It was now well past midnight. He felt exhilarated. It had been a good birthday, even if his conversation with Hong Qiu had not turned out as he'd expected. She no longer understood what was happening in the world. She refused to acknowledge that times were changing. He felt sad at the realization that they would drift farther and farther apart. But it was necessary. For the sake of his country. She might understand one day, despite everything.

However, most important, this evening was the end of all the preparations, all the complicated searches and planning. It had taken Ya Ru ten years to establish exactly what had happened in the past and draw up his plan. He had almost given up on many occasions. But whenever he read Wang San's diary, he had been able to find the necessary strength once again. He had the power to do what San could never have achieved.

There were a few empty pages at the end of the diary. That is where Ya Ru would write the final chapter when everything was over. He had chosen his birthday as the time to send Liu Xin out into the world to do what had to be done. He now felt relieved.

Ya Ru stood motionless by the window for a long

time. Then he switched off the lights and left through a back door leading to his private elevator.

When he got in his car, which was waiting in the underground lot, he asked the chauffeur to stop at Tiananmen. Through the tinted glass he could see the square, deserted but for the permanent presence of soldiers in their green uniforms.

This is where Mao had proclaimed the birth of the new People's Republic. Ya Ru had not even been born then.

The great events that would soon take place would not be proclaimed in this square in the Middle Kingdom.

The new world order would develop in deepest silence. Until it was no longer possible to prevent what was going to happen.

PART 3

The Red Ribbon (2006)

Wherever battles are waged there are casualties, and death is a common occurrence. But what is closest to our hearts is the best interests of the people and the suffering of the vast majority, and when we die for the people, it is an honorable death. Nevertheless we should do our best to avoid unnecessary casualties.

Mao Zedong, 1944

The Rebels

17

Birgitta Roslin found what she was looking for at the very back in a corner of the Chinese restaurant. One of the red ribbons was missing from the lamp hanging over the table.

She stood absolutely still and held her breath.

Somebody was sitting here, she thought. Then from here headed for Hesjövallen.

It must have been a man. Definitely a man.

She looked around the restaurant. The young waitress smiled. Loud Chinese voices were coming from the kitchen.

It struck her that neither she nor the police had begun to understand the scope of what had happened. It was bigger, more profound, more mysterious, than they could possibly have realized.

They knew nothing, in fact.

She sat at the table, poking absentmindedly at the food from the buffet. She was still the only guest in the restaurant. She beckoned to the waitress and pointed at the lamp.

"There's a ribbon missing," she said.

At first the waitress didn't seem to understand what she meant. She pointed again. The waitress nodded in surprise. She knew nothing about the missing ribbon. She bent down and looked under the table, in case it had fallen down there.

"Gone," she said. "I no see."

"How long has it been missing?" asked Roslin.

The waitress looked at her in confusion. Roslin repeated the question, as she thought the waitress hadn't understood.

The waitress shook her head impatiently. "Don't know. If this table is not good, please change."

Before Roslin could answer, the waitress had gone off to attend to a group of customers who had just entered the restaurant. She guessed that they were local government officials. When she heard them talking, she realized that they were conference delegates discussing the high levels of unemployment in Hälsingland. Roslin continued poking and nibbling at her food as the restaurant began to fill up. There was far too much for the young waitress to cope with on her own. Eventually, a man emerged from the kitchen and helped her to clear away the dishes and wipe the tables.

After two hours, business began to slacken. Roslin was still playing with her food, but she ordered a cup of green tea and passed the time by thinking through everything that had happened to her since she had arrived in Hälsingland.

The waitress came back to her and asked if there was anything else the lady wanted. Roslin said, "I'd like to ask you a few questions."

There were still some customers eating. The waitress spoke to the man who had been helping her, then came back to Roslin's table.

"If you want to buy the lamp, I can fix it," she said with a smile.

Birgitta Roslin smiled back.

"No lamp," she said. "Were you open on New Year's?"

"We are always open," said the waitress. "Chinese working times. Always open when others are closed."

"Can you remember your customers?" she asked, not expecting an answer.

"You have been here before," said the waitress. "I remember customers."

"Can you remember if anybody was sitting at this table on New Year's?"

The waitress shook her head.

"This is good table. There are always customer here. You are sitting here now. Tomorrow somebody else is sitting here."

Birgitta Roslin could see that it was hopeless asking such vague questions. She must be more precise. After a short pause, it struck her how to proceed.

"At New Year's," she began, "was there a customer you had never seen before?"

"Never?"

"Never. Neither before nor after."

She could see that the waitress was racking her brain.

The last of the lunch customers were leaving. The telephone on the counter rang. The waitress answered and noted down a take-out order. Then she came back to Roslin's table. In the meantime someone in the kitchen had started playing music.

"Beautiful music," said the waitress with a smile. "Chinese music. You like it?"

"Nice," said Birgitta Roslin. "Very nice."

The waitress hesitated. Finally she nodded, hesitantly at first, but then more confidently.

"Chinese man," she said.

"Sitting here?"

"On the same chair as you. He ate dinner."

"When was that?"

She thought for a moment.

"In January. But not New Year's. Later."

"How much later?"

"Maybe nine, ten days?"

Roslin bit her lip. That could fit in. The violence at Hesjövallen took place during the night between January 12 and 13.

"Could it have been a couple of days later?"

The waitress fetched a diary in which all bookings were recorded.

"January twelfth," she said. "He sat here then. He had not booked a table, but I remember other customers who were here."

"What did he look like?"

"Chinese. Thin."

"What did he say?"

The waitress's answer was immediate and surprised her.

"Nothing. He pointed at what he wanted."

"But he was definitely Chinese?"

"I tried to speak Chinese with him, but he said only 'silent.' And pointed. I think he wanted to be alone. He ate. Soup, spring rolls, **nasi goring**, and dessert. He was very hungry."

"Did he have anything to drink?"

"Water and tea."

"And he said nothing from start to finish?"

"He wanted to be alone."

"Then what happened?"

"He paid. Swedish money. Then he left."

"And he never came back?"

"No."

"Was he the one who took the red ribbon?"

The waitress laughed. "Why he do that?"

"Does that red ribbon have any special meaning?"

"It's a red ribbon. What can it mean?"

"Did anything else happen?"

"What do you mean?"

"After he'd left?"

"You ask many strange questions. Are you from Internal Revenue? He does not work here. We pay tax. All who work here have papers."

"I just wondered. Did you ever see him again?"

The waitress pointed to the window.

"He went to right. It was snowing. Then he was gone. He never came back. Why do you ask?"

"I might know him," said Birgitta Roslin.

She paid and left. She turned right outside the restaurant. She came to a crossroads and paused to look around. One side road contained several boutiques and a parking lot. The other one was a cul-de-sac. At the end was a little hotel with a sign behind a pane of glass that had cracked. She looked around in all directions once more, studied the hotel sign again.

She went back to the Chinese restaurant. The waitress was sitting down, smoking, and gave a start when the door opened. She stubbed out her cigarette immediately.

"I have another question," said Roslin. "That man sitting at the table in the corner—was he wearing an overcoat, or some other kind of outdoor clothes?"

The waitress thought for a moment. "No, no coat," she said. "How you know that?"

"I didn't know. Finish your cigarette. Thank you for your help."

The hotel door was broken. Somebody had tried to break it open, and the lock looked as if it had only been mended temporarily. She walked up a few steps to reception, which was simply a counter in front of a doorway. There was nobody there. She shouted. Nothing. She discovered a bell and was about to ring it when she suddenly realized there was somebody standing behind her. It was a man, so thin that he was almost transparent, as if he were seriously ill. He was wearing strong glasses and smelled of alcohol.

"Are you looking for a room?"

She could detect traces of a Gothenburg dialect in his voice.

"I just want to ask some questions. About a friend of mine who I think stayed here."

The man shuffled away, his slippers making a clopping noise with each step. He eventually turned up behind the desk. Hands shaking, he produced a hotel ledger. Roslin could never have imagined that hotels like the one she now found herself in still existed. It felt like she had been whisked back through time to a film from the 1940s.

"What's the name of the guest?"

"All I know is that he's Chinese."

The man pushed the ledger aside, staring hard at her and shaking his head. Roslin guessed he must be suffering from Parkinson's disease.

"It's normal to know the names of one's friends. Even if they are Chinese."

"He's a friend of a friend."

"When is he supposed to have stayed here?"

How many Chinese guests have you had here? she wondered. If there's been even just one staying here, you must know about it.

"In the beginning of January."

"I was in the hospital then. A nephew of mine looked after the hotel while I was away."

"Perhaps you could call him?"

"I'm afraid not. He's on an Arctic cruise at the moment."

The man peered nearsightedly at the pages of the ledger.

"We have in fact had a man from China staying here," he said suddenly. "A Mr. Wang Min Hao from Beijing. He stayed here for one night. On the twelfth of January. Is that the man you're looking for?"

"Yes," said Birgitta Roslin, scarcely able to contain her excitement. "That's the one."

The man turned the ledger so that she could read it. She took a piece of paper from her purse and made a note of the details. Name, passport number, and something that was presumably an address in Beijing.

"Thank you," said Birgitta Roslin. "You've been a big help. Did he leave anything behind in the hotel?"

"My name's Sture Hermansson," said the man. "My wife and I have been running this hotel since 1946. She's dead now. I will soon be dead as well. This is the last year the hotel will exist. The building is going to be demolished."

"It's sad when things turn out like that."

Hermansson grunted disapprovingly.

"What's sad about that? The place is a ruin. I'm also a ruin. There's nothing odd about old people dying. But I think this Chinaman actually did leave something behind."

He disappeared into the room behind the counter. Birgitta Roslin waited.

She was just beginning to wonder if he'd died when he finally reappeared. He had a magazine in his hand.

"This was in a wastebasket when I came back from the hospital. A Russian woman does the cleaning for me. As I have only eight rooms, she can manage it on her own. But she's careless. When I came back from the hospital I checked through the hotel. This was still in the Chinaman's room."

Sture Hermansson handed her the magazine. It was Chinese, detailing Chinese exteriors and people. She suspected that it was a PR brochure for a company rather than a magazine as such. On the back of it were carelessly written Chinese characters in ink.

"You're welcome to take it," said Hermansson. "I can't read Chinese."

She put it in her bag and prepared to leave.

"Many thanks for your help."

Hermansson smiled. "It was nothing. Are you satisfied?"

"More than satisfied."

She was heading for the exit when she heard Hermansson's voice behind her.

"I might have something else for you. But you seem to be in a hurry—perhaps you don't have time?"

Birgitta Roslin went back to the counter. Hermansson smiled. Then he pointed toward something behind his head. Roslin didn't understand at first what she was supposed to see. There was a clock hanging on the wall and a calendar from a service station promising quick and efficient service on all Ford cars.

"I don't understand what you mean."

"Your eyes must be even worse than mine," said Hermansson.

He took a wooden pointer from underneath the counter.

"The clock's slow," he explained. "I use this pointer to adjust the hands. It's not a good idea for a rickety old body like mine to stand on a stepladder."

He pointed up at the wall, next to the clock. All she could see was a ventilator. She still didn't understand what he was trying to show her. Then she realized: it wasn't a ventilator, but an opening in the wall for a camera lens.

"We can find out what this man looked like," said Sture Hermansson, looking pleased with himself.

"Is it a surveillance camera?"

"It certainly is. I made it myself."

"So you take pictures of everybody who stays in your hotel?"

"Video films. I don't even know if it's legal. But I have a button I press under the counter. The camera films whoever is standing there."

He looked at her with an amused smile.

"I've just filmed you, for instance," he said. "You're in exactly the right place to make a good picture."

Roslin accompanied him into the room behind the counter. This was evidently where he slept, as well as being his office. Through an open door she could see an old-fashioned kitchen where a woman stood washing dishes.

"That's Natasha," said Hermansson. "Her real

name's something different, but I think all Russian women should be called Natasha."

He looked at Roslin, and his face clouded over.

"I hope you're not a police officer," he said.

"Certainly not."

"I don't think she has all the right papers. But as I understand it, that applies to most of our immigrant workers."

"I don't think that's true," said Birgitta Roslin. "But I'm not a police officer."

He started sorting through the videocassettes, all of which were dated.

"Let's hope my nephew remembered to press the button," he said. "I haven't checked the films from the beginning of January. We had hardly any guests then."

After a lot of fumbling around that made Birgitta Roslin want to snatch the cassettes out of his hands, he found the right one and switched on the television. Natasha flitted through the room like a silent shadow, and disappeared.

Hermansson pressed the PLAY button. Roslin leaned forward. The picture was surprisingly clear. A man with a large fur hat was standing at the counter.

"Lundgren from Järvsö," said Hermansson. "He comes to stay here once a month in order to be left in peace so that he can drink himself silly in his room. When he's drunk, he sings hymns. Then he goes back home. A nice man. Scrap dealer. He's been coming to stay with me for nearly thirty years. I give him a discount."

The television screen started flickering. When the picture became clear again, two middle-aged women were standing in front of the counter.

"Natasha's friends," said Hermansson solemnly. "They come now and then. I'd rather not think about what they do for a living. But they're not allowed to entertain guests in this hotel. Mind you, I suspect they do so when I'm asleep."

"Do they also get a discount?"

"Everybody gets a discount. I don't have any set prices. The hotel's been operating at a loss since the end of the 1960s. I actually live off a little portfolio of stocks and shares. I rely on forestry and heavy industry. There's only one piece of advice I give to my trusted friends."

"What's that?"

"Swedish industrial stocks. They're unbeatable."

A new picture appeared on the screen. Birgitta Roslin sat up and took notice. The man's picture was very clear. A Chinese man, wearing a dark overcoat. He glanced up at the camera. It seemed almost as if he were looking her in the eye. Young, she thought. No more than thirty, unless the camera's telling a lie. He collected his key and disappeared from the screen, which went black.

"My eyes are not too good," said Hermansson. "Is that the man you're looking for?"

"Was it January twelfth?"

"I think so. But I can check with the ledger and see if he checked in after our Russian friends."

He stood up and went to the reception counter. While he was away Birgitta Roslin managed to play through the pictures of the Chinese man several times. She froze the picture at the moment when he looked straight at the camera. He's noticed it, she thought. Then he looks down and turns his face away. He even changes the way he is standing, so that his face can't be seen. It all went very quickly. She rewound the tape and watched the sequence again. Now she could see that he was on his guard all the time, looking for the camera. She froze the picture again. A man with close-cropped hair, intense eyes, tightly closed lips. Quick movements, alert. Perhaps older than she'd first thought.

Hermansson came back.

"It looks like we're right," he said. "Two Russian ladies checked in, using false names as usual. And then came this man, Mr. Wang Min Hao from Beijing."

"Would it be possible to make a copy of this film?"

Hermansson shrugged.

"You can have it. What use is it to me? I installed this camera and video setup for my own amusement. I wipe the cassettes every six months. Take it."

He put the cassette in its case and handed it to her. They went back into the lobby. Natasha was cleaning the globes over the lights that illuminated the hotel entrance.

Sture Hermansson gave Birgitta Roslin's arm a friendly squeeze.

"Are you going to tell me now why you're so interested in this Chinese man? Does he owe you money?"

"Why on earth should he?"

"Everybody owes everybody else something. If somebody starts asking about people, there's usually money involved somewhere."

"I think this man can provide the answers to certain questions," said Roslin. "But I'm afraid I can't tell you what they are."

"And you're not a police officer?"

"No."

"But you don't come from these parts, do you?"

"No, I don't. My name is Birgitta Roslin, and I come from Helsingborg. I'd be grateful if you'd get in touch if he turns up again."

She wrote her address and telephone number on a piece of paper and gave it to Sture Hermansson.

When she emerged into the street she noticed that she was sweating. The Chinese man's eyes were still following her. She put the cassette into her bag and looked around, unsure of what to do next. She really should be on her way back to Helsingborg—it was already late afternoon. She went into a nearby church and sat down in a pew at the front. It was chilly. A man was kneeling by one of the thick walls, repairing a plaster joint. She tried to think straight. A red ribbon had been found in Hesjövallen. It had been lying in the snow. By coincidence she had succeeded in tracing it to a Chinese restaurant. A Chinese man had eaten there the evening of January 12. Later that night or early the next morning, a large number of people had died in Hesjövallen.

She thought about the picture on Sture Hermansson's videotape. Was it really feasible for one lone man to carry out all those murders? Were there others involved whom she didn't know about yet? Or had the red ribbon ended up in the snow at Hesjövallen for an entirely different reason?

She found no answer. Instead she took out the brochure that had been left in the wastebasket. That also made her doubt whether there was any connection between Wang Min Hao and what had happened at Hesjövallen. Would a murderer really leave such obvious clues behind?

The light inside the church was dim. She put on her glasses and leafed through the brochure. One of the spreads was a picture of a skyscraper in Beijing and Chinese characters. On other pages were columns of figures and photographs of smiling Chinese men.

What interested her most was the Chinese writing on the back of the brochure. It brought Wang Min Hao very close to her. He was probably the one who had written it. As a reminder of something? Or for some other reason?

Who could read this stuff? The moment she asked the question, she knew the answer. Her distant and Red revolutionary youth suddenly came to mind. She left the church and stood in the churchyard with her cell phone in her hand. Karin Wiman, a friend from her student days in Lund, was a Sinologist and worked at the university in Copenhagen. No one answered, but she left a message asking Karin to call her back. Then she returned to her car and found a large hotel in the center of Hudiksvall with vacant rooms. Hers was spacious and on the top floor. She switched on the television and saw on teletext that snow was forecast for that night.

She lay on her bed and waited. She heard a man laughing in one of the neighboring rooms.

The ringing phone woke her. It was Karin Wiman, who sounded somewhat baffled. When Birgitta Roslin explained what she wanted, her friend urged her to find a fax machine and send her the page with the Chinese characters.

She was able to use the fax at the front desk, then went back to her room to wait. It was dark outside now. She would soon call home and explain that, because the weather had taken a turn for the worse, she would be staying another night.

Karin Wiman called at half past seven.

"The characters are carelessly drawn, but I think I can work out what they mean."

Birgitta Roslin held her breath.

"It's the name of a hospital. I've tracked it down. It's in Beijing. Called Longfu. It's in the center of town, on a street called Mei Shuguan Hutong. It's not far from China's biggest art gallery. I can send you a map if you like."

"Please do."

"Okay, now you can tell me why you want to know all this. I'm very curious. Has your old interest in China been resurrected?"

"Perhaps. I'll tell you more later. Can you send the map to the fax machine I used?"

"You'll have it in a few minutes. But you're being too secretive."

"Just be patient for a while. I'll tell you everything."

"We should get together."

"I know. We see far too little of each other."

Birgitta Roslin went down to the front desk and waited. The map of central Beijing arrived momentarily. Karin had marked it with an arrow.

Roslin noticed that she was hungry. Her hotel didn't have a restaurant, so she grabbed her jacket and went out. She would study the map when she came back.

It was dark in town, few cars, hardly any pedestrians. The man at the front desk had recommended an Italian restaurant in the vicinity. She went there and ate in the sparsely occupied dining room.

By the time she left, it had started snowing. She headed back to her hotel.

She suddenly stopped. For some reason she had the feeling she was being watched. But when she looked around, she couldn't see anybody.

She hurried back and locked her room door, securing it with the chain. Then she stood behind the curtains and looked down onto the street.

The same as before. Nobody to be seen. Just the snow falling, more and more densely.

18

Birgitta Roslin slept badly that night. She woke up several times and went to the window. It was still snowing. The wind was creating high drifts along house walls. The streets were deserted. At about seven she was woken up once and for all by snowplows clattering past.

Before going to bed she had called home with the details of the hotel she had checked into. Staffan had listened but not said much.

That he didn't express any surprise on hearing she wasn't on her way back made her both angry and disappointed. There was a time when we learned not to dig too deeply into each other's emotional lives, she thought. Everyone needs some private space. But that shouldn't develop into indifference. Is that where we're headed? Are we there already?

There was an electric teakettle in her room. She made a cup of tea and sat down with the map Karin Wiman had sent her. The room was in semidarkness, the only light coming from a reading lamp and from the muted television. The map was difficult to read, but she found the Forbidden City and Tiananmen Square. It brought back memories.

Roslin put the map down and thought about her daughters and their generation. The conversation with Karin had reminded her of the person she had once been herself. So near and yet so far, she thought.

Those days were crucial. In the midst of all my naïve chaos, I was convinced that the way to a better world was via solidarity and liberation. I've never forgotten that feeling of being at the very center of the world, at a time when it was possible to change everything.

But I've never lived up to the insights I had at that time. In my worst moments I've felt like a traitor. Not least to my mother, who encouraged me to rebel. But I suppose, if I'm honest with myself, my political will was really no more than a sort of varnish I spread over my existence. The only thing that really penetrated was my determination to be an honest judge. That's something nobody can take away from me, she concluded.

She drank her tea and made plans for the day. She would visit the police again and tell them what she'd discovered. This time they would have to listen. They hadn't exactly achieved a breakthrough in the investigation so far. When she checked into her hotel she had heard some Germans in the lobby discussing what had happened in Hesjövallen. This was news abroad as well as at home. A blot on the copybook of innocent Sweden, she thought. Mass murder has no place in this country. Such things only happen in the United States, or occasionally in Russia, but not here, in a little remote and peaceful village in the depths of the Swedish forests.

It was still snowing when Birgitta Roslin went to the police station again. The temperature had fallen. The thermometer outside the hotel said negative seven degrees Celsius. The sidewalks had not yet been cleared. She walked carefully to avoid slipping.

It was quiet in the station's reception area. A lone officer was reading messages on a notice board. The woman at the telephone switchboard was motionless, staring into space.

Roslin had the impression that the Hesjövallen massacre hadn't occurred, that the whole thing was a fantasy someone had made up.

"I'm looking for Vivi Sundberg."

"She's in a meeting."

"Erik Huddén?"

"He's there as well."

"Is everybody in the meeting?"

"Everybody. Apart from me."

"How long is it going to last?"

"Impossible to say. Maybe all day."

The woman in reception opened the door to let in the officer who had been reading the notice board.

"I think there's been a breakthrough," she said in a low voice, and left.

Birgitta Roslin sat down and leafed through a newspaper. Police officers occasionally came and went through the glass door. Journalists and a television team arrived. She half expected to see Lars Emanuelsson.

A quarter past nine. She closed her eyes and leaned back against the wall. Then she gave a start on hearing a voice she recognized. Vivi Sundberg was standing in front of her. She looked very tired, with black shadows around her eyes.

"You wanted to speak to me."

"If I'm not disturbing you."

"Of course you're disturbing me. But I assume it's important. You know the drill by now."

Birgitta Roslin followed her through the glass door and into an empty office.

"This isn't my office," said Sundberg. "But we can talk here."

Birgitta Roslin sat down on an uncomfortable visitor's chair. Vivi Sundberg remained standing, leaning against a bookcase filled with red-backed files.

Roslin braced herself, thinking that the situation was preposterous. Sundberg had already decided that no matter what she had to say, it would be irrelevant to the investigation.

"I think I've found something," she said. "A clue, I suppose you could call it."

Sundberg's face was expressionless. Roslin felt challenged.

"What I have to say is so important you should ask someone else to be present."

"Why?"

"I'm convinced of it."

Vivi Sundberg left the room and returned swiftly with a man who introduced himself as District Prosecutor Robertsson.

"I'm in charge of the preliminary investigation. Vivi tells me you have something to tell us. You are a judge in Helsingborg, is that right?"

"That's correct."

"Is Prosecutor Halmberg still there?"

"He's retired."

"But he still lives in Helsingborg, doesn't he?"

"I think he's moved to France. Antibes."

"Lucky man. He enjoyed a decent cigar, that one. Jurors often used to faint when he lit up in the back rooms during breaks in a trial. He started to lose cases when they introduced a smoking ban. He figured it was due to melancholy and cigar deprivation."

"I've heard stories about that."

The prosecutor sat down at the desk. Sundberg had returned to her place by the bookcase. Birgitta Roslin described in detail what she had discovered. How she had recognized the red ribbon, traced it to the restaurant, then found out that a Chinese man had been visiting Hudiksvall. She put the videocassette on the desk together with the brochure in Chinese and explained what the roughly written characters on the back cover meant.

Robertsson was staring hard at her. Vivi Sundberg was examining her hands. Then Robertsson grabbed hold of the cassette and stood up.

"Let's take a look at this. Now, right away."

They went to a conference room where an Asian lady was clearing away coffee mugs and paper bags. Birgitta Roslin bristled at the brusque way in which Vivi Sundberg ordered the cleaning woman to leave the room. After a great deal of difficulty and a succession of curses, Robertsson eventually managed to make the VCR work.

Somebody knocked on the door. Robertsson raised his voice and said they couldn't be disturbed. The Russian women appeared on the screen but soon left. The picture flickered. Wang Min Hao took center stage, looked at the camera, then left. Robertsson rewound and paused the tape at the moment when Wang looked at the camera. Sundberg had also become interested now. She closed the blinds on the nearest window, and the picture became clearer.

"Wang Min Hao," said Birgitta Roslin. "Assuming that's his real name. He turns up here in Hudiksvall out of nowhere on January twelfth. He spends the night in a little hotel, having first plucked a red ribbon out of a lampshade hanging over a table in a restaurant. That ribbon is later found at the crime scene in Hesjövallen."

Robertsson had been standing in front of the television screen, leaning over it. He sat down again. Vivi Sundberg opened a bottle of mineral water.

"Strange," said Robertsson. "I take it you've checked that the red ribbon really did come from that restaurant?"

"I'm sure it did."

"What's going on?" said Vivi Sundberg vehemently. "Are you conducting some kind of private investigation?"

"I don't want to get in your way," said Birgitta Roslin. "I know you're very busy."

Suddenly Sundberg left the room.

"I've asked them to bring the lamp from that restaurant," she said when she came back.

"They don't open until eleven o'clock," said Roslin.

"This is a small town," said Sundberg. "We'll get hold of the owner and order him to open up."

"Make sure the media mob doesn't hear about this," warned Robertsson. "Just imagine the headlines if they do. 'Chinaman behind the Hesjövallen Massacre'?"

"That's hardly likely after our press conference this afternoon," said Sundberg.

So the girl on the switchboard had been right, Roslin thought. Something has happened and will be made public today. That's why they're only half interested.

Robertsson started coughing. It was a violent attack, and he turned red in the face.

"Cigarettes," he said. "I've smoked so many cigarettes that if they were laid out end to end they would stretch from the center of Stockholm to somewhere south of Södertälje. From about Botkyrka onward they had filters. Not that they improved things at all."

"Let's talk this over," said Vivi Sundberg, sitting

down. "You've caused a lot of trouble and irritation in this building."

Now she's going to bring up the diaries, Roslin thought. Today will end with Robertsson digging up something to charge me with. Hardly obstructing justice, but there are other possibilities.

But Sundberg made no mention of the diaries, and Birgitta Roslin had the feeling there was a mutual understanding between them, despite Sundberg's attitude. What had happened was nothing her coughing colleague needed to know about.

"We will definitely look into this," said Robertsson. "We have no preconceived ideas, but there are no other clues indicating a Chinese man."

"What about the weapon?" Roslin asked. "Have you found it?"

Neither Sundberg nor Robertsson answered. They've found it, Roslin thought. That's what's going to be announced this afternoon. Of course it is.

"We can't comment on that at the moment," said Robertsson. "Let's wait for the lamp to arrive and compare the ribbons. If they are in fact the same, then this information will become a serious part of the evidence. We'll keep the cassette, of course."

He reached for a notepad and started writing.

"Who has seen this Chinese man?"

"The waitress in the restaurant."

"I often eat there. The young one or the old one? Or the miserable old crank in the kitchen? The one with the wart on his forehead?"

"The young one."

"She varies from being modestly shy to very cheekily flirty. I think she's bored to tears. Anybody else?"

"Anybody else who did what?"

Robertsson sighed.

"My dear colleague, you've surprised us all with this Chinaman that you've pulled out of your hat. Who else has seen him? The question couldn't be more straightforward."

"A nephew of the hotel owner. I don't know his name, but Sture Hermansson said he was in the Arctic."

"In other words, this investigation is beginning to take on unheard-of geographical proportions. First you produce a mysterious Chinese man. And now you tell us there's a witness in the Arctic. They've been writing about this business in **Time** and **Newsweek,** the **Guardian** phoned me from London, and the **Los Angeles Times** has also expressed interest. Has anybody else seen this Chinese person? I hope whoever you mention isn't currently in the Australian outback at the moment."

"There's a maid at the hotel. She's Russian."

Robertsson sounded almost triumphant when he responded.

"What did I tell you? Now we've got Russia involved as well. What's her name?"

"She's known as Natasha. But according to Sture Hermansson her real name is something different."

"Maybe she's here illegally," said Vivi Sundberg.

"We sometimes find Russians and Poles who shouldn't be here."

"But that's hardly relevant at the moment," said Robertsson. "Is there anyone else who's seen this Chinese man?"

"I don't know of anyone," said Birgitta Roslin. "But he must have come and gone somehow. By bus? Or taxi? Surely someone must have noticed him?"

"We'll look into it," said Robertsson, putting down his pen. "Assuming this turns out to be important."

Which you don't believe it is, Roslin thought. Whatever other line of investigation you have, you think it's more important.

Sundberg and Robertsson left the room. Roslin felt tired. The probability of what she'd discovered having anything to do with the case was low and getting lower. Her own experience was that strange facts often turned out to be red herrings.

While she waited, growing more and more impatient, she paced up and down the conference room. She had come across so many prosecutors like Robertsson in her life. Sundberg was also typical of the women police officers who gave evidence in her courts, but they rarely had hair as red as hers.

Sundberg came back, followed shortly by Robertsson and Tobias Ludwig. He was holding the plastic bag containing the red ribbon, and Vivi Sundberg was carrying the lamp from the restaurant.

The ribbons were laid out and compared. There was no doubt that they were identical.

They sat around the table again. Robertsson summarized briefly what Birgitta Roslin had told them. He's good at making an effective presentation, she noted.

When he finished, nobody had any questions. The only one to speak was Tobias Ludwig.

"Does this change anything with regard to the press conference we'll be holding later today?"

"No," said Robertsson. "We'll look into this. But in due course."

Robertsson declared the meeting closed. He shook hands and left. When Birgitta Roslin stood up, she received a look from Vivi Sundberg she interpreted as meaning she should stay behind.

When they were alone, Vivi Sundberg closed the door and came straight to the point.

"I'm surprised you're still involving yourself in this investigation. Obviously, what you've discovered is remarkable. We will investigate further. But I think you've already gathered that we have other priorities at the moment."

"Can you tell me anything?"

Sundberg shook her head.

"Nothing at all?"

"Nothing."

"Do you have a suspect?"

"As I've said, we'll make an announcement at the press conference. I wanted you to stay behind for an entirely different reason."

She stood up and left the room. When she came

back she was carrying the diaries Roslin had been forced to hand over a couple of days earlier.

"We've been through them," said Vivi Sundberg. "I have decided that they're irrelevant to the investigation. And so I thought I would demonstrate my goodwill by allowing you to borrow them. You'll have to sign for them. The only condition is that you return them when we ask for them back."

Roslin wondered for a moment if she was about to fall into a trap. What Sundberg was doing was not permissible, even if it wasn't criminal. Birgitta Roslin had nothing to do with the investigation. What might happen if she accepted the diaries?

Vivi Sundberg noticed that she was hesitating.

"I've spoken to Robertsson," she said. "He had nothing against it provided you sign a receipt."

"From what I've read so far they contain information about the Chinese working on the transcontinental railroad line in the United States."

"In the 1860s? That's nearly one hundred fifty years ago."

Sundberg put the diaries into a plastic bag on the table. In her pocket she had a receipt that Roslin duly signed.

Sundberg accompanied her to the reception area. They shook hands at the glass door. Roslin asked when the press conference was scheduled.

"Two o'clock. Four hours from now. If you have a press pass you can come in. It will be packed. This is too big a crime for a little town like ours."

"I hope you've made a breakthrough."

Vivi Sundberg paused before replying.

"Yes," she said eventually. "I think we're on the way toward a result."

She nodded slowly, as if to emphasize what she was saying.

"We now know that all the people in the village were related," she said. "All the dead, that is. There's a family connection."

"Everybody except the boy?"

"He was related as well. But he was just visiting."

Birgitta Roslin left the police station, thinking hard about what was going to be announced a few hours later.

A man caught up with her on the snow-covered sidewalk.

Lars Emanuelsson smiled. Birgitta Roslin felt an urge to hit him. At the same time, she couldn't help being impressed by the man's persistence.

"We meet again," he said. "Over and over you visit the police. The judge from Helsingborg hovers indefatigably on the periphery of the investigation. You must understand why I'm curious."

"Put your questions to the police, not to me."

Lars Emanuelsson turned serious.

"Rest assured, I already have. But I still haven't gotten any answers, which is annoying. I'm forced to speculate. What is a judge from Helsingborg doing in Hudiksvall? How is she involved in the horrific things that have been happening here?"

"I have nothing to say."

"Just tell me why you're so unpleasant and dismissive."

"Because you won't leave me in peace."

Lars Emanuelsson nodded in the direction of the plastic bag.

"I noticed that you were empty-handed when you went in the station earlier this morning. And now you're coming out with a heavy plastic bag. What's in there? Documents? Files? Something else?"

"That's none of your business."

"Never talk to a journalist like that. Everything is my business. What's in the bag, what isn't. Why don't you want to answer?"

As Birgitta Roslin started to walk away, she slipped and fell down in the snow. One of the old diaries tumbled out of the bag. Lars Emanuelsson rushed to help, but she pushed away his hand as she put the book back. Her face was red with anger as she hurried away.

"Old books," Emanuelsson shouted after her. "Sooner or later I'll find out what they mean."

She didn't stop to brush off the snow until she reached her car. She started the engine and switched on the heater. When she came out onto the main road, she started to calm down. She put Lars Emanuelsson and Vivi Sundberg out of her mind, took the inland route, stopped in Borlänge for a meal, then turned into a parking lot just outside Ludvika shortly before two o'clock.

The radio news bulletin was short. The press conference had just begun. According to what they had heard, the police had arrested a man on suspicion of mass murder in Hesjövallen. More information was promised in the next bulletin.

Birgitta Roslin resumed her journey, then stopped again an hour later. She turned off cautiously onto a timber track, afraid that the snow would be so deep that her car might get stuck. She switched on the radio. The first thing she heard was Robertsson's voice. A suspect was being interrogated. Robertsson expected him to be charged that afternoon or evening. That was all he could say at the moment.

A hubbub of sound filled the radio when he had finished speaking, but Robertsson declined to comment further.

When the news bulletin was over, she turned off the radio. Some heavy chunks of snow fell from a fir tree next to the car. She unbuckled her seat belt and got out. The temperature was still falling. She shuddered. What had Robertsson said? A male suspect. Nothing more. But he had sounded confident, just as Sundberg had given the impression of being confident that a breakthrough had been achieved.

This is not the Chinese man, she thought.

She restarted the engine and continued her journey. She forgot about the next news bulletin.

She stopped in Örebro and took a room for the night. She left the bag of diaries in the car.

Before falling asleep, she felt an almost irresistible

longing for another human being. Staffan. But he wasn't there. She could hardly remember what his hands felt like.

The following day, at about three in the afternoon, she arrived back home in Helsingborg. She put the plastic bag of diaries in her study.

By then she knew that a man in his forties, as yet unnamed, had been charged by Prosecutor Roberts-son. But there were no details—the media ranted on about the lack of information.

Nobody knew who he was. Everybody was waiting.

19

That evening Birgitta Roslin watched the television news with her husband. Prosecutor Robertsson talked about a breakthrough in the investigation. Vivi Sundberg was hovering in the background. The press conference was chaotic. Tobias Ludwig failed to keep the reporters under control, and they almost tipped over the podium at which Robertsson was standing. He was the only one who remained calm. Eventually he was interviewed alone on camera and explained what had happened. A man aged about forty-five had been arrested in his home outside Hudiksvall. There had been no drama, but to be on the safe side they had called in reinforcements. The man had been charged on suspicion of involvement in the Hesjövallen massacre. For technical reasons Robertsson was not prepared to reveal his identity.

"Why won't he do that?" wondered Staffan.

"Any other people involved could be warned, evidence could be destroyed," said Birgitta, hushing him.

Robertsson released no details, but the breakthrough had come as a result of several tips from the general public. They were checking various leads and had already held a preliminary interrogation.

The interviewer pressured Robertsson with more questions.

Has he confessed?

No.

Has he admitted to anything at all?

I can't comment on that.

Why not?

We are at a crucial stage in the investigation.

Was he surprised when he was arrested?

No comment.

Does he have a family?

No comment.

But he lives near Hudiksvall.

Yes.

What's his job?

No comment.

In what way is he connected to all the people who have been killed?

You must realize that I can't comment on that.

But you must also understand that our viewers are interested in what has happened. This is the second most serious outbreak of violence that has ever taken place in Sweden.

Robertsson raised his eyebrows in surprise.

What was worse?

The Stockholm Bloodbath.

Robertsson couldn't help laughing out loud. Birgitta Roslin groaned at the sheer cheek of the interviewer.

The two incidents can hardly be compared. But I'm not going to argue with you.

What happens next?

We will interrogate the suspect again.

Who is his defending counsel?

He's asked for Tomas Bodström, but he probably won't get him.

Are you sure you have arrested the right man?

It's too early to say. But for the moment I'm happy with the fact that he's been charged.

The interview ended. Birgitta turned down the sound. Staffan looked at her.

"Well, what does the judge have to say about this?"

"They obviously have some evidence, or they would never have been allowed to charge him. But he's been locked up on grounds of suspicion. Either Robertsson is being cautious, or he doesn't have anything more concrete."

"Did just one man do all this?"

"It doesn't necessarily follow that he was alone just because he's the only one who's been arrested."

"Can it really be anything but an act of madness?"

Birgitta sat in silence for a moment before replying.

"Can an act of madness be meticulously planned? Your answer is as good as mine."

"So we'll have to wait and see."

They drank tea and went to bed early. He stretched out his hand and stroked her cheek.

"What's on your mind?" he said.

"I was thinking about what a lot of forest there is in Sweden."

"I thought perhaps you might be thinking it was good to get away from everything."

"From what? You?"

"Me. And all the trials. A little midlife crisis."

She snuggled up closer.

"Sometimes I think: What's going on? It's unfair, I know. You, the children, my job, what else can I ask for? But there are other things. What used to make us tick when we were younger. Not only understanding, but making a difference. If you take a look around, the world has only gotten worse."

"Not in every way. We smoke less, we have computers, cell phones."

"It's as if the whole world is falling apart. And our courts are pretty useless when it comes to preserving any kind of moral decency in this country."

"Is this what you were thinking about when you were up there in the north?"

"I suppose so. I'm a little depressed. But perhaps you need to be a little depressed sometimes."

They lay there without speaking. She expected him to reach for her, but nothing happened.

We're not there yet, she thought, disappointed. But at the same time she couldn't understand why she didn't feel able to make the move herself.

"We should go away for a while," he said eventually. "Some conversations are better during daylight hours rather than right before going to sleep."

"Maybe we should go on a pilgrimage," she said. "Do what tradition tells us to do, take the route to Santiago de Compostela. Put rocks in our backpacks, every one representing a problem we're wrestling with. Then, when we've found solutions, we take the rocks out and lay them by the roadside, one by one."

"Are you serious?"

"Of course. But I don't know if my knees are up to it."

"If you carry things that are too heavy, you might get heel spurs."

"What's that?"

"Something nasty in your heels. A good friend of mine's had it. Ture, the vet. He's been through hell."

"We should become pilgrims," she mumbled. "But not just yet. I need to get some sleep. So do you."

The next day Birgitta Roslin contacted her doctor to confirm her follow-up appointment in five days. Then she gave the house a thorough clean, no more than glancing at the plastic bag with the diaries. She spoke to her children about arranging a surprise party for Staffan's birthday. Everybody agreed it was an excellent idea, and she called to invite their friends. She listened to the occasional news bulletins from Hudiksvall. Information seeping out from the embattled police HQ was scanty, to say the least.

It was not until late afternoon that she sat down at her desk and took out the diaries. Now that a man had been charged with the murders, her own theories seemed less important. She thumbed through until she came to the last page she had read.

The telephone rang. It was Karin Wiman. They set up a time for Birgitta to visit the following day.

In his diary notes JA continued complaining about nearly everybody he had to work with and was responsible for. The Irish are idle drunkards, the few black men the railroad company employs are strong but unwilling to make an effort. JA longs for slaves from the Caribbean islands that he's heard about. Only lashes of the whip can induce these strong men to really make use of their strength. He wishes he were able to whip them like one could whip oxen or donkeys. Birgitta Roslin was unable to establish which race he disliked most. Perhaps the "Red Indians," the Native Americans for whom he had so much contempt. Their reluctance to work, their two-faced cunning, were worse than anything he'd come across among the scum he was forced to kick and beat into submission to ensure the eastern advancement of the railroad. He also wrote regularly about the Chinese: he would be only too pleased to drive them into the Pacific Ocean and make them choose between drowning and swimming back to China. But he can't deny that the Chinese are good workers. They don't drink hard liquor, they keep themselves clean, and they obey the rules. Their only weakness is their predilection for gambling and strange religious ceremonies. JA continually tries to justify his reasons for disliking these people who in fact are making his job easier. Some lines were almost impossible to make out, but Birgitta Roslin thought he must be suggesting that the industrious Chinese were cut out for this work, and nothing else. They had reached a level that would never be raised, no matter what was done to help them.

The people JA holds in highest esteem are the ones from Scandinavia. The army of workers building the railroad contains a little colony of Nordic laborers: a few Norwegians and Danes, but more Swedes and Finns. **I trust these people. They don't try to fool me, as long as I keep an eye on them. And they're not afraid of hard work. But if I turn my back on them, they're transformed into the same gang of thugs as all the rest of them.**

Birgitta Roslin pushed the diary aside and stood up. Whoever this railroad foreman had been, she found him more and more repulsive. A man from a simple background who had immigrated to America. And then he suddenly found himself with enormous power over other people. A brutal person who had become a little tyrant. She got dressed to go out and went for a long walk through the city in order to shake off the disgust she felt.

It was six o'clock when she switched on the radio in the kitchen. The news bulletin began with Robertsson's statement. She stood as if transfixed, listening. In the background was the noise of flashbulbs and scraping chairs.

As on earlier occasions, he was clear and precise. The man who had been charged the day before had now confessed that he, and he alone, had committed all the murders at Hesjövallen. At eleven o'clock in the morning he had requested, through his lawyer, to speak again to the female police officer who had first interrogated him. He had also asked for the prosecutor to be present. His motive, he said, was revenge. There would have to be several more interrogations before it could be established just what he had been taking revenge for.

Robertsson concluded with the details that everybody had been waiting for.

"The man charged is Lars-Erik Valfridsson. He is a bachelor, employed by a firm that carries out excavation and rock-blasting operations. He has been sentenced several times in the past for assault and battery."

The flashbulbs continued to pop. Robertsson began answering questions from the barrage fired at him by the mass of journalists. The female broadcaster faded out Robertsson's voice and embarked on a summary of what had happened so far. Roslin left the radio on but turned her attention to teletext. There was nothing new, only a summary of what Robertsson had said. She switched off both the television and the radio and sat down on the sofa. Robertsson's voice had convinced her that he was sure they had found the murderer. She had listened to enough prosecutors to be able to draw conclusions about the sincerity of what he had said. He was convinced he was right. And honest prosecutors never based their indictments on revelations or guesses, but on facts.

It was too soon to draw conclusions. But she did so nevertheless. The man who had been arrested and charged was certainly not Chinese. She went back to her study and replaced the diaries in the plastic bag. There was no longer any need for her to study these unpleasantly racist and misanthropic jottings from more than a hundred years ago.

In the evening she and Staffan had a late dinner. They only referred in passing to what had happened. The evening papers he had brought home from the train had nothing to add to what she already knew. In one of the photographs from the press conference she noticed Lars Emanuelsson with his hand raised, wanting to ask a question. She shuddered at the thought of their meetings. She mentioned that she would be going to visit Karin Wiman the following day and would probably stay overnight. Staffan knew Karin and had known her late husband.

"Go," he said. "It'll do you good. When do you have to see the doctor again?"

"In a few days. He's bound to say I'm ready to go back to work."

The next morning the telephone rang shortly after Staffan had left for the railroad station, when she was packing her suitcase. It was Lars Emanuelsson.

"What do you want? How did you get this number? It's unlisted."

Emanuelsson snorted. "A journalist who doesn't know how to dig up a telephone number, no matter how secret it is, should take up another profession."

"What do you want?"

"A comment. Big earth-shattering events are taking place in Hudiksvall. A prosecutor who doesn't seem all that self-confident nevertheless looks us straight in the eye. What do you say to that?"

"Nothing."

Lars Emanuelsson's friendly tone, artificial or not, disappeared. His voice became sharper, more impatient.

"Let's cut the crap. Answer my questions. Otherwise I'll start writing about you."

"I have absolutely no information at all about what that prosecutor has announced. I'm just as surprised as the rest of the nation."

"Surprised?"

"Use whatever word you like. Surprised, relieved, indifferent, take your pick."

"Now I'm going to ask you some simple questions."

"I'm going to hang up."

"If you do I'll write that a judge in Helsingborg who recently left Hudiksvall in a hurry refuses to answer any questions. Have you ever had your house besieged by paparazzi? It's very easy to make that happen. In the old days in this country a few carefully placed rumors would soon lead to the gathering of lynch mobs. A flock of excited journalists is very reminiscent of a mob like that."

"What do you want?"

"Answers. Why were you in Hudiksvall?"

"I'm related to some of the victims. I'm not saying which ones."

She could hear him breathing heavily while he thought that over, or perhaps noted it down.

"That's probably true. Why did you leave?"

"Because I wanted to go home."

"What were those old books in that plastic bag you took out of the police station?"

She thought briefly before answering.

"Some diaries that belonged to one of my relatives."

"Is that true?"

"It's true. If you come here to Helsingborg I'll hold one of them out of the door to show you. I look forward to seeing you."

"I believe you. You must understand that I'm only doing my job."

"Is that it, then?"

"Yes, that's it."

Birgitta Roslin slammed the phone down hard. The call had made her sweat. But the answers she had given had been true and unevasive. Lars Emanuelsson wouldn't have anything to write about. But she was impressed by his persistence.

Although it would have been easier to take the ferry to Elsinore, she drove down to Malmö and over the long bridge she used to cross only by bus. Karin Wiman lived in Gentofte, north of Copenhagen. Birgitta Roslin lost her way twice before she finally connected to the right highway and then the coast road north. It was cold and windy, but the sky was clear. It was eleven o'clock by the time she found Karin's attractive house. It was the house she lived in when she got married, and it was the house in which her husband had died ten years ago. It was white, two stories, surrounded by a large, mature garden. Birgitta recalled that you could see the sea over the rooftops from the top floor.

Karin Wiman emerged from the front door to greet her. She had lost weight, and she was paler than Birgitta remembered. Was she ill, perhaps? They embraced, went inside, left Birgitta's suitcase in the room she would be sleeping in, and toured the house. Not much had changed since Birgitta was last there. Karin had evidently wanted to leave everything as it was when her husband was still alive. What would Birgitta have done in that situation? She didn't know.

But she and Karin Wiman were very different. Their lasting friendship was based upon that very fact. They had developed armor that absorbed or deflected the metaphorical blows they sometimes landed on each other.

Karin had made lunch. They sat in a conservatory full of plants and perfumes. Almost immediately, after the first tentative sentences, they began talking about their student years in Lund. Karin, whose parents had a stud farm in Skåne, had enrolled in 1966, Birgitta the following year. They had met in the Students' Union at a poetry reading and soon became friends despite their differences. Karin, given her background, was very self-confident. Birgitta, on the other hand, was insecure and tentative.

They became involved in National Liberation Front activities, sat as quiet as mice and listened to speakers, mainly young men who seemed to know everything, going on about the necessity of rebelling and stirring up trouble. But what inspired them most was the fantastic feeling of being able to create a new world order, a new reality—they were involved in shaping the future. And it wasn't only the NLF that gave them a grounding in political agitation. There were lots of other organizations expressing their solidarity with the freedom movements mushrooming in the poverty-stricken countries of the developing world and working to evict the old colonial powers. And a similar mood prevailed in local politics. Young Swedes were rebelling against everything old-fashioned and out of date. It was, to coin a phrase, a wonderful time to be alive.

Both of them had joined a radical group in left-wing Swedish politics known as the Rebels. For a few hectic months they had led a cultlike existence where the mainstay was brutal self-criticism and a dogmatic adherence to Mao Zedong's interpretations of revolutionary theory. They had cut themselves off from all other left-wing alternatives, which they regarded with contempt. They had smashed their classical music records, emptied their bookshelves, and lived a life modeled after that of Mao's Red Guard in China.

Karin asked if Birgitta remembered their notorious visit to the spa resort of Tylösand. She remembered it, all right. The Rebel cell they belonged to had held a meeting. Comrade Moses Holm, who later became a medical practitioner but was barred because he not only used drugs but also provided them to others, had proposed that they should "infiltrate the bourgeois group-sex decadents who spend the summer bathing and sun-bathing at Tylösand." After lengthy discussions it was agreed, and a strategy was drawn up. The following Sunday, in the beginning of July, nineteen comrades hired a bus and went to Halmstad and Tylösand. Parading behind a portrait of Mao, surrounded by red flags, they marched down to the beach, past all the astonished sunbathers. They chanted slogans, waved Mao's Little Red Book, then swam out into the sea with the portrait of Mao raised. Then they assembled on the beach, sang "The

Red Flag," condemned fascist Sweden in a short speech, and urged the collected workers to unite, arm themselves, and prepare for the revolution that was just around the corner. Then they returned home and spent the next few days evaluating their "attack."

"What do you remember about it?" asked Karin.

"Moses. Who maintained that our invasion of Tylösand would be recorded in the history of the imminent revolution."

"What I remember is that the water was really cold."

"But I have no memory of what we thought at the time."

"We didn't think anything. That was the point. We obeyed the thoughts of other people. We didn't realize that we were supposed to act like robots in order to liberate mankind." Karin shook her head and burst out laughing. "We were like little kids. We took ourselves so seriously. We claimed that Marxism was science, just as true as anything said by Newton or Copernicus or Einstein. But we were also believers. Mao's Little Red Book was our Bible. We didn't realize that what we were waving was not the word of God, but a collection of quotations from a great revolutionary."

"I remember having doubts," said Birgitta. "Deep down. Just as I did when I visited East Germany. I remember thinking: This is absurd, it can't go on for much longer. But I didn't say anything. I was always afraid that my uncertainty would be noticed. And so

I always yelled out the slogans louder than anybody else."

"We lived in a state of unparalleled self-delusion, even though we meant well. How could we possibly believe that Swedish workers enjoying a bit of sun would be prepared to arm themselves and overthrow the present system in order to start something new?"

Karin Wiman lit a cigarette. Birgitta recalled that she had always been a smoker, always felt instinctively for a pack of cigarettes and a book of matches.

They carried on talking until evening about friends they had known and what had become of them. Then they went for a walk through the little town. Birgitta realized that both she and Karin had the same need to think their way back into the past in order to understand more of their current life.

"Still, it wasn't all naïveté and lunacy," said Birgitta. "The idea of a world based on solidarity is still very much alive in me today. I like to think that, despite everything, we stood up to be counted, we questioned conventions and traditions that could have tipped the world even farther to the right."

"I've stopped voting," said Karin. "I don't like it, but I can't find any political truth that I can subscribe to. But I do try to support movements that I believe in. And they do still exist, in spite of it all, just as strong and intractable. How many people today do you think care about the feudal system in a little country like Nepal? I do. I sign petitions and send money."

"I barely know where Nepal is," said Birgitta. "I have to admit that I've become lazy. But sometimes I still long for that feeling of goodwill that was everywhere. We weren't just crazy students who thought we were at the center of the world, where nothing was impossible. There really was such a thing as solidarity."

Karin burst out laughing.

They made dinner together. Karin mentioned that the following week she would be going to China to take part in a major conference on the early Qin dynasty, whose first emperor laid the foundations for China as a united realm.

"What was it like when you first visited the land of your dreams?" Birgitta asked.

"I was twenty-nine when I went there for the first time. Mao had already gone, and everything was changing. It was a big disappointment, difficult to cope with. Beijing was a cold, damp city. Thousands and thousands of bicycles that sounded like an enormous swarm of grasshoppers, but then I realized that, even so, an enormous change had come about. People had clothes to wear. Shoes on their feet. I never saw anybody in Beijing starving, no beggars. I remember feeling ashamed. I had flown into this country from all the riches we take for granted; I had no right to regard developments in China with contempt or arrogance. I began to fall in love with the thought that the Chinese had won the trial of strength in which they had been embroiled. That was when I finally made up my mind what I was going to do with my life: become a Sinologist. Before that moment I'd had other ideas."

"Like what?"

"You'll never believe me."

"Try me!"

"I'd thought of becoming a professional soldier."

"Whatever for?"

"You became a judge. How does anyone make these decisions?"

After dinner they returned to the conservatory. The lights made the white snow outside glow. Karin had lent her a sweater, as it was becoming rather cold. They had drunk wine with the meal, and Birgitta was feeling a bit tipsy.

"Come with me to China," said Karin. "The flight doesn't cost an arm and a leg now. I'm bound to be given a big hotel room. We can share it. We've done that before. I remember the summer camps when you and I and three others shared a little tent. We were lying more or less on top of one another."

"I can't," said Birgitta. "I'll probably be cleared to go back to work."

"Come with me to China. Work can wait."

"I'd like to. But you'll be going there again sometime, right?"

"Of course. But when you get to our age, you shouldn't put things off unless you have to."

"We'll live for a long time yet. We'll live to an old age."

Karin said nothing. Birgitta realized that she'd put her foot in it. Karin's husband had died at the age of forty-one. She had been a widow since then.

Karin understood what her friend was thinking. She stretched out her hand and stroked Birgitta's knee.

"It's okay."

They continued talking. It was almost midnight when they retired to their rooms. Birgitta lay down on her bed with her cell phone in her hand. Staffan was due home at midnight and had promised to call.

She had almost dozed off when the telephone in her hand began to vibrate.

"Did I wake you up?"

"Nearly."

"Did everything go well?"

"We've been talking nonstop for more than twelve hours."

"Will you be coming home tomorrow?"

"I'll sleep as long as I can. Then I'll head home."

"I assume you've heard what's happened? He's said how he went about it."

"Who?"

"The man in Hudiksvall."

She sat up immediately.

"I know nothing at all. Tell me!"

"Lars-Erik Valfridsson. The man they charged. The police are looking for the weapon at this very moment. He evidently told them where he'd buried it. A homemade samurai sword, according to the news."

"Is that really true?"

"Why would I tell you something that isn't true?"

"Of course you wouldn't. But anyway. Has he said why?"

"Nobody has said anything apart from it being revenge."

When the call was over, she remained sitting up. During the whole day with Karin she hadn't devoted a single thought to Hesjövallen. Now everything that had happened came flooding back into her mind.

Perhaps the red ribbon would have an explanation that nobody had foreseen?

Why couldn't Lars-Erik Valfridsson also have eaten at that Chinese restaurant?

She lay down and switched off the light. She would go home tomorrow. She would send the diaries back to Vivi Sundberg and start work again.

There was no way she would go to China with Karin, even if that was what she would really like to do above all else.

20

When Birgitta Roslin got up the next morning, Karin Wiman had already left for Copenhagen, as she had an early lecture. She had left a message on the kitchen table.

Birgitta. I sometimes think that I have a path inside my head. For every day that passes it gets a bit longer and penetrates deeper into an unknown landscape where it will eventually peter out one of these days. But that path also meanders backward. Sometimes I turn around, like I did yesterday during all the hours we were talking, and I see things that I'd forgotten about, or prevented myself from remembering. I want us to continue with these conversations. The bottom line is that friends are all we have left. Or rather, perhaps, the last line of defense we can fight to maintain. Karin.

Birgitta put the letter in her purse, drank a cup of coffee, and prepared to leave. Just as she was about to close the front door, she noticed some flight tickets on a table in the hall. She noted that Karin was booked to fly with Finnair from Helsinki to Beijing.

She took the ferry from Elsinore. It was windy. After landing she stopped at a corner shop displaying placards announcing that Lars-Erik Valfridsson had confessed. She bought a bundle of newspapers and drove home. Her reserved, taciturn Polish cleaning lady was waiting for her in the hall. Birgitta had forgotten that this was the day she was scheduled to come. They exchanged a few words in English as Birgitta paid her. When she was finally alone in the house, she sat down to read the newspapers. As usual, she was amazed to see how many pages the evening papers could devote to facts that were extremely sparse. What Staffan had said in their brief telephone conversation the previous evening contained at least as much information as the newspapers made a fuss about.

The only new item was a photograph of the man assumed to have committed the murders. The picture was probably an enlargement of a passport or driver's license photograph and showed a man with a featureless face, narrow mouth, high forehead, and thin hair. She found it hard to imagine this man committing the barbaric murders in Hesjövallen. He looks like a Low Church pastor, she thought. Hardly a man with hell in his head and his hands. But she knew that she was going against her better judgment. She had seen so many criminals come and go in her court whose appearance suggested they couldn't possibly have committed the crimes they were charged with.

It was only when she had discarded the newspapers and switched on teletext that her interest was really aroused. The main item there was the discovery by the police of what was presumably the murder weapon. The precise location had not been revealed, but it had been dug up where Lars-Erik Valfridsson had said they would find it. It was a rather poor homemade copy of a Japanese samurai sword. But the edge was very sharp. The weapon was currently being examined in the hope of finding fingerprints and, above all, traces of blood.

Something wasn't right. She had an advertising pamphlet for the Chinese restaurant in her purse. She called the number and recognized the voice of the waitress she had spoken to. She explained who she was. It took a few seconds before the waitress caught on.

"Have you seen the newspapers? The picture of the man who murdered all those people?"

"Yes. Terrible man."

"Can you remember if he's ever had a meal at your restaurant?"

"No, never."

"Are you sure?"

"Never while I'm on duty. But other days my sister or my cousin work. They live in Söderhamn. They have restaurant there. We take turns. Family firm."

"Will you do something for me?" asked Birgitta Roslin. "Ask them to look at the picture in the news-papers. If they recognize him, please call me."

The waitress made a note of Roslin's telephone number.

"What's your name?" asked Roslin.

"Li."

"Mine's Birgitta. Thank you for helping me."

"You're not here in Hudiksvall?"

"I'm at home in Helsingborg."

"Helsingborg? We have a restaurant there. Also family. It's called Shanghai. Food as good as here."

"I'll go there for a meal. Provided you help me."

She remained seated by the telephone, waiting. When it rang, it was her son. She asked him to call back later, as she was expecting a call. Half an hour later, the call came.

"Maybe," said Li.

"Maybe?"

"My cousin thinks the man might have been in restaurant once."

"When?"

"Last year."

"But he's not certain?"

"No."

"Can you tell me his name?"

Birgitta made a note of the name and the telephone number of the restaurant in Söderhamn, then hung up. After a brief pause to think things over, she called police headquarters in Hudiksvall and asked to speak to Vivi Sundberg. She expected to have to leave a message, so was surprised when Vivi Sundberg came to the phone.

"How's it going with the diaries?" Vivi asked. "Still finding them interesting?"

"They're not easy to read. But I have time. Anyway, congratulations on your breakthrough. If I understand things correctly you have both a confession and a possible murder weapon."

"This can hardly be the reason that you're calling."

"Of course not. I wanted to bring your attention back to my Chinese restaurant one more time."

She told Vivi about the Chinese cousin in Söderhamn, and that Lars-Erik Valfridsson might have eaten at the restaurant in Hudiksvall.

"That could explain the red ribbon," said Birgitta in conclusion. "A loose thread."

Vivi Sundberg seemed only vaguely interested.

"We're not worried about that ribbon at the moment. I think you can understand that."

"But I wanted to tell you even so. I can give you the name of the waiter who might have served the man, and his telephone number."

"Thank you for letting us know."

When the call was over Roslin phoned her boss, Hans Mattsson. She had to wait for some time before he could take the call. She told him she expected to be cleared for work when she went to see her doctor in a couple of days.

"We're drowning," said Mattsson. "Or perhaps it might be more accurate to say we're being choked. All the cutbacks have strangled Swedish courts. I never thought I'd live to see it."

"To see what?"

"A price put on having a state governed by law. I didn't think it was possible to give democracy a monetary value. If you don't have a state functioning on the basis of law, you don't have democracy. We're on our knees. There's a creaking and scraping and groaning coming from under the floorboards of this society of ours. I'm really worried."

"It's hardly possible for me to take care of all the things you're talking about, but I promise to look after my own trials again."

"You're more than welcome."

She dined alone that evening as Staffan had to spend the night in Hallsberg between two shifts. She continued to leaf through the diaries. The only entries she paused to read properly were those at the end of the last volume. It was June 1892. JA was now an old man. He lived in a little house in San Diego, suffering pains in his legs and his back. After a lot of haggling he would buy ointments and herbs from an old Indian medicine man; he found they were the only medications that helped him. He wrote about his extreme loneliness, about the death of his wife, and the children who had moved so far away—one of his sons now lived in the Canadian wilderness. He never mentioned the railroad.

The diary ended in the middle of a sentence. It's June 19, 1892. He notes that it has been raining during the night. His back is aching more than usual. He had a dream.

And his notes stopped there. Neither Birgitta Roslin nor anybody else in this world would ever know what he had dreamed about.

She leafed backward through the diary. There was nothing to indicate that he knew the end was nigh, nothing in his notes paving the way for what was soon to happen. A life, she thought. My death could look the same, my diary, if I had kept one, would be unfinished. Come to that, whoever does manage to conclude his or her story, to write a final period before lying down and dying?

She put the diaries back into the plastic bag and decided to mail them the next day. She would follow what was happening in Hudiksvall the same way as everybody else.

She looked up a list of chief judges in the different regions of Sweden. The chief judge at the Hudiksvall district court was Tage Porsén. This will be the trial of his life, she thought. I hope he's a judge who enjoys publicity. Birgitta knew that some of her colleagues both hated and were afraid of being confronted by journalists and television cameras.

At least, that was the case among her generation and those who were older. She didn't know what the younger generation thought about publicity.

The thermometer outside the kitchen window indicated that the temperature had fallen. She switched on the television to watch the evening news. Then she would go to bed. The day spent with Karin Wiman had been very eventful, but also very tiring.

She had missed the beginning of the news bulletin, but it was obvious that something dramatic had happened in connection with the Hesjövallen case. A reporter was interviewing a criminologist who was verbose but serious. She tried to work out what was going on.

When the crime expert had finished speaking, the screen was filled with pictures from Lebanon. She cursed, switched over to teletext and discovered immediately what had happened.

Lars-Erik Valfridsson had taken his own life. Despite being checked every fifteen minutes, he had managed to tear a shirt into strips, make a noose, and hang himself. Although he had been discovered almost immediately, it had not been possible to revive him.

Birgitta Roslin switched off the television. Her head was swimming. Had he been unable to live with all the guilt weighing him down? Or was he mentally ill?

Something doesn't add up, she thought. It can't be him. Why did he kill himself, why did he confess, and why did he lead the police to a buried samurai sword?

It simply doesn't make sense.

She sat down in the armchair she used for reading, but switched off the lamp. The room was in semi-darkness. Somebody laughed as they went past in the street. She would often sit here and contemplate her work.

She returned to the beginning. It was too much, she thought. Perhaps not too much for a ruthless and obsessed man to carry out. But too much for a man from Hälsingland with no more of a criminal background than a few cases of assault. He confesses to something he didn't do. Then he gives the police a weapon he's made himself and hangs himself in his cell. I might be wrong, of course, but I don't think it adds up. They arrested him far too quickly. And what on earth could be the revenge he claimed was his motive?

It was midnight when she finally got up from her armchair. She wondered if she ought to call Staffan, but he might well be asleep by now. She went to bed and turned off the light. In her thoughts she was wandering around the village once more. Over and over again she envisaged the red ribbon that had been found in the snow, and the picture of the Chinese man from the hotel's homemade surveillance camera. The police must know something I don't know: why Lars-Erik Valfridsson was arrested and what might have been a plausible motive. But they are making a mistake by locking themselves into one single line of investigation.

She couldn't sleep. When she could no longer deal with all the tossing and turning, she put on her robe and went downstairs again. She sat at her desk and wrote a summary of all the events that linked her to Hesjövallen. It took her almost three hours to relive in detail all the things she knew. As she wrote she was nagged by the feeling that there was something she'd missed, a connection she hadn't seen. Her pen seemed to her like a chain saw clearing the under-growth in a forest, and she needed to be careful in case there was a young deer hiding there. When she finally straightened her back and raised her arms over her head, it was four in the morning. She took her notes to her chair, adjusted the lamp, and started reading them through, trying to look between the words, or rather behind them, searching for some-thing she'd overlooked. But nothing unusual attracted her attention, no link that she should have noticed sooner.

But she was convinced: this couldn't be the handiwork of a lunatic. It was too well organized, too cold-blooded, to have been carried out by anyone but a totally calm and cool killer. Possibly, she noted in the margin, one should ask if the man had been in the place before. It was pitch-dark, but he might have had a powerful flashlight. Several of the doors were locked. He must have known exactly who lived where, and probably also had keys. His motive must have been very compelling, so that he never hesitated for one second.

A thought suddenly struck her, something that hadn't occurred to her before. Had the man who committed the murders shown his face to those over whom he raised his sword or saber? Did he want them to see him?

That's a question for Vivi Sundberg to answer, she thought. Was the light on in the rooms where the dead bodies were found? Had they looked into the face of death before the sword fell?

She put her notes away; it was nearly five. She checked the thermometer outside the kitchen window and saw that the temperature had fallen to negative eight Celsius. She drank a glass of water and went to bed. She was on the point of falling asleep when she was dragged up to the surface again. There was something she'd missed. Two of the dead bodies had been tied to each other. Where had she seen that image before? She sat up in bed in the darkness, suddenly wide awake. She had seen a description of a similar scene somewhere.

The diaries. She went downstairs, laid them all out on the table, and started looking. She found the passage she was searching for almost immediately.

It's 1865. The railroad is meandering eastward, every sleeper, every rail, is torture. The workers are struck down by illnesses. They're dropping like flies. But the flood of replacement workers from the West means the work can continue at the high speed that is essential if the whole of the gigantic railroad program is not to be crippled by financial collapse. On one occasion, to be more precise on November 9, JA hears that a Chinese slave ship is on its way from Canton. It's an old sailing ship, only used now for shipping kidnapped Chinese to California. Trouble breaks out on board when food and water begin to run out as the vessel is becalmed for an unusually long period. In order to quash the revolt, the captain resorts to methods of unparalleled cruelty. Even JA, who doesn't hesitate to use both fists and whips to make his laborers work harder, finds what he hears distressing. The captain seizes some of the leading troublemakers, kills them, and ties them to other Chinese who are still alive, two at a time. Then they are forced to lie on deck, one of each pair slowly starving to death, the other decomposing. JA notes in his diary that "the punishment is excessive."

Could there be a link? Perhaps one of them in Hesjövallen had been forced to lie with a dead body lashed to his or her own? For a whole hour perhaps, maybe less, maybe more? Before the final blow brought release?

I missed that, she thought. Did the Hudiksvall police miss it as well? They can't have read the diaries all that carefully before I was allowed to borrow them.

But another question suggested itself, even if it seemed to be basically implausible. Did the murderer know about the events described in JA's diary? Was there a remarkable link spanning both time and space?

Maybe Vivi Sundberg was more cunning than Roslin thought.

Perhaps Vivi Sundberg even appreciated her stubbornness. She was a woman who had probably experienced problems with her annoying male colleagues.

Birgitta Roslin slept until ten, got up, and saw from Staffan's schedule that he was due back in Helsingborg at about three o'clock. She was just about to sit down and make a call to Sundberg when there was a ring at the front door. When she answered it, she found a short Chinese man standing with a take-out meal wrapped up in plastic in his hand.

"I haven't ordered anything," said Birgitta Roslin in surprise.

"From Li in Hudiksvall," said the man with a smile. "It costs nothing. She wants you to call her. We are family business."

"The Shanghai Restaurant?"

The man smiled.

"Restaurant Shanghai. Very good food."

He bowed and handed over the package, then left through the gate. Birgitta unpacked the food, sniffed at it and enjoyed the aroma, and put it in the refrigerator. Then she called Li. This time it was the irritable man who answered. She assumed it was the temperamental father, who held sway in the kitchen. He shouted for Li, who came to the phone.

"Thank you very much for the food," said Birgitta Roslin. "It was a lovely surprise."

"Have you tasted it?"

"Not yet. I'm waiting until my husband comes home."

"He also likes Chinese food?"

"Yes, he likes it a lot. You wanted me to call."

"I spoke to Mother about the lamp," she said. "That red ribbon is missing."

"I don't think I've met her."

"She's at home. Comes here to clean sometimes. But she notes down when she here. On January twelve she did cleaning. In morning before we opened."

Birgitta Roslin held her breath.

"She say that on this very day she dusted down all the paper lamps in this restaurant, and she was sure no ribbons were missing. She would have noticed."

"Could she have been mistaken?"

"Not my mother. Is it important?" Li asked.

"It could very well be," said Birgitta. "Many thanks for telling me about it."

She replaced the receiver. It rang again immediately. This time it was Lars Emanuelsson.

"Don't hang up," he said.

"What do you want?"

"Your opinion of what's happened."

"I have nothing to say."

"Were you surprised?"

"About what?"

"That he turned up as a suspect? Lars-Erik Valfridsson?"

"I know nothing about him apart from what I've read in the newspapers."

"But not everything is printed there."

He was egging her on. She was curious.

"He has ill-treated his two ex-wives," said Lars Emanuelsson. "The first one managed to run away. Then he found a lady from the Philippines and enticed her here through a mass of false pretenses. Then he beat her up to within an inch of her life before some neighbors caught on and reported him, and he was duly sentenced. But he's done worse things than that."

"What?"

"Murder. As early as 1977. He was still young then. There was a fight over a moped. He hit the young man on the head with a large stone, killing him instantly. He was examined by a forensic psychiatrist who judged that Lars-Erik could well turn to violence again. He presumably belonged to that small group of people regarded as potentially dangerous to society. I expect the police and the prosecutor thought they'd found the right man."

"But you don't think so?"

"Time will tell. But you can gather the way I'm thinking. That should be enough of an answer to your question. I wonder what conclusions you've drawn. Do you agree with me?"

"I've been paying no more attention to this case than any other member of the general public. Surely it must have dawned on you that I grew tired of your calls a long time ago."

Lars Emanuelsson didn't seem to hear what she said. "Tell me about the diaries. They must have something to do with this case."

"I don't want to receive any more calls from you."

She hung up. The phone rang again immediately. She ignored it. After five minutes of silence she called police HQ in Hudiksvall. It took ages before she got through to the operator, whose voice she recognized. She sounded both jittery and tired. Sundberg was not available. Birgitta Roslin left her name and telephone number.

"I can't promise anything," said the girl. "It's chaos here."

"I can understand that. Please ask Vivi Sundberg to call me when she gets the chance.

"Is it important?"

"She knows who I am. That's a sufficient answer to your question."

Vivi Sundberg called the following day. The news

bulletins were dominated by the scandalous happenings in the Hudiksvall jail. The minister of justice
had gone out of his way to promise an investigation
into the circumstances and to find out who was
responsible. Tobias Ludwig gave as good as he got in
his sessions with journalists and television cameras.
But the consensus was that the suicide should never
have happened.

Sundberg sounded tired. Birgitta Roslin decided
not to ask any questions about the latest developments. Instead, she explained about the red ribbon
and spelled out the thoughts she had noted down in
the margin of her notes.

Sundberg listened without comment. Birgitta
could hear voices in the background and didn't envy
Sundberg the tension that must have police headquarters in its grip.

Birgitta ended by asking if the lights had been on
in the rooms where the dead bodies had been found.

"Your suspicions are in fact justified," said Vivi.
"We've been wondering about that. All the lights
were on. In all the rooms but one."

"The one with the dead boy?"

"That's right."

"Do you have an explanation?"

"You must realize that I can't discuss that with you
over the telephone."

"Of course not. I beg your pardon."

"No problem. But I'd like to ask you to do something. Write down all you know and think about

what happened in Hesjövallen. I'll take it upon myself to look into the red ribbon business. But all the rest of it. Write everything down, and send it to me."

"It wasn't Lars-Erik Valfridsson who committed these murders," said Birgitta Roslin.

Those words came from nowhere. She was just as surprised as Vivi Sundberg must have been.

"Write it down and send it to me," said Vivi Sundberg again. "Thank you for getting in touch."

"What about the diaries?"

"I suppose you'd better send them back to us now."

When the call was finished, Birgitta felt relieved. Despite everything, her efforts had not been in vain. Now she could hand everything over to somebody else. With luck the police would be able to track down the true murderer, whether he had acted alone or had accomplices. She would not be surprised in the least if a man from China had been involved.

The following day Birgitta Roslin went to see her doctor. It was a windy winter's day with gusts blowing in from the sound. She felt impatient, couldn't wait to get back to work.

She only had to wait for a few minutes before it was her turn. The doctor asked how she was, and she said she felt fully restored. A nurse took a blood sample, and Birgitta sat down in the waiting room once more.

When she was called into the exam room, the doctor took her blood pressure and came straight to the point.

"You seem to be in good form, but your blood pressure is still way too high. We'll have to keep on trying to pin down the cause. I'm going to put you on sick leave for two more weeks. And I'm also going to refer you to a specialist."

It was only when she was back out on the street and hit by the freezing-cold wind that the results really sunk in. She was very worried about the possibility of being seriously ill, despite her doctor's assurances that this was not the case.

She stood in the middle of the square with the wind behind her. For the first time in many years, she felt helpless. While she was standing motionless, she felt her cell phone vibrating in her overcoat pocket. It was Karin, who wanted to thank Birgitta for having visited her.

"What are you doing?" she asked.

"I'm standing in a square," said Birgitta. "And at this very moment I haven't the slightest idea what I'm going to do with the rest of my life."

She told Karin about her visit to the doctor. It was a frozen telephone call. She promised to call back before Karin left for China.

When she got home and opened her garden gate, it started snowing, and the wind increased.

21

That same day she went to the district court and spoke to Hans Mattsson, She could see that he was worried and dejected when she told him that she was still on sick leave.

He peered pensively at her over his glasses.

"That doesn't sound good. I'm starting to worry about you."

"You don't need to, according to my doctor. The blood counts aren't what they should be, and my blood pressure needs to be reduced. I'm being referred to a specialist. But I don't feel ill, just a bit tired."

"Aren't we all?" said Hans Mattsson. "I've been feeling tired for the last thirty years. The biggest pleasure I have to look forward to nowadays is when I can sleep in."

"I'll be off for another two weeks. Then we'll just have to hope that it's sorted itself out."

"Take as long as you need. I'll speak to the National Courts Administration and see what they can do to help us out. As you know, you're not the only one who's away. Klas Hansson has a leave of absence to chair an inquiry for the EU in Brussels. I doubt if he'll ever come back. I've always suspected that he's been tempted by grander things than presiding over a court of law."

"I'm sorry to cause you problems."

"You're not causing me problems. It's your blood pressure that's doing that. Have a rest. Look after your roses and come back when you are healthy again."

She looked at him in surprise. "I don't grow roses. I certainly don't have a green thumb."

"That's what my grandmother used to say. When you were told not to work so much, she thought you should concentrate on growing your imaginary roses. I think it's a nice image. My grandmother was born in 1879. The same year as Strindberg published **The Red Room.** An odd thought. The only thing she ever did in her life, apart from giving birth to children, was darn socks."

"Okay, I'll do that," said Birgitta Roslin. "I'll go home and look after my roses."

The next day she mailed the diaries and her notes to Hudiksvall. When she handed over the parcel and was given the receipt, she had the feeling she was closing a door on the happenings in Hesjövallen. She felt relieved, and committed herself to the preparations for Staffan's birthday party.

Most of the family plus several friends were assembled when Staffan Roslin came home after being in charge of an afternoon train from Alvesta to Malmö and then traveling off-duty to Helsingborg. He stood in the doorway in his uniform plus a shaggy old fur hat, struck dumb, while the welcoming party sang "Happy Birthday to You." It was a relief for Birgitta to see everyone sitting around the table. What had happened in Hälsingland, as well as her high blood pressure, seemed less important when she was able to drink in the feeling of calm that only her family could give her. Naturally, she wished Anna had been able to come home from Asia, but she had declined the invitation when Birgitta finally reached her via a noisy cell phone connection in Thailand. It was very late by the time the guests had left, and only family members remained. She had talkative children who loved to spend time together. She and her husband sat on the sofa, listening with amused interest to the conversations. She occasionally topped up everybody's glass. The twins, Siv and Louise, were going to sleep in the spare room, but David had booked himself into a hotel, despite Birgitta's protests. It was four in the morning when the party broke up. Only the parents were left to clean up, fill the dishwasher, and put the empty bottles in the garage.

"That really was a lovely surprise," said Staffan when they eventually sat down at the kitchen table. "I'll never forget it. I feel so positive. Earlier on I was feeling utterly fed up with wandering back and forth through train carriages. I spend all my time traveling, but I never arrive anywhere. That's the curse of train drivers and conductors. We spend all our time in our glass bubbles."

"We should do this more often. Let's face it, it's at

moments like this that life takes on a different meaning. Not just duty and doing what needs to be done."

"And now?"

"What do you mean?"

"You're going to be off work for another two weeks. What are you going to do?"

"Hans Mattsson talks passionately about his longing to sleep in. Maybe that's what I should do for a few days."

"Go somewhere warm for a week. Take one of your girlfriends with you."

She shook her head doubtfully. "I don't know. Maybe. But who?"

"Karin Wiman?"

"She's going to China, to work."

"Isn't there anybody else you could ask? Maybe you could go away with one of the twins?"

That was a very tempting thought. "I'll see what they have to say. But first I need to find out if I really can go off somewhere. Don't forget that I need to see a specialist."

He stretched out a hand and placed it on her arm. "I hope you're telling me the whole story. Do I need to be worried?"

"No. Not unless my doctor is lying to me. But I don't think he is."

They sat up for a bit longer before going to bed. When she woke up the next morning Staffan had already left. So had the twins. She had slept until half past eleven. A Hans Mattsson morning, she thought.

She spoke on the telephone to Siv and Louise after lunch, but neither of them had time to travel, although they would both have loved to take a holiday with their mother. She also received a call informing her that due to a cancellation, she would be able to see the specialist the following day.

At about four there was a ring at the door. She wondered if she was about to receive another free Chinese meal. But when she opened it, she found Detective Chief Inspector Hugo Malmberg standing there with snow in his hair and old-fashioned overshoes on his feet.

"I happened to bump into Hans Mattsson. He mentioned that you were unwell—in confidence, as he knows we're old friends."

She let him in. Despite his huge size, he had no problem bending down to take off his overshoes.

They sat in the kitchen and drank coffee. She told him about her high blood pressure and blood counts, and that it was not unusual for women of her age.

"My high blood pressure is ticking away like a time bomb inside me," said Malmberg glumly. "I take medication, and my doctor says the readings are okay; but I'm worried even so. Nobody in my family has ever died of a tumor. Everybody, women as well as men, has been floored by strokes and heart attacks. Every day I have to make an effort to overcome my worries."

"I've been in Hudiksvall," said Roslin. "You were the one who gave me Vivi Sundberg's name. Did you know I went there?"

"It comes as a surprise, I have to admit."

"Do you remember the circumstances? I discovered that I was related to one of the families murdered in Hesjövallen. Since then it's become clear that all the murder victims were related through marriage. Do you have time?"

"My answering machine says I'm out on police business for the rest of the day. As I'm not on standby, I can sit here all night if need be."

"Until the cows come home? Isn't that what they say?"

"Or until the riders of the Apocalypse thunder past and annihilate us all. Anyway, entertain me with all the horrors I don't need to get involved in."

"Are you being cynical?"

He frowned, and growled. "Don't you know me better than that? After all these years? I'm offended."

"That wasn't the intention."

"Fire away. I'm listening."

As he seemed to be genuinely interested, Birgitta told him in detail what had happened. He listened carefully, interpolated the occasional question, but seemed convinced that she was being meticulous. When she had finished he sat for a while without speaking, staring at his hands. Birgitta knew that Hugo Malmberg was regarded as an exceptionally competent police officer. He combined patience with speed, a methodical approach with intuition. She had heard that Malmberg was one of the most-sought-after teachers in the Swedish police academy.

Although his day job was in Helsingborg, he was often called in by the national CID to assist in especially difficult cases elsewhere in the country.

It suddenly occurred to her that it was odd he hadn't been summoned to help out with the investigation into the Hesjövallen murders.

She put it to him point-blank, and he smiled.

"They have in fact asked. But nobody told me that you had been involved and made some remarkable discoveries."

"I don't think they like me," Birgitta Roslin said.

"Police officers tend to be very keen on protecting their own feeding bowls. They were eager for me to travel up there and advise, but they lost interest once Valfridsson had been arrested."

"He's dead now."

"But the investigation continues." Malmberg sighed.

"Nevertheless, you know now that he didn't do it."

"Do I?"

"You've heard what I had to say." She looked at him in earnest.

"Remarkable goings-on, plausible facts. Things that obviously ought to be fully investigated. But the main line of investigation, Valfridsson, doesn't get any worse simply because the man happens to commit suicide."

"He didn't do it. What happened that night between January twelfth and thirteenth was much bigger than anything a man with a few assault convictions and an ancient homicide would be capable of."

"You may be right. But you could also be wrong. Over and over again it turns out that the biggest fishes swim around in the most placid of pools. Bicycle thieves become bank robbers; rowdies turn into professional hitmen willing to kill anybody for a sum of money. So why shouldn't a guy who gets drunk and beats up a few people and maybe even kills the odd one simply go to pieces and commit a horrific crime like the one in Hesjövallen?"

"But there was no motive," she insisted.

"The prosecutor talks about revenge."

"For what? What could justify revenge on a whole village? It just doesn't make sense."

"If the crime doesn't make sense, the motive doesn't need to either," Malmberg said.

"Whatever. I think Valfridsson was a red herring."

"**Is** a red herring. What did I say? The investigation continues even if he's dead. Let me ask you a question. Is your idea of a mysterious Chinese man being responsible much more plausible? How in God's name can you link a little village in the north of Sweden with a Chinese motive?"

"I don't know."

"We shall have to wait and see. And you must make sure to get better soon."

It was snowing even more as he prepared to leave.

"Why don't you take a vacation? Go somewhere warm?"

"Everybody keeps saying that. I'll have to clear it with my doctor first."

She watched him disappear into the swirling snow. She was touched to think that he'd taken the time to visit her.

By the following day the snow had moved on. She kept her appointment with the specialist, had blood samples taken, and was informed that it would be a week or more before all the test results were available.

"Are there things I'm not allowed to do?" she asked her new doctor.

"Avoid unnecessary exertions."

"Am I allowed to go on vacation?"

"That would do you good."

"I have another question. Should I be afraid?"

"No. As you don't have any other symptoms, you've no reason to worry."

"So I'm not going to die?"

"Of course you are. Eventually. So am I. But you'll be okay as long as we can get your blood pressure down to reasonable levels."

When she emerged into the street, she recognized that she had been anxious, not to say afraid. Now she felt relieved. She decided to go for a long walk. But she hadn't gone far before she paused.

The thought struck her from out of the blue. Or maybe she had already reached a decision without knowing it. She went into a café and telephoned Karin Wiman. The line was busy. She waited impatiently, ordered a coffee, leafed through a newspaper.

Tried again. Still busy. She didn't get an answer until her fifth attempt.

"I'm going with you to Beijing."

Birgitta couldn't get the same flight—she would arrive a day later. Staffan was fine with the idea, even pleased for her.

The evening before she left, Birgitta rummaged through a cardboard carton in the garage. Down at the very bottom she found what she was looking for: her old well-thumbed copy of Mao's Little Red Book. On the inside of the red plastic cover she had written a date: **April 19, 1966.**

I was a little girl then, she thought. Innocent in almost every way. I'd only once been with a young man, Tore, from Borstahusen, who dreamed of becoming an existentialist and regretted not having much of a beard. I lost my virginity to him in a freezing-cold garden shed smelling of mold. All I remember is that he was almost unbearably awkward. Afterward, all the sticky goo on our bodies became such an embarrassment that we parted as quickly as possible and never again looked each other in the eye. I still wonder what he told his friends. And then came the political storm that carried me away. But I never managed to live up to the knowledge of the world that I acquired. After some time with the Rebels, I hid myself away. I never managed to work out why I'd allowed myself to be lured into what was almost a religious cult. Karin joined the Communist Party. I became linked with Amnesty International, and now I have no political connections at all.

She sat on a pile of old car tires and skimmed the Little Red Book. She came across a photograph between two of the pages: it was of her and Karin Wiman. She remembered the occasion. They had squeezed into a photo booth at Lund railroad station—it was Karin's idea as usual. She laughed out loud when she saw the photo, but was also scared by the thought of how long ago it was.

The cold wind, she thought. Old age comes creeping up behind me. She put the book of quotations in her pocket and left the garage. Staffan had just come home. She sat down opposite him in the kitchen as he ate the evening meal she had prepared for him.

"So, is my Red Guard wife ready to go?" he asked.

"I've just fetched my Little Red Book."

"Spices," he said. "If you want to give a present, bring back some spices. I always maintain there are smells and tastes in China that you don't find anywhere else."

"What else do you want?"

"You, healthy and happy."

"I think I can deliver that."

He offered to drive her to Copenhagen the next day, but she thought it would be enough if he took her to the station.

It was a beautiful, clear winter's day when Staffan Roslin drove his wife to the railroad station and waved as her train left the platform. At Kastrup airport she checked in without difficulty and got the aisle seats she wanted on both flights, to Helsinki and Beijing. As the plane took off, and she had the feeling that she was emerging from a locked room, she smiled at the elderly Finn sitting beside her. She closed her eyes, declined anything to eat or drink before reaching Helsinki, and thought back to the time when China had been her paradise, both on earth and in her dreams.

She woke up as the plane began its descent into Helsinki. The wheels came into contact with the concrete of the runway, and she had two hours to fill before her flight to Beijing was due to depart. She sat down on a bench underneath an old airplane hanging from the ceiling of the departure hall. It was cold. Through the large picture windows facing the runways, she could see the breath of the ground staff as they worked. She thought about the latest conversation she'd had with Vivi Sundberg, a couple of days earlier. Birgitta had asked if they had made any stills from the film in the homemade surveillance camera. They had, and Sundberg didn't even ask why when Birgitta had asked for a copy of the picture of the Chinese man. The following day an enlargement of the photograph was delivered to her mailbox. Now it was in her purse. She took the picture out of the envelope.

So you are one in a billion Chinese faces, Birgitta thought. I shall never find you. I shall never discover who you are. And if the name you gave was genuine. And above all, what you did.

She slowly made her way to the departure gate for the flight to Beijing. A line was already forming. This is where Asia begins, she thought. Borders are distorted by airports, closer but at the same time farther away.

Her seat was 22C. Next to her was a dark-skinned man working for a British company in the Chinese capital. They exchanged a few pleasantries, but neither of them wished to become involved in a serious conversation. She curled up under her blanket. Her excitement had now given way to a feeling of having embarked upon a journey without being properly prepared. What would she actually do in Beijing? Wander the streets, look at people, and track down museums? It was quite certain that Karin Wiman wouldn't have much time to spend with Birgitta. She wondered if something of the insecure Rebel still survived inside her.

Halfway through the flight, just as they crossed the border into China, the captain announced that a sandstorm had made it impossible to land in Beijing. They would land in a town called Taiyuan and wait for the weather to improve. After landing they were bused to a freezing-cold terminal where well-wrapped-up Chinese were waiting in silence. The time difference was making her feel tired and unsure of her first impressions of China. The countryside was covered in snow, the airport surrounded by hills, and on a nearby road she could see buses and ox carts.

Two hours later the sandstorm in Beijing had died down. The flight took off, then landed again. When she had passed through all the controls, she found Karin waiting for her.

"The Rebel has landed," she said. "Welcome to Beijing!"

"Thank you. It hasn't sunk in yet that I'm really here."

"You are in the Middle Kingdom. At the center of the world. In the center of life."

That evening of the first day, she found herself standing on the nineteenth floor of the hotel, in the room she was sharing with Karin. She gazed out over the glittering, gigantic city and felt a shiver of expectation.

In another skyscraper at the same time stood a man looking out over the same city and the same lights as Birgitta Roslin.

He was holding a red ribbon in his hand. When he heard a subdued knock on the door behind him, he turned around slowly to receive the visitor for whom he had been waiting impatiently.

The Chinese Game

22

On her first morning in Beijing, Birgitta Roslin went out early. She had breakfasted in the gigantic dining room with Karin Wiman, who then hurried off to attend her conference, having explained how she was looking forward to hearing what was to be said about the old emperors. For Karin Wiman history was in many ways more alive than the real world in which she lived.

Birgitta had been given a map by a young lady at the front desk who was very beautiful and spoke almost perfect English. A quotation came into her mind. **The current upswing of the peasants' revolt is of enormous significance.** It was one of Mao's sayings that kept cropping up in the heated debates that were held in the spring of 1968.

The current upswing of the peasants' revolt is of enormous significance. The words echoed in her mind as she left the hotel and passed the silent and very young men dressed in green who were guarding the entrance. The carriageway in front of her was wide with many traffic lanes. Cars everywhere, hardly any bicycles. The street was lined with imposing bank buildings and also a five-story bookstore. People were standing outside the store with large plastic sacks full of bottles of water. After only a few paces Birgitta could feel the pollution in her throat and nose and the taste of metal in her mouth. In sites not already occupied by buildings, the arms of tall cranes were in constant motion. It was obvious that she was in a city undergoing fundamental and hectic change.

A man was pulling an overloaded cart piled high with what looked like empty chicken cages; he seemed to be in the wrong century. Apart from that she could have been anywhere else in the world.

When I was young, she thought, I saw in my mind's eye an endless mass of Chinese peasants in identical quilted clothes toiling with picks and spades, surrounded by chanting revolutionaries waving red flags, transforming rocky hills into fertile fields. The teeming crowds are still here, but in Beijing at least, in the street where I am now standing, the people are not as I anticipated. They are not even on bicycles; they have cars, and the women are wearing elegant high-heeled shoes as they march along the sidewalks.

During those days when the Swedish masses were preparing to assemble in town squares and chant the sayings of the great Chinese leader, in Birgitta's imagination all Chinese people were dressed in identical baggy gray-blue uniforms, wore identical caps, had the same close-cropped hair and furrowed brows.

Occasionally, in the late 1960s, when she had received an issue of the illustrated magazine **China,** she had been surprised by all the healthy-looking people with glowing cheeks and sparkling eyes raising their arms to the god that had come down from heaven, the Great Helmsman, the Eternal Teacher, and all the other names he had been given, the mysterious Mao. But he had not actually been mysterious. That would become clearer as time passed. He was a politician with a shrewd feeling for what was happening in the gigantic Chinese empire. Until independence in 1949 he had been one of those unique leaders that history very occasionally produces. But after coming to power he brought about much suffering, chaos, and confusion. Nevertheless, nobody could take away from him the fact that, like a modern emperor, he had resurrected the China that was by this stage well on the way to becoming a world power.

Standing now outside her gleaming hotel with its marble portals and elegantly dressed receptionists speaking flawless English, she felt as if she'd been transported into a world she knew nothing about. Was this really the society in which the upswing of the peasants' revolt had been such a major event?

That was forty years ago, she thought. More than a generation. Then I was enticed like a fly to a pot of honey by something reminiscent of a religious cult offering salvation. We were not urged to commit collective suicide, because the Day of Judgment was nigh, but to give up our individuality for the benefit of a collective intoxication, at the heart of which was a Little Red Book that had replaced all other forms of enlightenment. It contained all wisdom, the answers to all questions, expressions of all the social and political visions the world needed in order to progress from its present state and install once and for all paradise on earth, rather than a paradise in some remote kingdom in the sky. But what we didn't even begin to understand was that the sayings comprised living words. They were not inscribed in stone. They described reality. We read the sayings without interpreting them. As if the Little Red Book was a dead catechism, a revolutionary liturgy.

It took Birgitta Roslin more than an hour to get to Tiananmen Square—the Square of Heavenly Peace. It was the biggest square she had ever seen. She approached it via a pedestrian passage under Jianguomennei Dajie. The place was teeming with people on all sides as she walked across it. Wherever she turned there were people taking photographs, waving flags, selling bottles of water and picture postcards.

She stopped and looked around. The sky above her was hazy. Something was missing. It was some time before it dawned on her what it was.

There were no birds at all. But people were milling around everywhere, people who wouldn't notice if she stayed or suddenly left.

She remembered the images from 1989, when the young students had demonstrated in support of their demands to be able to think and speak freely, and the final solution when tanks had rumbled into the square and many of the demonstrators had been massacred. This is where a young man had been standing with a white plastic bag in his hand, she thought. The whole world saw him on television, and people held their breath. He had stood in front of a tank and refused to give way. Like an insignificant little tin soldier he personified all the resistance a human being is capable of. When they tried to pass by the side of him, he moved sideways as well. What happened in the end she didn't know. She had never seen a picture of that. But all those crushed by the tracks of the tanks or shot by the soldiers had been real people.

These events were the second starting point for her relationship with China. A large part of her life was embedded in the period between being a Rebel who invoked Mao Zedong to proclaim absurdly that the revolution had already begun among Swedish students in 1968 and the image of the young man standing in front of the tank in 1989. In just over twenty years she had developed from a young and idealistic student to a mother of four children and a district judge. The concept of China had always been a part of her. First as a dream, then as something she realized she didn't really understand at all, as it was so big and full of contradictions. She discovered that her children had a very different idea of China. They associated it with enormous future possibilities, just as the dream of America had characterized her own generation and that of her parents. To her surprise, David had recently told her that when he had children he would try to hire a Chinese nanny so that they could learn the language from the very start.

She wandered around Tiananmen Square, watching people take photographs and the police who were a constant presence. In the background was the building where, in 1949, Mao had proclaimed the birth of the Republic. When she started to feel cold, she walked the long way back to her hotel. Karin had promised to skip the formal lunches and eat with her instead.

There was a restaurant on the top floor of the skyscraper in which they were staying. They were given a window table with views over the vast city. Birgitta told her about her long walk to the enormous square and her reflections on their youth.

They ate several small Chinese dishes and finished off the meal with tea. Birgitta produced the brochure with the handwritten Chinese characters Karin had deciphered as the name of the hospital Longfu.

"I intend to devote my afternoon to visiting that hospital," she said.

"Why?"

"It's always a good idea to have something specific to do when you're wandering around in a city you don't know. Anything at all would do. If you don't have a plan, your feet get tired. I don't have anybody to visit, and nothing in particular that I want to see. But who knows, I might find a sign with these characters on it. I can come back here and tell you that you were right."

They parted outside the elevators. Karin needed to hurry back to her conference. Birgitta went to their room on the nineteenth floor and lay down on the bed to rest.

She had started to sense it during her morning walk through the streets—a feeling of listlessness that she couldn't quite pin down. Surrounded by people, or alone in this anonymous hotel in the gigantic city, she felt her identity starting to fade away. Who would miss her if she got lost? Who would even notice that she existed?

She had had a similar experience previously, when she was very young. Suddenly ceasing to exist, losing her grip on her identity.

She felt impatient and got up, then stood by the window. A long way down below was the city, all the people, each one with his or her dreams that Birgitta knew nothing about.

She gathered the clothes that were scattered around the room and locked the door behind her. All she was doing was whipping up feelings of unrest that were becoming increasingly difficult to handle. She needed to move about, get to know the city. Karin had promised to take her to a performance of the Peking Opera that evening.

According to the map, Longfu was quite a trek.

But she had plenty of time. She walked along the straight and apparently endless streets until she finally came to the hospital, after having passed a large art gallery.

Longfu consisted of two buildings. She counted seven stories, all in white and gray. The windows on the ground floor were barred. The blinds were closed, and old flower boxes filled with withered leaves stood on the window ledges. The trees outside the hospital were bare; the brown, parched lawns were covered in dog crap. Her first impression was that Longfu looked more like a prison than a hospital. She entered the grounds. An ambulance drove past, then another. Next to the main entrance was a notice in Chinese. She compared it with what was written in the brochure—she had come to the right place. A doctor in a white coat was standing outside the entrance, smoking and talking loudly into a cell phone.

She went back out onto the street and wandered around the big residential area. Wherever she looked old men were sitting on the sidewalks playing board games.

It was when she came to the corner of the extensive hospital grounds that it dawned on her what she had seen without thinking about it. On the other side of the street was a new skyscraper. She took the Chinese brochure out of her pocket. There was the building. There was no doubt about it. On the very top floor was a terrace, the likes of which she had never seen before. It projected from the side of the building like the forecastle of a ship. The façade of the skyscraper was covered in dark-tinted glass panels. Armed guards stood outside the high entrance. Presumably the building contained offices rather than residences. She stood on the lee side of a tree, where she was partly protected from the freezing-cold wind. Some men came out of the tall doors, which seemed to be made of copper, and stepped into waiting black cars. A tempting thought struck her. She checked that she still had the photograph of Wang Min Hao in her pocket. If he was somehow connected with this building, perhaps one of the guards might recognize him. But what would she say if they nodded and said he was indeed in there?

She couldn't make up her mind what to do. Before she showed anybody the photograph, she must think up a reason for wanting to see him. Obviously, she couldn't mention the murders in Hesjövallen. But whatever she said would need to be plausible.

A young man stopped by her side. He said something that she couldn't make out. Then she realized that he was speaking English to her.

"Are you lost? Can I help you?"

"I'm just looking at that handsome building over there. Do you know who owns it?"

He shook his head in surprise.

"I study to be veterinarian. I know nothing of tall buildings. Can I help you? I try to teach me speak better English."

"Your English is very good." She pointed up at the projecting terrace. "I wonder who lives there?"

"Somebody who is very rich."

"Can you help me?" she said. She took out the photograph of Wang Min Hao. "Can you go over to the guards and ask them if they know this man. If they ask why you want to know, just say somebody asked you to give him a message."

"What message?"

"Tell them you'll fetch it. Come back here. I shall wait by the hospital entrance."

"Why not ask them yourself?" he said.

"I'm too shy. I don't think a Western woman on her own should ask about a Chinese man."

"Do you know him?"

"Yes."

She tried to look as casual as possible, but was beginning to regret her ploy. However, he took the photograph and was about to leave.

"One more thing," she said. "Ask them who lives up there, on the top floor. It looks like an apartment with a big terrace."

"My name is Huo," he said. "I will ask."

"My name's Birgitta. Just pretend to be interested."

"Where you from? U.S.A.?"

"Sweden. Ruidian, I think it's called in Chinese."

"I do not know where that is."

"It's almost impossible to explain."

As he started to cross the road, she turned and hurried back to the hospital entrance.

An old man on crutches came slowly out of the open entrance door. She suddenly had the feeling that she was exposing herself to danger. She calmed herself down by noting that the street was full of people. A man who had killed a lot of people in the north of Sweden might get away with it. But not someone who murdered a Western tourist in a busy street. In broad daylight. China couldn't afford that.

The man with the crutches suddenly fell over. The young police officers on guard by the entrance made no move. She hesitated, but then helped the man back onto his feet. A mass of words came tumbling out of his mouth, but she didn't understand, nor could she tell if he was grateful or angry. He smelled strongly of spices—or alcohol. He continued walking through the grounds toward the street.

Huo came back. He appeared to be calm and wasn't looking furtively around. Birgitta went to meet him.

He shook his head.

"Nobody has seen this man."

"Nobody knew who he was?"

"Nobody."

"Who did you show the picture to?"

"The guards. Another man came as well. From inside the house. He had sunglasses. Do I pronounce that right? 'Sunglasses'?"

"Very good. Who lives on the top floor?"

"They did not answer that."

"But somebody lives there?"

"I think so. They did not like the question."

"Why not?"

"They told me to go away."

"So what did you do?"

He looked at her in surprise.

"I went away."

She took an American ten-dollar bill from her purse. He didn't want to accept it at first. He returned the photograph of Wang Min Hao and asked which hotel she was staying at, made sure she knew her way back there, then bowed politely as he said good-bye.

On the way back to the hotel she once again had the vertiginous feeling that she could be swallowed up by the mass of humanity at any moment and never found again. She felt so dizzy that she was obliged to lean against a wall. There was a teahouse not far away. She went in, ordered tea and cookies, and tried to take long, deep breaths. Here it was again, the feeling of panic that had occasionally overwhelmed her in recent years. The long journey to Beijing had not provided any release from the worries that were weighing her down.

She thought about Wang again. I could track him here, but no farther.

She paid her bill, surprised by how expensive it was, then braced herself once more to face the bitterly cold wind.

That evening they went to the theater located inside the enormous Qianmen Jianguo Hotel. Earphones were available, but Karin Wiman had arranged the services of interpreters. During the whole of the four-hour performance, Birgitta sat leaning to one side, listening to the young woman's frequently incomprehensible summaries of what was happening onstage. Both she and Karin were disappointed, as they soon realized that the performance consisted of extracts from various classical Peking operas, no doubt top class, but aimed exclusively at tourists. When the show finished and they were finally able to leave the freezing-cold auditorium, they both had stiff necks.

Outside the theater they waited for the car the conference had placed at Karin's disposal. At one point Birgitta had the impression she had caught sight of the young man Huo, who had earlier addressed her in English amid the hustle and bustle of the street.

It happened so quickly that she hadn't really registered his face before it had vanished again.

When they arrived at their hotel, Birgitta looked over her shoulder, but nobody was there—nobody she recognized, at least.

She shuddered. The fear she felt seemed to have come from nowhere. But it **was** Huo she had seen outside the theater; she was certain of it.

Karin asked if she fancied a nightcap, and she did.

An hour later, Karin was asleep. Birgitta was standing by the window, gazing out over the glittering neon lights.

She was still worried. How could Huo have known that she was there? Why had he followed her?

When she finally crept into bed beside her sleeping friend, she regretted having produced the photograph of Wang Min Hao.

She felt cold. She lay awake for many hours. The chill of the Beijing winter's night embraced her.

23

There were snow flurries the following day. Karin had risen at six o'clock in order to check through the lecture she was due to deliver. Birgitta woke up and saw her friend on a chair near the window, reading by the light from a standard lamp; it was still dark outside. She experienced a vague feeling of envy. Karin had chosen a life involving travels and contact with foreign cultures. Her own life was played out in courtrooms featuring a constant duel between truth and lies, arbitrary decisions and justice: outcomes were usually uncertain and often frustrating.

Karin noticed that Birgitta was awake.

"It's snowing," she said. "Not a lot. You never get heavy snowfalls in Beijing. It's powdery, but quite sharp, like grains of sand from the desert."

"You are a busy bee. Up so early."

"I'm nervous. There'll be so many people listening

to what I have to say, bending over backward to find errors."

Birgitta sat up and moved her head tentatively.

"I still have a stiff neck."

"Peking operas demand a high level of physical stamina."

"I wouldn't mind seeing another one. But without an interpreter."

Karin left shortly after seven. They arranged to meet again that evening. Birgitta slept for another hour, and by the time she'd finished breakfast it was nine o'clock. Her worries from the previous day had vanished. The face she thought she had recognized outside the theater must have been a figment of her imagination. The range of her fantasies sometimes surprised her, although she should have been used to them.

She sat in the large reception area, where silent servants armed with feather dusters were busy cleaning marble columns. She felt annoyingly idle and decided to look for a department store where she could buy a Chinese board game. And she had also promised Staffan some spices. A young male concierge marked the way to a suitable store on her map. She changed some money in the hotel, then went out. It was not quite as cold as it had been. Occasional snowflakes were whirling around in the air. She pulled her scarf up over her mouth and nose and set off.

It took her almost an hour to get to the department store. It was on a street called Wangfuijing Dajie, occupied a whole block, and, when she stepped in through the imposing entrance doors, felt like a gigantic labyrinth. She was immediately caught up in the crush. She noticed people on all sides giving her curious looks and commenting on her clothes and appearance. She looked in vain for a notice in English. As she made her way toward one of the moving staircases, she was shouted at in bad English by various sales staff.

On the third floor she found a department selling books, paper goods, and toys. She spoke to a young shop assistant, but unlike the hotel staff she didn't understand what Birgitta said. The assistant said something into an intercom, and within seconds an older man appeared beside her and smiled.

"Board games," said Birgitta. "Where can I find those?"

"Mah-jongg?"

He led her to another floor, where she suddenly found herself surrounded by shelves containing all kinds of board games. She picked out two, thanked the man for his help, and went to one of the cash registers. Once the games had been wrapped up and placed in a large, colorful plastic bag, she found her own way to the food department. She could smell spices and soon found a large selection in small, pretty paper packets. After buying some she sat down in a cafeteria near the entrance. She drank tea and ate a Chinese cake that was so sweet she had trouble getting it down. Two small children came to stand and stare at her until they were called brusquely back by their mother at a neighboring table.

Just before getting up to leave, Birgitta had the feeling she was being watched. She looked around, tried to scrutinize several faces, but there was no one she recognized. She was annoyed by these imaginings and left the store. As the plastic bag was heavy, she took a taxi back to the hotel and wondered what to do for the rest of the day. She wouldn't be able to see Karin until late that evening—Karin had a formal dinner that she would have liked to skip, but couldn't. Birgitta decided to visit the art gallery she had passed the previous day. She knew the way there. She remembered having seen several restaurants where she could have a meal if she felt hungry. It had stopped snowing now, and the clouds had broken up. She felt younger, more energetic than in the morning. Just now, I'm that freely rolling stone we used to dream of becoming when we were young, she thought. A rolling stone with a stiff neck.

The main building of the gallery looked like a typical Chinese tower with small platforms and projecting roof details. Visitors entered through two majestically imposing doors. As the gallery was so big, she decided to restrict herself to the ground floor. There was an exhibit on how the People's Liberation Army had used art as a propaganda weapon. Most of the paintings were in the familiar style she recalled from the illustrated Chinese magazines in the 1960s. But there were also some nonfigurative paintings depicting war and chaos in bright colors.

Wherever she went, she was surrounded by guards and guides, mainly young women in dark blue uniforms. None of them spoke English.

She spent a few hours in the art gallery. It was nearly three o'clock when she left, glancing at the hospital and behind it the skyscraper with the jutting-out terrace. Quite close to the gallery was a simple restaurant; she was given a place at a corner table after she had pointed at various plates of food on other diners' tables. She also pointed at a bottle of beer and noticed how thirsty she was when she began drinking. She ate far too much, then drank two cups of strong tea in order to overcome her drowsiness while thumbing through several picture postcards she'd bought at the gallery.

Then it hit her. She had had enough of Beijing, although she'd only been there for two days. She felt restless, missed her work, and had the feeling that time was simply slipping through her fingers. She couldn't continue wandering aimlessly around the streets. She needed something specific to do, now that the board games and the spices had been bought. First she needed to go back to her hotel and rest, then come up with a proper plan—she had another three days, two of them alone.

When she came back out onto the street, the sun had disappeared behind the clouds again, and it felt much colder. She wrapped her jacket tightly around her and wound her scarf over her mouth and nose.

A man came up to her with a piece of paper and a small pair of scissors in his hand. In broken English he begged her to allow him to clip her silhouette. He produced a file with plastic pockets with other silhouettes he had made. Her first reaction was to say no, but she changed her mind and took off her woolly hat, removed her scarf, and posed in profile.

The silhouette he made was astonishingly good. He asked for five dollars, but she gave him ten.

The man was old and had a scar on one cheek. She would have loved to hear his life story, if only that had been possible. She put the silhouette into her bag; they bowed to each other and went their separate ways.

She hadn't the slightest idea of what was happening when the attack took place. She felt an arm wrapped around her neck, bending her backward, and at the same time somebody snatched her purse. When she screamed and tried to hang on to it, the arm around her neck tightened. She was punched in the stomach and left gasping for breath. She collapsed onto the sidewalk. It had come about so quickly and lasted no more than ten or fifteen seconds. A passing cyclist stopped to try to lift her to her feet, together with a woman who put down her heavy grocery bags in order to help. But Birgitta Roslin was unable to stand up. She sank down onto her knees and passed out.

When she recovered consciousness she was on a stretcher in an ambulance with sirens blaring. A doctor was pressing a stethoscope onto her chest. Everything was a blur. She remembered having her purse stolen. But why was she in an ambulance? She tried to ask the doctor with the stethoscope. But he answered in Chinese: she deduced from his gestures that he wanted her to keep quiet and not move. Her throat felt very tender. Perhaps she had been seriously injured? The thought scared her stiff. She might have been killed. Whoever had attacked her hadn't hesitated to do so, despite the broad daylight in a busy street.

She started crying. The doctor reacted by feeling her pulse. Even as he did so the ambulance came to a halt, and the back doors were opened. She was transferred to another stretcher and wheeled along a corridor with very bright lights. She was sobbing uncontrollably and didn't notice being given a tranquilizer. She drifted away as if on a groundswell, surrounded by Chinese faces that seemed to be swimming in the same waters as she was: their heads, bobbing up and down in the waves, were preparing to accept the Great Helmsman as he approached the shore after a long and strenuous swim.

When she regained consciousness she was in a room with dimmed lights and drawn curtains. A man in uniform was sitting on a chair next to the door. When he saw that she had opened her eyes, he stood up and left the room. Shortly afterward two other men in uniform entered the room, accompanied by a doctor who spoke to her in English with a strong American accent.

"How are you feeling?"

"I don't know. I'm tired. My throat hurts."

"We have examined you carefully. You survived that unfortunate incident without serious injury."

"Why am I here? I want to go back to my hotel."

The doctor bent down closer to her face.

"The police need to talk to you first. We don't like it when foreign visitors are treated badly in our country. We are ashamed. Whoever attacked you must be found."

"But I didn't see anything."

"I'm not the one you need to talk to."

The doctor stood up and nodded to the two men in uniform, who carried their chairs over to her bed and sat down. One of them, the interpreter, was young, but the man asking the questions was in his sixties. He had tinted glasses, which meant that she couldn't see his eyes. He started asking questions without either of the men having introduced themselves. She had the vague impression that the elderly man didn't like her at all.

"We need to know what you saw."

"I didn't see anything. It all happened so quickly."

"All the witnesses have agreed that the two men were not masked."

"I didn't even know there were two of them."

"What did register with you?"

"I felt an arm around my neck. They attacked me from behind. They snatched my purse and punched me in the stomach."

"We need to know everything you can tell us about these two men."

"But I didn't see anything."

"No faces?"

"No."

"Did you hear their voices?"

"I didn't even know they said anything."

"What happened just before you were attacked?"

"A man cut my silhouette. I'd paid him and was about to leave."

"When your silhouette had been cut—did you see anything then?"

"Such as?"

"Anybody waiting?"

"How many times do I have to tell you that I didn't see anything at all?"

When the interpreter had translated her answer the police officer leaned toward her and raised his voice.

"We are asking these questions because we want to catch the men who attacked you and stole your purse. That's why you should answer without losing your temper."

The words cut her. "I'm just telling you the way it was."

"What did you have in your purse?"

"Some cash, not a lot, Chinese, and some American dollars. A comb, a handkerchief, some tablets, a pen, nothing important."

"We found your passport in an inside pocket of your jacket. I gather you are Swedish. Why are you here in China?"

"I came here on vacation, with a friend."

The elderly man thought that over. His face was expressionless.

"We didn't find a silhouette," he said eventually.

"It was in my purse."

"You didn't say that when I asked you. Is there anything else you've forgotten?"

She thought for a moment, then shook her head. The interrogation was over. The elderly police officer said something, then left the room.

"When you feel better we'll take you back to your hotel. We'll come back to you later and ask a few more questions for the records."

The interpreter mentioned the name of her hotel without her having said it.

"How do you know the name of the hotel I'm staying at? The key was in my purse."

"We know things like that."

He bowed and left the room. Before the door closed, the doctor with the American accent came back into the room.

"We need you for a few more minutes," he said. "Some blood tests, an assessment of your X-rays."

My watch, she thought. They didn't take that. She checked it. A quarter to five.

"When can I go back to my hotel?"

"Soon."

"My friend will be very worried if I'm not there."

"We'll arrange transportation back to your hotel. We're very keen to make sure that our foreign guests are not disappointed by our hospitality, despite the fact that unfortunate incidents do occasionally take place."

She was left alone in the room. Somewhere in the distance she heard somebody screaming, a lonely cry echoing down the corridor.

She chewed over what had happened. The whole episode seemed surreal—the sudden shock at having been grabbed from behind, the punch in the stomach, and the people who had helped her.

But they must have seen something, she thought. Have the police asked them? Were they still there when the ambulance arrived? Or did the police get there first?

She had never been attacked before in her life. She had been threatened, but never physically assaulted. This was the first time she was the victim.

She felt afraid but knew this was usual after a person had been attacked. Fear, but also anger, a feeling of having been humiliated, distress. And a lust for revenge. Just now, lying in bed, she would not have protested if the two men who had mugged her had been forced to kneel down and shot through the back of the head.

A nurse came into the room and helped her to

dress. She had a pain in her stomach and a graze on her knee. When the nurse gave her a comb and held up a mirror in front of her, she could see that she was very pale. So this is what I look like when I'm scared, she thought. I won't forget it.

The doctor returned as she sat on the bed, ready to go back to her hotel.

"The pain in your neck will pass, probably as soon as tomorrow," he said.

"Thank you for all you've done for me."

Three police officers were standing in the corridor, waiting for her. One of them was carrying a frightening-looking automatic weapon. She accompanied them down in the elevator and stepped into a police car. She had no idea where she was, didn't even know the name of the hospital where she had been treated. At one point she thought she might have recognized one side of the Forbidden City, but wasn't sure.

The sirens had been switched off. She was grateful not to have to return to her hotel in a car with flashing blue lights. She recognized the hotel entrance and got out of the car, which moved away even before she had time to turn around. She was still wondering how they could have known where she was staying.

She explained at the front desk that she had lost her key and was given another without question. It happened so quickly that she realized it must have been prepared in advance. The woman behind the counter smiled. She knows, Birgitta thought. The police have been here, told the staff about the assault, and prepared them for her return with no key.

As she walked toward the elevators, she thought she should be grateful, but instead she felt uneasy. That feeling was not banished when she entered her room. She could see that somebody had been there. But the maid had come earlier in the day. It was possible of course that Karin had stopped in briefly, to pick up something or to change clothes. But what was there to prevent the police from making a discreet search? Or somebody else, for that matter?

What betrayed the unknown visitor was the plastic carrier bag with the board games. She saw immediately that it wasn't where she had left it. She looked around the room, slowly, so that nothing would escape her notice. But it was only the bag that had been moved and not replaced.

She went to the bathroom. Her toiletrics bag was exactly where she had left it that morning. None of the contents were missing.

She went back into the room and sat on a chair by the window. Her suitcase was lying with the lid open. She went to examine the contents, lifting out each item of clothing, one by one. If somebody had searched through it, they had done it carefully to avoid detection.

It was only when she came to the bottom of the case that she stopped dead. There ought to be a flashlight and a box of matches there. She always took them with her on her travels, ever since the year before she married Staffan when she had visited Madeira and there had been a power outage that lasted for more than a day. She had been out for an evening walk by the steep cliffs on the outskirts of Funchal when everything went black. It had taken her hours to grope her way back to the hotel. After that she always carried a flashlight and a box of matches in her suitcase. The flashlight was there, but no sign of the matches. The matchbox had a green label and came from a restaurant in Helsingborg.

She went through the clothes once more without finding the box. Had she put it in her purse? She did sometimes do that, but she had no memory of moving it from her suitcase. But who would take a box of matches from a room being searched surreptitiously?

She sat down on the chair by the window again. That last hour in the hospital, she thought. Even at the time I had the feeling that I was being kept there unnecessarily. What were the test results they were waiting for? Was the real reason that they wanted me out of the way while the police searched my hotel room? But why? After all, I was the one who had been mugged.

There was a knock on the door. Birgitta gave a start. She could see through the peephole that there were police officers in the corridor. She opened the door anxiously. These were new officers, not the ones she had seen at the hospital. One was a woman, short, about the same age as Birgitta. She was the one who did the talking.

"We just want to make sure that everything is all right."

"Thank you."

The policewoman indicated that she wanted to enter the room. Birgitta stepped to one side. One policeman stood outside the door, another one inside. The woman led the way to the chairs by the window and placed a briefcase on the table. Something about her behavior surprised Birgitta Roslin, without her being able to put her finger on what it was.

"I'd like you to study some pictures. We have information from some witnesses and think we might know who carried out the attack."

"But I didn't see anything. An arm, perhaps? How can I identify an arm?"

The police officer wasn't listening. She produced some photographs and placed them on the table in front of Birgitta Roslin. All of them were of young men.

"Perhaps you saw something without having registered it."

There was obviously no point in protesting. Birgitta leafed through the pictures, and it occurred to her that these were young men who might eventually commit a crime that would result in their being executed. Naturally, she didn't recognize any of them. She shook her head.

"I've never seen any of them before."

"Are you sure?"

"Certain."

"None of them?"

"None."

The policewoman replaced the photographs in the briefcase. Birgitta noticed that her fingernails were badly bitten.

"We shall catch the people responsible for the attack," said the woman. "How much longer will you be staying in Beijing?"

"Three days."

The officer nodded, bowed, and left the room.

You knew that, Birgitta thought as she fastened the safety chain. That I would be staying for three more days. Why ask me something you knew already? You can't fool me as easily as that.

She closed her eyes and thought that she should call home.

When she woke up it was dark outside. The pain in her neck was beginning to subside. But the attack seemed even more menacing now. She had a strange feeling that the worst hadn't actually happened yet. She took out her cell phone and called Helsingborg. Staffan wasn't at home, nor did he answer his cell phone. She left a message, then considered calling her children but decided not to.

She went through the contents of her purse in her head one more time. She had lost sixty dollars. But most of her cash was locked up in the little safe in the wardrobe. She stood up and went to check the safe. It was still locked. She keyed in the code and went through the contents. Nothing was missing. She closed the door and relocked it. She was still trying to work out what had struck her as odd about the policewoman's behavior. She stood by the door and tried to call up the scene in her mind's eye. But in vain. She lay down on the bed again. Thought again about the photographs the policewoman had taken out of her briefcase.

She suddenly sat up. **She had opened the door. The policewoman had indicated that she wanted to come in and Birgitta had moved to one side. Then the woman had walked straight over to the chairs by the window. She hadn't even cast a glance at the open bathroom door, or the part of the room with the large double bed.**

Birgitta Roslin could think of only one explanation. The policewoman had been in the room before. She didn't need to look around. She already knew where everything was.

Birgitta stared at the table where the briefcase and the photographs had been lying. She hadn't recognized any of the faces she had been asked to study. But was that perhaps really what the police wanted to check? That she couldn't identify anybody in the pictures? It was not a question of her possibly being able to recognize one of her attackers. On the contrary. The police wanted to make sure that she really hadn't seen anything.

But why? She stood by the window. A thought she had entertained while still in Hudiksvall came back into her mind.

What has happened is big, too big for me alone.

Fear flooded her before she had time to prepare herself. It was more than an hour before she could pluck up the courage to take the elevator to the dining room.

Before she went in through the glass doors, she looked around. But there was nobody there.

24

Birgitta Roslin had been crying in her sleep. Karin Wiman sat up in bed and gently touched her shoulder in order to wake her up.

Karin came back very late that evening. To make sure that she didn't lie awake for hours, Birgitta had taken one of the sleeping pills she so seldom used but always had with her.

"You must have been dreaming," said Karin. "Something sad that made you cry."

Birgitta couldn't remember any dreams. The inner landscape she had just left was completely empty.

"What time is it?"

"Nearly five. I'm tired, I need to sleep a bit longer. Why were you crying?"

"I don't know. I must have been dreaming, even if I don't remember what."

Karin lay down again. She soon fell back to sleep.

Birgitta got up and opened a little gap in the curtains. The early morning traffic was already under way. A few flags straining at their moorings told her that it was going to be another windy day in Beijing.

The fear she had felt after being mugged returned. But she resolved to fight against it, just as she had when she had received numerous threats as a judge. She ran through in her mind once again what had happened, this time being as critical as she possibly could. In the end she was left with the almost embarrassing feeling that her imagination had gotten the better of her. She suspected conspiracy at every turn, a chain of events that she made up, whereas in reality they were unconnected. She had been mugged; her purse had been snatched. Why the police should be involved in the attack now seemed beyond her comprehension—no doubt they were doing all they could to help. Perhaps she had been crying about herself and her fantasies?

She switched on the lamp and tilted it backward so that the light didn't fall on Karin's side of the bed. Then she started to leaf through the Beijing guidebook she had brought with her. She ticked off in the margin things she wanted to see during the days she had left. First of all she wanted to visit the Forbidden City that she had read so much about and been entranced by ever since she first became interested in China. Another day she wanted to visit one of the Buddhist temples in the city. She and Staffan had often agreed that if by any chance they felt the need to become more closely acquainted with the spiritual world, only Buddhism would fit the bill. Staffan had pointed out that it was the one religion that had never gone to war nor resorted to violence in order to spread its message. It was important for Birgitta that Buddhism recognized only the god that everybody had latent inside his or her self. Understanding its creed meant slowly waking up that inner god.

She went back to bed and slept for a few more hours, then woke up to see Karin naked, stretching and yawning in the middle of the room. An old Rebel with a body that was still quite well preserved, she thought.

"Now there's a pretty sight," she said.

Karin gave a start, as if she'd been caught doing something wrong.

"I thought you were asleep."

"I was until a minute ago. This time I woke up without crying."

"Did you dream?"

"I expect so. But I don't remember anything. The dreams slipped away and hid. No doubt I was a teenager and unlucky in love."

"I never dream about my youth. But I do sometimes imagine myself very old."

"We're not far from that state."

"Not yet. I'm concentrating on lectures that I hope are going to be interesting."

She went into the bathroom, and when she emerged she was fully dressed.

Birgitta still hadn't mentioned the mugging. She wondered if she should keep it to herself. Among all the emotions surrounding the event was a feeling of embarrassment, as if she should have been able to avoid what had happened. She was normally very alert.

"I'm going to be just as late this evening again," said Karin. "But it will be all over by tomorrow. Then it'll be our turn."

"I have long lists," said Birgitta. "Today it's going to be the Forbidden City."

"Mao used to live there," said Karin. "Some people maintain that he consciously tried to imitate one of the old emperors. Most likely Qin, who we talk about day after day. But I think that's malicious slander. Political slander."

"His spirit no doubt hovers over the whole conference," said Birgitta. "Off you go now; work hard and think clever thoughts."

Karin left, full of energy. Instead of giving in to envy, Birgitta leaped out of bed, did a few halfhearted push-ups, and prepared to spend a day in Beijing without any conspiracies or worried glances over her shoulder. She devoted the morning to exploring the mysterious labyrinth that made up the Forbidden City. Over the middle gate in the vividly pink-colored wall, once used exclusively by emperors, hung a large portrait of Mao. Birgitta noticed that all the Chinese who passed through the red gates touched their gold mountings. She assumed it was some kind of superstition. Perhaps Karin could explain it.

She walked over the worn stones that paved the inner courtyard of the palace and recalled that when she had been a Red Rebel, she had read that the Forbidden City comprised 9,999 and a half rooms. As the Divine God had 10,000 rooms, naturally, the Divine Son could not have more. She doubted if that were true.

There were lots of visitors despite the cold wind. Most were Chinese, moving with reverence through the rooms to which their ancestors had been denied entrance for generations. What a gigantic revolution this was, Birgitta Roslin thought. When a people liberates itself, every individual acquires the right to dream his own dreams and has access to the forbidden rooms where oppression was created.

Every fifth person in the world is Chinese. When my family is gathered together, if we were the world, one of us would be Chinese. So we were right after all when we were young. Our Red revolutionary prophets, not least Moses, who was the most educated theoretically, reminded us over and over again that it was impossible to discuss the future without taking China into account.

Just as she was about to leave the Forbidden City, she discovered to her surprise a café from an American chain. The sign screeched at her from a redbrick wall. She watched to see how passing Chinese reacted. Some stopped and pointed, others even went inside, while most didn't seem to take any notice of what Birgitta considered to be a disgraceful sacrilege. China had become a different kind of mystery since the first time she had tried to understand the Middle Kingdom. But that's not right, she told herself. It must be possible to understand how there can be an American café in the Forbidden City given how the world moves on.

She had lunch at a little restaurant and was again surprised to see how expensive the bill was. Then she decided to try to find an English newspaper at the hotel and drink a cup of coffee in the bar in the huge reception area. She found a copy of the **Guardian** at the newspaper kiosk and sat down in a corner where an open fire was burning merrily. Some American tourists stood up and announced in very loud voices that they were now going to climb the Great Wall of China. She took an instant dislike to them.

When would she go to see the Wall? Perhaps Karin would have time on the last day before they had to fly home? How could one possibly visit China and not see the Wall, which, according to modern legend, was one of the few human constructions that could be seen from space?

The Wall really is something I have to see, she thought. No doubt Karin has been there before. But she'll have to do it for my sake.

A woman suddenly appeared in front of her table. She was about the same age as Birgitta, with sleek hair. She smiled and gave the impression of great dignity. She addressed Birgitta Roslin in immaculate English.

"Mrs. Roslin?"

"That's me."

"Do you mind if I sit down and join you? I have an important errand."

"Please do."

The woman was wearing a dark blue suit that must have been very expensive.

She sat down.

"My name is Hong Qiu," she said. "I wouldn't dream of disturbing you if I didn't have something very important to talk to you about."

She gestured discreetly to a man hovering in the background. He came up to their table and placed upon it Birgitta's purse, as if it were an exceedingly valuable gift, before bowing and withdrawing.

Birgitta looked at Hong Qiu in surprise.

"The police found your purse," said Hong Qiu. "It is humiliating for us to accept that one of our guests has been exposed to an unfortunate incident, and so I was asked to return it to you."

"Are you a police officer?"

Hong Qiu continued to smile.

"Certainly not. But I'm sometimes asked to perform certain services for our authorities. Is there anything missing?"

Birgitta opened her purse. Everything was still there, apart from the money. To her surprise she also discovered that the box of matches she'd been unable to find was actually there in her purse.

"The money is missing."

"We are confident of catching the criminals. They will be severely punished."

"But they won't be condemned to death, I hope?"

There was an almost indiscernible reaction in Hong Qiu's face, but Birgitta noticed it.

"Our laws are strict. If they have committed serious crimes before, it's possible that they might receive the death sentence. But if they show signs of having reformed, they may get away with prison."

"But what happens if they don't express any regret?"

The response was evasive. "Our laws are clear and unambiguous. But nothing is certain. We make judgments according to the particulars of a case. Punishment doled out in accordance with routines can never be justified."

"I work in the law—I'm a judge. Only an extremely primitive legal system can ever resort to capital punishment, which seldom if ever has a preventative effect."

Birgitta Roslin regretted the meddlesome tone of her comments. Hong Qiu listened attentively, but her smile had disappeared. A waitress approached them, but Hong Qiu dismissed her with a shake of the head. Birgitta Roslin had the distinct impression that a pattern was being repeated. Hong Qiu didn't react to the news that Birgitta was a judge—she knew that already.

In this country they know all there is to know about me, she thought. Or am I imagining it?

"Naturally I'm pleased to have my purse back. But you must realize that I'm surprised by the way this has happened. You bring it to me, but you are not a police officer—I don't know what or who you are. Have the people who stole my purse been arrested, or did I misunderstand what you said? Did somebody find it after the muggers had thrown it away?"

"Nobody has been arrested, but the police have their suspicions. The purse was found not far from where it was stolen."

Hong Qiu started to stand up. Birgitta Roslin stopped her.

"Tell me who you are. An unknown woman suddenly appears from nowhere and returns my purse."

"I work on security matters. As I speak both English and French, I am sometimes asked to perform certain tasks."

"Security? So you are in fact a police officer. Despite what you said."

Hong Qiu shook her head.

"Security goes beyond police responsibility. It goes deeper, down to the very roots of society. I'm sure that's true in your country as well."

"Who asked you to look me up and return my purse?"

"A duty officer at Beijing's central lost property office."

"Lost property? Who had handed in my purse?"

"I don't know."

"How could he know the purse belonged to me? It doesn't contain any identity card or anything with my name."

"I assume he was informed by the relevant police authorities investigating the case."

"Are you saying there is more than one department dealing with muggings?"

"It's normal for police officers with various specialties to work together."

"In order to find a lost purse?"

"In order to solve a serious attack on a guest in our country."

She's going around and around in circles, Birgitta thought. I'll never get a proper answer out of her.

"I'm a judge," said Birgitta Roslin again. "I'll be staying here in Beijing for a few more days. As you seem to know all about me I hardly need to tell you that I've come here with a friend who is spending every day talking about your first emperor at an international conference."

"A knowledge of the Qin dynasty is important for an understanding of my country. But you are wrong if you think I know much about who you are and why you have come to Beijing."

"Since you were able to produce the purse I had lost, I'm going to ask you for some advice. What do I need to do to get entry into a Chinese court of law? It doesn't need to be an especially remarkable trial, I just want to follow the proceedings and perhaps ask a few questions."

"I can arrange that for tomorrow. I can go with you."

The immediate answer startled Birgitta Roslin. "I don't want to be a nuisance. You seem to have an awful lot to do."

"No more than I decide is important." Hong Qiu stood up. "I'll contact you later this afternoon to let you know where we can meet tomorrow."

Birgitta was about to mention her room number, but then it struck her that Hong Qiu no doubt knew that already.

She watched Hong Qiu walk through the bar toward the entrance. The man who had been carrying the purse and another man joined her before they disappeared from Birgitta's sight.

She looked at the purse and burst out laughing. There is an entrance, she thought, and also an exit. A purse is lost, and found again. But what actually happens in between, I have no idea. There's a risk that I won't be able to distinguish between what's going on in my mind and what actually happens in reality.

Hong Qiu called an hour later, just after Birgitta had returned to her room. Nothing surprised her anymore. It was as if unseen people were observing every move she made and could say exactly where she was at any given moment. Like now. She came into the room, and the telephone rang immediately.

"Nine o'clock tomorrow morning," said Hong Qiu.

"Where?"

"I'll pick you up. We shall visit a court in an out-lying suburb of Beijing. I chose it because a female judge will be on duty there tomorrow."

"I'm most grateful."

"I want to do everything we possibly can to make up for that unfortunate incident."

"You've already done that. I feel surrounded by guardian angels."

After the phone call Birgitta emptied her purse onto the bed. She still found it hard to accept that the box of matches had been in there rather than in her suitcase. She opened the box. It was half empty. Somebody's been smoking, she thought. The box was full when I put it in my case. She took out the matches and looked inside. She didn't really know what she expected to find. All it is is a matchbox, she thought. She felt annoyed as she put the matches back into the box and replaced it in her purse. She was going too far again. Her imagination was running away with her.

She devoted the rest of the day to a Buddhist temple and a long drawn-out dinner in a restaurant not far from her hotel. She was asleep when Karin tiptoed into their room, and she merely turned over when the light was switched on.

The next day they got up at the same time. As Karin had overslept, she didn't have a chance to do much more than confirm that the conference would come to an end at two o'clock. After that she would be free. Birgitta told her about the visit she was going to make to a Chinese court, but still didn't mention her mugging.

Hong Qiu was waiting in reception. She was wearing a white fur coat today; Birgitta felt almost embarrassingly underdressed standing by her side. But Hong Qiu noted that she was wearing warm clothes.

"Our courts of law can be rather chilly," she said.

"Like your theaters?"

Hong Qiu smiled. She couldn't know that we'd attended a Peking opera a few nights ago, Birgitta thought—or could she?

"China is still a very poor country. We are approaching the future with great humility and hard work."

Not everybody's poor, Birgitta thought cynically. Even my untrained eye can see that your fur coat is genuine and extremely expensive.

A car with a chauffeur was waiting outside the hotel. Birgitta had a vague feeling of reluctance. What did she actually know about this woman she was following into a car with an unknown man behind the wheel?

She persuaded herself that there was no danger. Why couldn't she just be thankful for the kindness and consideration they were surrounding her with? Hong Qiu sat silently in a corner of the backseat with her eyes half closed. They traveled very fast down a very long street. After a few minutes Birgitta Roslin hadn't the slightest idea in which part of Beijing she was.

They stopped outside a low, concrete building with two police officers guarding the entrance. Over the door was a row of Chinese characters in red.

"The name of the district court," said Hong Qiu, who had noticed what Birgitta was looking at.

As they walked up the steps to the entrance, the two police officers presented arms. Hong Qiu didn't seem to react. Birgitta wondered who her companion really was. She could hardly be simply a messenger girl whose job was to return stolen purses to foreign visitors.

They continued along a deserted corridor and came to the courtroom itself, which was wood-paneled and austere. On a high dais at one of the short sides sat two men in uniform. The place between them was empty. There were no members of the public present. Hong Qiu led the way to the front bench, where two cushions had been placed. Everything has been prepared, Birgitta thought. The performance can begin. Or is it simply that I'm being courteously received even in this courtroom?

They had barely sat down when the accused was escorted in between two security officers. A middle-aged man with close-cropped hair, dressed in a dark blue prison uniform. His head was bowed. Sitting beside him was a defense lawyer. Sitting at another table was the man Birgitta assumed to be the prosecutor. He was dressed in civilian clothes, a bald, elderly man with a furrowed face. The woman judge entered the courtroom from a door behind the podium. She was in her sixties, small and stout. When she sat down, she looked almost like a child sitting at the table.

"Shu Fu has been the leader of a criminal gang that specializes in stealing cars," said Hong Qiu in a low voice. "The others have already been sentenced. As Shu is the leader of the gang and a recidivist, he'll probably get a stiff sentence. He's been treated mildly in the past, but because he's betrayed the trust put in him and continued his criminal activities, the court is bound to give him a more severe punishment."

"But not the death penalty?"

"Of course not."

Hong Qiu had not liked her last question. The answer sounded impatient, almost dismissive. That wiped the smile off her face, Birgitta thought. But is this a real trial or is the whole thing being staged and the sentence already decided?

The voices were shrill and echoed around the courtroom. The only one who never said a word was the accused, who just sat there, staring down at the floor. Hong Qiu occasionally translated what was being said. The defense lawyer was not making any great effort to support his client—but then that was not unusual in a Swedish court either, Birgitta thought. The whole trial became a dialogue between the prosecutor and the judge. She couldn't work out the function of the two assistants sitting on the podium.

The trial was over in less than half an hour.

"He'll get about ten years' hard labor," said Hong Qiu.

"I didn't hear the judge say anything that sounded like a sentence."

Hong Qiu made no comment. When the judge stood up, everybody else followed suit. The convicted man was led away. Birgitta never managed to catch his eye.

"Now we shall meet the judge," said Hong Qiu. "She has invited us to tea in her office. Her name is Min Ta. When she's not working, she spends her time looking after two grandchildren."

"What's her reputation?"

Hong Qiu didn't understand the question.

"All judges have a reputation, more or less accurate. Seldom very wide of the mark. I'm reputed to be a mild but very firm judge," Birgitta explained.

"Min Ta follows the law. She's proud of being a judge. And so she is also a true representative of our country."

They went through the low door at the back of the dais and were received by Min Ta in her spartan and freezing-cold office. A clerk served tea. They sat down. Min Ta immediately began to talk in the same shrill voice as she had used in the courtroom. When she finished, Hong Qiu translated what she had said.

"It is a great honor to meet a colleague from Sweden. She has heard many positive comments about the Swedish legal system. Unfortunately she has another trial coming up shortly, otherwise she'd have loved to discuss the Swedish legal system with you."

"Please thank her for inviting me," said Birgitta Roslin. "Ask her what she thinks the sentence will be. Were you right in guessing about ten years?"

"I never go into a courtroom without being thoroughly prepared," said Min Ta when she had heard the translation of the question. "It's my duty to use my time and that of the other legal officers efficiently. There was no doubt in this case. The man had confessed; he's a recidivist; there were no extenuating circumstances. I think I'll give him between seven and ten years in prison, but I shall ponder carefully before deciding."

That was the only question Birgitta had the possibility of asking. Then it was Min Ta who fired a whole series of questions for her to answer. Birgitta wondered in passing exactly what Hong Qiu said in her translations. Perhaps she and Min Ta were in fact conducting a conversation about something entirely different?

After twenty minutes Min Ta stood up and explained that she would have to return to the courtroom. A man came in with a camera. Min Ta stood next to Birgitta Roslin, and a photograph was taken. Hong Qiu was standing to one side, out of camera range. The two judges shook hands, and they both went into the corridor together. When Min Ta opened the door Birgitta noticed that the courtroom was now packed.

They returned to the car and drove off at high speed. When they stopped, it was not at the hotel but outside a pagoda-like teahouse on an island in an artificial lake.

"It's cold," said Hong Qiu. "Tea warms you up."

Hong Qiu led her to a room screened off from the rest of the teahouse. Two teacups were waiting on a table, beside which stood a waitress with a teapot in her hand. Everything that happened to Birgitta today was meticulously planned. From having been just another tourist, she had been transformed into an especially important visitor to China. She still didn't know why.

Hong Qiu suddenly started talking about the Swedish legal system. She gave the impression of being very well read. She asked questions about the murders of Olof Palme and Anna Lindh.

"In an open society you can never guarantee a person's safety one hundred percent," said Birgitta Roslin. "You have to pay prices in all kinds of societies. Freedom and safety are always jostling for position."

"If you are really intent on murdering somebody, it can never be prevented," said Hong Qiu. "Not even an American president can be protected."

Birgitta Roslin detected an undertone in what Hong Qiu had said, but was unable to put her finger on it.

"We don't often hear about Sweden," said Hong Qiu. "But just recently news has reached our papers about a horrific mass murder."

"I happen to know a bit about it," said Birgitta Roslin. "Even though I wasn't involved. A suspect was arrested, but he committed suicide. Which is a scandal in itself, no matter how it happened."

As Hong Qiu was displaying polite interest, Birgitta described what had happened in as much detail as she could. Hong Qiu listened attentively, asked no questions, but occasionally asked for something to be repeated.

"A madman," said Birgitta Roslin in conclusion. "Who managed to take his own life. Or another madman the police haven't succeeded in finding yet. Or something completely different, with a motive and a cold-blooded, brutal plan."

"What would that be?"

"As nothing seems to have been stolen it must be a combination of hatred and revenge."

"What do you think?"

"Who should they be looking for, do you mean? I don't know. But I find it hard to accept the theory of a lone madman."

Birgitta elaborated on what she called the Chinese lead. She started from the beginning, when she discovered she was related to some of the dead, and then the astonishing next phase involving the Chinese visitor to Hudiksvall. When she noticed that Hong Qiu really was listening intently, she found it impossible to stop. In the end she took out the photograph and showed it to Hong Qiu.

Hong Qiu nodded slowly. Just for a moment she

seemed lost in her own thoughts. It suddenly occurred to Birgitta that Hong Qiu recognized the face. But that was implausible. One face in a billion?

Hong Qiu smiled, returned the photograph, and asked what Birgitta intended to do for the remainder of her time in Beijing.

"Tomorrow I hope my friend will be able to take me to see the Great Wall of China. Then we'll be flying home the following day."

"I'm afraid I'm busy and won't be able to help you."

"You have already done more than I could ever have asked for."

"In any case, I shall come to bid you farewell before you leave."

They said good-bye outside the hotel. Birgitta Roslin watched the car with Hong Qiu leaving through the hotel gates.

Karin came back at three o'clock and, with a sigh of relief, threw most of the conference material into the wastebasket. When Birgitta suggested a trip to the Great Wall of China the following day, Karin agreed immediately. But first, she wanted to go shopping. Birgitta accompanied her from one store to the next, to semiofficial markets in side streets and dimly lit boutiques filled with all kinds of bargains, from old lamps to wooden sculptures depicting evil demons. Weighed down with parcels and packages, they hailed a taxi as dusk began to fall. Karin was feeling tired, so they ate at the hotel. Birgitta spoke to the concierge and arranged a trip to the Wall for the following day.

Karin was asleep, but Birgitta curled up in a chair and watched Chinese television with the sound turned down. She occasionally felt stabs of fear originating from the previous day's events. But she had made up her mind once and for all to say nothing about it, not even to Karin.

The following day they drove out to the Great Wall of China. There wasn't even a breath of wind, and the dry cold felt less intrusive. They wandered around the Wall, duly impressed, and took pictures of each other or handed the camera to a friendly local who was only too pleased to snap them.

"So, we came here in the end," said Karin. "With a camera in our hands, not Mao's Little Red Book."

"A miracle must have taken place in this country," said Birgitta. "Not brought about by gods but by people with astounding courage."

"In the cities, at least. But poverty is apparently still widespread in the countryside. What will they do when hundreds of millions of peasants finally decide they've had enough?"

" 'The current upswing of the peasants' revolt is of enormous significance.' Perhaps that mantra has a fundamental truth built in, despite everything?"

"Nobody in those days told me that China could be as cold as this. I've almost frozen to death."

They returned to their waiting car. Just as Birgitta was walking down the steps from the wall, she glanced back over her shoulder, for one last look at the Wall.

What she saw instead was one of Hong Qiu's men reading a guidebook. There was no doubt about it. He was the one who had walked up to her table with her purse.

Karin waved impatiently from the car. She was cold, wanted to get going.

When Birgitta turned around again, the man had vanished.

25

That last evening in Beijing, Birgitta Roslin and Karin Wiman stayed in their hotel. They sat around in the bar drinking vodka cocktails, discussing various possible ways of rounding off their visit to China. But the vodka made them so tipsy and tired that they decided to eat in the hotel. Afterward, they spent hours talking about how their lives had turned out. It was as if things had been predetermined by their youthful revolutionary dreams of a Red China. Now they had actually made the trip there and found a country that had undergone fundamental change, but perhaps hadn't turned out as they had once imagined it would. They stayed in the dining room until they were the only ones left. Several blue silk ribbons

hung down from the lampshade over their table. Birgitta leaned over toward Karin and whispered that
perhaps they should each take one of those ribbons as
a souvenir of their trip. Karin used a small pair of nail
scissors to snip off a couple of ribbons when none of
the waiters was watching.

Karin fell asleep when they had finished packing
their bags. The conference had been very tiring. Birgitta sat on the sofa with almost all the lights out. She
suddenly felt old. She'd come this far; there was a bit
still left to go, then the path would suddenly peter
out, and she would be consumed by darkness. She
had already begun to notice that the path was sloping
downward, only slightly; but the bottom line was
that she could do nothing to change its direction.
Think of ten things you still want to achieve, she
whispered to herself. Ten things you still have left to
do. She sat down at the little desk and began writing
in a notebook.

What did she still have left that she really wanted
to experience? One of the things she hoped for was to
see and enjoy a grandchild, perhaps even several.
Also, she and Staffan had often talked about visiting
various islands. The only ones they had been to so far
were Iceland and Crete. One of their dream journeys
was to Galápagos, another to Pitcairn Island, where
the blood from the mutineers on the **Bounty** was still
flowing through the veins of the inhabitants. Learn a
few more languages? Or at least improve her French,
a language she had once spoken quite well.

But the most important thing was for her and Staffan to succeed in reawakening their relationship. She sometimes felt very sad when the thought struck her that they might decline into old age without any of the old passion remaining alive.

No journey was more important than that.

She tore out the sheet of paper, crumpled it up, and tossed it into the wastebasket. Why should she need to write down what was already posted clearly and unmistakably on the church doors of her inner self?

She undressed and snuggled into bed. Karin was breathing calmly in the other bed. She suddenly had the feeling that it was time for her to go home, to be declared fit and start work again. Without her everyday routines she would never be able to fulfill any of the dreams lying in wait for her.

She hesitated for a moment, then reached for her cell phone and sent a text message to her husband. "On the way home. Every journey starts with a step forward. So does the journey home."

Birgitta woke up at seven o'clock. Although she had slept no more than five hours, she felt wide awake. A faint headache reminded her of the vodka cocktails the evening before. Karin was asleep, swaddled in her sheet, one hand hanging down to the floor. Birgitta carefully tucked it in under the sheet.

The breakfast room was already busy, despite the early hour. She looked around to see if she could recognize any of the faces. She had no doubt that the man she had recognized at the Great Wall was one of Hong Qiu's entourage. Perhaps it was just that the Chinese state had taken her under its wing, to ensure that no more accidents would happen?

She ate her breakfast, leafed through an English newspaper, and was just about to return to her room when Hong Qiu suddenly appeared at her table. She was not alone. Alongside her were two men Birgitta had not seen before. Hong Qiu nodded to the men, who withdrew and sat down. She said something to a waitress and shortly afterward was served a glass of water.

"I hope all's well," said Hong Qiu. "How was your trip to the Wall?"

"The Great Wall was impressive. But it was cold."

She looked Hong Qiu provocatively in the eye, hoping to see from her reaction if Hong Qiu realized that the scout had been noticed. But Hong Qiu's face remained expressionless. She did not reveal her cards.

"There's a man waiting for you in a room next to this dining room," said Hong Qiu. "His name's Chan Bing."

"What does he want?"

"He wants to inform you that the police have arrested a man who was involved in the attack when you lost your purse."

Birgitta felt her pulse rate increase. There was something sinister about what Hong Qiu said.

"Why doesn't he come in here if he wants to speak to me?"

"He's in uniform. He doesn't want to disturb your breakfast."

Birgitta Roslin flung her arms out wide in resignation. "I don't have a problem with talking to people in uniform."

She stood up and put her napkin down on the table. At that very moment Karin came into the dining room and looked at them in surprise. Birgitta was forced to explain what had happened, and introduced Hong Qiu.

"I don't really know what's going on," she said to Karin. "The police have evidently caught one of the men who mugged me. Have your breakfast in peace. I'll be back when I've heard what the police officer has to say."

"Why haven't you said anything about this before?"

"I didn't want to worry you."

"You're worrying me now instead. I think I'm getting angry."

"You don't need to."

"We have to leave for the airport at ten o'clock."

"That's two hours away."

Birgitta followed Hong Qiu. The two men were still hovering in the background. They went down the corridor leading to the elevators and stopped outside a door standing ajar. As she stepped inside, Birgitta could see that it was a little conference room. At the far end of the oval table sat an elderly man smoking a cigarette. He was wearing a dark blue uniform with lots of stripes. His cap was lying on the table in front of him. He stood up and bowed to her, gesturing to a chair by his side. Hong Qiu stood by the window in the background.

Chan Bing had bloodshot eyes and thin hair combed back. Birgitta Roslin had the impression that the man sitting next to her was very dangerous. He drew deeply on his cigarette. There were already three butts in the ashtray.

Hong Qiu said something, Chan nodded. Birgitta tried to remember if she had met anybody with more red stars on his epaulets than this man had.

Chan Bing's voice was hoarse when he spoke. "We arrested one of the two men who attacked you. We ask you to point him for us."

Chan Bing's English was hesitant, but he could make himself understood.

"But I didn't see anything."

"Always you see more than you think."

"They were behind me the entire time. I don't have eyes in the back of my head."

Chan's face was expressionless.

"You in fact do. In tense, dangerous situations you see through the back of your head."

"That might be true in China, but not in Sweden. I have never heard of an accused being found guilty because somebody saw him through eyes in the back of their head."

"There are other witnesses. It is not only you who will point out your attacker. Other witnesses will identify him also."

Birgitta looked appealingly at Hong Qiu, who was staring at a spot way above her head.

"I have to fly home," said Birgitta. "My friend and I must leave this hotel two hours from now and go to the airport. I have my purse back. The help I've received from the police in this country has been excellent. I might well write an article for a Swedish legal magazine describing my experiences and the gratitude I owe to China. But I will not be able to identify a possible attacker."

"Our request for your cooperation is not unreasonable. The laws in this country say you have a duty to be at the police's disposal when they are solving a serious crime."

"But I'm about to go home. How long will it take?"

"Unlikely more than a day."

"That's not possible."

Hong Qiu had approached without Birgitta noticing. "We will naturally help you to rebook your tickets," she said.

Birgitta Roslin slammed her hand down on the table. "I am going home today. I refuse to extend my stay by another day."

"Chan Bing is a very high-ranking police officer. What he says goes. He can force you to stay in China."

"Then I demand to speak to my embassy."

"Of course."

Hong Qiu placed a cell phone on the table in front

of Birgitta and a piece of paper with a telephone number. "The embassy will open one hour from now."

"Why should I be forced to go along with this?"

"We don't want to punish an innocent man, but nor do we want a guilty man to go free."

Birgitta Roslin stared at her and realized that she would be forced to stay in Beijing for at least one more day. They had made up their minds to keep her here. The best I can do is to accept the situation, she thought. But nobody is going to force me to identify an attacker I have never seen before.

"I must speak to my friend," she said. "What will happen to my baggage?"

"The room will still be reserved in your name," said Hong Qiu.

"I take it you've already arranged that. When was it decided that I should be forced to stay? Yesterday? The day before? Last night?"

She received no reply. Chan Bing lit another cigarette and said something to Hong Qiu.

"What did he say?" asked Birgitta.

"That we must hurry up. Chan Bing is a busy man."

"Who is he?"

Hong Qiu explained while they were walking along the corridor. "Chan Bing is a very experienced detective. He is responsible for incidents that affect people like you, guests in our country."

"I didn't like him."

"Why not?"

Birgitta Roslin stopped. "If I'm going to stay on for another day, I want you to be with me. Otherwise I'm not going to leave this hotel until the embassy is open and I've spoken to them."

"I'll be there."

They continued to the breakfast room. Karin Wiman was just about to leave her table when they arrived. Birgitta explained what had happened. Karin eyed her even more curiously.

"Why didn't you say anything about this before? Then we'd have been prepared for something like this, that you might have to stay on."

"Like I said, I didn't want to worry you. I didn't want to worry myself either. I thought it was all over. I'd gotten my purse back. But now I'm going to have to stay until tomorrow."

"Is it really necessary?"

"The policeman I just spoke to didn't seem the type to change his mind."

"Do you want me to stay as well?"

"No, you go. I'll follow tomorrow. I'll call home and explain what's happened."

Karin was still hesitant. Birgitta steered her toward the exit.

"Go. I'll stay and sort this business out. Apparently the laws in this country say that I'm not allowed to leave until I've helped them."

"But you said you didn't see whoever it was who attacked you."

"And that's what I'm going to tell them, and stick to it. Go now! When I get home we'll have to get together and look at our pictures of the Wall."

Birgitta watched Karin walk toward the elevators. As Birgitta had taken her coat down to the breakfast room, she was ready to leave right away.

She traveled in the same car as Hong Qiu and Chan Bing. Motorcycles with wailing sirens cleared a way through the dense traffic. They passed through Tiananmen Square and continued along one of the wide central streets until they turned off into the entrance of an underground garage guarded by police officers. They took an elevator up to the fourteenth floor, then walked along a corridor past uniformed men who eyed her curiously. Now it was Chan Bing walking beside her, not Hong Qiu. She is not the most important person in this building, Birgitta thought. Here it's Mr. Chan who calls the shots.

They came to the anteroom of a large office, where police officers jumped to attention. The door closed behind them in what she assumed was Chan's office. A portrait of the country's president hung on the wall behind his desk. She saw that Chan had a modern computer and several cell phones. He pointed to a chair. Birgitta sat down. Hong Qiu had remained in the anteroom.

"Lao San," said Chan Bing. "That's the name of the man you will soon meet and pick out from among nine others."

"How many times do I have to repeat that I didn't see the men who attacked me?"

She suddenly felt afraid. All too late it occurred to her that both Hong Qiu and Chan Bing might know that she was looking for Wang Min Hao. That was why she was here. In some way she had become a danger. The question was: to whom?

They both know, she thought. Hong Qiu is not present because she already knows what Chan Bing is going to talk to me about.

The photograph was still in the inside pocket of her coat. She wondered whether she ought to produce it and explain to Chan Bing why she had gone to the place where she was attacked. But something told her not to. Just now it was Chan Bing playing the cat, and she was the mouse.

Chan shuffled some papers on his desk—not because he was going to read them, she could see that, but to fill in time while he made up his mind what to say.

"How much money was stolen?" he asked.

"Sixty American dollars. And rather less in Chinese money."

"Rings? Jewelry? Credit card?"

"Everything else was returned to me."

There was a buzz from a telephone on his desk. Chan answered, listened, then hung up.

"They're ready," he said. "Now you see the man who attacked you."

"I thought there was more than one?"

"Only one of the men who attacked you can still be interrogated."

So the other man is dead, Birgitta thought, and began to feel sick. She wished she wasn't here in Beijing. She ought to have insisted on going home with Karin Wiman. She had entered some kind of trap.

They went along a corridor, down some steps and through a door. The light was dim. A police officer was standing next to a curtain.

"I'll leave you alone," said Chan Bing. "As you understand, the men can't see you. Speak into microphone on the table if you want somebody to walk forward or turn in profile."

"Who will I be speaking to?"

"You speak to me. Take good time."

"There's no point. I don't know how many times I have to say that I didn't see the faces of my attackers."

Chan Bing didn't reply. The curtain was pulled to one side, and Birgitta Roslin was left alone in the room. On the other side of the one-way mirror was a number of men in their thirties, simply dressed, some extremely thin. Their faces were new to her. She didn't recognize any of them—even if she thought for a brief moment the man on the far left was a bit like the man caught on Sture Hermansson's surveillance camera in Hudiksvall. But it wasn't him. This man's face was rounder, his lips thicker.

Chan Bing's voice came from an invisible speaker. "Take time."

"I have never seen any of these men before."

"Let the impressions mature."

"Even if I stay here until tomorrow, none of my impressions will change."

Chan Bing didn't answer. She pressed the microphone button in annoyance.

"I have never seen any of these men before."

"Are you sure?"

"Yes."

"Now look carefully at this one."

The man standing fourth from the left on the other side of the one-way mirror took a step forward. He was wearing a quilted jacket and patched trousers. His thin face was unshaven.

Chan Bing's voice sounded tense. "Have you seen this man before?"

"Never."

"He's one of the men who attacked you. Lao San, twenty-nine years, previously punished for many crimes. His father was executed for murder."

"I've never seen him before."

"He has confessed to the crime."

"So you don't need me anymore, then?"

A policeman who had been hidden in the shadows behind her stepped forward and closed the curtain. He beckoned her to follow him. They returned to the office where Chan Bing was already waiting. There was no sign of Hong Qiu.

"We want to thank you for your help," said Chan. "Now remains only some formality. A record is being written out."

"A record of what?"

"The confrontation with the criminal."

"What will happen to him?"

"I'm not a judge. What would happen to him in your country?"

"That depends on the circumstances."

"Naturally our law system works the same way. We judge the criminal, his will to confess, and the special circumstances."

"Is there any risk that he will be sentenced to death?"

"Hardly," said Chan drily. "It is Western prejudice that in our country we condemn simple thieves to death. If he had used weapon it would be different."

"But his accomplice is dead?"

"He resisted arrest. The two policemen he attacked are in intense care."

"How do you know that he was guilty?"

"He resisted arrest."

"He might have had other reasons for that."

"The man you recently saw, Lao San, has confessed that it was his accomplice."

"But there is no proof?"

"There is confession."

It was clear to Birgitta that she would never be able to overcome Chan's patience. She decided to do what she was asked to do, then leave China as quickly as possible.

A woman in police uniform came in with a file. She was careful to avoid looking at Birgitta.

Chan Bing read out what was written in the minutes. Birgitta thought he seemed to be in a hurry now. His patience is at an end, she thought. Or something else. He has what he wants, maybe.

In a long-winded document Chan Bing confirmed that Mrs. Birgitta Roslin, Swedish citizen, had been unable to identify Lao San, who was the perpetrator of the serious assault to which she had been subjected.

Chan Bing finished reading and handed the document over to her. It was written in English.

"Sign," said Chan Bing. "Then you can go home."

Birgitta Roslin read both pages carefully before adding her signature. Chan Bing lit a cigarette. He seemed to have forgotten already that she was there.

Hong Qiu entered the room. "We can go now," she said. "It's all over."

Birgitta said nothing on the way back to the hotel.

"I assume there wasn't a suitable flight available for me today?"

"I'm afraid you will have to wait until tomorrow."

There was a note for her at the front desk saying that she had been rebooked with Finnair the following day. She was about to say good-bye when Hong Qiu offered to collect her later for dinner. Birgitta agreed immediately. Being alone in Beijing was the last thing she wanted just now.

She entered the elevator and thought of Karin, on her way home, airborne and invisible high up in the sky.

She called home immediately, but had problems

working out the time difference. When Staffan answered, she could hear that she had woken him up.

"Where are you?"

"Still in Beijing."

"Why?"

"I was delayed."

"What time is it?"

"Here it's one in the afternoon."

"Aren't you on the way to Copenhagen now?"

"I'm sorry if I woke you. I'll be arriving at the same time I was supposed to arrive tomorrow, but a day later."

"Is everything okay?"

"Everything's fine."

The connection was cut off. She tried to call again, but couldn't get through. She sent a text confirming the change in plans.

When she finished, she looked around and had the feeling that somebody had been in her room while she had been detained by the police. Her suitcase was open. Her clothes were not as she had packed them. The night before, she had tried closing the lid to make sure that nothing was catching. She tried closing the lid again now, but it was impossible.

Then she realized—identifying an attacker was nothing more than a means of getting her out of her hotel room. Everything had gone very quickly once Chan Bing had finished reading the minutes to her. He must have been informed that whoever was searching her room had finished.

It's not about my case, she thought. The police are searching my room for other reasons. Just as Hong Qiu suddenly appears at my table out of thin air.

There's only one possible explanation. Somebody wants to know what I'm doing with a photograph of an unknown man outside the skyscraper next to a hospital. Perhaps that man isn't such a mystery after all?

The fear she had felt earlier now hit her with full force. She started searching for cameras and microphones, looking behind pictures, examining lampshades, but she found nothing.

At the agreed time she met Hong Qiu in the lobby. Hong Qiu suggested they go to a famous restaurant, but Birgitta didn't want to leave the hotel.

"I'm tired," she said. "Mr. Chan Bing is a very trying man. All I want to do is to have a quick bite to eat, then go to sleep. I'm going home tomorrow."

The final sentence was intended as a question. Hong Qiu nodded.

"Yes, you're going home tomorrow."

They sat down by one of the tall windows. A pianist was playing on a small stage in the middle of the huge room, which contained both aquariums and fountains.

"I recognize that tune," said Birgitta Roslin. "It's an English song from the Second World War. **We'll meet again, don't know where, don't know when.** Perhaps it's about us?"

"I've always wanted to visit the Nordic countries. Who knows?"

Birgitta drank red wine. It made her tipsy on an empty stomach.

"It's all over now," she said. "I can go home. I've got my purse back and I've seen the Great Wall of China. I've convinced myself that the Chinese peasants' revolt has made enormous strides forward. What has happened in this country is nothing less than a human miracle. When I was young I longed to be one of those marching with Mao's Little Red Book in my hand, surrounded by thousands of other young people. You and I are about the same age. What did you dream of?"

"I was one of the marchers."

"Convinced?"

"We all were. Have you ever seen a circus or a theater full of children? They screech with sheer joy. Not necessarily because of what they are seeing, but because they are together with a thousand other children in a tent or in a theater. No teachers, no parents. They rule the world. If there are enough of you, you can be convinced of anything at all."

"That's not an answer to my question."

"I'm about to answer it now. I was like those children in the tent. But I was also convinced that without Mao Zedong, China would never be able to raise itself out of its poverty. Being a Communist meant fighting against destitution and poverty."

"What happened next?"

"What Mao had constantly warned against. That restlessness and dissatisfaction would always be there.

But the dissatisfaction was caused by various different expectations. Only a fool thinks you can step into the same river twice. Today, I can see clearly how much of the future Mao predicted."

"Are you still a Communist?"

"Yes. So far nothing has convinced me that there is any other way to combat the poverty, still so widespread in our country, than working together with my comrades."

Birgitta gestured with one arm and accidentally knocked her wineglass, spilling a few drops on the tablecloth.

"This hotel. When I wake up and look around, I could be anywhere in the world."

"There's a long way to go yet."

The food was served. The pianist had stopped playing. Birgitta was wrestling with her thoughts. Eventually she put down her knife and fork and looked at Hong Qiu, who stopped eating immediately.

"Tell me the truth now. I'm about to go home. You don't need to play games with me any longer. Who are you? Why have I been kept under surveillance all the time? Who is Chan Bing? Who was that man I was supposed to pick out? I don't believe all that nonsense about it being connected with my purse and a foreigner being the victim of an unfortunate attack."

She had expected Hong Qiu to react in some way, to drop some of the defenses she had been hiding behind all the time, but she was unmoved.

"What else could it be about, apart from the attack?"

"Somebody has searched my room."

"Is anything missing?" Hong Qiu asked.

"No. But I know somebody has been there."

"If you like I can talk to the hotel's head of security."

"I want you to answer my questions. What's going on?"

"Nothing, apart from my wanting our guests to feel secure in our country."

"Am I really supposed to believe that?"

"Yes," said Hong Qiu. "I want you to believe what I say."

Something in her voice led Birgitta Roslin to lose the desire to ask any further questions. She knew she wouldn't get any answers. She would never know if it was Hong Qiu or Chan Bing who had been keeping watch on her all the time. There was an entrance and an exit, and Birgitta was running backward and forward down a corridor between them, with a blindfold over her eyes.

Hong Qiu accompanied her back to her room. Birgitta took hold of Hong Qiu's wrist.

"No more interference? No more muggers? No more people with faces I recognize suddenly turning up?"

"I'll collect you at twelve o'clock."

Birgitta Roslin slept fitfully that night. She got up at the crack of dawn and had a quick breakfast in the dining room. She didn't recognize any of the wait-resses or guests. Before leaving her room she had hung the DO NOT DISTURB notice and sprinkled some bath salts on the mat just inside the door. When she came back she could see that nobody had been in the room.

As agreed, she was collected by Hong Qiu. When they came to the airport, Hong Qiu led her through a special security gate so that she didn't need to stand in line.

They said their good-byes at passport control. Hong Qiu handed over a small parcel.

"A present from China."

"From you or the country?"

"From both of us."

Birgitta wondered if she might have been unfair to Hong Qiu after all. Perhaps she had only been doing her best to help the foreign visitor to forget the mugging.

"Have a good flight," said Hong Qiu. "Maybe we'll meet again one of these days."

Birgitta went through passport control. When she turned around, Hong Qiu had vanished.

Only when she had settled down in her seat and the plane had taken off did she open the parcel. It was a porcelain miniature of a young girl waving Mao's Little Red Book over her head.

Birgitta put it in her purse and closed her eyes. Her relief at being on the way home at last made her feel very tired.

When she arrived in Copenhagen, Staffan was there to meet her. That evening she sat by his side on the sofa and told him stories about the trip. But she said nothing about the mugging.

Karin Wiman called. Birgitta promised to visit her in Copenhagen as soon as possible.

The day after she got back, she went to see her doctor. Her blood pressure had gone down. If it stayed stable, she would be able to return to work in a few more days.

It was snowing lightly when she emerged into the street again. She could hardly wait to go back to work.

The next day she was in her office by seven in the morning and began sorting through the papers that had piled up on her desk, even though she was not officially back at work yet.

Snow was falling more heavily now, a layer growing thicker on her window ledge.

She placed the statuette from Hong Qiu, which had red cheeks and a big victorious smile, next to the telephone. She took the surveillance photograph out of her inside pocket and put it at the bottom of a drawer in her desk.

When she closed the drawer, she had the feeling that it was all over at last.

PART 4

The Colonizers (2006)

In your fight for the total liberation of oppressed peoples, rely first and foremost on their own efforts, and afterwards—and only afterwards—on international aid. The people who have succeeded in their own revolution should assist those who are still fighting for their freedom. That is our international duty.

Mao Zedong, conversation with
African friends, August 8, 1963

Bark Peeled Off by Elephants

26

Some thirty-five miles west of Beijing, not far from the ruins of the Yellow Emperor's palace, were several gray buildings surrounded by high walls. They were sometimes used by the leaders of the Chinese Communist Party. The buildings looked less than imposing from the outside and comprised several large conference rooms, a kitchen, and a restaurant and were surrounded by grounds where the delegates could stretch their legs or conduct intimate private conversations. Only those in the innermost circles of the Communist Party knew that these buildings, which were always referred to as the Yellow Emperor, were used to house the most important discussions about the future of China.

And that is precisely what was happening one winter's day in 2006. Early in the morning a number of black cars drove in at high speed through the gates in the wall, which closed again immediately. A fire was burning in the largest of the conference rooms. Nineteen men and three women were gathered there. Most of them were over sixty, the youngest about thirty-five. Everybody knew everybody else. As a group they formed the elite that in practice governed China, both politically and economically. The president and the commander in chief of the armed forces were absent. But delegates would report back to both when the conference was over and present the proposals they had all agreed upon.

There was only one item on the agenda for today. It had been formulated as a matter of great secrecy, and all those present had been sworn to silence. Anybody who broke that oath need have no doubt that he or she would disappear from public life without a trace.

In one of the private rooms a man in his forties was pacing restlessly. In his hand was the speech he had been working on for months, which he was due to deliver this morning. He knew that it was one of the most important documents ever to be presented to the inner circle of the Communist Party since China had become independent in 1949.

Yan Ba, who worked in futurology at Beijing University, had been given the assignment by the president of China himself two years previously. From that day onward he had been relieved of all his professorial duties and assigned a staff of thirty assistants. The whole project had been shrouded in maximum secrecy and supervised by the president's personal security service. The speech had been written on just one computer, to which only Yan Ba had access. Nobody else had seen the text he was now holding in his hand.

Not a single sound penetrated the walls. According to rumor, the room had once been a bedroom used by Mao Zedong's wife, Jiang Qing; after Mao's death she had been arrested together with three others, the so-called Gang of Four, put on trial, and had later committed suicide in prison. She had demanded absolute silence in whatever room she slept in. Builders and decorators had always traveled in advance to insulate her bedroom, and soldiers had been sent out to kill any dogs that might bark within hearing range of any temporary accommodation she was staying in.

Yan Ba checked his wristwatch. It was ten minutes to nine. He would begin his lecture at precisely a quarter past. At seven o'clock he had taken a pill prescribed by his doctor. It was supposed to make him calm but not drowsy. He could feel that the nervousness really was ebbing away. If what was written on the papers in his hand became reality, there would be earth-shattering consequences throughout the world, not merely in China. But nobody would ever know that he was the person who had devised and formulated the proposals that had been put into practice. He would simply return to his professorship and his students. His salary would increase, and he had already moved into a larger apartment in central Beijing. The pledge of secrecy he had signed would affect him for the rest of his life. Responsibility, criticism, and perhaps also praise for what happened would go to the relevant politicians to whom he, like all other citizens, owed allegiance.

He sat by the window and drank a glass of water. Big changes do not take place on the battlefield, he thought. They happen behind locked doors. Alongside the leaders of the United States and Russia, the president of China is the most powerful man in the world. He must now make some momentous decisions. The people assembled here are his ears. They will listen to what Yan Ba has to say and make their judgments. The outcome will slowly seep out from the Yellow Emperor to the world at large.

Yan Ba was reminded of a journey he had made a few years earlier with a geologist friend. They had traveled to the remote mountainous regions where the source of the Yangtze River is located. They had followed the winding and increasingly narrow stream to a point where it was no more than a trickle of water.

His friend had put down his foot and said: "Now I am stopping the mighty Yangtze in its tracks."

The memory of that incident had dogged him throughout the laborious months during which he had been working on his lecture about the future of China. He was now the person with the power to change the course of the mighty river.

Yan Ba picked up a list of the delegates who had begun to assemble in the conference room. He was familiar with all the names and never ceased to be astonished that they were gathering to listen to him.

This was a group of the most powerful people in China: politicians, a few military men, economists, philosophers, and not least the so-called gray mandarins who devised political strategies that were constantly being measured against reality. There were also a few of the country's leading commentators on foreign affairs and representatives from the security organizations. All were part of an ingenious mix that made up the center of power in China, with its population of more than a billion.

A door opened silently and a waitress dressed in white came in with the cup of tea he had ordered. The girl was very young and very beautiful. Without a word she put down the tray and left the room again.

When the time came at last, he examined his face in the mirror and smiled. He was ready to put down his foot and stop the river in its tracks.

It was completely silent when Yan Ba moved up to the lectern. He adjusted the microphone, arranged his papers, and peered out at his audience, which looked shadowy in the dim light.

He started talking about the future: the reason he was standing there, why the president and the polituro had called on him to explain what major changes were now necessary. He told his audience what the president had said to him when he was given his task.

"We have reached a point where a new and dramatic change of direction is required. If we don't make the change, or if we make the wrong one, there is a serious risk that unrest could break out. Not even our loyal armed forces would be able to stand up to hundreds of millions of furious peasants intent on rebellion."

That was how Yan Ba had seen his task. China was faced with a threat that had to be met by discerning and bold countermeasures. If not, the country could collapse into the same state of chaos it had experienced so many times before in its history.

Hidden behind the men and the few women sitting before him in the semidarkness were hundreds of millions of peasants waiting impatiently for a new life, like the lives the expanding middle classes in urban areas were enjoying. Their patience was running out, developing into boundless fury and demands for immediate action. The time was ripe; the apple would soon fall to the ground and begin to decay if they did not rush to pick it up.

Yan Ba began his lecture by miming a symbolic fork in the road with his hands. "This is where we are now," he said. "Our great revolution has led us here, to a point that our parents could never even have dreamed of. For a brief moment we can pause at this fork in the road and turn around and look back. In the distance is the destitution and suffering we come from. It is recent enough for the generation before ours to remember what it was like, living like rats. The rich landowners and the old public officials regarded the people as soulless vermin, fit for nothing apart from working themselves to death. We both can and should be astonished at how far we have progressed since then, thanks to our great party and the leaders who have led us along the right paths. We know that truth is always changing, that new decisions must constantly be made in order to ensure that the old principles of socialism and solidarity will survive. Life does not stop to wait; new demands are being made of us all the time, and we must seek out the knowledge to enable us to find the solutions to these new problems. We know that we can never attain an everlasting paradise to call our own. If we do believe that, paradise becomes a trap. There is no reality without struggle, no future without battles. We have learned that class differences will always manifest themselves, just as circumstances in the world keep on changing, countries going from strength to weakness and then back to strength. Mao Zedong said that there is constant unease under the skies, and we know that he was right—we are on a ship that requires us to navigate through channels whose depth we can never judge in advance. For even the seafloor is constantly shifting: there are threats to our existence and our future that cannot be seen."

Yan Ba turned a page. He could sense the total concentration in the room. No one moved; everyone waited for what came next. He had planned to talk for five hours. That is what the delegates were expecting. When he told the president his lecture was written, he had been told that no pauses would be allowed. The delegates would have to remain in their seats from start to finish.

"They must see the whole picture," the president had said. "The whole must not be split up. Every pause brings with it a risk that doubts would crop up, cracks in the coherent understanding that what we must do is necessary."

He devoted the next hour to a historic overview of China, which underwent a series of dramatic changes not just during the last century but throughout the many centuries since Emperor Qin first laid the foundation of a united country. It was as if within this Middle Kingdom a long chain of hidden explosive charges had been laid. Only the most outstanding leaders, the ones with the sharpest visionary eyesight, would be able to predict the moments when the explosions would take place. Certain of these men, including Sun Yat-sen and not least Mao, had possessed what the ignorant population regarded as an almost magic ability to interpret their times—and would bring about the explosions that someone else, let us call her the **nemesis divina** of history, had placed along the invisible path that the Chinese nation had to traverse.

Needless to say, Yan Ba spent most of this part of his lecture talking about Mao and his era. Mao founded the first Communist dynasty. Not that the word "dynasty" was used—that would have aroused echoes of the previous rule of terror—but everyone knew that was how the peasants who had spearheaded the revolution regarded Mao. He was an emperor, despite the fact that he allowed ordinary people to enter the Forbidden City and didn't force them to step to one side, at risk of being beheaded if they didn't, when the Great Leader, the Great Helmsman, went past. The time had now come, Yan Ba explained, to turn back once more to Mao and accept with humility that he had been right about how the future would evolve, even though he has been dead for thirty years. His voice was still very much alive; he had the capabilities of a prophet and a scientist to see into the future, to shine his own kind of light into the dark of future decades.

But what had Mao been right about? There was a lot he had gotten wrong. The leader of the first Communist dynasty had not always treated his contemporaries the way he should have. He had been at the forefront when the country had been liberated, and the dream of freedom, the spiritual content of the liberation struggle itself, according to Yan Ba, was about the right of even the poorest peasant to hope for a better future without risking being beheaded by some despicable landowner. Instead, the landowners were now the ones who would be decapitated; it would be their blood that enriched the earth, not that of the poor peasants.

But Mao had been wrong in thinking that China would be able to make enormous economic advances in just a few years. He maintained that one iron foundry should always be sufficiently close to another for the workers to see the smoke from each stack signaling to one another. The Great Leap Forward, which was supposed to project China into both the present and the future, was a huge mistake. Instead of large-scale industrial production, there were people in their backyards melting down old forks and saucepans in primitive furnaces. The Great Leap Forward failed; Chinese workers were unable to jump over the bar because their leaders raised it too high. It was now impossible for anyone to deny, even though Chinese historians had to be sparing with the truth when describing difficult times, that millions of people had starved to death. There was a period of some years when Mao's rule was not unlike earlier imperial dynasties. Mao had locked himself in his rooms in the Forbidden City and never admitted that the Great Leap Forward had been a failure. Nobody was allowed to talk about it. But nobody could know what Mao actually thought. In the writings of the Great Helmsman there was always an area conspicuous by its absence: he concealed his innermost thoughts. No one knows if Mao ever woke up at four in the morning, the bleakest time of day, and wondered just what he had done. Did he lie awake and see the shadows of all the starving, dying people who had been sacrificed at the altar of his impossible dream, the Great Leap Forward?

Instead, Mao counterattacked. Counterattacked what? Yan Ba asked rhetorically, and paused for several seconds before answering. Counterattacked his own defeat, his own failed policies, and the danger that there might be whispering in the shadows, a backstairs coup. Mao's exhortation to "bombard the headquarters"—a new kind of explosive charge, you might say—was his reaction to what he saw around him. Mao mobilized young people, just as everyone does in a state of war. Mao exploited young people the way France, England, and Germany did when they marched them off to the battlefields of the First World War to die with their dreams choked by the slushy mud. There was no need to go on about the Cultural Revolution—that was Mao's second mistake, an almost entirely personal vendetta against the forces in society that challenged him.

By then Mao had started to grow old. The question of his successor was always at the top of his agenda. When the next in line, Lin Biao, turned out to be a traitor and perished in a plane crash on his way to Moscow, Mao began to lose control. But to the very end he continued to issue challenges to those who would outlive him. There would be new class warfare; new groups would try to benefit at the expense of others. Or as Mao repeated as a mantra, "each individual will be replaced by his opposite." Only the stupid, the naïve, anyone who refused to see, would imagine that China's future was assured once and for all.

"Now," said Yan Ba, "Mao—our great leader—has been dead for thirty years. We can see that he was right. But he was unable to identify precisely the conflicts he predicted would come. Nor did he try to do so, because he knew that was impossible. History can never give us exact knowledge of what will happen in the future: rather, it shows us that our ability to prepare ourselves for change is limited."

Yan Ba noticed that the audience was still concentrating hard on every word he said. Now that he had finished his historical introduction, he knew they would be listening even more intently. Many no doubt had a premonition of what was about to come. Yan Ba was aware that he was giving one of the most important speeches in the history of the new China. One day his words would be repeated by the president.

There was a little clock placed discreetly next to the lamp on the lectern. Yan Ba began the second hour of his lecture by describing China's present situation and the changes that were necessary. He described the widening gap between different groups of citizens that was now threatening future developments. It had been necessary to strengthen the coastal areas and the big industrial centers that were at the very heart of economic progress. After Mao's death Deng had decided rightly that there was only one way to go: to emerge from isolation and open Chinese ports to the world. He quoted from Deng's famous speech, which declared that "our doors are now opening and can never again be closed." The future of China could only be fashioned by cooperation with the world around it. Deng's understanding of how capitalism and market forces worked so ingeniously together had convinced him that the moment when the apple could be picked was soon; China could once more and with conviction assume its role as the Middle Kingdom, a great power in the making and, in some thirty or forty years' time, the world's leading nation both politically and economically. During the past twenty years China had developed economically in a way that was without precedent. Deng had once expressed it by saying that the leap forward from every citizen owning a pair of trousers to a situation in which every citizen could choose to acquire a second pair was a leap greater than that first one. Those who understood Deng's way of expressing himself knew that he meant something very basic: not everybody could be in a position to acquire that second pair at the same moment. That hadn't been possible in Mao's time either: the poorest peasants living in the remotest areas in their squalid villages were the last in line, long after the urban dwellers had cast off their old clothes. Deng knew that progress could not take place everywhere simultaneously. That went against all economic laws. Progress was a sort of tightrope walk, attempting to ensure that neither wealth nor poverty grew so fast that the Communist Party and its inner circles, who were the tightrope walkers, fell off and hurtled down into the abyss. Deng was no longer with us, but the moment he had feared and warned us about, the point at which balance was in danger of being lost, was now upon us.

Yan Ba had reached the section of his lecture in which two words would dominate: one was "threat" and the other "necessity." The biggest threat came from the gap in living standards—while those who lived in the coastal cities could see their lot in life improving, the rural peasants found that nothing had changed, and they could barely make a living from their agriculture. The only course open to them was to migrate to urban areas in the hope of finding work. The authorities encouraged this, especially in the industries that made goods for the West, toys and clothes. But what would happen when these industrial cities, these seething building sites, could no longer cope with the influx? How would it be possible to prevent hundreds of millions of people, who had nothing to lose but their poverty, from rebelling? Mao had said it was always right to rebel. So why should it be wrong if those who were just as poor now as they were twenty years ago to rise up in protest?

Yan Ba knew that many of those listening to his lecture had spent a long time thinking about this problem. He also knew that a few copies had been printed of a plan incorporating an extreme solution. Nobody spoke about it, but everybody who was familiar with the Chinese Communist Party's way of thinking knew what it contained. The events that took place in Tiananmen Square in 1989 could be seen as a prologue proving the plan's existence. The party would never allow chaos to break out. If it came to the worst, if no other solution could be found, the army would be called in. No matter how large the confrontation—ten or fifty million people—the party would retain its power over the citizens and the country.

"The question is ultimately very simple," Yan Ba told them. "Is there any other solution?" He provided the answer: yes, but it would require the highest level of strategic thought in order to bring it about. "But, ladies and gentlemen," Yan Ba continued, "these preparations have already begun, even if they appear to be concerned with something quite different."

So far he had only spoken about China, history, and the present. Now, as the third hour approached, he left China and discussed Africa.

"Let us now travel," said Yan Ba, "to an entirely different continent, to Africa. In recent years, in order to secure sufficient supplies of raw materials, not least oil, to meet our needs, we have built up increasingly strong relationships with many African states. We have been generous with loans and gifts, but we do not interfere in the internal politics of these countries. We are neutral; we do business with everybody. As a result, it makes no difference to us if the land we are dealing with is Zimbabwe or Malawi, Sudan or Angola. Just as we reject any kind of foreign interference in our internal affairs and our legal system, we acknowledge that these countries are independent and that we cannot make any demands with regard to the way in which they are run. We are criticized for this approach, but this does not worry us because we know that behind such criticism is envy and fear, as the U.S.A. and Russia begin to realize that China is no longer the colossal nonentity they have imagined us to be for so long. People in the Western world refuse to understand that African nations prefer to cooperate with us. China has never oppressed them, nor colonized them. On the contrary, we supported them when they began to liberate themselves in the 1950s. Our friends in Africa turn to us when the International Monetary Fund or the World Bank rejects their applications for loans. We do not hesitate to help them. We do so with a clear conscience because we are also a poor country. We are still a part of the so-called Third World. As we have worked increasingly successfully with these countries, it has become clear that, in the long run, it may well be there that we find a part of the solution to the threat I talked about earlier this morning. For many of you, and perhaps also for me, my explanation for my thinking will be a historical paradox.

"Let me suggest a parallel to illustrate what it was

like in those countries fifty years ago. At that time Africa was made up almost exclusively of colonies suffering from the oppression of Western imperialism. We stood shoulder to shoulder with these people; we supported their liberation movements by supplying advice and weaponry. Not for nothing was Mao and his generation an example of how a well-organized guerrilla movement could overcome a superior enemy, how a thousand ants biting an elephant's foot could bring it down. Our support contributed to the liberation of one country after another. We have seen how the tail of imperialism began to droop more and more. When our comrade Nelson Mandela was released from prison on the island where he had spent so many years, that was the final blow that defeated Western imperialism in the guise of colonialism. The liberation of Africa tilted the axis of the earth in the direction we believe indicates that freedom and justice will eventually be victorious. Now we can see that large areas of land, often very fertile, are lying in waste. Unlike ours, the Dark Continent is sparsely populated. And we have now realized that it offers us at least part of a solution to the circumstances that threaten our own stability."

Yan Ba took a sip of water from the glass standing next to the microphone. Then he continued talking. He was coming to the point that he knew would lead to animated discussions not only among his listeners, but also within the Communist Party and the polit-buro.

"We must be aware of what we are doing," said Yan Ba, "but we must also be aware of what we are not doing. What we are proposing both to you and the Africans is not another wave of colonization. We are coming not as conquerors, but as friends. We have no intention of repeating the outrages that were insepara-ble from colonialism. We know what oppression means because so many of our forefathers lived in slavelike circumstances in the U.S.A. during the nine-teenth century. We ourselves were subjected to the bar-barity of European colonialism. The fact that on the surface, like reflections of the sun, there may appear to be similarities does not mean that we shall impose colonial regimes on the African continent for the sec-ond time. We shall simply solve a problem at the same time as we provide assistance to these people. In the deserted plains, in the fertile valleys through which the great African rivers flow, we shall farm the land by moving there millions of our peasants, who, with no doubt at all, will begin to farm land lying fallow. We shall not be getting rid of people; we shall simply be filling a vacuum, and everybody will benefit from what comes to pass. There are lands in Africa, especially in the south and southeast, where enormous areas could be populated by the poor people from our own coun-try. We would be making Africa fruitful and at the same time eliminating a threat that faces us. We know that we will meet with opposition, not only in the world at large, where it will be alleged that China has shifted from being a supporter of liberation movements to becoming a colonizer itself. We will also come up against resistance within the Communist Party. The reason I am delivering this lecture is to clarify this opposition. There will be many divergent opinions among the leading lights of our country. You, who are gathered here today, have the good sense and insight to realize that a large part of the threat undermining our stability can be eliminated in the way I have described. New ways of thinking always arouse opposition. Nobody was more aware of that than Mao and Deng. They were brothers in the sense that they were never afraid of new ideas and were always on the lookout for ways to give the poor people of this world a better life, in the name of solidarity."

Yan Ba continued for another hour and forty minutes to spell out what China's policy would be in the near future. When he eventually finished, he was so exhausted that his legs were shaking. But the applause was overwhelming. When silence returned and the lights went up, he checked his watch and found that the clapping had lasted for nineteen minutes. He had completed his task.

He left the podium the same way he had come and hurried to the car that was waiting for him outside one of the entrance doors. On the journey back to the university he tried to imagine the discussions that would follow. Or perhaps the delegates would have to disperse immediately? Each hastening back to his or her own territory to start preparing for the momentous developments in Chinese politics over the next few years?

Yan Ba didn't know, and he felt a certain sense of loss, now that he had vacated the stage. He had done his job. Nobody would ever mention his name when future historians came to examine the revolutionary events that could be traced back to China in 2006. Legend would have it that a significant meeting took place at the Yellow Emperor, but exact details would remain unclear. Those attending the meeting had been given strict instructions—note taking was not allowed.

When Yan Ba got back to his office, he closed the door, fed his speech into the shredder, and then took the trash to the boiler room in the university basement. A janitor opened one of the fire doors. He threw in the shredded paper and watched it transform into ashes.

And that was that. He spent the rest of the day working on an article about the significance of DNA research. He left his office soon after six and headed home. He felt a little flutter of excitement as he approached his new Japanese car, which was part of the remuneration for the lecture he had delivered.

There was a lot of winter still to come. He longed for the spring.

That same evening Ya Ru stood by the window of his large office on the top floor of the skyscraper he owned. He was thinking about the speech he had heard that morning. But what intrigued him most was not the content of the lecture. He had been aware for some time of the strategies being developed in the innermost party circles to counteract the major challenges that were in store. What had surprised him was the presence of his sister Hong Qiu, that she had been invited to take part. Even though she was a highly placed adviser to members of the inner circle of the Communist Party, he had not expected to meet her there.

He didn't like it. He was convinced that Hong Qiu was one of the old-style Communists who were bound to protest at what they would doubtless call a shameful neocolonization of Africa. As he was one of the keenest supporters of the policy, he wasn't looking forward to finding himself pitted against his sister. That could stir up trouble and threaten his position of power. If there was one thing the party leaders and those who governed the country disapproved of, it was conflicts between members of the same family in influential posts. Nobody had forgotten the bitter antagonism between Mao and his wife, Jiang Qing.

San's diary lay open on Ya Ru's desk. He still hadn't filled in the empty white pages. But he knew that Liu Xin had returned from his mission and would soon be face-to-face with him, delivering his report.

A thermometer on the wall indicated that the temperature was falling.

Ya Ru smiled and dismissed thoughts about his sister and the cold weather. Instead he thought about how he would very soon be leaving the cold behind as a member of a delegation of politicians and businessmen, visiting four countries in southern and eastern Africa.

He had never been to Africa before. But now, when the Dark Continent would become increasingly significant for China's development—perhaps even in the long run a Chinese satellite continent—it was important that he be present when fundamental business contacts were established.

The next weeks would be intensive, involving a lot of traveling and a lot of meetings. But he had resolved to leave the delegation for a few days before returning to Beijing. He would venture into the bush and hoped to see a leopard.

Beijing lay before him. One thing he knew about leopards was that they often sought out elevated viewpoints from which they had an overview of the countryside.

This is my hillock, he thought. My cliff top. From my vantage point up here, nothing escapes my notice.

27

In the morning of March 7, 2006, the businessman Shen Weixian had his death sentence confirmed by the People's Supreme Court of Justice in Beijing. He had already been given a suspended death sentence the previous year. Despite the fact that he had spent the past twelve months expressing his regret for accepting bribes worth millions of yuan, the court was unable to change his sentence to life imprisonment. Popular objections to corrupt businessmen with good connections in the Communist Party had increased dramatically. The party had realized that it was now of vital importance to put the fear of death into people who amassed fortunes through bribery.

Shen Weixian was fifty-nine when he had his sentence confirmed. He had worked his way up from simple circumstances to become head of a large chain of abattoirs that specialized in pork products. He had been offered bribes to give preference to various suppliers and quite soon started to accept them. At first, in the early 1990s, he had been cautious and only taken small sums, careful not to adopt a lifestyle that was obviously beyond his apparent means. Toward the end of the 1990s, however, when nearly all his colleagues were accepting bribes, he became increasingly careless, demanding bigger and bigger sums as well as making no attempt to disguise his opulent lifestyle.

He would never have guessed that he would eventually become the scapegoat in order to scare the others. Until his final appearance in the dock he had been sure that his death sentence would be reduced to several years in jail and that he would be released early. When the judge passed the sentence, adding that the execution would be carried out within the next forty-eight hours, he was dumbfounded. Nobody in the courtroom dared look him in the eye. When the police led him away, he started protesting, but it was too late. Nobody listened. He was moved immediately onto death row, where prisoners were kept under round-the-clock observation before being led out, alone or with others, to a field, made to kneel down, their hands bound, and shot in the back of the head.

Under normal circumstances, prisoners sentenced to death for murder, rape, robbery, or similar crimes were taken directly from court to the place of execution. Until the middle of the 1990s Chinese society had demonstrated its positive support for the death penalty by transporting the condemned prisoners on the back of an open truck. Executions would take place in front of a large crowd that would be given an opportunity to make a last-minute decision on whether a prisoner would in fact be shot, or spared. But the crowds that assembled on such occasions were never in the mood to show mercy. In recent years, such events had been arranged more discreetly. No filmmakers or photographers who were not sanctioned by the state were allowed to document the executions. It was only after the sentence had been carried out that the newspapers reported the death. In order to avoid provoking what the political leaders regarded as hypocritical anger abroad, public announcements confirming executions were no longer made. Nobody but the Chinese authorities now knew the exact number carried out. Publicity was only allowed in the case of criminals like Shen Weixian, in order to send warnings to high-ranking officials and businessmen, and at the same time to calm public opinion, which was becoming increasingly critical of a society that made such corruption possible.

News of the confirmation of Shen Weixian's death sentence spread very rapidly in Beijing political circles. Hong Qiu heard about it only a couple of hours after the judgment was made. She had met Shen Weixian briefly some years previously at a reception in the French embassy and had taken an instant dislike to him, suspecting intuitively that he was greedy and corrupt. However, Shen Weixian was a close friend of her brother, Ya Ru. Obviously Ya Ru would distance himself from Shen and deny that they had been more than casual acquaintances, but Hong Qiu knew the truth was different.

Hong Qiu had seen a lot of people die. She had been present at decapitations, hangings, firing-squad executions. Being executed for cheating the state was the most despicable death she could imagine. Who would want to be chucked onto the scrap heap of history with a shot in the back of the head? She shuddered at the thought. But she did not oppose the death penalty. Hong Qiu regarded it as a necessary weapon for the state to use in its defense, and that serious criminals should be deprived of the right to live in a society they had sought to undermine.

Nevertheless, she decided to visit Shen. She knew the governor, and so thought she stood a chance of seeing the prisoner.

The car pulled up at the prison gate. Before opening the car door, Hong Qiu checked the sidewalk through the tinted-glass windows. She saw several people she assumed were journalists or photographers. Then she stepped out of the car and hurried over to the door in the wall next to the tall gate. A warden opened it and let her in.

It was almost half an hour later when she was ushered by a warden deeper into the labyrinthine prison to the warden Ha Nin, whose office was on the top floor. She hadn't seen him for many years and was surprised to see how much he had aged.

"Ha Nin," she said, stretching out both arms. "It's been so many years!"

He took her hands and squeezed them hard.

"Hong Qiu. I can see one or two gray hairs on

your head, just as you can on mine. Do you remember the last time we met?"

"When Deng gave his speech on the necessity of rationalizing our industries."

"Time passes quickly."

"It passes more quickly the older you are. I think death is approaching at great speed, so quickly that we perhaps won't be able to realize what is happening."

"Like a grenade with the pin pulled? Death will explode in our faces?"

She withdrew her hands. "Like the flight of a bullet from the barrel of a rifle. I've come to speak to you about Shen Weixian."

Ha Nin did not seem surprised. They sat down at a battered table. Ha Nin lit a cigarette. Hong Qiu came straight to the point. She wanted to see Shen, say good-bye, find out if there was anything she could do for him.

"It's very strange," said Ha Nin. "Shen knows your brother. He has begged Ya Ru to try and save his life. But Ya refuses to talk to Shen and says that the death sentence is correct. Then you appear, Ya's sister."

"A man who deserves to die doesn't necessarily deserve to have nobody do him a final favor or listen to his last words."

"I have received permission to let you visit him. If he wants you to."

"Does he?"

"I don't know. At this moment the prison doctor is in his cell, talking to him."

Hong Qiu nodded, then turned away from Ha Nin as a signal that she didn't want to discuss the matter further.

It was another half hour before Ha Nin was called out to his anteroom. When he came back, Hong Qiu was informed that Shen was prepared to receive her.

Shen was in the farthest cell, at the very end of the corridor. He normally had thick black hair, but it had been shaved off. He was wearing a blue prison uniform, the pants too big, the jacket too small. Ha Nin stepped back and instructed one of the guards to unlock the door. When Hong Qiu stepped inside, she could feel that the tiny room was steeped in angst and terror. Shen grasped her hand and sank down on his knees.

"I don't want to die," he whispered.

She helped him to sit down on the bed, where there was a mattress and a blanket. She pulled up a stool and sat down opposite him.

"You must be strong," she said. "That's what people will remember. The fact that you died with dignity. You owe that to your family. But nobody can save you. Neither I nor anybody else."

Shen stared wide-eyed at her. "I only did what everybody else was doing."

"Not everybody. But a lot of people. You must accept responsibility for what you did, and not degrade yourself further by lying."

"Why am I the one who has to die?"

"It could have been somebody else. But you were

the one. In the end everybody who is incorrigible will come to a similar end."

Shen looked at his trembling fingers and shook his head.

"Nobody wants to talk to me. It's as if I'm not only going to die, but I'm completely alone in the world. Not even my family wants to come here and talk to me. I'm dead already."

"Ya Ru hasn't come either."

"I don't understand what you mean."

"It's really his fault that I'm here."

"I have no desire to help him."

"You misunderstand me. Ya Ru doesn't need any help. He's keeping his head down and denying that he ever had anything to do with you. Part of your fate is that everybody speaks ill of you. Ya Ru is no exception."

"Is that really true?"

"I'm telling you the facts. There is just one thing I can do for you. I can help you to get revenge if you tell me about how you worked together with Ya Ru."

"But he's your brother."

"The family bonds were cut through long ago. Ya Ru is dangerous for our country. Chinese society was built on the basis of individual honesty. Socialism cannot work and develop unless citizens are honest and behave decently. The likes of you and Ya Ru corrupt not only themselves, but the whole of society."

At last Shen understood the point of Hong Qiu's visit. It seemed to give him renewed strength and for the moment counteracted the fear that had taken possession of him. Hong Qiu knew that at any moment Shen would relapse and become so paralyzed by the fear of death that he would no longer be able to answer her questions. And so she harried him, put him under pressure, as if he were once again undergoing a police interrogation.

"You are locked up in a cell, waiting to die. Ya Ru is sitting in his office in the skyscraper he calls the Dragon's Mountain. Is that fair?"

"He could easily have been sitting here instead of me."

"Rumors about him abound. But Ya Ru is clever. Nobody can trace his footprints after he has passed by."

Shen leaned toward her and lowered his voice. "Follow the money."

"Where will that lead?"

"To the people who loaned him large sums so that he could build his castle. Where else could he have got all the millions he needed?"

"From his business investments."

"In broken-down factories that make plastic ducks for Western children to play with in the bath? In backstreet sweatshops where they make shoes and T-shirts? He wouldn't even be able to earn money like that from his brick kilns."

Hong Qiu frowned. "Does Ya Ru have interests in factories making bricks? We have just heard that people are working there as slaves, burned as a punishment for not working hard enough."

"Ya Ru was warned of what was about to happen. He offloaded all his commitments before the big police raids took place. That's his strength. He's always tipped off in advance. He has spies everywhere."

Shen suddenly clutched at his stomach, as if he were in acute pain. Hong Qiu could see the anguish in his face and just for a moment was close to feeling sympathy for him. He was only fifty-nine years old, had made a brilliant career for himself, and was now about to lose everything: his money, his comfortable life, the oasis he had built for his family in the midst of all the poverty. When Shen was arrested and charged, the newspapers had been full of shocking but also voluptuous details about how his two daughters used to fly regularly to Tokyo or Los Angeles to buy clothes. Hong Qiu could still recall a headline that had doubtless been thought up by the security services and the Ministry of the Interior: "They buy clothes with the savings of pig farmers." That headline had cropped up over and over again. Letters to the editor had been published—no doubt written by the newspaper itself and checked by high-ranking civil servants with political responsibility for the outcome of Shen's trial. The letters had suggested that Shen's body be butchered and fed to the pigs. The only just way of punishing Shen was to turn him into pig swill.

"I can't save you," said Hong Qiu again. "But I can give you an opportunity to bring others down alongside you. I was given permission to speak to you for thirty minutes. That time is nearly up. You said that I should follow the money?"

"He's sometimes called Golden Hands."

"What does that mean?"

"Can it mean more than one thing? He is the golden intermediary. He makes black money white; he shifts money out of China; he puts money in accounts without the tax authorities having the slightest idea about what's going on. He charges fifteen percent on all the transactions he carries out. Not the least of his activities is laundering the money floating around in Beijing: the houses and arenas and other things that are currently being built for the Olympic Games two years from now."

"Is it possible to prove any of this?"

"You need two hands," said Shen slowly. "One hand takes. But there has to be another hand that's prepared to give. How often are they sentenced to death? The other hand, the one prepared to pay money in order to secure an advantage? Hardly ever. Why is one a bigger crook than the other? That's why you should track down the sources of the money. Start with Chang and Lu, the building contractors. They are scared, and they'll talk to protect themselves. They have the most amazing stories to tell."

Shen fell silent. Hong Qiu thought about the struggle taking place behind the newspaper headlines between those who wanted to preserve the old residential district in central Beijing and those hoping to see it demolished to make way for the Olympic Games. She belonged to those who passionately defended the old residential area and had often angrily dismissed the accusation that she did so for sentimental reasons. By all means construct new buildings and renovate old ones, but short-term interests such as the Olympic Games should not be allowed to dictate the city's appearance.

Hong Qiu could see that the questions she had been asking had managed to make Shen almost completely forget the execution that would soon be his fate. He started talking again.

"Ya Ru is a vindictive person. They say that he never forgets an injustice to which he thinks he's been subjected, no matter how minor it might have been. He also told me that he regards his family as a unique dynasty whose memory must be preserved at all costs. You had better look out and make sure he doesn't regard you as a defector, betraying the family's honor." Shen looked hard at Hong Qiu. "He will kill anybody who crosses him. I know that. Especially people who mock him. He has men he can always call upon when necessary. They crawl out from under stones and disappear again just as quickly. I heard recently that he sent one of his men to the U.S.A. Rumor has it that there were dead bodies lying around when the man returned to Beijing. They say he's been to Europe as well."

"The U.S.A.? Europe?"

"That's what rumor suggests."

"And does rumor tell the truth?"

"Rumor always tells the truth. When lies and exaggerations have been filtered out, there is always a kernel of truth left behind. That's what you need to look for."

"How do you know all this?"

"Power not based on knowledge and a constant flow of information will eventually become impossible to defend."

"That didn't help you."

Shen didn't reply. Hong Qiu thought about what he had said. It had surprised her.

She also thought about what the Swedish judge had said. Hong Qiu had recognized the man in the photograph Birgitta Roslin had shown her. Even if it was blurred, there was no doubt that it was Liu Xin, her brother's bodyguard. Was there a connection between what Birgitta Roslin had told her and what Shen had just said? Could that be possible?

The warden reappeared in the corridor. Her time was up. Shen's face suddenly turned white and he grabbed hold of her arm.

"Don't leave me," he said. "I don't want to be alone when I die."

Hong Qiu released herself from his hands. Shen started screaming. It was as if Hong Qiu was faced with a terrified child. The warden threw him down on the floor. Hong Qiu left the cell and hurried away as quickly as possible. Shen's desperate cries followed her. They echoed in her ears until she was back in Ha

Nin's office. That was when she made up her mind. She would not leave Shen alone in his final moments.

Shortly before seven the next morning Hong Qiu turned up at the cordoned-off field used for executions. According to what she had heard, it was the place where the military trained before going on the attack in Tiananmen Square more than a decade earlier. But now there were nine people to be executed. Alongside crying and freezing-cold relatives, Hong Qiu took up her position behind a barrier. Young soldiers with rifles in their hands were keeping watch. Hong Qiu observed the young man closest to her. He could hardly be more than nineteen years old.

She couldn't imagine what he must be thinking. He was about the same age as her own son.

A covered truck rumbled onto the field. The nine condemned prisoners were taken down from the back by impatient soldiers. Hong Qiu had always been surprised by how fast everything went on such occasions. There was no dignity in dying in this cold, wet field. She saw Shen fall over when he was pushed down from the back of the truck—he made no sound, but she could see tears rolling down his cheeks. One of the women was screaming. One of the soldiers barked an order at her, but she carried on screaming until an officer stepped forward and hit her hard in the face with a pistol butt. She fell silent and was dragged to her place in the row. All were forced to kneel down. Soldiers with rifles stood behind each of the prisoners. The gun barrels were barely a foot away from the backs of their heads. Then it all happened in a flash. An officer gave an order, shots were fired, and the prisoners fell forward with their faces buried in the wet mud. When the officer walked along the row and gave each of them the coup de grâce, Hong Qiu looked away. Now she didn't need to see any more. The next of kin of the dead would be billed for the cost of the two bullets. They would have to pay for the death of their relatives.

Over the next few days she thought about what Shen had told her. His words about Ya Ru's vindictiveness echoed around her head. She knew that in the past he hadn't hesitated to resort to violence. Brutally, almost sadistically. She sometimes thought her brother was a psychopath at heart. Thanks to Shen, who was now dead, she might get some insight into who he really was, this brother of hers.

Now the time was ripe. She would talk to one of the prosecutors who devoted themselves exclusively to accusations of corruption.

She didn't hesitate. Shen had spoken the truth.

Three days later, late in the evening, Hong Qiu arrived at a military airfield outside Beijing. Two of Air China's biggest passenger jets were standing there, bathed in light, waiting for the delegation of nearly four hundred people who were going to visit Zimbabwe.

Hong Qiu's role was to conduct discussions about closer cooperation between the Zimbabwean and Chinese security services—the Chinese would pass on knowledge and techniques to their African colleagues.

As a privileged passenger, she was allocated a place at the front end of the aircraft, where the seats were bigger and more comfortable. Hong Qiu fell asleep soon after the meal was served and the lights had been dimmed.

She was woken up by somebody sitting down on the empty seat beside her. When she opened her eyes, she found herself looking into Ya Ru's smiling face.

"Surprised, my dear sister? You couldn't find my name on the list of participants for the simple reason that not everybody on board is included on it. I knew you would be here, of course."

"I should have known you wouldn't let an opportunity like this slip through your fingers."

"Africa is a part of the world. Now that the Western powers are increasingly deserting the continent, it's time for China to step out of the wings, of course. I am anticipating huge successes for our fatherland."

"I see China drifting farther and farther away from its ideals."

Ya Ru raised his hands defensively. "Not now, not in the middle of the night. Way down below us the world is fast asleep. Perhaps we are flying over Vietnam at this very moment, or perhaps we've gone farther than that. But let's not argue. Let's get some sleep. The questions you want to ask me can wait. Or perhaps I should call them complaints?"

Ya Ru stood up and walked off down the aisle to the staircase leading up to the upper deck, which was directly behind the nose of the aircraft.

She closed her eyes again. It won't be possible to avoid this, she thought. The moment is approaching when the huge gap between us can no longer be concealed, nor should it be. Just as the enormous split running straight through the Communist Party cannot and should not be concealed. Our private feud mirrors the battle the country faces.

She eventually succeeded in falling asleep. She would never be able to do battle with her brother without a good night's sleep.

Over her head Ya Ru was sitting wide awake with a drink in his hand. He had realized in all seriousness that he hated his sister Hong Qiu. He would have to get rid of her. She no longer belonged to the family he worshipped. She interfered in too many things that were none of her business. Only the day before they left he had heard through his contacts that Hong Qiu had paid a visit to one of the prosecutors leading the investigation into corruption. He had no doubt that he had been the topic of discussion.

Moreover, his friend, the high-ranking police officer Chan Bing, had told him that Hong Qiu had been displaying an interest in a Swedish female judge who had been visiting Beijing. Ya Ru would talk to Chan Bing when he got back from Africa. He told himself that she would lose this battle before it had even begun in earnest.

Ya Ru was surprised to find that he didn't even hesitate. But now nothing would be allowed to stand in his way. Not even his dear sister, currently below him in the same airplane.

Ya Ru made himself comfortable on a chair that could be converted into a bed. Soon he was also asleep.

Underneath him was the Indian Ocean and in the distance the coast of Africa, still veiled in darkness.

28

Hong Qiu was sitting on the veranda outside the bungalow she would be staying in during the visit to Zimbabwe. The cold winter of Beijing seemed far away, replaced by the warm African night. She listened to the sounds emanating from the darkness, especially the high-pitched sawing of the cicadas. Despite the warmth of the evening she was wearing a long-sleeved blouse, as she had been warned of the profusion of mosquitoes carrying malaria. What she would most have liked to do was strip naked, move the bed out onto the veranda, and sleep directly under the night sky. She had never before experienced such heat as overwhelmed her when she stepped off the airplane into the African dawn. It was a liberation. The cold restrains us with handcuffs, she thought. Heat is the key that liberates us.

Her bungalow was surrounded by trees and bushes in an artificial village made for prominent guests of the Zimbabwean government. It had been built during Ian Smith's time, when the white minority proclaimed unilateral independence from England in order to retain a racist white regime in the former colony, then called Rhodesia. At that time there was only a large guesthouse with an accompanying restaurant and swimming pool. Ian Smith often used it as a weekend retreat where he and his ministers could discuss the major problems faced by the increasingly isolated state. After 1980, when the white regime had collapsed, the country had been liberated, and Robert Mugabe was in power, the area had been extended to include several bungalows, a network of country walks, and a long veranda with views of the Logo River, where you could watch herds of elephants come to the riverbank at sundown to drink.

Hong Qiu could just make out a guard patrolling the path that meandered through the trees. Never before had she experienced darkness as compact as this African night. Anybody could be hiding out there—a beast of prey, be it with two legs or four.

The idea that her brother could be watching, waiting, gave her pause. As she sat in the darkness, she felt for the first time an all-consuming fear of him. It was as if she had only now realized that he was capable of doing anything to satisfy his greed for power, for increased wealth, for revenge.

She shuddered at the thought. When an insect bumped into her face, she gave a start. A glass standing on the bamboo table fell onto the stone paving and smashed. The cicadas fell silent for a moment before beginning to play once more.

Hong Qiu moved her chair in order to avoid the risk of standing on the glass shards. On the table was her schedule. This first day had been spent watching and listening to an endless march of soldiers and military bands. Then the big delegation had been conveyed in a caravan of cars, escorted by motorcycles, to a lunch at which ministers had delivered long speeches and proposed toasts. According to the program, President Mugabe should have been present, but he never showed up. When the lengthy lunch was over, they had at last been able to move into their bungalows. The camp was a few dozen miles outside Harare, to the southwest. Through the car windows Hong Qiu could see the barren countryside and the gray villages, and it struck her that poverty always looks the same, no matter where you come across it. The rich can always express their opulence by varying their lives. Different houses, clothes, cars. Or thoughts, dreams. But for the poor there is nothing but compulsory grayness, the only form of expression available to poverty.

In the late afternoon there had been a meeting to plan the work to be done over the coming days, but Hong Qiu preferred to stay in her room and go through the material herself. Then she had gone for a long walk down to the river and watched the elephants moving slowly through the bush and the heads of the hippos popping out above the surface of the water. She had been almost alone down there, her only companions a chemist from Beijing University and one of the radical market economists who had trained during Deng's time. She knew that the economist, whose name she had forgotten, was in close contact with Ya Ru. At first she wondered if her brother had sent a scout to keep an eye on her activities. But Hong Qiu dismissed the idea as a figment of her imagination—Ya Ru was more cunning than that.

Was the discussion she wanted to have with her brother going to be feasible? Was it not the case that the split dividing the Chinese Communist Party had already passed the point where it was possible to bridge the gap? It was not a matter of straightforward and solvable differences about which particular political strategy was most appropriate. It concerned fundamental disagreements, old ideals versus new ones that could only superficially be regarded as communist, based on the tradition that had created the republic fifty-seven years previously.

If men like her brother were allowed to call the shots, the final fixed bastions of Chinese society would be demolished. A wave of capitalist-inspired irresponsibility would sweep away all the remnants of institutions and ideals built up on the basis of solidarity. For Hong Qiu it was an undeniable truth that human beings were basically reasonable creatures, that solidarity was common sense and not primarily an emotion, and that, in spite of all setbacks, the world was progressing toward a point where reason would hold sway. But she was also convinced that nothing was certain in itself, that nothing in human society happened automatically. There were no natural laws to account for human behavior.

Mao again. It was as if his face were beaming out there in the darkness. He knew what would happen, she thought. The future is never assured, once and for all. He repeated that wisdom, over and over again, but we didn't listen. New groups would always emerge and seize privileges for themselves, new revolutions would constantly take place.

She sat on the veranda and let her thoughts come and go. Dozed off. She was woken by a noise. She listened. There it was again. Somebody was knocking on her door. She checked her watch. Midnight. Who would want to visit her this late? She wondered whether she should open the door. There was another knock. Somebody knows that I'm awake, she thought; somebody has seen me on the veranda. She went inside and peered through the peephole. An

African was standing outside. He was wearing the hotel uniform. Curiosity got the better of her and she opened the door. The young man handed over a letter. She could see from her name on the envelope that it was Ya Ru's handwriting. She gave the boy a few Zimbabwe dollars, unsure if it was too much or too little, and went back to the veranda. She read the short message.

> **Hong Qiu,**
> **We ought to keep the peace, for the sake of the family, of the nation. I apologize for the rudeness of which I am sometimes guilty. Let us look one another in the eye again. During the last few days before we return home, please let me invite you to accompany me into the bush, to see the primitive nature, and animals. We can talk there.**
> **Ya Ru.**

She checked the text carefully, as if she expected to find a hidden message between the lines. She found none, nor could she fathom why he had sent her this message in the middle of the night.

She gazed out into the darkness and thought about the predators who have their prey in their sight, without the victims having the slightest idea of what is about to happen.

"I can see you," she whispered. "No matter where you come from, I shall discover you in time. Never again will you be able to sit down beside me without my having seen you coming."

Hong Qiu woke up early the next morning. She had slept fitfully, dreaming about shadows creeping up on her, menacing, faceless. Now she was on the veranda, watching the brief African dawn, the sun rising over the endless bush. A colorful kingfisher with its long beak landed on the veranda rail, then flew off immediately. The dew from the damp night glittered in the grass. From somewhere in the distance came African voices, somebody shouting, laughing. She was surrounded by strong aromas. She thought about the letter that had reached her in the middle of the night and urged herself to be alert. She somehow felt even more wary of Ya Ru in this foreign country.

At eight o'clock a specially selected group of delegates, headed by a trade minister and the mayors of Shanghai and Beijing, had gathered in a conference room off the hotel foyer. Mugabe's face looked down from several walls with a smile that Hong Qiu couldn't quite place: Was it friendly or scornful? In a loud voice the trade minister's state secretary called the assembly to attention.

"We shall now meet President Mugabe. The president will receive us in his palace. We shall enter in a single file, the usual distance between ministers and mayors and other delegates. We shall greet one another, listen to our national anthems, then sit down at a table in assigned seats. President Mugabe and our ministers will exchange greetings via interpreters, after which President Mugabe will deliver a short speech. We have not been given an advance copy. It could be anything from twenty minutes to three hours. Advance visits to the restrooms are strongly advised. The speech will be followed by a question-and-answer session. Those of you who have been given prepared questions will raise your hands, introduce yourselves when called to speak, and remain standing while President Mugabe answers. No follow-up questions are allowed, nor is anybody else in the delegation permitted to speak. After the meeting with the president, most of the delegation will visit a copper mine called Wandlana while the minister and selected delegates will continue their discussion with President Mugabe and an unknown number of his ministers."

Hong Qiu looked at Ya Ru, who was leaning with half-closed eyes against a column at the back of the conference room. It was only when they left the room that they established eye contact. Ya Ru smiled at her before clambering into one of the cars intended for ministers, mayors, and specially selected delegates. Hong Qiu sat down in one of the buses waiting outside the hotel.

Her apprehension was growing all the time. I must speak to somebody, she thought, somebody who will understand my fear. She looked around the bus. She had known many of the older delegates for a long time. Most of them shared her view of political developments in China. But they are tired, she thought. They are now so old that they no longer react when danger threatens.

She continued searching, but in vain. There was nobody there she felt she could confide in. After the meeting with President Mugabe she would work once more through the whole list of participants. Surely there must be someone whom she could trust.

The bus headed for Harare at high speed. Through the window Hong Qiu could see the red soil stirred up by the people walking by the side of the road.

The bus suddenly stopped. A man sitting on the other side of the aisle explained to her.

"We can't all arrive at the same time," he said. "The cars with the most important people must arrive first. Then we will arrive, the political and economic ballet to make up the pretty background."

Hong Qiu smiled. She had forgotten the name of the man who had spoken, but she knew that during the Cultural Revolution he had been a hard-pressed professor of physics. When he returned from his many privations in the country, he had immediately been put in charge of what was to become China's space research institute. Hong Qiu suspected that he shared her views about the direction China ought to be taking. He was one of the old school still managing to keep going, not one of the youngsters who have never understood what it means to live a life in which something is more important than they are.

They had stopped close to a little marketplace running along both sides of the road. Hong Qiu knew that Zimbabwe was close to economic collapse. That was one of the reasons that their large delegation was visiting the country. Although this would never be made public, it was in fact President Mugabe who had begged the Chinese government to make a contribution toward helping Zimbabwe out of the country's severe economic depression. The sanctions imposed by the West meant that the basic infrastructure of the country was close to collapse. Only a few days before leaving Beijing, Hong Qiu had read in a newspaper that inflation in Zimbabwe was now approaching five thousand percent. People tramping along by the edge of the road were moving very slowly. It seemed to Hong Qiu that they were either hungry or tired.

Hong Qiu suddenly noticed a woman kneeling down. She had a child in a carrier on her back and a head ring made from folded cloth for supporting heavy loads. Two men by her side helped each other to lift up a heavy sack of cement and balance it on her head. Then they helped her to stand up. Hong Qiu watched her stagger away. Without a second thought she stood up, hurried down the aisle, and spoke to the interpreter.

"Please come with me."

The interpreter, who was a young woman, opened her mouth to protest, but Hong Qiu prevented her from speaking. The driver had opened the front door to allow a flow of air into the bus, which had already started to become stuffy, as the air-conditioning wasn't working. Hong Qiu dragged along the interpreter to the other side of the road, where the two men had settled down in the shade and were sharing a cigarette. The woman with the heavy burden on her head had already disappeared into the haze.

"Find out how much the sack they put on the woman's head weighs."

"About fifty kilos," the interpreter informed her after asking.

"But that's a horrific burden. Her back will be ruined before she's thirty."

The men merely laughed.

"We're proud of our women. They're very strong."

Hong Qiu could see in their eyes that they didn't understand what the problem was. Women here suffer the same difficulties that our poor Chinese peasants have to put up with, she thought. Women always carry heavy burdens on their heads, but even worse are the burdens they have to bear inside their heads.

She returned to the bus with the interpreter. Shortly afterward they set off—now they had an escort of motorcycles. Hong Qiu let the wind from the open window blow into her face.

She would not forget the woman with the sack of cement on her head.

The meeting with President Robert Mugabe lasted four hours. When he came into the room, he looked more like a friendly schoolmaster than anything else. When he shook hands with her, he was looking beyond her, a man in another world who just brushed against her in passing. After the meeting he would have no memory of her. She knew that this little man, who radiated strength despite being both old and frail, was described by some as a bloodthirsty tyrant who tormented his own people by destroying their homes and chasing them off their land whenever it suited him. But others regarded him as a hero who never gave up the fight against the remnants of colonial power he stubbornly insisted lay behind all of Zimbabwe's problems.

What did she think herself? She knew too little about the politics to be able to form a definite opinion, but Robert Mugabe was a man who in many ways deserved her admiration and respect. Even if not everything he did was good, he was basically convinced that the roots of colonialism grew very deep and needed to be cut away not just once but many times. Not least of the reasons she respected him was she had read how he was constantly and brutally attacked in the Western media. Hong Qiu had lived long enough to know that loud protests from landowners and their newspapers were often intended to drown the cries of pain coming from those who were still suffering from torture inflicted by colonialism.

Zimbabwe and Robert Mugabe were under siege. The West's indignation had been extreme when, a few years previously, Mugabe had forcibly annexed land owned by the white farmers who still dominated the country and made hundreds of thousands of Zimbabweans landless. The hatred of Mugabe increased for every white farmer who, in open confrontation with the landless blacks, was injured by rocks or bullets.

But Hong Qiu knew that as early as 1980, when Zimbabwe, then called Rhodesia, was liberated from Ian Smith's fascist regime, Mugabe had offered the white farmers open discussions aimed at finding a peaceful solution to the vital question of landownership. His overtures had been greeted by silence on that first occasion and then many more times over the following fifteen years. Over and over again Mugabe had repeated his offer of negotiations but had received no response, only contemptuous silence. His patience had finally run out, and large numbers of farms were handed over to the landless. This was immediately condemned by the West, and protests flowed in from all sides.

At that moment the image of Mugabe was changed from that of a freedom fighter to that of the classical African tyrant. He was depicted just as anti-Semites used to depict the Jews, and this man who had spearheaded the liberation of his country was ruthlessly defamed. Nobody mentioned that the former leaders of the Ian Smith regime, not least Smith himself, had been allowed to remain in Zimbabwe. Mugabe did not send them into the law courts and then to the gallows as the British used to do with rebellious black men in the colonies. But a refractory white man was not the same as a refractory black man.

She listened to Mugabe's speech. He spoke slowly, his voice was mild, he never raised it even when talking about the sanctions that led to an increase in the infant mortality rate, widespread starvation, and more and more illegal immigration to South Africa alongside millions of others. Mugabe spoke about the opposition in Zimbabwe. "There have been incidents," Mugabe admitted. "But the foreign media never reports the attacks on those loyal to me and the party. We are always the ones who throw stones or make baton charges, but the others never throw firebombs, never maim or beat up their opponents."

Mugabe spoke for a long time, but he spoke well. Hong Qiu reminded herself that this man was more than eighty years old. Like so many other African leaders he had spent a long time in jail during the drawn-out years when the colonial powers still believed they would be able to face down attacks on their supremacy. She knew that Zimbabwe was a corrupt country. It still had a long way to go. But it was too simple to place all the blame on Mugabe. The truth was more complicated.

She could see Ya Ru sitting at the other end of the table, closer to both the minister of trade and the lectern where Mugabe was speaking. He was doodling in his notepad. He used to do that even as a child, drawing matchstick men while he thought or listened, usually small devils jumping around, surrounded by burning bonfires. Nevertheless, Hong Qiu thought, he is most probably listening more intently than anybody else. He is sucking in every word to see what advantages he can gain in future business between the two countries, which is the real reason for our visit. What raw materials does Zimbabwe have that we need? How will we be able to get access to them at the cheapest price?

When the meeting was over and President Mugabe had left the big conference room, Ya Ru and Hong Qiu met each other by the doors. Her brother had been standing there, waiting for her. They each took a plate and filled it from the buffet table. Ya Ru drank wine, but Hong Qiu was content with a glass of water.

"Why do you send me letters in the middle of the night?"

"I had the irresistible feeling that it was important. I couldn't wait."

"The man who knocked on my door knew that I was awake. How could he know that?"

Ya Ru raised an eyebrow in surprise.

"There are different ways of knocking on a door, depending on whether the person behind it is awake or asleep."

Ya Ru nodded. "My sister is very cunning."

"And don't forget that I can see in the dark. I sat out on my veranda for a long time last night. Faces light up in the moonlight."

"But there wasn't any moonlight last night?"

"The stars produce a light that I'm able to intensify. Starlight can become moonlight."

Ya Ru eyed her thoughtfully. "Are you challenging me to a trial of strength? Is that what you're up to?"

"Isn't that what you're doing?"

"We must talk. In peace and quiet. Revolutionary things are taking place out here. We have closed in on Africa with a large but friendly armada. Now we are involved in the landings."

"Today I watched two men lift a sack containing over a hundred pounds of cement onto a woman's head. My question to you is very simple. Why have we come here with an armada? Do we want to help that woman to alleviate her burden? Or do we want to join those lifting sacks onto her head?"

"An important question that I'd be happy to discuss. But not now. The president is waiting."

"Not for me."

"Spend your evening on your veranda. If I haven't knocked on your door by midnight, you can go to bed."

Ya Ru put down his glass and left her with a smile. Hong Qiu noticed that the brief conversation had made her sweat. A voice announced that Hong Qiu's bus would be leaving in thirty minutes. Hong Qiu filled her plate once more with tiny sandwiches. When she felt she had eaten enough, she made her way to the back of the palace, where the bus was waiting. It was very hot, the sun reflecting off the white stone walls of the palace. She put on her sunglasses and a white hat she had brought in her purse. She was about to enter the bus when somebody spoke to her. She turned around.

"Ma Li? What are you doing here?"

"I came as a substitute for old Zu. He's been struck down with thrombosis and couldn't make it. I was called in to replace him. That's why I'm not on the list of participants."

"I didn't notice you on the way here this morning."

"Somebody pointed out to me rather sternly that I'd sat myself in one of the cars, which protocol forbade me to do. Now I'm where I ought to be."

Hong Qiu reached out and grasped hold of Ma Li's wrists. She was exactly what Hong Qiu had been hoping for. Somebody she could talk to. Ma Li had been a friend ever since her student days, after the Cultural Revolution. Hong Qiu recalled an occasion early one morning, in one of the university's dayrooms, when she had found Ma Li asleep on a chair. When she woke up, they started talking.

It seemed to be preordained that they should be friends. Hong Qiu could still remember one of the first conversations they'd had. Ma Li had said that it was now time to stop "bombarding headquarters." That had been one of the things Mao had urged the cultural revolutionaries to do. Not even the very top officials in the Communist Party should be spared the necessary criticism. Ma Li maintained that, instead, it was now necessary for her to "bombard the vacuum inside my head, all the lack of knowledge that I have to fight against."

Ma Li trained to become an economic analyst and was employed by the Ministry of Trade as one of a group of experts whose job it was to keep a constant check on currency variations throughout the world. Hong Qiu had become an adviser to the minister responsible for homeland security, for coordinating the top military leaders' views on the country's internal and external defense, especially protection for the political leaders. Hong Qiu had been at Ma Li's wedding, but after the birth of Ma Li's two children their meetings had been irregular.

But now they had met once again, on a bus behind Robert Mugabe's palace. They spoke nonstop during the journey back to the camp. Hong Qiu noticed that Ma Li was at least as pleased as she was at their reunion. When they reached the hotel, they decided to take a walk to the big veranda with the magnificent views over the river. Neither of them had any important engagements until the following day, when Ma Li was due to visit an experimental farm and Hong Qiu was supposed to attend a discussion with a group of Zimbabwean military leaders at Victoria Falls.

The heat was oppressive as they walked down to the river. They could see flashes of lightning in the distance and hear faint rumbles of thunder. There was no sign of animal life. It seemed that the whole place had suddenly been deserted. When Ma Li took hold of Hong Qiu's arm, she gave a start.

"Did you see that?" asked Ma Li, pointing.

Hong Qiu looked but couldn't see any sign of movement in the thick bushes that lined the riverbank.

"Behind that tree where the bark has been peeled off by elephants, next to the rock sticking up out of the ground like a spear."

Now Hong Qiu saw it. The lion's tail was swinging slowly, whipping against the red earth. Its eyes and mane were occasionally visible through the leaves.

"You've got very good eyes," said Hong Qiu.

"I've learned to notice things. Otherwise your surroundings can be dangerous. Even in a city, or a conference room, there can be traps to stumble into, if you're not careful."

In silence, almost reverentially, they watched the lion venture down to the river and begin lapping up the water. Out in the middle of the river, a few hippos' heads bobbed up and down. A kingfisher just as colorful as the one on Hong Qiu's veranda alighted on the rail, with a dragonfly in its beak.

"Peace and quiet," said Ma Li. "I long for it more and more, the older I become. Perhaps it's the first sign of getting old? Nobody wants to die surrounded by the noise from machines and radios. The progress we make costs us a lot in the way of silence. Can a person really live without the kind of quiet we are experiencing right now?"

"You're right," said Hong Qiu. "But what about the invisible threats to our lives? What do we do about them?"

"I suppose you are thinking about pollution? Poisons? Plagues that are constantly mutating and changing their appearance?"

"According to the World Health Organization, Beijing is currently the dirtiest city in the world. Recent measurements recorded up to one hundred forty-two micrograms of dirt particles per cubic meter of air. The equivalent figure in New York is twenty-seven, in Paris twenty-two. As we know only too well, the devil is always in the details."

"Just think of all the people who discover that for the first time in their lives it's possible for them to buy a moped. How can you persuade them not to?"

"By strengthening the party's control over developments. What is produced by goods, and what is produced by thoughts."

Ma Li stroked Hong Qiu's cheek gently.

"I'm so pleased every time I realize that I'm not alone. I'm not ashamed to maintain that **baoxian yundong** is what can rescue our country from disintegration and decay."

"A campaign to preserve the Communist Party's right to lead," said Hong Qiu. "I agree with you. But at the same time we both know that the danger threatens to come from within. Once upon a time it was Mao's wife who was the mole for the new upper class, despite the fact that she waved her red flag more ardently than anybody else. Today there are others hiding within the party who want nothing more than to undermine it and replace the stability we enjoy with a sort of capitalist freedom that nobody will be able to control."

"The stability has been lost already," said Ma Li. "As I'm an analyst who knows the way in which money flows in our country, I know much that neither you nor anybody else is aware of. But, of course, I'm not allowed to say anything."

"We are alone. The lion isn't listening."

Ma Li eyed her up and down. Hong Qiu knew exactly what she was thinking—can I trust her or can't I?

"Don't say anything if you are in doubt," said Hong Qiu. "If you make the wrong choice when it comes to people you can rely on, you are both defenseless and helpless. That is insight we were given by Confucius."

"I trust you," said Ma Li. "Nevertheless, you can't get away from the fact that one's natural instincts for self-preservation always encourage caution."

Hong Qiu pointed to the riverbank.

"The lion has gone now. We didn't notice when he left."

Ma Li nodded.

"This year the government has increased military expenditure by almost fifteen percent," Hong Qiu continued. "In view of the fact that China doesn't have any real enemies close at hand, naturally enough the Pentagon and the Kremlin wonder what is going on. Their analysts can see without too much of an effort that the state and the armed forces are preparing to cope with an inner rebellion. In addition we are spending almost ten billion yuan on our Internet surveillance systems. These are figures impossible to conceal. But there's another statistic that very few people know about. How many riots and mass protests do you think took place in our country during the past year?"

Ma Li thought for a moment before answering. "Five thousand, perhaps?"

Hong Qiu shook her head. "Nearly ninety thousand. Work out how many that is every day. It's a figure that casts a shadow over everything the politburo undertakes. What Deng did fifteen years ago, when he liberalized the economy, was enough to tamp down most of the unrest in the country. But not anymore, it isn't. Especially when the cities are no longer able to find space and work for the hundreds of millions of peasants who are waiting impatiently for their turn to enjoy the good life we all dream about."

"What will happen?"

"I don't know. Nobody knows. It makes sense to be worried and on the alert. There's a power struggle going on in the party that's more serious than it ever was in Mao's day. Nobody can foresee what the outcome will be. The military is afraid of chaos that can't be brought under control. You and I know that the only thing we can do, the one thing we have to do, is restore the basic principles that used to apply."

"Baoxian yundong."

"The only way. Our only way. It's not possible to take a shortcut to the future."

A herd of elephants was making its way slowly down toward the river to drink. When a party of Western tourists came onto the veranda, the pair returned to the hotel foyer. Hong Qiu had intended to suggest that they eat together, but Ma Li forestalled her by saying that she had an engagement that evening.

"We're going to be here for two weeks," said Ma Li. "We'll have plenty of time to talk about everything that's happened."

"Everything that's happened and is going to happen," said Hong Qiu. "All the things we don't yet have an answer to."

Hong Qiu watched Ma Li walk off on the other side of the big swimming pool. I'll talk to her tomorrow, she thought. Just when I badly needed to talk to somebody, one of my oldest friends turned up out of the blue.

She dined alone that evening. A large party from the Chinese delegation had gathered around two long tables, but Hong Qiu preferred to be on her own.

Moths danced around the lamp over her head.

When she had finished eating, she sat for a while at the bar by the swimming pool and drank a cup of tea. Some of the Chinese delegation got drunk and tried to make advances on the beautiful young waitresses moving from table to table. Hong Qiu was annoyed and left. In another China that would never have been allowed, she thought angrily. The security guards would have intervened by now. Anybody who got drunk and started throwing his weight around would never again have been allowed to represent China. They might even have been imprisoned. But these days, nobody pays any attention.

She sat down on her veranda and thought about the arrogance that followed in the wake of the licentious belief that a less regulated capitalist market system would be good for the country's development. It had been Deng's aim to make the Chinese wheels roll more quickly. But today the situation was different. We live with the risk of overheating, not only in our industries but also in our own brains, she thought. We don't see the price we're paying, in the form of polluted rivers, air that suffocates us, and millions of people desperate to flee from the rural areas.

Once, we came to the country that used to be called Rhodesia to support a liberation struggle. Now, almost thirty years after liberation was achieved, we come back as poorly disguised colonizers. My own brother is one of those selling out all our old ideals. He has none of the honest belief in the power and prosperity of the people that once liberated our own country.

She closed her eyes and listened to the sounds of the night. All thoughts of Ma Li and their conversation slowly ebbed away from her weary head.

She had almost fallen asleep when she heard a noise that pierced the song of the cicadas. It was a twig snapping.

She opened her eyes and sat up straight. The cicadas were silent. She knew that there was somebody in the vicinity.

She ran into her bungalow and locked the glass door. She switched off the light.

Her heart was pounding. She was scared.

Somebody was out there in the darkness. He had inadvertently stepped on a twig and snapped it under his foot.

She threw herself onto the bed, afraid that someone would force his way in.

But nobody emerged from the darkness. After waiting for almost an hour, she closed the curtains, sat down at the desk, and wrote a letter that had been formulating itself in her head during the course of the day.

29

It took Hong Qiu several hours to write her summary of what had happened recently, with her brother and the strange information from the Swedish judge, Birgitta Roslin, as the starting point. She did it to protect herself. She established once and for all that her brother was corrupt and one of the people well on the way to taking over China. In addition, he and his bodyguard Liu Xin might be involved in several brutal murders far outside the country's borders. She didn't switch on the air-conditioning so that she would be better able to hear any sounds from outside. The night insects were buzzing around the lamp in the stiflingly hot room, and heavy drops of sweat kept dripping onto the desk. She had every reason to feel worried. She had lived long enough to be able to distinguish between real and imagined dangers.

Ya Ru was her brother, but above all else he was a man who didn't hesitate to use any means in order to attain his goals. She was not opposed to development heading off in new directions. Just as the world around them was changing, so must China's leaders think up new strategies to solve present and future problems. What Hong Qiu and many others of like mind questioned was that leaders were not combining socialistic foundations with development toward an economy in which free markets played a major role. Was the alternative impossible? A powerful country like China didn't need to sell its soul in the hunt for oil and raw materials and new markets in which to place its industrial products. Was not the big challenge to demonstrate to the world that brutal imperialism and colonialism were not an inevitable consequence when one's country developed?

Hong Qiu had seen greed take possession of young people who, by means of contacts, relatives, and not least ruthlessness, had managed to create huge fortunes. They felt untouchable, and that made them even more brutal and cynical. She wanted to offer resistance to them and to Ya Ru. The future was not a foregone conclusion; everything was still possible.

When she had finished writing, read through the letter, and made some corrections and clarifications, she sealed the envelope, wrote Ma Li's name on it, then lay down on top of the bed to sleep. There was no sound from the darkness outside. Although she was very tired, it was some time before she fell asleep.

She got up at seven o'clock and watched the sunrise from her veranda. Ma Li was already in the breakfast room when she arrived. Hong Qiu joined her, ordered tea from the waitress, and looked around the room. Members of the Chinese delegation were sitting at most of the tables. Ma Li announced that she intended to go down to the river to watch the animals.

"Come to my room an hour from now," said Hong Qiu in a low voice. "I'm in number twenty-two."

Ma Li nodded and asked no questions. Just like me, she's lived a life that has taught us that secrets are a constant presence, Hong Qiu thought.

She finished her breakfast, then retired to her room to wait for Ma Li. The trip to the experimental farm wasn't scheduled until half past nine.

After exactly an hour Ma Li knocked on her door. Hong Qiu gave her the letter she'd written during the night.

"If anything happens to me," she said, "this letter will be important. If I die in my bed of old age, you can burn it."

Ma Li looked hard at her. "Should I be worried about you?"

"No. But the letter's important even so. For the sake of others. And for our country."

Hong Qiu could see that Ma Li was surprised. But she asked no more questions, merely put the letter in her purse.

"What's on the agenda today for you?" Ma Li wondered.

"A discussion with members of Mugabe's security service. We're going to assist them."

"Weapons?"

"Partly. But first and foremost helping to train their staff, teach them close combat, and also the art of keeping watch on people."

"Something we're expert at."

"Do I detect hidden criticism in what you just said?"

"Of course not," said Ma Li in surprise.

"You know I've always maintained the importance of our country protecting itself from the enemy within just as much as from the one without. Many countries in the West would like nothing better than to see Zimbabwe collapse into bloody chaos. England has never accepted totally that the country liberated itself in 1980. Mugabe is surrounded by enemies. It would be stupid of him not to demand that his security service should operate at the very top end of its ability."

"And he's not stupid, I suppose?"

"Robert Mugabe is bright enough to realize that he must resist all attempts from the former colonial power to kick the legs from beneath the ruling party. If Zimbabwe falls, there are many other countries that could go down the same road."

Hong Qiu accompanied Ma Li to the door and watched her disappear along the paved path meandering through the luxuriant greenery.

Right next to Hong Qiu's bungalow was a jacaranda tree. She gazed at its light blue blossoms, and tried to think of something to compare the color with, but in vain. She picked up a flower that had fallen to the ground. She placed it between the pages of her diary in order to press and preserve it. She took her diary with her wherever she went, but seldom got around to writing in it.

She was just about to settle down on the veranda and study a report on the political opposition in Zimbabwe when there was a knock on the door. Standing outside was one of the Chinese tour guides, a middle-aged man by the name of Shu Fu. Hong Qiu had noticed earlier he seemed scared stiff that something would go wrong with the arrangements. He seemed to be highly unsuitable as a guide on a big venture like this one, especially because his English was far from satisfactory.

"Hong Qiu," said Shu Fu. "There's been a change of plan. The minister of trade wants to visit a neighboring country, Mozambique, and he wants you to be one of the party that accompanies him."

"Why?"

Hong Qiu's surprise was genuine. She had never been in close contact with the minister of trade, Ke, and indeed had barely done more than shake hands with him before leaving for Harare.

"The trade minister has just asked me to inform you that you will be traveling with him. There will be a small delegation."

"When shall we be leaving? And where to?"

Shu Fu wiped the sweat from his brow, then flung out his arms. He pointed to his watch. "I am unable to tell you any more details. The cars will be leaving for the airport in forty-five minutes. No delay will be tolerated. Everyone involved is requested to take light baggage only and to be prepared for an overnight stay. But it's possible that you will return as soon as this evening."

"Where are we going? What's the point?"

"Minister of Trade Ke will explain that."

"But surely you can tell me the name of the town we're headed for?"

"To the city of Beira on the Indian Ocean. According to the information I have, the flight will be less than an hour."

Hong Qiu had no opportunity to ask any more questions. Shu Fu hurried back to the path.

Hong Qiu stood motionless in the doorway. There is only one explanation, she thought. Ya Ru wants me to be there. He is obviously one of those going with Ke. And he wants me there as well.

She remembered something she had heard during the flight to Africa. President Kaunda of Zambia had demanded that the national airline Zambia Airways should invest in one of the world's biggest passenger jets at that time, a Boeing 747. There was no market to justify such a large aircraft flying regularly between Lusaka and London. But it soon transpired that President Kaunda's real aim was to use the 747 on his regular journeys to and from other countries. Not because he wanted to travel in luxury but to have enough space for the opposition, or those in his government and among the top military leaders that he didn't trust. He crammed his aircraft full of those who were prepared to plot against him or even to engineer a coup d'état while he was out of the country.

Was Ya Ru trying something similar? Did he want to have his sister close by so that he could keep tabs on her?

Hong Qiu thought about the twig that had snapped in the darkness outside her bungalow. It could hardly have been Ya Ru standing out there in the shadows. More likely somebody he had sent to spy on her.

As Hong Qiu didn't want to oppose Ke, she packed the smaller of her two suitcases and prepared for the journey. A few minutes before departure she went to the front desk. There was no sign of either Ke or Ya Ru. On the other hand, she thought she had caught sight of Ya Ru's bodyguard Liu Xin, though she wasn't sure. Shu Fu escorted her to one of the waiting limousines. Also in her car were two men she knew worked in the Ministry of Agriculture in Beijing.

The airport was only a few miles outside Harare. The three cars in the convoy drove very fast with a motorcycle escort. Hong Qiu noticed that there were police officers at every street corner, holding up other traffic. They drove straight in through the airport gates and without further ado boarded a waiting Zimbabwe air force jet. Hong Qiu boarded through the rear entrance and noted that there was a screen separating the front half of the cabin. She assumed that this was Mugabe's private airplane, which he had lent the Chinese delegation. After only a few minutes of waiting, the plane took off. Sitting next to Hong Qiu was one of Ke's female secretaries.

"Where are we going?" Hong Qiu asked when they had reached cruising altitude and the pilot announced the journey would be fifty minutes.

"To the Zambezi Valley," said the woman by her side.

Her tone made it obvious to Hong Qiu that there was no point in asking any more questions. She would eventually find out what was involved in this sudden trip.

Or was it really so sudden? It occurred to her that not even this was something she could be sure of. Perhaps it was all part of a plan that she knew nothing about?

When the aircraft prepared for descent, it swung out over the sea. Hong Qiu could see the blue-green water glittering down below and little fishing boats with simple triangular sails bobbing up and down on the waves. Beira was glistening white in the sunlight. Encircling the concrete center of the city were endless shantytowns, possibly slums.

The heat hit her as she stepped out of the airplane. She saw Ke walking toward the first of the waiting cars, which was not a black limousine but a white Land Cruiser with Mozambican flags on the hood. She watched Ya Ru get into the same car. He didn't turn around to look for her. But he knows I'm here, Hong Qiu thought.

They headed northwest. Together with Hong Qiu in the car were the same two men from the Ministry of Agriculture. They were poring over small topographic maps, carefully checking them against the countryside they could see through the car windows. Hong Qiu still felt as uncomfortable as she had when Shu Fu first appeared outside her door and announced a change of plan. It was as if she had been forced into something that her experience and intuition warned her about, all alarm bells ringing. Ya Ru wants to have me here, she thought. But what arguments did he present to Ke that resulted in my sitting and bumping along in a Japanese car whipping up thick clouds of red soil? In China the soil is yellow; here it's red, but it blows around just as easily and gets into your eyes and every pore.

The only plausible reason for her being present on this visit was that she was one of many in the Communist Party who were skeptical about current policies, not least those of Ke. But was she here as a hostage, or in the hope of seeing her change her mind about the policies she found so distasteful? High-ranking Ministry of Agriculture officials and a minister of trade on an uncomfortable car ride in the heart of Mozambique had to mean that the aim of the journey was of major significance.

The countryside flashing past outside the car windows was monotonous—low trees and bushes, occasionally intersected by small rivers and streams, and here and there clumps of huts and small well-tended fields. Hong Qiu was surprised that such fruitful ground was so sparsely populated. In her imagination the African continent was like China or India, a part of the poverty-stricken Third World where endless masses of people fell over one another in their efforts to survive. But what I've always imagined is a myth, she thought. The big African cities are not much different from what we see in Shanghai or Beijing. The culmination of catastrophic development that impoverishes both people and nature. But I knew nothing at all about African rural areas until now as I actually see them and travel through them.

They continued in a northwesterly direction. In some places the roads were so bad that the cars had to slow to a walking pace. The rain had penetrated the hard-packed red earth, loosened up the road surface, and turned it into deep ruts.

They eventually came to place called Sachombe. It was an extensive village with huts, a few shops, and some semiderelict concrete buildings from the colonial period when the Portuguese administrators and their local **assimilados** had ruled over the country's various provinces. Hong Qiu recalled reading about how Portugal's dictator Salazar had described the gigantic landmasses of Angola, Mozambique, and Guinea-Bissau, which he ruled with an iron fist. In his linguistic world these distant countries were called "Portugal's overseas territories." That was where he had sent all his poor, often illiterate, peasants, partly to solve a domestic problem and at the same time to build up a colonial power structure concentrated on the coastal areas even as late as the 1950s. Are we about to do something similar? Hong Qiu wondered. We are repeating the injustice, but we have dressed ourselves in different costumes.

When they left their cars and wiped the dust and sweat from their faces, Hong Qiu discovered that the whole area was cordoned off by military vehicles and armed soldiers. Behind the barriers she could see curious natives observing the strange foreign guests. The poor are always there, she thought—the ones whose interests we say we are looking after.

Two large tents had been erected on the flat stretch of sand in front of the white buildings. Even before the convoy came to a halt a large number of black limousines had assembled, and there were also two helicopters from the Mozambique air force. I don't know what's in store, Hong Qiu thought, but whatever it is, it's something important. What can have made Minister of Trade Ke suddenly agree to visit a country that isn't even on our program? A small part of the delegation was due to spend a day in Malawi and Tanzania, but there was no mention of Mozambique.

A brass band came marching up. At the same time a number of men emerged from one of the tents. Hong Qiu immediately recognized the short man leading the way. He had gray hair, wore glasses, and was powerfully built. The man who was now greeting Minister of Trade Ke was none other than Mozambique's newly elected president Guebuza. Ke introduced his delegation to the president and his attendants. When Hong Qiu shook his hand, she found herself looking into a pair of friendly yet piercing eyes. Guebuza is no doubt a man who never forgets a face, she thought. After the introductions, the band played the two national anthems. Hong Qiu stood stiffly at attention.

As she listened to the Mozambique national anthem she looked around for Ya Ru but could see no sign of him. She hadn't seen him since they arrived in Sachombe. She continued scrutinizing the group of Chinese present and established that several others had vanished after the landing in Beira. She shook her head. There was no point in her worrying about what Ya Ru was up to. More important just now was that she should try to understand what was about to happen here, in the valley through which the Zambezi River flowed.

They were led into one of the tents by young black men and women. A group of older women danced alongside them to the persistent rhythm of drums. Hong Qiu was placed in the back row. The floor of the tent was covered in carpets, and every member of the delegation had a soft armchair. When everybody was comfortably seated, President Guebuza walked up to the lectern. Hong Qiu put on her earphones. The Portuguese was translated into perfect Chinese. Hong Qiu guessed that the interpreter came from the leading school in Beijing that exclusively trained interpreters to accompany the president, the government, and the most important business delegations in their negotiations. Hong Qiu had once heard that there wasn't a single language, no matter how small and insignificant, that didn't have qualified interpreters in China. That made her proud. There was no limit to what her fellow citizens could achieve—the people who, until a generation ago, had been condemned to ignorance and misery.

Hong Qiu turned to look at the entrance to the tent, which was flapping gently in the breeze. She caught a glimpse of Shu Fu standing outside, a few soldiers, but no sign of Ya Ru.

The president spoke very briefly. He welcomed the Chinese delegation and said a few introductory words. Hong Qiu listened intently in order to understand what was going on around her.

She gave a start when she felt a hand on her shoulder. Ya Ru had slipped into the tent unnoticed and was kneeling behind her. He slid aside one of her earphones and whispered into her ear.

"Listen carefully now, my dear sister, and you will understand something of the major events that are going to change our country and our world. This is what the future will look like."

"Where have you been?"

She blushed when she realized how idiotic the question must sound. It felt like when he was a child and was late coming home. Hong Qiu had often taken on the role of Mom when their parents were away at one of their frequent political meetings.

"I go my own way. But I want you to listen now and learn something. About how old ideals are exchanged for new ones, without losing their content."

Ya Ru placed the earphone back over her ear and hurried out through the door of the tent. She caught sight of his bodyguard Liu Xin and wondered once again if it really was he who had killed all those people Birgitta Roslin had spoken about. She made up her mind that as soon as she got back to Beijing she would speak to one of her friends in the police force. Liu Xin never did anything without having been ordered to do so by Ya Ru. She would confront Ya Ru eventually, but first she must find out more about what actually happened.

The president handed the podium over to the chairman of the committee that had made the preparations for this meeting on the Mozambique side. He was strikingly young, with a bald head and frameless glasses. Hong Qiu thought they said his name was Mapito, or possibly Mapiro. He spoke enthusiastically, as if what he was saying really inspired him.

And Hong Qiu understood. The circumstances slowly became clear, what the meeting was all about, the secrecy surrounding it. Deep in the Mozambique bush a gigantic project was getting under way, involving two of the poorest countries in the world—but one of them a great power, the other a small country in Africa. Hong Qiu listened to what was being said, the soft Chinese voice translating after each pause, and she understood why Ya Ru had wanted her to be present. Hong Qiu was a vigorous opponent of everything that could lead to China being transformed into an imperial power—and hence, as Mao used to say, a paper tiger that would be crushed sooner or later by united popular resistance. Perhaps Ya Ru had a faint hope that Hong Qiu would be convinced that what was now going on would bring advantages to both countries? But more important was that the group Hong Qiu belonged to did not frighten those in power. Neither Ke nor Ya Ru were scared of Hong Qiu and those who shared her views.

When Mapito paused to take a sip of water, Hong Qiu thought that this was precisely what she feared most of all: China had reverted to a class society. Even worse than what Mao had warned against, it would become a country divided between powerful elites and an underclass locked into its poverty. And worse still, it would allow itself to treat the rest of the world as imperialists always had done.

Mapito continued speaking.

"Later today we shall travel by helicopter along the Zambezi River, as far up as Bandar, and then downstream to Luabo, where the huge delta linking the river to the sea begins. We shall fly over fertile areas that are sparsely populated. According to the calculations we have made, over the next five years we will be able to accommodate four million Chinese peasants who can farm the areas currently lying fallow. Not one single person will be obliged to move. Nobody will lose his livelihood. On the contrary, our fellow citizens will benefit from big changes. Everybody will have access to roads, schools, hospitals, electricity, all the things that have previously been available to very few in rural areas and a privilege for those living in towns."

Hong Qiu had already heard rumors about Chinese authorities, working on the enforced removal of peasants because of the construction of huge dams, promising those affected that one day they would be able to live the life of landed gentry in Africa. She could see the large-scale migration in her mind's eye. The fine-sounding words conjured up an idyllic image of the poor Chinese peasants—illiterate and ignorant—immediately settling down in this alien milieu. There would be no problems, thanks to the friendship and will to cooperate; no conflicts would arise between the newcomers and those already living on the banks of the river. But nobody would be able to convince her that what she was now listening to was not the first stage of China's transformation into a predatory nation that would not hesitate to grab for itself all the oil and other raw materials needed to maintain the breakneck speed of its economic development. The Soviet Union had supplied weapons—often old, outdated ones—during the drawn-out liberation war that led to the withdrawal of the Portuguese colonizers from Mozambique in 1974. In return the Soviets had asserted the right to overfish in Mozambique's teeming fishing grounds. Was China now about to follow in this tradition based on the one and only commandment: always put your own advantage before everything else?

So as not to draw attention to herself, she applauded with everybody else when the speaker sat down. Then Minister of Trade Ke began to address the delegation. There were no dangers, he assured his audience: everything and everyone was uncompromisingly conjoined in equal and mutual advantage.

Ke's speech was brief. Then the guests were ushered into the other tent, where a buffet table had been prepared. Hong Qiu was handed an ice-cold glass of wine. She looked around for Ya Ru, but could see no trace of him.

An hour later the helicopters took off and headed northwest. Hong Qiu gazed down on the mighty river. The few places where people lived, where the land had been cleared and cultivated, were in sharp contrast to the huge areas that were totally untouched. Hong Qiu wondered if she had been wrong after all. Perhaps China really was doing something to help Mozambique that wasn't based on the expectation that China would put in far, far less than what it would take out?

The sound of the engines made it impossible for her to marshal her thoughts. The question remained unanswered.

Before climbing into the helicopter she had been handed a little map. She recognized it. The two men from the Ministry of Agriculture had been studying it during the car journey from Beira.

They reached the most-northerly point, then turned eastward. When they reached Luabo, the helicopters made a short diversion over the sea before returning and landing at a place Hong Qiu identified, with the aid of the map, as Chinde. There new cars were waiting to take them along new roads made from the same tightly packed red earth that was everywhere.

They drove straight into the bush and stopped when they came to a small tributary of the Zambezi. The cars pulled up to a lot that had been cleared of bushes and undergrowth. Some tents had been pitched in a semicircle facing the river. When Hong Qiu left the car, Ya Ru was waiting to greet her.

"Welcome to Kaya Kwanga. That means 'My Home' in one of the local languages. We'll be spending the night here."

He pointed to the tent closest to the river. A young black woman took her suitcase.

"What are we doing here?" Hong Qiu asked.

"Enjoying the silence of Africa after a long day's work."

"Is this where I'm going to see the leopard?"

"No. Most of the wildlife here is snakes and lizards. Plus the hunter ants that everybody is so scared of. But no leopards."

"What happens now?"

"Nothing. The work is over and done with. You'll discover that not everything is as primitive as it seems. There's even a shower in your tent. And a comfortable bed. Later this evening we'll have a communal meal. Anyone who wants to sit around the campfire afterward is welcome to do so; those who want to sleep can do that, too."

"You and I must talk things through," said Hong Qiu. "It's essential."

Ya Ru smiled. "After dinner. We can sit outside my tent."

He didn't need to point out which one it was. Hong Qiu had already gathered that it was the one next to hers.

Hong Qiu sat by the door of her tent and watched the sun setting rapidly over the bush. A fire was already burning in the open area in the middle of the semicircle of tents. She could see Ya Ru there. He was wearing a white tuxedo. It reminded her of a picture she had seen long ago in a Chinese magazine in connection with a major article describing the colonial history of Africa and Asia. Two white men wearing tuxedos had been sitting deep in the African bush, eating at a table with a white tablecloth, using expensive crockery, and drinking chilled white wine. The African waiters were standing motionless, but at the ready, behind their chairs.

Hong Qiu was the last of all those present to take her place at the set table by the fire.

She thought about the letter she had written the previous evening. And about Ma Li—and suddenly she was not even sure that she could still rely upon her.

Nothing, she thought, is certain any longer. Nothing at all.

30

After dinner, enveloped by the shadows of the night, they were entertained by a troupe of dancers. Hong Qiu, who had not even tasted the wine served with the meal as she wanted to keep a clear head, watched the dancers with a mixture of admiration and the remains of an old longing. Once upon a time, when she was very young, she had dreamed of a future as an artiste in a Chinese circus, or perhaps at the classical Peking Opera.

Hong Qiu observed Ya Ru sitting in his camp chair, a glass of wine balanced on his knee, his eyes half closed, and she thought about how little she knew of his childhood dreams. He had always existed in a little world of his own. She had been able to get close to him, but not so close that they had ever talked about dreams.

A Chinese interpreter introduced the dances. That wasn't necessary, Hong Qiu thought. She could have worked out for herself that the traditional dances had roots in everyday life or in symbolic meetings with devils or demons or benign spirits. Popular rites come from the same source, no matter what country you come from or what color your skin is. The climate has a role to play—those used to the cold generally danced fully dressed. But when in a trance, searching for lines to the spiritual world or the underworld, with what has been or what is to come, Chinese and Africans behave in more or less the same way.

Hong Qiu continued to look around. President Guebuza and his retinue had left. The only ones remaining in the camp where they would spend the night were the Chinese delegation, the waiters and waitresses, the cooks, and a large number of security guards skulking in the shadows. Many of those sitting and watching the frantic dances seemed to be deep in thought about other matters. A great leap forward is being planned in the African night, Hong Qiu thought. But I refuse to accept that this is the path we ought to be following. There's no way that this can happen: four million, perhaps more, of our poorest peasants migrating to the African wilderness— without our demanding substantial recompense from the country that receives them.

A woman suddenly started singing. The Chinese interpreter informed her listeners that it was a lullaby. Hong Qiu listened and was convinced that the melody could also calm a Chinese child. She recalled stories about cradles she had heard many years ago. In poor countries women always carried their children in bundles tied to their backs because they needed to have their hands free for working, especially in the fields—in Africa with hoes, in China while wading knee-deep in water for planting rice. Somebody had compared this to cradles rocked with the foot, which were common in other countries, and even in certain parts of China. The rhythm of the foot rocking the cradle was the same as the hip movements of the women walking. And the children slept, no matter what.

Hong Qiu closed her eyes and listened. The woman finished on a note that lingered before seeming to fall like a feather to the ground. The performance was over, and the guests applauded. Some members of the audience moved their chairs closer together and conducted conversations in low voices.

Others stood up, went back to their tents, or hovered around the edge of the light from the fire as if waiting for something to happen but not sure what.

Ya Ru came and sat down on a chair by Hong Qiu that had been left vacant.

"A remarkable evening," he said. "Absolute freedom and calm. I don't think I've ever been as far away from the big city as this."

"What about your office?" said Hong Qiu. "High up above ordinary people, all the cars and all the noise."

"That's not the same. Here I am on the ground. The earth is holding on to me. I'd like to own a house in this country, a bungalow on a beach, so that I could go for a swim in the evening and then straight to bed."

"No doubt you could ask for that? A plot of land, a fence, and somebody to build the house exactly as you want it?"

"Perhaps. But not yet."

Hong Qiu noticed that they were on their own now. The chairs around them were empty. Hong Qiu wondered if Ya Ru had made it clear that he wished to have a private talk with his sister.

"Did you see the woman dancing like a sorceress on a high?"

Hong Qiu thought for a moment. The woman had exuded strength, but had nevertheless moved rhythmically. "Her dancing was very powerful."

"Somebody told me she's seriously ill. She'll soon be dead."

"From what?"

"Some blood disease. Not AIDS, maybe they said cancer. They also said that she dances in order to generate strength. Dancing is her fight for life. She is postponing death."

"But she'll die even so."

"Like the stone, not the feather."

Mao again, Hong Qiu thought. Perhaps he's there in Ya Ru's thoughts about the future more often than I realize. He knows that he is one of those who have become a part of a new elite, far removed from the people he's supposed to take care of.

"What's all this going to cost?" she asked.

"This camp? The whole visit? What do you mean?"

"Moving four million people from China to an African valley with a wide river. And then perhaps ten or twenty or even a hundred million of our poorest peasants to other countries on this continent."

"In the short term, an awful lot of money. In the long term, nothing at all."

"I take it," said Hong Qiu, "that everything's been prepared already. The selection processes, transport and the armada of ships needed, simple houses that the settlers can erect themselves, food, equipment, shops, schools, hospitals. Are the contracts between the two countries already drawn up and signed? What does Mozambique get out of this? What do we get out of it apart from the chance to offload a chunk of our poor onto another poor country? What happens if it turns out that this enormous migration goes wrong? What's behind all this, apart from the desire to get rid of a problem that's growing out of control in China—and what are you going to do with all the other millions of peasants who are threatening to rebel against the current government?"

"I want you to see with your own eyes. To use your common sense and grasp how important it is for the Zambezi Valley to be populated. Our brothers will produce a surplus here that can be exported."

"You're making it sound like we're doing the world a favor by dumping our people here. I think we're treading the same path that imperialists have always trodden. Put the screws on the colonies, and transfer the profits to us. New markets for our products, a way of giving capitalism more staying power. Ya Ru, that's the truth behind all your fancy words. I know we're building a new Ministry of Finance for Mozambique. We call it a gift, but I see it as a bribe. I've also heard that the Chinese foremen beat the natives when they didn't work hard enough. Naturally, it was all hushed up. But I feel ashamed when I hear things like that. And I'm frightened. I don't believe you, Ya Ru."

"You're starting to get old, Hong Qiu. Like all old people you're frightened of anything new. You suspect conspiracies against old ideals wherever you turn. You think that you're standing up for the right way when in fact you've started to become the thing you are more afraid of than anything else. A conservative, a reactionary."

Hong Qiu leaned forward quickly and slapped his face. Ya Ru jerked back and stared at her in surprise.

"Now you've gone too far. I will not allow you to insult me. We can discuss things, disagree. But I'm not having you hit me."

Ya Ru stood up without another word and disappeared into the darkness. Nobody else seemed to have noticed what happened. Hong Qiu already regretted her reaction. She ought to have had enough patience and verbal skills to continue to try to convince Ya Ru that he was wrong.

Ya Ru did not return. Hong Qiu went to her tent. Kerosene lamps illuminated the area outside as well as inside. Her mosquito net was already in place, and her bed prepared for the night.

Hong Qiu sat outside the tent. It was a sultry evening. Ya Ru's tent was empty. She knew he would get revenge for the slap she had given him. But that didn't scare her. She could understand and accept that he was angry at his sister hitting him. When she next saw him she would apologize immediately.

Her tent was so far away from the fire that the sounds of nature were much clearer than the mumble of voices and conversations. The light breeze carried with it the smell of salt, wet sand, and something else she couldn't pin down.

Hong Qiu slept fitfully and was awake for much of the night. The sounds of darkness were foreign to her, penetrated her dreams, and dragged her to the surface. When the sun rose over the horizon, she was already up and dressed.

Ya Ru suddenly appeared in front of her. He smiled.

"We are both early birds," he said. "Neither of us has the patience to sleep any longer than is absolutely necessary."

"I'm sorry I hit you."

Ya Ru shrugged and pointed at a green-painted jeep on the road next to the tent.

"That's for you," he said. "A driver will take you to a place only half a dozen miles from here. When you get there, you'll see the remarkable drama that takes place at every watering hole as dawn breaks. For a short while beasts of prey and their potential victims observe a truce while they are drinking."

A black man was standing beside the jeep.

"His name's Arturo," said Ya Ru. "He's a trusted driver who also speaks English."

"Many thanks for your consideration," said Hong Qiu. "But we need to talk."

Ya Ru brushed aside her last comment. "We can do that later. The African dawn doesn't last long. There's coffee and some breakfast in a basket."

Hong Qiu realized that Ya Ru was trying to make peace. What had happened the day before must not come between them. She went over to the jeep, greeted the driver, who was a thin, middle-aged man, and sat down in the back of the open vehicle. The road winding its way into the bush was almost nonexistent, just a faint track in the dry earth. She fended off thorny branches from the low trees that lined the track.

When they came to the watering hole, Arturo parked near the edge of a steep drop down to the river below and handed Hong Qiu a pair of binoculars. Several hyenas and buffalo were drinking, and Arturo pointed out a herd of elephants. The gray, lumbering animals were approaching the watering hole almost as if they were walking straight out of the sun.

Hong Qiu had the feeling that this was what the world must have looked like at the beginning of time. Animals had come and gone here for countless generations.

Arturo served her a cup of coffee without speaking. The elephants were coming closer now, dust whirling around their enormous bodies.

Then the silence was broken.

Arturo was the first to die. The bullet hit him in the forehead and split his head in two. Hong Qiu had no time to gather what was happening before she was also hit by a bullet that smashed her jaw, was deflected downward, and broke her spine. The loud bangs made the animals raise their heads for a moment and listen. Then they resumed drinking.

Ya Ru and Liu Xin approached the jeep, used their combined strength to overturn it, and sent it tumbling down the steep slope. Liu Xin drenched it with a drum of gasoline, stepped to one side, then threw a burning box of matches at the vehicle, which burst into flames with a roar. The animals ran away from the watering hole at high speed.

Ya Ru was waiting in the backseat of their own jeep. His bodyguard settled down behind the wheel and prepared to start the engine. Ya Ru hit him hard on the back of the head with a steel rod. He kept on hitting until Liu Xin no longer moved, then pushed the bodyguard's corpse into the fire, which was still burning with full force.

Ya Ru drove the jeep into the thick vegetation and waited. After half an hour he returned to the camp and raised the alarm concerning an accident that had happened at the watering hole. The jeep had tumbled over the edge of the cliff and rolled down into the watering hole, where it had caught fire. His sister and the driver had both been killed. When Liu Xin tried to rescue them, he had also been engulfed by the flames.

Everybody who saw Ya Ru that day commented on how upset he was. But at the same time people were impressed by his self-control. He had insisted that the accident should not be allowed to interfere with their important work. Minister of Trade Ke gave his condolences to Ya Ru, and the negotiations continued as planned.

The bodies were taken away in black plastic bags and cremated in Harare. Nothing was written in the newspapers about the incident, neither in Mozambique nor in Zimbabwe. Arturo's family, who lived in the town of Xai-Xai in the south of Mozambique, was awarded a pension after his death. It gave all six of his children the possibility of studying, and his wife, Emilda, was able to buy a new house and a car.

When Ya Ru traveled back to Beijing with the rest of the delegation, he had with him two urns containing ashes. One of the first evenings home, he went out onto his huge terrace high above the city and let the ashes drift away into the darkness.

He was already beginning to miss his sister and the conversations they used to have. But he also knew that what he had done had been absolutely essential.

Ma Li lamented what had happened in a state of silent dismay. But deep down, she never did believe the story about the car accident.

31

On the table was a white orchid. Ya Ru stroked a finger over the soft petals.

It was an early morning, a month after returning from Africa. In front of him on the table were the plans for a house he had decided to build on the edge of the beach outside the town of Quelimane in

Mozambique. As a bonus to the big deals agreed to by the two countries, for an advantageous price Ya Ru had been able to buy a large area of unspoiled beach. In the long term he intended to build an exclusive tourist resort for wealthy Chinese, increasingly large numbers of whom would be venturing out into the world.

Ya Ru had been standing on a high sand dune, gazing out over the Indian Ocean. It was the day after the deaths of Hong Qiu and Liu Xin. With him were the governor of Zambezi Province and a South African architect who had been specially called in. Suddenly the governor had pointed toward the reef farthest from the shore. A whale was basking there and blowing. The governor explained that it was not unusual to see whales along this stretch of coast.

"What about icebergs?" wondered Ya Ru. "Has a lump of ice from the Antarctic ever drifted as far north as this?"

"There is a legend," said the governor. "Many generations ago, just before the first white men—the Portuguese sailors—landed on our shores, it's said that an iceberg was spotted off this coast. The men who paddled out in their canoes to investigate were frightened by the cold given off by the ice. Later, when the white men came ashore from their big sailing ships, people said that the iceberg had been a harbinger of what was soon to happen. The white men were the same color as the iceberg, their thoughts and actions just as cold. Nobody knows if it's true or not."

"I want to build here," said Ya Ru. "Yellow icebergs will never drift past this beach."

After a day of frantic measuring, a large plot of land was marked out and transferred to one of Ya Ru's many companies. The price for the land and the beach was barely more than symbolic. For a similar sum Ya Ru also bought the approval of the governor and the most important officials, who would ensure that he received the ratification documents and all the necessary building permission without undue delay. The instructions he gave the South African architect had already produced a set of plans and a watercolor sketch of what his palatial house would look like, with two swimming pools filled with water pumped up from the sea, surrounded by palm trees and an artificial waterfall. The house would have eleven rooms plus a bedroom with a roof that could slide open to reveal the starry sky. The governor had promised that special electrical and telecommunication cables would be laid for Ya Ru's remote property.

Now, as he sat contemplating what would become his African home, he decided that one of the rooms would be arranged as a tribute to Hong Qiu. Ya Ru wanted to honor her memory. He would furnish this room with a bed made for a guest who would never arrive. Irrespective of what had happened, she would remain a member of the family.

The telephone rang. Ya Ru frowned. Who would want to speak to him this early in the morning? He picked up the receiver.

"Two men from the security services are here."

"What do they want?"

"They are high-ranking officials from the Special Intelligence Section. They say it's urgent."

"Let them in ten minutes from now."

Ya Ru replaced the receiver. He held his breath. The SIS only dealt with matters involving men at the very top of the government or, like Ya Ru, men who lived between the political and economic power brokers—the modern bridge builders picked out by Deng to be of crucial importance for the country's development.

What did they want? Ya Ru went to the window and looked out over the city in the morning haze. Could it have anything to do with Hong Qiu's death? He thought of all the known and unknown enemies he had. Was one of them trying to exploit Hong Qiu's death in order to destroy his good name and reputation? Or was there something he had over-looked, despite everything? He knew that Hong Qiu had been in touch with a prosecutor, but he belonged to quite a different authority.

Hong Qiu could naturally have spoken to other people he didn't know about.

He couldn't think of any explanation. All he could do was listen to what the men had to say.

After ten minutes had passed he put the plans into a drawer and sat down at his desk. The two men Mrs. Shen showed in were in their sixties. That increased Ya Ru's uneasiness. The officers sent out were usually younger. The fact that these two men were older indicated that they were very experienced and the matter they wanted to discuss was serious.

Ya Ru stood up, bowed, and invited them to sit down. He didn't ask their names, as he knew that Mrs. Shen would have checked their identity papers very carefully.

They sat down in armchairs around a low table in front of the window. Ya Ru offered them tea, but the men declined.

It was the elder of the two men who did the talking. Ya Ru detected an unmistakable Shanghai accent.

"We have received information," said the man. "We can't say where the information came from, but it is so detailed that we can't ignore it. Our instructions have become stricter when it comes to dealing with crimes against the state and the constitution."

"I have been involved in tightening up on action against corruption," said Ya Ru. "I don't understand why you are here."

"We have received information suggesting that your construction companies are seeking advantages using forbidden methods."

"Forbidden methods?"

"Forbidden exchange of favors."

"In other words, bribery and corruption? Taking bribes?"

"The information we have received is very detailed. We are worried."

"So you have come here at this early hour of the morning to tell me that you are investigating irregularities in my companies?"

"We would prefer to say that we are informing you of the suspicions."

"To warn me?"

"If you like."

Ya Ru understood. He was a man with powerful friends, even in the anticorruption authority. And so he had been given a head start. To eradicate the trail, get rid of proof, or demand explanations if he was not personally aware of what was going on.

He thought of the shot in the back of the head that had recently killed Shen Weixian. It was as if the two gray men sitting opposite him were emitting a cold chill, just as, according to legend, the African iceberg had.

Ya Ru wondered again if he had been careless. Perhaps on one occasion or another he had felt too secure and allowed himself to be carried away by his arrogance. If so, that had been a mistake. Such mistakes are always punished.

"I need to know more," he said. "This is too vague, too general."

"Our instructions don't allow us to say more."

"The accusations, even if they are anonymous, must come from somewhere."

"We can't answer that either."

Ya Ru wondered for a moment if it might be possible to pay the two men to give him more information. But he dare not take the risk. One or perhaps both of them might be carrying concealed microphones recording the conversation. There was of course also a chance that they were honest and didn't have a price—unlike so many government officials.

"These vague accusations are totally without foundation," said Ya Ru. "I'm grateful to have heard about the rumors that are evidently surrounding me and my companies. But anonymity is often a source of falsehood, envy, and insidious lies. I make sure that my enterprises are beyond reproach, I have the confidence of the government and the party and have no hesitation in maintaining that I am sufficiently in control to know that my managing directors follow my directives. Obviously I'm not able to claim that there are no minor irregularities; my employees number more than thirty thousand."

Ya Ru stood up as a signal that, as far as he was concerned, the meeting was over. The two men bowed and left the room. When they had gone, he rang through to Mrs. Shen.

"Get hold of one of my security chiefs and tell him to find out who these two are," he said. "Find out who their bosses are. Then summon my nine managing directors to a meeting three days from now. Everybody must attend, no excuses accepted. Anybody who doesn't turn up will be fired on the spot. This has to be sorted out."

Ya Ru was furious. What he did was no worse than what anybody else did. A man like Shen Weixian frequently went too far and in addition had been rude to the state officials who cleared the way for him. He had been an appropriate scapegoat, and nobody would miss him now that he was gone.

Ya Ru spent several hours of intensive activity working out a plan for what to do next and puzzling over which of his managing directors could have secretly opened up the poison cupboard and given away information about his dodgy deals and secret agreements.

Three days later his managing directors assembled in a hotel in Beijing. Ya Ru had chosen the location with care. It was there that he used to call a meeting once a year and fire one of his directors in order to demonstrate that nobody was safe. The group of men gathered in the conference room shortly after ten in the morning looked distinctly pale. None of them had been informed precisely what the meeting was about. Ya Ru kept them waiting for more than an hour before putting in an appearance. His strategy was very simple. First he confiscated their cell phones, so that they were unable to contact one another or be in touch with the outside world, then he sent them out of the room. Each of them had to sit in a small room with one of the guards summoned by Mrs. Shen at his side. Then Ya Ru interviewed them one at a time and told them without beating about the bush what he had heard a couple of days previously. What did they have to say? Any explanations? Was there something Ya Ru ought to know? He observed their faces closely and tried to detect if any of them seemed to have prepared what to say in advance. If there was such a person, Ya Ru could be sure that he had found the source of the leak.

But all the directors displayed the same degree of surprise and indignation. At the end of the day, he was forced to conclude that he hadn't found a guilty person. He let them go without firing anybody. But all of them received strict instructions to look into the security of their own setups.

It was only some days later, when Mrs. Shen reported on what his investigators had discovered about the men from the security services, that he realized he had been following a false trail. Once again he'd been studying the plans for his house in Africa when she came in. He asked her to sit down and adjusted the desk lamp so that his face was in shadow. He liked listening to her voice. No matter what she told him, be it a financial report or a summary of new directives from some government authority, he always had the feeling that she was telling him a story. There was something in her voice that reminded him of the childhood he had long since forgotten about, or been robbed of—he couldn't make up his mind which.

"Somehow or other it seems to be connected with your dead sister, Hong Qiu. She was in close contact

with some of the top men at the State Security
Bureau. Her name keeps cropping up whenever we
try to link the men who came to visit us the other
morning and others hovering in the background. We
think the information can only have been circulating
for a short time before she died so tragically. Nevertheless, somebody at the very highest level seems to
have given the go-ahead."

Ya Ru noticed that Mrs. Shen broke off. "What is
it you are not telling me?"

"I'm not sure."

"Nothing is sure. Has somebody at the very top
authorized this investigation into my activities?"

"I can't say if it's true or not, but rumor has it that
those in authority are not satisfied with the outcome
of the sentence passed on Shen Weixian."

A shiver ran down Ya Ru's spine. He understood
the implications before Mrs. Shen had time to say
any more.

"Another scapegoat? Do they want to condemn
another rich man in order to demonstrate that this is
now a campaign and not merely an indication that
patience is running out?"

Mrs. Shen nodded. Ya Ru shrank farther back into
the shadows. "Anything else?"

"No."

"You may go."

Mrs. Shen left the room. Ya Ru didn't move. He
forced himself to think, although what he wanted to
do most of all was run away.

When he had made the difficult decision to kill Hong Qiu, and that the murder would take place in Africa, he had been sure that she was still his loyal sister. To be sure, they had different views, they often argued. In this very room, on his birthday, she had accused him of taking bribes.

That was when he had realized that sooner or later Hong Qiu would become too big a danger to him. He now saw that he ought to have acted sooner. Hong Qiu had already abandoned him.

Ya Ru shook his head slowly. He now understood something that had never occurred to him before. Hong Qiu had been prepared to do the same thing to him as he had done to her. She hadn't intended to use a weapon herself—Hong Qiu preferred to proceed via the laws of the land. But if Ya Ru had been condemned to death, she would have been one of those declaring it the right thing to do.

Ya Ru thought of his friend Lai Changxing, who some years previously had been forced to flee the country when the police raided all his companies early one morning. The only reason he managed to save himself and his family had been that he owned a private airplane that was always ready to take off at a moment's notice. He had fled to Canada, which did not have an extradition treaty with China. He was the son of a peasant who had made an amazing career for himself when Deng created a free market. He had started by digging wells but later became a smuggler and invested all he earned in companies that within a few years generated an enormous fortune. Ya Ru had once visited him in the Red Manor he had built in his home district of Xiamen. He had also taken upon himself major social responsibilities by constructing old people's homes and schools. Even in those days Ya Ru had been put off by Lai Changxing's arrogant ostentation and had warned his friend that he could be heading for a fall. They had sat one evening discussing the envy many people felt with regard to the new capitalists, the Second Dynasty, as Lai Changxing called them ironically—but only when talking in private with people he trusted.

Ya Ru had not been surprised when the gigantic house of cards collapsed and Lai had to flee the country. After he'd left, several of those involved with his businesses were executed. Others—hundreds of them—had been imprisoned. But at the same time, he was revered as a generous man in his poor home district. He would give fortunes to taxi drivers in the form of tips or give generous gifts to impoverished families whose names he didn't even know, for no obvious reason. Ya Ru also knew that Lai was now writing his memoir—which worried many high-ranking officials and politicians in China. Lai was in possession of many truths, and as he now lived in Canada, nobody could censure him.

But Ya Ru had no intention of fleeing his country.

There was another thought beginning to gnaw away at his mind. Ma Li, Hong Qiu's friend, had also been on the visit to Africa. Ya Ru knew that the two women had had long conversations. Moreover, Hong Qiu had always been a letter writer.

Perhaps Ma Li was in possession of an incriminating letter from Hong Qiu? Something she had passed on to people who had in turn informed the security services?

Three days later, when one of the winter's severe sandstorms was raging over Beijing, Ya Ru visited Ma Li's office not far from Ritan Gongyuan, the Sun God's Park. Ma Li worked in a government department devoted to financial analyses and wasn't sufficiently senior to cause him any serious problems. Mrs. Shen and her assistants had investigated Ma Li and found no links with the inner circles of government and the party. Ma Li had two children. Her current husband was an insignificant bureaucrat. As her first husband had died in the war with the Vietnamese in the 1970s, nobody had objected to her remarrying and having another child. Both of the children now led lives of their own: the elder, a daughter, was an educational adviser in a teacher training college, and the son worked as a surgeon in a hospital in Shanghai. Neither of them had contacts that caused Ya Ru any worries. But he had been careful to note that Ma Li had two grandchildren to whom she devoted a large amount of her time.

Mrs. Shen fixed an appointment with Ma Li. She hadn't mentioned what the meeting was about, only that it was urgent and probably connected with the trip to Africa. That ought to worry her a bit, Ya Ru thought as he sat in the backseat of his car observing the city they were driving through. As he had plenty of time, he had asked the driver to make a diversion past some of the construction sites he had business interests in. His main priority was the Olympic Games. One of Ya Ru's big contracts was for the demolition of a residential area that had to be cleared in order to make way for roads to the new sports stadia. Ya Ru expected to earn billions, even after he had subtracted the massive payments made to civil servants and politicians.

The car pulled up outside an unremarkable building, where Ma Li worked. She was standing on the steps, waiting for him.

"Ma Li," said Ya Ru. "Seeing you now makes me think that our trip to Africa, which ended in such tragedy, was a very long time ago."

"I think about my dear friend Hong Qiu every day," said Ma Li. "But I allow Africa to drift away into the past. I shall never go back there."

"As you know, we sign new contracts with many countries on the African continent every day. We are building bridges that will last for a long time to come."

As they talked they walked along a deserted corridor to Ma Li's office, whose windows looked out onto a little garden surrounded by a high wall. In the middle of the garden was a fountain that had been turned off for the winter.

Ma Li switched off her telephone and served tea. Ya Ru could hear somebody laughing in the distance.

"Searching for truth is like watching a snail chasing a snail," Ya Ru said pensively. "It moves slowly, but it is persistent."

Ya Ru looked her straight in the eye, but Ma Li did not avert her gaze.

"There are rumors circulating," Ya Ru continued, "that I don't like at all. Rumors about my companies, about my character. I wonder where they are coming from. I have to ask who would want to do me damage. Not the usual crowd that is jealous of me, but somebody else, with motives I don't understand."

"Why should I want to damage your reputation?"

"That's not what I mean. My question is quite different. Who knows, who has got hold of this information, who is spreading the rumors?"

"Our lives are totally different. I'm a civil servant; you do big business deals that we read about in the newspapers. Compared with my life as an insignificant nobody, you lead a life that I can barely imagine."

"But you knew Hong Qiu," said Ya Ru, "my sister, who was very close to me. After not having seen each other for ages, you and she meet in Africa. You have long talks, she makes a hurried visit to you early one morning. When I get back to China, rumors start spreading."

Ma Li turned pale. "Are you accusing me of slandering you in public?"

"You must understand, and I'm sure you do, that in my situation I wouldn't say anything like that without first having done some thorough research. I have ruled out one possibility after another. In the end I have only one explanation. One person."

"Me?"

"Not really, no."

"You mean Hong Qiu? Your own sister?"

"It's no secret that we disagreed about fundamental questions regarding the future of China: political developments, the economy, our views on history."

"But were you enemies?"

"Enmity can develop over a very long time, almost invisibly, the way land slowly rises out of the sea. All of a sudden you find you have an enemy you knew nothing about."

"I find it hard to believe that Hong Qiu would use anonymous complaints as a weapon. She wasn't that kind of person."

"I know. That's why I'm asking you the question. What did you actually talk about?"

Ma Li didn't answer. Ya Ru continued without giving her any time to think.

"Perhaps there's a letter," he said slowly. "Perhaps she gave you a letter that morning. Am I right? A letter? Or some kind of document? I have to know what she said to you and what she gave you."

"It was as if she sensed that she was going to die," said Ma Li. "I've been thinking a lot about it, but I can't understand the strength of the worry she must have felt. She just asked me to make sure that her body was cremated after she died. She wanted her ashes spread over Longtanhu Gongyuan, the little lake in the park. She also asked me to look after her belongings, her books, to give away her clothes and empty her house."

"Nothing else?"

"No."

"Was this something she said, or did she write it down?"

"It was a letter. I memorized it. Then I burned it."

"So it was only a short letter?"

"Yes."

"But why did you burn it? You could almost call it a will."

"She said nobody would question what I said."

Ya Ru continued to observe her face while he thought over her words. "She didn't give you another letter as well?"

"What could that have been?"

"Maybe a letter you didn't burn. But that you passed on to somebody else?"

"I received one letter. It was addressed to me. I burned it. That's all."

"It would not be good if you haven't told me the truth."

"Why on earth should I lie?"

Ya Ru flung out his arms. "Why do people lie? Why do we have that ability? Because in certain circumstances it can be advantageous for us. Lies and truth are weapons, Ma Li, that skillful operators can make good use of, just as other people are very handy with a sword."

He was still looking her in the eye, but she didn't look away. "Nothing else? There's nothing else you want to tell me?"

"No. Nothing."

"You realize, of course, that sooner or later I'll find out all I need to know?"

"Yes."

Ya Ru nodded thoughtfully. "You are a good person, Ma Li. So am I. But I can be bitter and twisted if anybody is dishonest with me."

"There's nothing I haven't told you."

"Good. You have two grandchildren, Ma Li. You love them more than anything else in the world."

He saw that she gave a start.

"Are you threatening me?"

"Not at all. I'm merely giving you an opportunity to tell me the truth."

"I've told you everything. Hong Qiu told me about the fears she had regarding developments in China. But no threats, no rumors."

"Then I believe you."

"You scare me, Ya Ru. Do I really deserve that?"

"I haven't scared you. Hong Qiu did that, with her secret letter. Talk to her soul about that. Ask her to set you free from the worries you have."

Ya Ru stood up. Ma Li accompanied him out into the street. He shook her hand, then stepped into his car. Ma Li went back to her office and threw up in the washbasin.

Then she sat down at her desk and memorized word for word the letter she had received from Hong Qiu, which was lying hidden in one of her desk drawers.

She was angry when she died, Ma Li thought. No matter how it happened. Nobody has yet been able to give me a satisfactory explanation of how the car accident took place.

Before leaving her office that evening she tore the letter into tiny pieces and flushed it down the lavatory.

Ya Ru spent the evening in one of his nightclubs in the entertainment district of Beijing, Sanlitun. In a back room he relaxed on a bed and allowed Li Wu, one of the hostesses at the club, to massage the back of his head and neck. They were the same age and had once been lovers. She still belonged to the small group of people that Ya Ru trusted. He was very careful about what he did and didn't say to her. But he knew that she was loyal.

She was always naked when she massaged him. The distant sound of music from the nightclub filtered in through the walls. The lights inside the room were dim, the wallpaper red.

Ya Ru again ran through the conversation he'd had with Ma Li. It all started with Hong Qiu, he thought.

It was a grave error on my part, trusting her family loyalty for so long.

Li continued massaging his back. Suddenly he took hold of her hand and sat up.

"Did I hurt you?"

"I need to be alone, Li. I'll shout when I need you again."

She left the room as Ya Ru wrapped himself up in a sheet. He wondered if he'd been thinking along the wrong lines. Perhaps the key question wasn't what was in the letter that Hong Qiu had handed over to Ma Li.

What if Hong Qiu had been talking to somebody, he wondered. Somebody she assumed I would never worry about.

He recalled what Chan Bing had said about the Swedish judge Hong Qiu had displayed an interest in. What was there to prevent Hong Qiu from talking to her? Passing on confidential information?

Ya Ru lay down on the bed again. The back of his neck felt less painful now, after being stroked by Li's sensitive fingers.

The next morning he called Chan Bing. He came straight to the point.

"You mentioned something about a Swedish judge my sister had been in contact with. What was that about?"

"Her name was Birgitta Roslin. She'd been mugged,

a routine incident. We brought her in to identify her attacker. She didn't recognize anybody, but she had evidently been talking to Hong Qiu about a number of murders in Sweden that she suspected had been carried out by a man from China."

This was worse than he'd thought, and potentially more damaging than any accusations of corruption. He politely brought the conversation to a close.

He was already steeling himself for a task he would have to carry out himself, now that Liu Xin was no longer around.

One more thing to finish off. Hong Qiu was not yet defeated, once and for all.

Chinatown, London

32

It was raining in the morning at the beginning of May when Birgitta Roslin accompanied her family to Copenhagen, where they were due to catch a flight for Madeira. After a lot of soul-searching and many discussions with Staffan, she had decided not to go with them on their vacation. The long sick leave she had taken earlier in the year had made it impossible for her to ask for more time off. She simply couldn't make the trip.

The rain was bucketing down when they arrived in Copenhagen. Staffan, who traveled free on Swedish railways, had wanted to take the train to Kastrup, where their children were waiting, but she was just as insistent on taking him to the airport by car. She waved good-bye to all of them in the departure terminal, then settled down in a café and watched the crowds of people lugging their baggage and dreaming of journeys to distant lands.

A few days earlier she had called Karin Wiman

and said she would be going to Copenhagen. Although it was several months since they had returned from Beijing, they still hadn't had an opportunity to meet. Birgitta had been snowed under with work after being declared fit again. Hans Mattsson had welcomed her return with open arms, placed a vase of flowers on her desk, and immediately followed it with a large number of cases. At that precise moment, at the end of March, a debate had been raging in the local newspapers in southern Sweden about the scandalously long waiting times in district courts. According to Birgitta Roslin's colleagues, Hans Mattsson, who could hardly be called bellicose by nature, had not been sufficiently outspoken in making clear the hopeless situation the courts had been placed in by the National Judiciary Administration and more especially the government, which were intent on saving money. While her colleagues groaned and fumed about their workload, Birgitta had felt extremely pleased to be back in the thick of it. She had often stayed behind in her office so late that Hans Mattsson, in his gentle way, had warned her not to overstretch herself and fall ill again.

And so she and Karin Wiman had only spoken on the telephone. They had arranged to meet twice, but on both occasions something had come up to prevent it. Now, however, on this rainy day in Copenhagen, Birgitta was free. She didn't need to appear in court again that day and would spend the night at Karin's place. She had the pictures from China in her bag and was looking forward with childlike eagerness to seeing the photographs Karin had taken.

They had agreed to meet for lunch at a restaurant in one of the streets off Strøget. Birgitta had intended to wander around the shops looking for a dress she could wear in court, but the heavy rain made that an unattractive activity. She stayed at Kastrup until it was time to meet, then took a taxi into town, as she was unsure of the way. Karin waved cheerfully to her as she entered the packed restaurant.

"They got away all right, I hope?"

"It's only after they've left that it hits you. The horrific possibilities when your whole family is on the same plane."

Karin shook her head.

"Nothing will happen," she said. "If you really want to travel safely, an airplane is your best bet."

They had lunch, looked at the photographs, and recalled memories from their trip. While Karin was talking, Birgitta found herself thinking for the first time in ages about the mugging. Hong Qiu suddenly appearing at her breakfast table. The stolen purse that had been found. The whole strange and frightening business she had become involved in.

"Are you listening?" Karin asked.

"Of course I'm listening. Why do you ask?"

"You don't seem to be."

"I keep thinking of my family up there in the sky."

They ordered coffee to round off the meal. Karin

suggested they should each drink a brandy in protest against the cold spring weather.

"Of course, we'll have a brandy."

They took a taxi to Karin's house. When they got there, it stopped raining, and the clouds were beginning to break.

"I need to stretch my legs," said Birgitta. "I spend far too much time sitting in my office or in court."

They strolled along the beach, which was deserted apart from a few elderly people walking their dogs.

They paused and watched a yacht scudding northward through the sound.

"Don't you think it's high time you told me now?" Karin asked.

"Told you what?"

"What really happened in Beijing. I know what you said wasn't true. Or at least, not the whole truth and nothing but the truth, as they say in court."

"I was attacked. And my purse was stolen."

"I know that. But the circumstances, Birgitta. I don't believe what you said. There was something missing. Even if we haven't met very often in recent years, I know you. I would never try to tell you an untruth. Or to fool you, as my father used to say. I know you would see through me."

This came as a relief to Birgitta.

"I don't understand it myself," she said. "I don't understand why I concealed half the story. Perhaps because you were too busy with your First Dynasty. Perhaps because I didn't even really understand what had happened."

They kept walking and took off their jackets when the sun started to warm up. Birgitta told her about the photograph taken by the surveillance camera in the little hotel in Hudiksvall and her attempt to track down the man on the film. She explained it in precise detail, as if she were in the witness box under the watchful eye of a judge.

"You didn't say anything about that," said Karin when Birgitta came to the crucial point. They had turned and started to walk back.

"When you left I was scared," said Birgitta. "I thought I might rot away in some underground dungeon. And afterward the police would simply say that I'd disappeared."

"I take that as a lack of confidence in me. I should be angry with you."

Birgitta stopped and turned to confront Karin.

"We don't know each other all that well," she said. "Maybe we think we do. Or wish we did. When we were young our relationship was quite different from what it is now. We're friends. But we're not that close. Perhaps we never have been."

Karin nodded. They continued walking along the beach, where the sand was driest higher up than the seaweed.

"You always want things to stay the same, for everything to be just as it used to be," said Karin. "But as you get older you have to be careful to avoid sentimentality. If friendships are going to last, they have to keep being reexamined and renewed. Maybe old love never goes rusty. But old friendships do."

"The fact that we're talking about it is a step in the right direction. It's like scraping away the rust with a steel brush."

"What happened next? How did it all end?"

"I went home. The police, or some branch of the secret service, had searched my room. I have no idea what they hoped to find."

"But you must have wondered. A mugging?"

"It's all about the photograph from the hotel in Hudiksvall, of course. Somebody wanted to prevent me from looking for that man. But I think Hong Qiu was telling the truth. China doesn't want foreign visitors to go back home and talk about so-called unfortunate incidents. Not now, when the country is preparing for the Olympic Games."

"A whole country with more than a billion inhabitants waiting in the wings to make its brilliant entry onto the world stage. A remarkable thought."

"Hundreds of millions of people, our beloved poor peasants, probably don't realize what these Olympics mean. Or else they realize that nothing will get better for them simply because the young people of the world are gathering in Beijing to play games."

"I have a vague memory of her—that woman called Hong Qiu. She was very beautiful. There was something evasive about her, as if she were on edge."

"Could be. I remember her differently. She helped me."

"Was she the servant of several masters?"

"That's something I've thought a lot about. I don't know. But you're probably right."

They walked out onto a jetty. Several of the mooring berths were empty. A woman was squatting in an old wooden boat, bailing out. She nodded to them with a smile and said something in a dialect Karin couldn't understand.

Afterward they drank coffee in Karin's living room. Karin talked about her current work, studying several Chinese poets and their work from liberation in 1949 to the present day.

"I can't devote my whole life to empires that died long ago. The poems make a pleasant change."

Birgitta came close to mentioning her own secret and impassioned pop lyrics, but said nothing.

"Many of them were courageous," said Karin. "Mao and the rest at the top of the political tree were rarely tolerant of criticism. But Mao tolerated the poets. I suppose you could say that was because he wrote poetry himself. But I think he knew that artists could show the big political stage in a new light. When other political leaders wanted to clamp down on artists who wrote the wrong words or painted with dodgy brushstrokes, Mao always put his foot down and stopped them. To the bitter end. What happened to artists during the Cultural Revolution was of course his responsibility, but not his intention. Even if the last revolution he set in motion had cultural overtones, it was basically political. When Mao realized that some of the young rebels were going too far, he slammed on the brakes. Even if he couldn't express it in so many words, I think he regretted the havoc caused during those years. But he knew better

than anybody else that if you want to make an
omelette, you have to break an egg. Isn't that what
people used to say?"

"Or that the revolution wasn't a tea party."

They both burst out laughing.

"What do you think about China now?" asked Birgitta. "What exactly is going on there?"

"I'm convinced there's a tremendous tug of war.
Within the party, within the country. The Communist Party is trying to show the rest of the world, people like you and me, that it's possible to combine
economic development with a state that isn't democratic. Even if all the liberal thinkers in the West deny
it, a one-party dictatorship is reconcilable with economic development. That causes unrest in our part
of the world. That's why so much is spoken and written about human rights in China. The lack of freedom and transparency, the human rights so central to
Western values, become the target of Western attacks
on China. For me it's hypocritical, since our part of
the world is full of countries—not least the United
States and Russia—in which human rights are violated every day. Besides, the Chinese know that we
want to do business with them, at any price. They
saw through us in the nineteenth century when we
decided to brand them all as opium addicts and
award ourselves the right to do business with them
on our terms. The Chinese have learned lessons, and
they won't repeat our mistakes. That's the way I see
things, and obviously, I'm aware that my conclusions

aren't perfect. What's happening is much bigger than anything I can take in. We can't apply our way of looking at things to China. But no matter what we think about it, we have to respect what's going on. Nowadays only an idiot would think that what's happening there won't affect our own future. If I had small children today I'd employ a Chinese nanny to make sure they become acquainted with the Chinese language."

"That's exactly what my son says."

"He has vision."

"I was overwhelmed by the visit to China," said Birgitta. "The country is so enormous, I wandered around with the constant feeling that I could just disappear at any moment. And nobody would ask questions about one individual when there are so incredibly many others. I wish I'd had more time to talk to Hong Qiu."

That evening they had dinner and once more immersed themselves in memories of the past. Birgitta felt increasingly strongly that she didn't want to lose contact with Karin again. There was nobody else with whom she had shared her youth, nobody who could understand what she was talking about.

They sat up until late, and before going to bed promised themselves that in the future they would meet more often.

"Commit some minor traffic offense in Helsingborg," Birgitta suggested. "Don't admit anything when the police interview you at the scene. Then you'll eventually end up in the dock. When I've sentenced you we can go and have dinner somewhere."

"I find it hard to imagine you in court."

"So do I. But that's where I spend most of my days."

The next day Karin went with Birgitta to the main railroad station.

"Well, I'd better be getting back to my Chinese poets," said Karin. "What are you going to do?"

"I'll spend this afternoon reading up on a couple of forthcoming trials. I envy you your poets. But I'd prefer not to think about it."

They were just about to go their different ways when Karin took hold of Birgitta's arm.

"I haven't asked you at all about the events in Hudiksvall. What's happening?"

"The police are convinced that, no matter what, the man who committed suicide did it."

"On his own? All those dead bodies?"

"Maybe. But they still haven't managed to find a motive."

"Lunacy?"

"I didn't think that at the time, and I still don't think so."

"Are you in touch with the police?"

"Not at all. I just read what's written in the newspapers."

Birgitta watched Karin hurrying off through the big central hall, then caught a train to Kastrup, tracked down her car in the parking lot, and drove home.

Growing older involves a kind of retreat, she thought. You don't just keep rushing forward. Like the conversations Karin and I had. We're trying to find our real selves, who we are, both now and then.

She was back in Helsingborg by about twelve o'clock. She went straight to her office, where she read a memorandum from the National Judiciary Administration before turning her attention to the two cases she needed to prepare.

She suddenly felt happiness bubbling up inside her. She closed her eyes and breathed deeply. Nothing is too late, she thought. Now I've seen the Great Wall of China. There are other walls and especially islands I want to visit before my life is over and the coffin lid nailed down. Something inside me says that Staffan and I will manage to handle the situation we find ourselves in.

It was eleven o'clock before she was at home and began to get ready for bed. There was a ring at the front door. She frowned, but went to answer: there was nobody. She stepped out and looked up and down the street. A car drove past, but apart from that it was deserted. The gate was closed. Kids, she thought. They ring the bell, then run away.

She went back in and fell asleep before midnight. She woke up soon after two without knowing what had disturbed her. She didn't remember having had a dream and listened into the darkness without hearing anything. She was just about to roll over and go back to sleep when she sat up. Switched on the bedside light and listened. Got up and opened the door onto the landing. She still couldn't hear anything. She put on her robe and went downstairs. All the doors and windows were locked. She stood by a window over-looking the street and pulled the curtain to one side. She thought she might have glimpsed a shadow hur-rying away down the sidewalk, but she blamed her overactive imagination. She had never been afraid of the dark. Perhaps she had woken up because she was hungry. After a sandwich and a glass of water she went back to bed and soon fell asleep again.

The next morning when she was about to pick up her briefcase, she had the feeling someone had been in her study. It was the same kind of feeling as she'd had in connection with her suitcase in the hotel room in Beijing. When she had gone to bed the previous evening, she had put all the documents into the brief-case. Now some of the edges of those documents were protruding from the top.

Although she was in a rush, she checked the base-ment. Nothing was missing; nothing had been touched. My imagination's running away with me, she thought. I had enough of a persecution complex in Beijing—I don't need any more of the same here in Helsingborg.

Birgitta Roslin locked her front door and walked down the hill to the town and the district court. When she arrived, she went to her office, switched off the telephone, leaned back in her chair with her eyes closed, and thought over the case she had to deal with

about a Vietnamese gang accused of smuggling cigarettes. In the back of her mind she ran through the
most important parts of the case against the two Tran
bothers, which had resulted in their being arrested
three separate times before finally being charged.
Now they faced being tried and sentenced. Two more
Vietnamese men, Dang and Phan, had been arrested
during the investigation.

Birgitta Roslin was pleased to have prosecuting
counsel Palm in her court. He was a middle-aged
man who took his professional duties seriously. On
the basis of the material she had access to, Palm had
insisted on a thorough police investigation, which
didn't always happen.

As the clock struck ten she entered the courtroom
and sat at her desk. The lay assessors and recording
clerks were already in their places. The public gallery
was packed. There were both police officers and security guards on duty. Everybody had been required to
pass through metal detectors. She opened proceedings,
noted down names, checked that all involved were present, then let the prosecutor take over. Palm spoke
slowly and clearly and occasionally addressed his
remarks to the public gallery. There was a large group of
Vietnamese present, most of them very young. Birgitta
Roslin also recognized journalists and a sketch artist
working for several national newspapers. Birgitta had a
drawing of herself, done by the same artist, that she had
cut out of the paper. She had put it in a desk drawer, as
she didn't want her visitors to think she was vain.

It was a hard day. Although the police investigation had made it obvious how the crimes had been committed, the four young men started blaming one another. Two of them spoke Swedish, but the Tran brothers needed an interpreter. Roslin was forced to point out on several occasions that the translation was not clear enough—indeed, she wondered if the girl really understood what the brothers were saying. She also needed to instruct some of the people in the public gallery to be quiet and threatened to remove them if they didn't calm down.

While she was having lunch, Hans Mattsson stopped in to ask how things were going.

"They're lying," Birgitta said. "But the case against them is solid. The only question is whether the interpreter is up to it."

"She has a good reputation," said Hans Mattsson in surprise. "She's supposed to be the best one available in Sweden."

"Perhaps she's having an off day."

"Are you?"

"No. But it's taking time. I doubt we'll be finished by tomorrow."

During the afternoon proceedings Birgitta continued to observe the people in the public gallery. She noticed a middle-aged Vietnamese woman sitting alone in a corner of the courtroom, half hidden from those sitting in front of her. Every time Birgitta glanced over, the woman seemed to be looking at her, whereas the rest of the Vietnamese were mainly watching their accused friends or family members.

Birgitta remembered when she had sat in the Chinese courtroom a few months earlier. Maybe I have a colleague from Vietnam observing me, she thought ironically. But surely somebody would have mentioned it. Besides, that woman doesn't have an interpreter sitting next to her.

When she concluded the day's proceedings, she was uncertain how much more time was necessary to wrap up the case. She sat in her office and made an assessment of what still needed to be done. One more day might be enough, if nothing unexpected happened.

She slept deeply that night, without being disturbed by strange noises.

When the trial resumed the following day, the woman was in the same seat again. Something about her made Birgitta feel insecure. During a brief adjournment she summoned an usher and asked him to check if the woman kept to herself even outside the courtroom. Just before the court reconvened, he came by to report that she did indeed—she hadn't spoken to anybody at all.

"Please keep an eye on her," said Birgitta Roslin.

"I could remove her if you like."

"On what grounds?"

"That she worries you."

"No, I'm just asking you to keep an eye on her. No more than that."

Although she was doubtful until the last minute, she did manage to conclude proceedings late that afternoon. She announced that sentences would be passed on June 20 and declared the case closed. The last thing she saw before going back to her office, having thanked her various assistants, was the Vietnamese woman, who had turned to watch Birgitta leave the courtroom.

Hans Mattsson came by. He had been listening to the closing arguments by the prosecuting and defending counsels on the internal speaker system.

"Palm has had a few good days."

"The only question is how to hand down the sentences. There's no doubt the brothers are the ringleaders. The other two are also guilty, of course, but they seem to be afraid of the brothers. It's hard to avoid the suspicion that they might have shouldered more guilt than they deserve."

"Just let me know if you want to discuss anything."

Birgitta gathered her notes and prepared to go home. Staffan had left a message on her cell phone to say that all was well. She was about to leave when her office phone rang. She hesitated. Then she picked up the receiver. It was the usher.

"I just wanted to say that you have a visitor."

"Who?"

"The woman you asked me to keep an eye on."

"Is she still around? What does she want?"

"I don't know."

"If she's related to any of the accused Vietnamese, I'm not allowed to talk to her."

"I don't think she's a relative."

Birgitta was beginning to get impatient. "What do you mean?"

"I mean that she's not from Vietnam. She speaks excellent English. She's Chinese. And she wants to speak to you. She says it's very important."

"Where is she?"

"Waiting outside. I can see her from here. She's just plucked a leaf from a birch tree."

"Does she have a name?"

"I'm sure she does. But she hasn't told me what it is."

"I'm coming. Tell her to wait."

Birgitta walked over to the window. She could see the woman, standing on the sidewalk.

A few minutes later she left the courthouse.

33

The woman, whose name was Ho, could have been Hong Qiu's younger sister. Birgitta was struck by the resemblance, not only the sleek hair but also the dignified posture.

Ho introduced herself in excellent English, just as Hong Qiu had done.

"I have a message for you," said Ho. "If I'm not disturbing you."

"I've just finished work for the day."

"I didn't understand a single word of what was said in court," said Ho, "but I could see the respect that was shown to you."

"A few months ago I attended a trial in China. The judge on that occasion was also a woman. And she was also treated with great respect."

Birgitta asked if Ho would like to go to a café or restaurant, but Ho simply pointed to a nearby park where there were several benches.

They sat down. Not far away a group of elderly drunks was arguing noisily. Birgitta had seen them many times before. She had a vague memory of having found one of them guilty of some misdemeanor, but she couldn't remember what. Drunks in parks and the lonely men who rake dead leaves in churchyards are the very hub of Swedish society, she often said to herself. Take them away, and what's left? She noticed that one of the drunks was a dark-skinned man. The new Sweden was asserting its identity even here. Birgitta smiled.

"Spring has sprung," she said.

"I'm here to tell you that Hong Qiu is dead."

Birgitta hadn't known what to expect—but it wasn't that. She felt a wrench deep down inside her. Not of sorrow, but of immediate fear.

"What happened?"

"She died in a car accident while on a trip to Africa. Her brother was there as well. But he survived. He may not have been in the same car. I don't know all the details."

Birgitta stared at Ho in silence, chewing over the words, trying to understand. The colorful spring was suddenly surrounded by shadows.

"When did it happen?"

"Several months ago."

"In Africa?"

"My dear friend Hong Qiu was part of a big delegation to Zimbabwe. Our minister of trade, Ke, was the leader of the visit, which was considered very important. The accident happened on an excursion to Mozambique."

Two of the drunks suddenly started screaming and pushing each other.

"Let's go," said Birgitta, rising to her feet.

She took Ho to a nearby café, where they were almost the only customers. Birgitta asked the girl behind the counter to turn down the music. Ho drank a bottle of mineral water, Birgitta a cup of coffee.

"Tell me about it," she said. "In detail, slowly, as much as you know. During the few days I met Hong Qiu she became a sort of friend. But who are you? Who has sent you all the way from Beijing? And above all, why?"

Ho shook her head.

"I've come from London. Hong Qiu had a lot of friends who are now mourning her loss. Ma Li, who was with Hong Qiu in Africa, gave me the sad news. And she asked me to contact you as well."

"Ma Li?"

"One of Hong Qiu's other friends."

"Start at the beginning," said Birgitta. "I still find it hard to believe that what you say is true."

"All of us do. But it is. Ma Li wrote to me and described what happened."

Birgitta waited. She had the impression that the silence also contained a message. Ho was creating a space around them, closing them in.

"The information is not consistent," said Ho. "The official story of Hong Qiu's death seems to have been sanitized."

"Who told Ma Li about it?"

"Ya Ru, Hong Qiu's brother. According to him Hong Qiu had chosen to go on a trip deep into the bush, to see wild animals. The driver was going too fast, the car overturned, and Hong Qiu died instantly. The car burst into flames; gasoline had leaked out."

Birgitta shook her head. And shuddered at the same time. She simply couldn't imagine Hong Qiu dead, a victim of a banal car accident.

"A few days before Hong Qiu died she'd had a long conversation with Ma Li," Ho continued. "I don't know what about; Ma Li is not the type to betray the confidence of a friend. But Hong Qiu had given her clear instructions. If anything happened to her, you should be told."

"Why? I barely knew her."

"I can't answer that."

"But surely Ma Li must have explained?"

"Hong Qiu wanted you to know where I could be found in London, if you needed any help."

Birgitta could feel her fear growing. I'm attacked in a street in Beijing; Hong Qiu has an accident in Africa. The two events are somehow connected.

The message scared her. **If you ever need help you should know that there is a woman in London called Ho.**

"But I don't understand what you're saying. Have you come here to give me a warning? What might happen?"

"Ma Li didn't give any details."

"But whatever was in the letter was sufficient to make you come here. You knew where I lived, you knew how to get in touch with me. What did Ma Li write?"

"Hong Qiu had told her about a Swedish judge called Mrs. Roslin who had been a close friend of hers for many years. She described the regrettable mugging, and the meticulous police investigation."

"Did she really say that?"

"I'm quoting from the letter. Word for word. Hong Qiu also told her about a photograph you had shown her."

Birgitta gave a start.

"Really? A photograph? Did she say anything else?"

"That it was of a Chinese man you thought had something to do with incidents that had taken place in Sweden."

"What did she say about the man?"

"She was worried. She had discovered something."

"What?"

"I don't know."

Birgitta said nothing. She tried to work out what was implied by the message from Hong Qiu. It could only be a warning cry out of silence. Had Hong Qiu suspected that something might happen to her? Or did she know that Birgitta was in danger? Had Hong Qiu discovered the identity of the man in the photograph? In which case, why didn't she say so?

Birgitta could feel her discomfort growing. Ho sat in silence, watching her, waiting.

"There's one question I must have an answer to. Who are you?"

"I've been living in London since the beginning of the 1990s. I first went there as a secretary in the Chinese embassy. Then I was appointed head of the English-Chinese chamber of commerce. Now I'm an independent consultant to Chinese companies that want to establish themselves in England. But not only there. I'm also involved in a big exhibition complex that's going to be built near a Swedish city called Kalmar. My work takes me all over Europe."

"How did you get to know Hong Qiu?"

The reply surprised Birgitta.

"We're relatives. Cousins. Hong Qiu was ten years older than I, but we've known each other since we were young."

Birgitta thought about Hong Qiu evidently having

said that she and Birgitta had been friends for many years. There was a message in that. Birgitta could only interpret it as meaning that their brief acquaintance had formed deep links. Significant trust was already possible. Or perhaps, rather, necessary?

"What did it say in the letter? About me?"

"Hong Qiu wanted you to be informed as soon as possible."

"What else?"

"As I've already said. You should know where I live, in case something happens."

"What might happen?"

"I don't know."

Something in Ho's tone of voice put Birgitta on her guard. So far Ho had been telling the truth. But now she was being evasive. Ho knows more than she's saying, Birgitta thought.

"China is a big country," said Birgitta. "For a Westerner it's easy to confuse its size with the impression that it's secretive. The lack of knowledge is transformed into mystery. I'm sure that's what I'm doing. That's how I experienced Hong Qiu. No matter what she said to me, I could never understand what she meant."

"China is no more secretive than any other country. It's a Western myth that our country is incomprehensible. The Europeans have never accepted that they simply don't understand the way we think. Nor that we made so many crucial discoveries and inventions before you acquired the same knowledge. Gunpowder, the compass, the printing press, everything is originally Chinese. You weren't even first to learn the art of measuring time. Thousands of years before you started making mechanical clocks we had water clocks and hourglasses. You can never forgive us for that."

"When did you last meet Hong Qiu?"

"Four years ago. She came to London. We spent a few evenings together. It was in summer. She wanted to go for long walks on Hampstead Heath and interrogate me on how the English regarded developments in China. Her questions were demanding, and she was impatient if my answers were unclear. She also wanted to go to cricket matches."

"Why?"

"She never said. Hong Qiu had a number of surprising interests."

"I'm not all that interested in sports, but cricket seems to me totally incomprehensible—it's impossible to work out how one of the teams wins or loses."

"I think her enthusiasm was due to the fact that she wanted to understand how Englishmen work by studying their national sport. Hong Qiu was a very obstinate person."

Ho checked her wristwatch. "I have to go back to London from Copenhagen later today."

Birgitta wondered whether she ought to ask the question that had been forming in the back of her mind.

"You weren't by chance in my house the night before last? In my study?"

"I was staying in a hotel. Why should I have wanted to creep into your house like a thief?" she said, bemused.

"It was just a thought. I was woken up by a noise."

"Had somebody been there?"

"I don't know."

"Is anything missing?"

"I thought somebody had disturbed my papers."

"No," said Ho. "I haven't been there."

"And you are here on your own?"

"Nobody knows I'm in Sweden. Not even my husband and children. They think I'm in Brussels. I often go there."

Ho took out a business card and put it on the table in front of Birgitta. On it was her full name, Ho Mei Wan, her address, and various telephone numbers.

"Where exactly in London do you live?"

"In Chinatown. In summer it can be very noisy in the streets all night long. But I like living there even so. It's a little China in the middle of London."

Birgitta tucked the business card into her purse. She accompanied Ho to the railroad station to make sure she caught the right train.

"My husband's a conductor on the railway," Birgitta said. "What does your husband do?"

"He's a waiter," said Ho. "That's why we live in Chinatown. He works in a restaurant on the ground floor."

Birgitta watched the Copenhagen train disappear into a tunnel. She went home, prepared a meal and felt how tired she was. She decided to watch the news, but fell asleep soon after lying down on the sofa. She was woken up by the telephone ringing. It was Staffan calling from Funchal. It was a bad connection. He had to shout in order to make himself heard over all the crackling. She gathered that all was well and they were enjoying themselves. Then they were cut off. She waited for him to call again, but nothing happened. She lay down on the sofa again. She had difficulty taking in the fact that Hong Qiu was dead. But even when Ho told her what had happened, she had the feeling that something didn't add up.

She began to regret not having asked Ho more questions. But she had simply been too tired after the complicated trial and hadn't felt up to it. And now it was too late. Ho was on her way home to her English Chinatown.

Birgitta lit a candle for Hong Qiu and searched through maps in the bookcase before finding one of London. Ho's husband's restaurant was adjacent to Leicester Square. Birgitta had once sat with Staffan in the little park there, watching people come and go. It was late fall, and they had made the journey on the spur of the moment. Looking back, they had often talked about that trip as a one-off but very precious memory.

She went to bed early, as she had to be in court the following day. The case, concerning a woman who had beaten up her mother, was not as complicated as the one involving the four Vietnamese, but she couldn't afford to be tired when she took her place on the bench. Her self-respect wouldn't allow that. To make sure that she didn't spend the night awake, she took half a sleeping pill before switching off the lights.

The case turned out to be simpler than she had expected. The accused woman suddenly changed her plea and admitted all the charges against her. And the defense did not produce any surprises that would have extended proceedings. As early as a quarter to four Birgitta Roslin was able to sum up and announce that the sentence would be made public on June 1.

When she returned to her office, she called the police in Hudiksvall, off the top of her head. She thought she recognized the voice of the young woman who answered. She sounded less nervous and overworked than last winter.

"I'm looking for Vivi Sundberg. Is she in today?"

"I saw her walk past only a few minutes ago. Who's calling?"

"The judge in Helsingborg. That'll be sufficient."

Vivi Sundberg came to the phone almost immediately. "Birgitta Roslin. Long time no hear."

"I just thought I'd check in."

"Some new Chinamen? New theories?"

Birgitta could hear the irony in Vivi's voice and was very tempted to reply that she had lots of new Chinamen to pull out of her hat. But she merely said that she was curious to know how things were going.

"We still think the man who unfortunately managed to take his own life is the murderer," Vivi said. "But even though he's dead, the investigation is continuing. We can't sentence a dead man, but we can give those who are still alive an explanation of what happened and, not least, why."

"Will you succeed?"

"It's too early to say."

"Any new leads?"

"I can't comment on that."

"No other suspects? No other possible explanations?"

"I can't comment on that either. We are still embroiled in a large-scale investigation with lots of complicated details."

"But you still think it was the man you arrested? And that he really had a motive for killing nineteen people?"

"That's what it looks like. What I can tell you is that we've had help from every kind of expert you can think of—criminologists, profile makers, psychologists, and the most experienced detectives and technicians in the country. Needless to say, Professor Persson is extremely doubtful. But when isn't he? There's still a long way to go, though."

"What about the boy?" Birgitta asked. "The victim who died, but didn't fit the pattern. How do you explain that?"

"We don't have an explanation per se. But of course we do have a picture of how it all happened."

"There's one thing I've been wondering about," said Birgitta. "Did any of the dead seem to be more important than the other victims?"

"What do you mean?"

"Anybody who was exposed to especially brutal treatment? Or maybe the one who was killed first? Or last?"

"Those are questions I can't comment on."

"Just tell me if my questions come as a surprise."

"No."

"Have you found an explanation for the red ribbon?"

"No."

"I've been in China," said Birgitta. "I saw the Great Wall of China. I was mugged and spent an entire day with some very intense police officers."

"Really?" said Vivi. "Were you hurt?"

"No, only scared. But I got back the purse they stole from me."

"So perhaps you were lucky after all?"

"Yes," said Birgitta. "I was lucky. Thanks for your time."

Birgitta remained at her desk after replacing the receiver. She had no doubt that the specialists who had been brought in would have had something to say if they'd felt the investigation was going nowhere.

That evening she went for a long walk, and spent a few hours leafing through wine brochures. She made a note of several from Italy that she wanted to order, then watched an old film on TV that she had seen with

Staffan when they first started going out together. Jane Fonda played a prostitute, the colors were pale and faded, the plot peculiar, and she couldn't help but smile at the strange clothes, especially the vulgar platform shoes that had been highly fashionable at the time.

She had almost dozed off when the telephone rang. The clock on the bedside table said a quarter to midnight. The ringing stopped. If it had been Staffan or one of the children they would have called her cell phone. She switched off the light. Then the telephone rang again. She jumped up and answered using the phone on her desk.

"Birgitta Roslin? My apologies for calling at this late hour. Do you recognize my voice?"

She did recognize it, but couldn't put a face to it. It was a man, an elderly man.

"No, not really."

"Sture Hermansson."

"Do I know you?"

"Know is perhaps too strong a word. But you visited my little Hotel Eden in Hudiksvall a few months ago."

"Now I remember."

"I want to apologize for calling so late."

"You already have. I take it you have a special reason for calling?"

"He's come back."

Hermansson lowered his voice when he spoke these last words. The penny dropped, and she realized what he was talking about.

"The Chinaman?"

"Precisely."

"Are you sure?"

"He arrived not long ago. He hadn't booked in advance. I've just given him his key. He's in the same room as last time. Number twelve."

"Are you sure it's the same man?"

"You have the film. But he seems to be the same person. He uses the same name, at least."

Birgitta tried to think what to do. Her heart was pounding.

Her train of thought was broken by Hermansson.

"One more thing."

"What?"

"He asked about you."

Birgitta held her breath. The fear inside her hit home with full force.

"That's not possible."

"My English is not good. To be honest, it took me some time before I realized who he was asking after. But I'm sure it was you."

"What did you tell him?"

"That you lived in Helsingborg. He seemed surprised. I think he assumed you were from Hudiksvall."

"What else did you say?"

"I gave him your address, because you'd left it with me and asked me to get in touch if anything happened."

You half-witted imbecile, Birgitta thought. She was suddenly panic-stricken.

"Do me a favor," she said. "Call me when he goes out. Even if it's the middle of the night. Call."

"I take it you want me to tell him I've been in touch with you?"

"It would be good if you didn't mention that."

"Okay, I won't. I won't say a thing."

The call was over. Birgitta didn't understand what was going on.

Hong Qiu was dead. But the man with the red ribbon had come back.

34

After a sleepless night Birgitta Roslin called the Hotel Eden just before seven a.m. The phone rang for a considerable amount of time without anybody answering.

She had tried to deal with her fear. If Ho hadn't come from London and told her that Hong Qiu was dead, she wouldn't have reacted so strongly to Sture Hermansson's call. But she assumed that because Hermansson hadn't been in touch again during the night, nothing further had happened. Perhaps the man was still asleep.

She waited another half hour. She had several days ahead of her without any trials and hoped to work her way through all the piled-up paperwork and spend some time pondering her final decision regarding the sentence for the four Vietnamese criminals.

The telephone rang. It was Staffan from Funchal.

"We're taking a side trip," he said.

"Over the mountains? Down in the valleys? Along those beautiful paths through all the flowers?"

"We've booked tickets on a big sailboat that's going to take us out to sea. We may be out of cell phone range for the next couple of days."

"Where are you going?"

"Nowhere. It's the children's idea. We'll be unqualified crew members together with the captain, a cook, and two real sailors."

"When are you leaving?"

"We're already at sea. It's lovely weather. But unfortunately there's no wind yet."

"Are there lifeboats? Do you have life jackets?"

"You're underestimating us. Tell me you hope we have a good time. If you like I can bring you a little bottle of seawater as a souvenir."

It was a bad connection. They yelled out a few words of farewell. When Birgitta replaced the receiver, she suddenly wished she had gone to Funchal with them, even though Hans Mattsson would have been disappointed and her colleagues irritated.

She called the Hotel Eden again. Now the line was busy. She waited, tried again after five minutes—still busy. She could see through the window that the beautiful spring weather was continuing. She was too warmly dressed and changed her clothes. Still busy.

She decided to try from downstairs in her office. After checking the refrigerator and making a grocery list, she dialed the Hudiksvall number one more time.

A woman replied in broken Swedish. "Eden."

"Can I speak to Sture Hermansson, please?"

"You can't," yelled the woman.

Then she shouted something hysterically in a foreign language that Birgitta assumed was Russian.

It sounded as if the telephone had fallen onto the floor. Somebody picked it up. Now it was a man who answered. He spoke with a Hälsingland accent.

"Hello?"

"Can I speak to Sture Hermansson, please?"

"Who's asking?"

"Who am I speaking to? Is this Hotel Eden?"

"Yes. But you can't speak to Sture."

"My name's Birgitta Roslin and I'm calling from Helsingborg. I was contacted around midnight by Sture Hermansson. We arranged to speak again this morning."

"He's dead."

She took a deep breath. A brief moment of dizziness. "What happened?"

"We don't know. It looks as if he's managed to cut himself with a knife and bled to death."

"Who am I speaking to?"

"My name's Tage Elander. Not the former prime minister, my surname doesn't have an **r** before the **l**. I run a wallpaper factory in the building next door.

The hotel maid, the Russian woman, came running in a few minutes ago. Now we're waiting for the police and an ambulance."

"Has he been murdered?"

"Sture? Who the hell would want to murder Sture? He seems to have cut himself on a kitchen knife. As he was alone in the hotel last night, nobody heard his cries for help. It's tragic. He was such a friendly man."

Birgitta wasn't sure she had understood correctly. "He can't have been alone in the hotel."

"Why not?"

"Because he had guests."

"According to the maid, the hotel was empty."

"He had at least one paying guest. He told me that last night. A Chinese man in room number twelve."

"It's possible I misunderstood. I'll ask her."

Birgitta could hear the conversation in the background. The Russian maid was still hysterical.

Elander came back to the telephone. "She insists there were no guests here last night."

"All you need to do is check the ledger. Room number twelve. A man with a Chinese name."

Elander put down the phone again. Birgitta could hear that the maid whose name might be Natasha had started to cry. She also heard a door shutting and different voices speaking in the background. Elander picked up the receiver again. "I'll have to stop there. The police and the ambulance have arrived. But there is no hotel ledger."

"What do you mean?"

"It's vanished. The maid says it's always on the counter. But it's gone."

"I'm certain there was a guest staying in the hotel last night."

"Well, he's not here now. Maybe he's the one who stole the ledger?"

"It could be worse than that," said Birgitta. "He might have been the one holding the kitchen knife that killed Sture Hermansson."

"I don't understand what you're saying. Maybe it's best if you speak to one of the police officers."

"I'll do that. But not right now."

She replaced the receiver. She had remained standing while taking the call, but now she had to sit down. Her heart was hammering in her chest.

Everything was falling into place. If the man she thought had murdered the inhabitants of Hesjö-vallen had returned, asked about her, and then vanished with the hotel ledger, leaving behind a dead hotel owner, it could mean only one thing. He had come back in order to kill her. When she asked the young Chinese man to show the guards the photograph from Sture Hermansson's camera, she could never have imagined the consequences. For obvious reasons the murderer had assumed she lived in Hudiksvall. Now that mistake had been corrected. He had been given the correct address by Hermansson.

Her panic increased. The mugging, Hong Qiu's

death, the purse that had been stolen and then recovered, the visit to her hotel room—everything was connected. But what would happen now?

She dialed her husband's number, feeling desperate. But no signal. She cursed his sailing adventure under her breath. She tried the number of one of their daughters, with the same result.

She called Karin Wiman. No response there either.

The panic gave her no breathing room. She had to get out of there.

Once she had reached that decision, she acted as she always did in difficult situations: rapidly and firmly, with no hesitation. She called Hans Mattsson and got through to him even though he was in a meeting.

She told him she had a virus and ended the call abruptly.

Birgitta went upstairs and packed a small suitcase. Hidden inside an old textbook from her student days were some five- and ten-pound notes from a previous trip to England. She was sure that the man who had killed Sture Hermansson must be on his way southward. He might even have set off during the night if he was traveling by car. Nobody had seen him leave.

It dawned on her that she had forgotten the hotel's surveillance camera. She called the Hotel Eden. This time a coughing man answered. She didn't bother to explain who she was.

"There's a surveillance camera in the hotel. Sture Hermansson used to take pictures of his guests. It's not true that the hotel was empty last night. There was at least one guest."

"Who am I speaking to?"

"Are you a police officer?"

"Yes."

"You heard what I said. Who I am is unimportant."

She replaced the receiver. It was half past eight by now. She left the house, hailed a taxi, asked to be taken to the train station, and was soon on board a train to Copenhagen. Her panic was now being transformed into a defense of her actions. She was convinced that she wasn't imagining the danger. Her only hope now was to take advantage of the assistance Ho had offered her.

In the departure hall at Kastrup she saw on a display that there was a flight to London in two hours. She bought a ticket with an open return. After checking in she sat down with a cup of coffee and called Karin Wiman. But she hung up before Karin had a chance to answer. What could she say to her? Karin wouldn't understand, despite what Birgitta had told her when they met a few days earlier. The kind of things that happened to Birgitta Roslin didn't happen in Karin Wiman's world. They didn't happen in her own world either, truth be told, but an unlikely chain of events had driven her into the corner where she now found herself.

She arrived in London after an hour's delay: the airport was in a state of chaos due to a terror alert after an unattended suitcase had been discovered in one of the departure lounges. It was late in the afternoon before she managed to get to central London and found herself a room in a two-star hotel on a street off Tottenham Court Road. Once she had settled in and, with the aid of a sweater, sealed the drafty window overlooking a grim courtyard, she lay down on the bed feeling exhausted. She had dozed for a few minutes during the flight, but was kept up by a child that kept screaming until the wheels hit the tarmac at Heathrow. The mother, who seemed far too young to be one, had eventually collapsed in tears herself, thanks to the screeching child.

When Birgitta woke with a start she found she had slept for three hours. Dusk was already falling. She had intended to look for Ho at her home address in Chinatown that same day, but now she decided to wait until tomorrow. She took a short walk to Piccadilly Circus and went into a restaurant. Shortly afterward a large party of Chinese tourists came in through the glass doors. She stared at them in a state of rising panic but managed to gain control of herself. After her meal she returned to the hotel and sat in the bar with a cup of tea. When she collected her room key she noticed that the hotel had a Chinese night porter. She wondered if it was only now that Chinese people were popping up all over Europe, or if it was an earlier development that she hadn't noticed before.

She thought back over what had happened, with

the return of the Chinese man to the Hotel Eden and Sture Hermansson's death. She was tempted to call Vivi Sundberg but resisted the urge. If the hotel register was missing, a photograph in the do-it-yourself surveillance camera was unlikely to make much of an impression on the police. Moreover, if the police thought the death was an accident, there would be no point in making a call. But she did dial the hotel's number. There wasn't even an answering machine to say the place was closed—not for the season, but probably for good.

Unable to shake off her fear, she barricaded the door with a chair and checked the window locks carefully. She went to bed, surfed through the television channels, but rather than whatever was flickering past on the screen, she kept seeing a sailboat beating its way over the sea from Madeira.

She woke up in the middle of the night to find the television still on, now showing an old black-and-white James Cagney gangster movie. She switched off the lamp that was shining directly into her face and tried to go back to sleep. But failed. She lay awake for the rest of the night.

It was drizzling outside when she got up and drank coffee without eating anything. After borrowing an umbrella from reception, where there was now a young woman of Asian apparance, perhaps from the Philippines or Thailand, Birgitta stepped out into the streets of London. Most of the restaurants were still closed. Hans Mattsson, who traveled the world in search of new taste sensations, had once said that the best way of finding really good restaurants, be they Chinese, Iranian, or Italian, was to look out for ones that were open in the mornings, because they didn't only cater to tourists. At Ho's address there was a restaurant on the ground floor, as she had described. It was closed. The building was constructed of red brick, with an alley on either side. She decided to ring the bell by the door leading to the building's apartments.

But something made her hesitate. She crossed the street to a café—open in the morning—and ordered a cup of tea. What did she actually know about Ho? And what did she know about Hong Qiu, come to that? One day Hong Qiu had suddenly turned up at her restaurant table out of nowhere. Who had sent her? Could it have been Hong Qiu who sent one of her burly bodyguards after Karin Wiman and Birgitta when they visited the Great Wall? There was one fact Birgitta couldn't avoid: both Hong Qiu and Ho knew a great deal about who she was. And all this was because of a photograph.

Were her suspicions on the mark? Had Hong Qiu turned up in order to entice her away from the hotel? Perhaps it wasn't even true that Hong Qiu had died in a car accident. Maybe Hong Qiu and the man who called himself Wang Min Hao were somehow or other both involved in what had happened at Hesjö-vallen. Had Ho come to Helsingborg for the same reason? Could she have known that a man was on his way once more to the little Hotel Eden?

She tried to recall what she had told Hong Qiu in their various conversations. Too much, she now realized. What surprised her was that she hadn't been more careful. Hong Qiu had been the one who raised the matter. A throwaway remark that the mass murders in Hesjövallen had been an item in the Chinese mass media? Was that really plausible? Or had Hong Qiu merely enticed Birgitta to walk out onto the ice in order to watch her slip and then helped her back onto dry land once she had found out what she wanted to know?

Why had Ho spent so much time in the public gallery of Birgitta's courtroom? She didn't understand Swedish. Or perhaps she did? And then she had suddenly had to rush back to London. What if Ho had only been there in order to keep an eye on Birgitta? Perhaps Ho had an accomplice who had spent hours rummaging through Birgitta's home while the judge was sitting in court?

Right now I need somebody to talk to, she thought. Not Karin Wiman, she wouldn't understand. Staffan or my children. But they are out at sea and unreachable.

Birgitta was just about to leave the café when she saw the door on the other side of the street open. Out came Ho, who started walking toward Leicester Square. It seemed to Birgitta that Ho was on her guard. Birgitta hesitated before emerging into the street and following her. When they came to the square, Ho entered the little park, then turned off toward the Strand. Birgitta kept expecting Ho to turn around to check if anybody was following her. She finally did just before they came to Zimbabwe House. Birgitta had time to lower her umbrella to hide her face but almost lost Ho until she caught sight of her yellow raincoat again. As they approached the Savoy Hotel, Ho opened the heavy door to a big office block. Birgitta waited for a few minutes before going up to read on the well-polished brass nameplate that it was the English-Chinese chamber of commerce.

She retraced her steps and selected a café in Regent Street just off Piccadilly. Sitting down with a cup of coffee she dialed one of the numbers on Ho's business card. An answering machine invited her to leave a message. She hung up, prepared what she wanted to say in English, then dialed the number again.

"I did as you said. I came to London because I think I'm being pursued. Right now I'm sitting in Simon's, a café next to Rawson's fashion house on Regent Street, just off Piccadilly. It's now ten o'clock. I'll stay for an hour. If you haven't been in touch before then, I'll call you again later."

Ho arrived forty minutes later. Her garish yellow raincoat stood out among the dark clothes most people were wearing. Birgitta had the feeling that even this was of some significance.

"What's happened?"

A waitress took Ho's order for tea before Birgitta could answer. She explained in detail about the man who had turned up at the hotel in Hudiksvall, that it was the same man she'd told her about before, and that the hotel owner had been killed.

"Are you sure about this?"

"I haven't come all the way to London to tell you about something I'm not sure of. I've come here because this all really happened, and I'm scared. This man asked specifically about me. He was given my address, the house where I live. Now I'm here. I'm doing what Ma Li or actually Hong Qiu said to you and you said to me. I'm scared, but I'm also angry because I suspect that neither you nor Hong Qiu has been telling the truth."

"Why should I lie? You've come a long way to London, but don't forget that my journey to visit you was just as long."

"I'm not being told everything that's going on. I'm not hearing any explanations, although I'm convinced they exist."

"You're right," said Ho. "But you're forgetting that it's possible neither Hong Qiu nor Ma Li knew any more than they said."

"I didn't see it clearly when you came to Sweden to visit me," said Birgitta, "but I do now. Hong Qiu was worried that somebody would try to kill me. That's what she said to Ma Li. And the message was passed on to you, three women in succession to warn a fourth that she was in danger. But not just any old danger. Death. Nothing less than that. Without realizing it, I've put myself at risk, the extent of which I'm only now beginning to comprehend. Am I right?"

"That's why I went to see you."

Birgitta leaned forward and took Ho by the hand. "Help me to understand. Answer my questions."

"If I can."

"You can. It wasn't the case that you had somebody with you when you came to Helsingborg, was it? It's not the case that at this very moment there's somebody keeping an eye on us, is it? You could have called somebody before coming here."

"Why would I have done that?"

"That's not an answer, it's a new question. I want answers."

"I didn't have anybody with me when I went to Helsingborg."

"Why did you sit in my courtroom for two whole days? You couldn't understand a word of what was said, after all."

"No."

Birgitta changed over into Swedish. Ho frowned and shook her head. "I don't understand."

"Are you sure? Or do you actually understand Swedish very well?"

"If that were the case, surely I'd have spoken to you in Swedish."

"You must realize that I'm very unsure. You might find it advantageous to pretend that you don't understand my language. I even wonder if you're wearing a yellow raincoat to make it easier for somebody to see you."

"Why should I?"

"I don't know. I don't know anything at all at the

moment. Most important of course is that Hong Qiu wanted to warn me. But why should I turn to you for help? What can you do?"

"Let me start with your last question," said Ho. "Chinatown is a world of its own. Even though thousands of English people and tourists wander around our streets—Gerrard Street, Lisle Street, Wardour Street, all the alleys—we only allow you to see the surface. Concealed behind your Chinatown is my Chinatown. It's possible to hide away there, change identity, survive for months and even years without being discovered. Even if most of the people living here are Chinese who have become naturalized English citizens, the bottom line is that we all feel that we are in our own world. I can help you by giving you entry into my Chinatown, a place you would otherwise never be allowed into."

"What exactly should I be scared of?"

"Ma Li wasn't at all clear when she wrote to me. But you mustn't forget that Ma Li was also scared. She didn't say as much, but I could sense it."

"Everybody's scared. Are you scared?"

"Not yet. But I **can** be."

Her cell phone rang. She checked the display and stood up. "Where are you staying?" she asked. "Which hotel? I have to go back to work."

"Sanderson."

"I know where that is. What room?"

"One thirty-five."

"Can we meet tomorrow?"

"Why do we have to wait that long?"

"I can't get away from work before then. I have a meeting this evening that I can't skip."

"Is that really true?"

Ho took hold of Birgitta Roslin's hand. "Yes," she said. "A Chinese delegation is going to talk business with the bosses of several big British companies. I have to be there."

"Right now you're the only one I can turn to."

"Call me tomorrow morning. I'll try to get time off."

Ho went out into the rain, her yellow coat fluttering as she walked. Birgitta Roslin stayed for quite some time, feeling incredibly weary, before walking back to her hotel, which of course was not the Sanderson. She still didn't trust Ho, just as these days she mistrusted anyone vaguely Asian in appearance.

She ate in the hotel's restaurant that evening. It had stopped raining by the time she finished dinner. She decided to go out to the park and sit for a while on the same bench that she and Staffan had sat on once upon a time.

She watched people coming and going. A young couple sat briefly on her bench, kissing and cuddling, followed by a man carrying yesterday's paper, rescued from a trash can.

She made another attempt to call Staffan on his sailboat off Madeira, even though she knew it was a waste of time.

She noted how many fewer and fewer people were

strolling through the park, and eventually stood up to return to her hotel.

Then she saw him. He came along one of the paths diagonally behind where she had been sitting. He was dressed in black and could only have been the man whose photo was taken by Sture Hermansson's surveillance camera. He was walking straight toward her, carrying something shiny in his hand.

She screamed and took a step back. As he came closer, she fell over backward and hit her head against the iron edge of the bench.

The last thing she saw was his face; it was as if her eyes had taken one more picture of him. Then she faded away into an all-embracing and silent darkness.

35

Ya Ru loved the shadows. He could make himself invisible there, just like the beasts of prey he both admired and feared. But others had the same ability. It had often occurred to him that young entrepreneurs were in the process of taking over the economy, and hence before long would be demanding a seat at the table where political decisions were made. Everybody starts in the shadows, where they can watch and observe without being seen.

But the shadow he was hiding behind on this particular evening in rainy London had a different aim. He watched Birgitta Roslin, sitting on a bench in a little park off Leicester Square. From where he was standing he could see only her back. But he didn't dare risk discovery. He had already noticed that she was on her guard like a restless animal. Ya Ru didn't underestimate her. If Hong Qiu had trusted Birgitta Roslin, he needed to take her extremely seriously.

He had been following her all day, ever since she turned up outside the building where Ho lived. He had been amused to realize he owned the restaurant where Ho's husband, Wa, worked. They didn't know that, of course—Ya Ru seldom owned anything under his own name. The Ming Restaurant belonged to Chinese Food, Inc., a limited company registered in Liechtenstein, where Ya Ru had placed his European restaurant portfolio. He kept a careful eye on the accounts and quarterly reports produced by young, gifted Chinese employees he had recruited from the top English universities. Ya Ru hated everything English. He would never forget what history told him. He was delighted to rob the country of talented young businessmen who had taken advantage of the best universities.

Ya Ru had never eaten a meal at the Ming Restaurant. He didn't intend to do so on this occasion either. As soon as he had fulfilled his mission he would return to Beijing.

There had been a time in his life when he'd regarded airports with almost religious emotions.

They were the modern equivalent of harbors. In those days Ya Ru had never traveled anywhere without a copy of **The Travels of Marco Polo**. The man's fearless desire to investigate the unknown had been an inspiration. Nowadays he thought more and more that traveling was a pain, even if he did have a private jet and was usually spared the agony of hanging around in disconsolate and soul-destroying airports. The feeling that one's mind was revitalized by all these sudden changes of location, the intoxicating delight of passing through time zones, was negated by all the pointless time spent waiting for departures or baggage. The neon-lit shopping malls at airports, the moving walkways, the echoing corridors, the ever-smaller glass cages in which smokers were crammed together, were not places where new thoughts or new philosophical ideas could be developed. He thought back to the time when people traveled by train or by transatlantic liners. In those days intellectual discussions and learned arguments had been taken for granted, as much a part of the accepted environment as luxury and idleness.

That was why he had fitted his private jet, the big Gulfstream he now owned, with antique bookshelves, in which he kept the most significant works of Chinese and foreign literature.

He felt like a distant relative—with no blood relationship, only a mystical one—of Captain Nemo, who traveled in his underwater vessel like a lone emperor without an empire but with a large library and a devastating hatred of the people who had ruined his life. It was believed that Nemo modeled himself after a vanished Indian prince who had opposed the British Empire. Ya Ru could feel an affinity to this, but what he really sympathized with was the gloomy and embittered figure of Nemo himself, the inspired engineer and widely read philosopher. He named the Gulfstream **Nautilus II**. An enlargement of one of the original etchings in the book, depicting Nemo with his reluctant visitors in the extensive library of the **Nautilus,** was displayed on the wall next to the entrance to the flight deck.

But now everything was about the shadows. He concealed himself efficiently and observed the woman he would have to kill. Another thing he had in common with Nemo was his belief in revenge. The necessity of revenge left its mark through history like a leitmotif.

It would all soon be over. Now that he was in Chinatown in London, with raindrops falling on the collar of his jacket, it struck him that there was something remarkable about the end of this story taking place in England. It was from here that the Wang brothers had commenced their journey back to China, the country that only one of them would ever see again.

Ya Ru didn't mind waiting when he was in control of the time involved, unlike at airports. This attitude often surprised his friends, who regarded life as all too short, created by a god that could seem like a miserable old mandarin who didn't want the joy of existence to last too long. Ya Ru had argued that, on the contrary, the gods responsible for creating life knew exactly what they were doing. If humans were allowed to live too long, their knowledge would increase to such an extent that they would be able to see through the mandarins and join forces to exterminate them. A short life span prevents many revolutions, Ya Ru maintained. And his friends usually agreed, though they didn't always understand his thinking.

Ya Ru always looked to animals when he wanted to understand his own behavior and that of others. He was the leopard, and he was also the stallion that fought off all challengers in order to become the sole emperor.

If Deng was the colorless cat that hunted mice better than any other, Mao was the owl, the wise bird but also the ice-cold raptor that knew exactly when to swoop down in silence and seize its prey.

His line of thought was broken by Birgitta Roslin standing up. During the day he had spent following her, one thing had become abundantly clear: She was scared. She was always looking around, never still. Worries were flowing constantly through her head. He would be able to make use of that observation, even if he hadn't yet decided how.

But now she stood up. Ya Ru hung back in the shadows.

Then something happened he was totally unprepared for. She gave a start, screamed, then stumbled backward and hit her head on a bench. A Chinese man stopped and bent down to investigate what had happened. Several other people came hurrying over. Ya Ru stepped out of the shadows and approached the group standing around the prostrate woman. Two police officers came running. Ya Ru pushed his way forward to get a better view. Birgitta Roslin sat up. She had evidently lost consciousness for a few seconds. He heard the police officers asking if she needed an ambulance, but she said no.

It was the first time Ya Ru had heard her voice. He memorized it—a deep, expressive voice.

"I must have stumbled," he heard her saying. "I thought somebody was coming toward me. I was frightened."

"Were you attacked?"

"No. It was just my imagination."

The man who had frightened her was still there. Ya Ru noticed that there was a certain similarity between Liu Xin and this man, who by sheer coincidence had entered into a story he had nothing to do with.

Ya Ru smiled to himself. She is indeed scared and on her guard.

The police officers escorted Birgitta Roslin back to her hotel. Ya Ru remained in the background. But now he knew where she was staying. After checking once more that she was steady on her feet, the police officers walked off while she went in through the hotel doors. Ya Ru saw her being given her key by a receptionist who took it from one of the highest shelves. He waited a few more minutes before entering the hotel lobby. The receptionist was Chinese. Ya Ru bowed and held out a sheet of paper.

"The lady who just came in, she dropped this in the street outside."

The receptionist took the paper and put it into the empty mail slot. It was for room 614, on the very top floor of the hotel.

The sheet of paper was white, and blank. Ya Ru suspected that Birgitta would ask the receptionist who had handed it in. A Chinese man, she would be told. And she would become even more on edge. There was no risk to himself.

Ya Ru pretended to be reading a brochure advertising the hotel while thinking about how he could find out how long Birgitta Roslin was staying. The opportunity came when the Chinese receptionist disappeared into a back room and was replaced by a young Englishwoman. Ya Ru went up to the counter.

"Mrs. Birgitta Roslin," he said. "From Sweden. I'm supposed to pick her up and drive her to the airport. It's not clear if she's expecting to be picked up tomorrow or the day after."

Without more ado the receptionist tapped away at the computer keyboard.

"Mrs. Roslin is booked in for three days," she said. "Shall I call her so that you can sort out when she needs to be collected?"

"No, I'll sort it out with the office. We don't like to disturb our clients unnecessarily."

Ya Ru left the hotel. It had started drizzling again. He turned up his collar and walked toward Gower Street to find a taxi. Now he didn't need to worry about how much time he had at his disposal. A very long time has passed since all this began, he thought. A few more days until it reaches its inevitable conclusion are of no significance.

He hailed a taxi and gave the address in Whitehall where his company in Liechtenstein owned an apartment he stayed at on his visits to England. He had often felt that he was betraying the memory of his forefathers by staying in London when he could just as well go to Paris or Berlin. As he sat in the taxi he made up his mind to sell the Whitehall apartment and look for a new place in Paris.

It was time to bring that part of his life to a close as well.

He lay down on top of the bed and listened to the silence. He had insulated all the walls when he first bought the apartment. Now he couldn't even hear the distant hum of traffic. The only sound was the sighing of the air conditioner. It gave him the feeling of being on board a ship. He felt very much at peace.

"How long ago was it?" he said aloud into the room. "How long ago was it when this story that is now coming to a close first started?"

He did the calculation in his head. It was 1868 when San first sat down in his little room at the mission station. Now it was 2006. One hundred thirty-eight years ago. San had sat down in the candlelight and meticulously chronicled the story of himself and his two brothers, Guo Si and Wu. It had begun the day they left their squalid home and set off on the long trek to Canton. There they had been exposed to a wicked demon in the guise of Zi. From then onward death followed them wherever they went. In the end the only one left alive was San, with his stubborn determination to tell his story.

They died in a state of deepest humiliation, Ya Ru thought. The succession of emperors and mandarins followed Confucius's advice to keep the population on such a tight rein that rebellion could never be possible. But just as the English maltreated the natives in their colonies, the brothers were tortured by Americans when they were building the railroads. At the same time, the English displayed icy contempt for the Chinese and attempted to make them all drug addicts by swamping the markets in China with opium. That is how I see those brutal Englishmen, as drug dealers standing on street corners selling their dope to people they hate and regard as inferior creatures. It's not so long since Chinese were depicted in European and American cartoons as apes with tails. But the caricatures were true: We were born to be humiliated and turned into slaves. We were not human. We were animals. We had tails.

When Ya Ru used to wander around the streets of London, he would think about how many of the buildings surrounding him were built with enslaved people's money, their toil and their suffering, their backs and their deaths.

What had San written? That they had built the railroad through the American desert using their own ribs as sleepers under the rails. Similarly, the screams and pains of slaves were infused into the iron bridges that spanned the Thames, or in the thick stone walls of the enormous buildings in the fine old financial district of London.

Ya Ru's train of thought was broken when he dozed off. On waking he went into the living room, where all the furniture and lamps were Chinese. On the table in front of the dark red sofa was a light blue silk bag. He opened it, having first placed a sheet of white paper on the table. Then he poured out a pile of finely ground glass. It was an ancient method of killing people, mixing the almost invisible grains of glass into a bowl of soup or a cup of tea. There was no escape for anybody who drank it. The thousands of microscopic grains of glass cut the victim's intestines to shreds. In ancient times it was known as the invisible death because it was sudden and couldn't be explained.

The pulverized glass would bring San's story to an end. Ya Ru carefully tipped the glass back into the silk bag and tied it with a knot. Then he switched off all the lamps except for one with a red shade inset with dragons in gold brocade. He sat down in an easy chair that had once belonged to a rich landowner in

Shandong Province. He was breathing slowly and sank into the peaceful state in which he thought most clearly.

It took him an hour to decide how he would conclude this last chapter by killing Birgitta Roslin, who in all probability had given his sister Hong Qiu information that could harm him. Information that she could well have passed on to others without his knowing. When he had made up his mind, he pressed a button on the table. A few minutes later he heard old Lang starting to prepare dinner in the kitchen.

She used to clean Ya Ru's office in Beijing. Night after night he had observed Lang's silent movements. She was a better cleaner than any of the others who between them kept his skyscraper clean.

When he heard that, in addition to her cleaning work, she also prepared traditional dinners for weddings and funerals, he asked her to cook him a dinner the following evening. He then appointed her his cook and paid her a wage she would otherwise never have been able to dream of. She had a son who had immigrated to London, and Ya Ru arranged for her to fly to Europe in order to look after him during his many visits.

That evening Lang served a series of small dishes. Without Ya Ru having said anything, she had divined what he wanted. She placed his tea on a small kerosene-flamed heater in the living room.

"Breakfast tomorrow?" she asked before leaving.

"No, I'll see to that myself. But dinner—fish."

Ya Ru went to bed early. He hadn't had many uninterrupted hours of sleep since leaving Beijing. First the flight to Europe, then the complicated connections to the town in the north of Sweden, then the visit to Helsingborg, where he had broken into Birgitta's study and found the word "London" underlined on a scrap of paper next to her telephone. He had flown to Stockholm in his private jet and then on to Copenhagen, followed by London. He had assumed that Roslin would be going to visit Ho.

He made a few notes in his diary, switched off the lamp, and soon fell asleep.

The next day London was enveloped in thick clouds. Ya Ru got up as usual at five o'clock and listened to the Chinese news on his shortwave radio. Then he checked the world stock markets on a computer, spoke to two of his managing directors about various ongoing projects, and made himself a simple breakfast of fruit.

At seven he left the apartment with the silk bag in his pocket. There was one potential shortcoming in his plan. He didn't know what time Birgitta Roslin usually ate breakfast. If she was already in the dining room when he got there, he would have to wait until the following day.

He paused for a couple of minutes to listen to a lone cellist playing on the sidewalk with an upturned hat at his feet. He donated a few coins and continued. He turned onto Irving Street and came to the hotel. There was a man at the reception desk he hadn't seen before. He went up to the counter and took one of the hotel's business cards. As he did so he noticed that the sheet of paper had disappeared from Birgitta Roslin's mail slot.

The door to the dining room was standing open. He saw Birgitta Roslin right away. She was sitting at a table by the window, evidently just beginning her breakfast, and was being served coffee by a waiter.

Ya Ru held his breath and thought for a second. He decided not to wait after all. This was his moment. He took off his overcoat and approached the headwaiter. He explained that he wasn't a guest but would like to have breakfast. The headwaiter was from South Korea. He led Ya Ru to a table diagonally behind the one where Birgitta Roslin was leaning over her plate.

Ya Ru looked around the restaurant. There was an emergency exit in the wall closest to his table. As he went to collect a newspaper, he tried the door and discovered it was unlocked. He returned to his table, ordered tea, and waited. Many of the tables were still empty, but Ya Ru had noted that most of the keys were not behind the desk at reception. The hotel was almost full.

He took out his cell phone and the business card he had picked up. Then he dialed the number and waited. When the receptionist answered, he said he had an important message for one of the guests, Birgitta Roslin.

"I'll put you through to her room."

"She'll be in the dining room," said Ya Ru. "She always has breakfast at this time. I'd be grateful if you could find her. She usually sits at a window table. She'll be wearing a blue dress; her hair is dark and cut short."

"I'll ask her to come and take the call."

Ya Ru held the phone in his hand with the line open until he saw the receptionist enter the dining room. Then he hung up, slipped it into his pocket, and at the same time took out the silk bag of ground glass. As Birgitta Roslin stood up and accompanied the receptionist out through the door, Ya Ru walked over to her table. He picked up her newspaper and looked around, as if making sure that the guest sitting there really had left. He waited while a waiter topped up cups of coffee at a neighboring table, all the time keeping a close eye on the door to reception. When the waiter had moved on, Ya Ru opened the bag and tipped the contents into the half-empty cup of coffee. Birgitta Roslin came back into the dining room. Ya Ru had already turned around and was about to return to his own table.

At that moment the windowpane shattered, and the sound of a rifle shot combined with the noise of falling glass. Ya Ru had no time to realize that something had gone wrong, catastrophically wrong. The bullet hit him in his right temple and killed him instantly. All his important bodily functions had already ceased when his body fell onto a table and knocked over a vase of flowers.

Birgitta Roslin stood there motionless, just like all the other guests in the dining room, the waiters and waitresses and a headwaiter clutching a dish of hard-boiled eggs. The silence was broken by somebody screaming.

Roslin stared at the dead body lying on the white tablecloth. It still hadn't dawned on her that it had anything to do with her. A vague thought that London was being subjected to a terrorist attack flew through her head.

Then she felt a hand grabbing hold of her arm. She tried to pull herself free as she turned around.

It was Ho standing behind her.

"Don't say a word," said Ho. "Just follow me. We can't stay here."

Ho ushered Birgitta out into the foyer.

"Give me your key. I'll pack your bag while you pay your bill."

"What's going on?"

"Don't ask any questions. Just do as I say."

Ho was gripping her arm so tightly that it hurt. Chaos had broken out in the hotel. People were screaming and yelling, running back and forth.

"Insist on paying," said Ho. "We have to get out of here."

Birgitta understood. Not what had happened, but what Ho said. She stood at the desk and bellowed at one of the bewildered receptionists that she wanted to settle her bill. Ho disappeared into one of the elevators and returned ten minutes later with Birgitta's suitcase. By then the hotel lobby was teeming with police officers and paramedics.

Birgitta had paid her bill.

"Now we're going to walk calmly out of the door," said Ho. "If anybody tries to stop you, just say that you have a plane to catch."

They elbowed their way out into the street without anybody hindering them. Birgitta paused and looked back. Ho dragged at her arm once again.

"Don't turn around. Just walk normally. We'll talk later."

They came to where Ho lived and went up to her apartment, on the second floor. There was a man there, in his twenties. He was very pale and talked excitedly to Ho. Birgitta could see that Ho was trying to calm him down. She took him into an adjacent room, where the agitated conversation continued. When they returned, the man was carrying a bundle that looked like it might contain a pool cue. He left the apartment. Ho stood by the window, looking down into the street. Birgitta slumped onto a chair. She had only just realized that the man who died had fallen onto the table next to the one where she'd been sitting.

She looked at Ho, who had now left the window.

She was very pale. Birgitta could see that she was trembling.

"What happened?" she asked.

"You were the one who was supposed to die," said Ho. "He was going to kill you. I must tell it exactly as it is."

Birgitta shook her head.

"You have to be clear," she said. "Otherwise I don't know what I'll do."

"The man who died was Ya Ru, Hong Qiu's brother."

"What happened?"

"He tried to kill you. We managed to stop him at the very last moment."

"We?"

"You could have died because you gave me false information about the hotel you were staying at. Why did you do that? Did you think you couldn't trust me? Are you so confused that you can't distinguish between friends and people who are anything but?"

Birgitta raised her hand. "You're going too fast. I can't keep up. Hong Qiu's brother? Why would he want to kill me?"

"Because you knew too much about what happened in your country. All those people who died. Ya Ru was presumably behind it all—that's what Hong Qiu thought, at least."

"But why?"

"I can't say. I don't know."

Birgitta was thinking. When Ho was about to speak again, Birgitta raised her hand to stop her.

"You said 'we,' " said Birgitta after a while. "The man who just left your apartment was carrying something. Was it a rifle?"

"Yes. I had decided that San should keep an eye on you. But there was nobody with your name at the hotel you told me you were staying at. It was San who realized that this hotel was closest. We saw you through the window. When Ya Ru came up to your table after you'd been called away, I realized that he was going to kill you. San took out his rifle and shot him. It all happened so quickly that nobody in the street caught on. Most people probably thought it was a motorbike backfiring. San had the rifle hidden in a raincoat."

"San?"

"Hong Qiu's son. She sent him to me."

"Why?"

"Hong Qiu wasn't only afraid for her own life and yours. She was just as afraid for her son. San was convinced that Ya Ru had killed his mother. So he didn't need much encouragement to get his revenge."

Birgitta felt sick. She was slowly beginning to realize what it was all about. It was as she had suspected earlier but rejected because it seemed so preposterous. Something in the past had triggered the deaths of all those people in Hesjövallen.

She reached out and grabbed hold of Ho. There were tears in her eyes.

"Is it all over now?"

"I think so. You can go home. Ya Ru is dead. Neither you nor I know what will happen next. But at least you won't be a part of the story anymore."

"How am I going to be able to live without knowing how it all ends?"

"I'll try to help you."

"What will happen to San?"

"No doubt the police will find witnesses who will say that a Chinese man who shot another Chinese man. But nobody will be able to finger San."

"He saved my life."

"He probably saved his own life by killing Ya Ru."

"But who is this man that everybody's afraid of?"

Ho shook her head. "I don't know if I can answer that. In many ways he's a representative of the new China that neither Hong Qiu nor I nor Ma Li, nor even San for that matter, want to have anything to do with. There are major struggles going on in our country about what's going to happen next. What the future is going to look like. Nobody knows; nothing is assured. You can only do what you think is right."

"Such as killing Ya Ru?"

"That was necessary."

Birgitta went into the kitchen and drank a glass of water. When she put the glass down, she knew that she had to go home now. Everything that was still unclear would have to wait. All she wanted to do was to go home, to get away from London and everything that had happened.

Ho accompanied her in a taxi to Heathrow. After a wait of four hours, she succeeded in finding a seat on a flight to Copenhagen. Ho wanted to wait until the plane had left, but Birgitta asked her to leave.

When she got back to Helsingborg, she opened a bottle of wine and emptied it during the course of the night. She slept most of the next day. She was woken up by Staffan's call to say that their boat trip was over. She couldn't stop herself from bursting into tears.

"What's the matter? Has something happened?"

"No, nothing. I'm tired."

"Should we pack up and come home?"

"No. It's nothing. If you want to help, just believe me when I say it's nothing. Tell me about your sailing adventure."

They spoke for a long time. She insisted on his telling her in detail about their trip, about their plans for that evening and for the next day. When they finished talking, she had calmed herself down.

The following day she declared herself fit again and went back to work. She also made a telephone call to Ho.

"Soon I'll have lots to tell you," said Ho.

"I promise to listen. How's San?"

"He's agitated, scared, and he misses his mother. But he's strong."

After hanging up Birgitta remained seated at the kitchen table.

She closed her eyes.

The image of the man lying in a heap over the

table in the hotel dining room was slowly fading away, and soon hardly any of it remained.

36

A few days before Midsummer Birgitta Roslin conducted her last trial before vacation. She and Staffan had rented a cottage on the island of Bornholm. They would stay there for three weeks, and the children would come to visit, one after the other. The trial, which she estimated would take two days, concerned three women and a man who had been robbing people in parking lots and roadside camping sites. Two of the women came from Romania; the man and the third woman were Swedish. What struck Roslin most was the brutality displayed, especially by the youngest of the women on two occasions, when they had attacked people in campers at overnight trailer parks. She had hit one of the victims, an elderly man from Germany, so hard on the head with a hammer that it split his skull. The man had survived, but if the hammer had landed an inch either way he could well have died. On the other occasion she had stabbed a woman with a screwdriver that missed her heart by a fraction of an inch.

The prosecutor, Palm, had described the gang as "entrepreneurs active in various branches of criminal activity." Besides spending nights touring parking lots between Helsingborg and Varberg, they had also spent days stealing from stores, especially fashion boutiques and salesrooms specializing in electronic equipment. Using specially prepared suitcases whose linings had been ripped out and replaced by metal foil, so that the alarm didn't go off when they left the stores, they had stolen goods worth almost a million kronor before they were caught. But they made the mistake of returning to the same fashion boutique near Halmstad and were recognized by the staff. They all confessed, and the stolen goods were recovered. To the surprise of the police, which Birgitta shared, they did not argue and blame one another when it came to sorting out who did what.

It was rainy and chilly the morning she walked to the courthouse. It was also mainly in the mornings that she was still troubled by the events that culminated in the London hotel.

She had spoken to Ho twice on the telephone. Both times she was disappointed because she thought Ho had been evasive, not telling her what happened after the shooting drama. But Ho had insisted that Birgitta must be patient.

"The truth is never simple," Ho said. "It's only in the Western world that you think knowledge is something you can acquire quickly and easily. It takes time. The truth never hurries."

But she had been told one piece of information by Ho, something that frightened her almost more than anything else. The police had discovered in the dead Ya Ru's hand a small silk bag containing the remains of extremely fine powder made from broken glass. The British detectives had been unable to work out what it was, but Ho told Birgitta it was an old, sophisticated Chinese method of killing people.

She had been as close to death as that. Sometimes, but always when she was alone, she was stricken by violent sobbing attacks. She hadn't even mentioned this to Staffan. She had kept it to herself ever since getting back home from London. Staffan had no idea of how she really felt.

A week after Ya Ru's death, she received a call from somebody she would have preferred not to talk to: Lars Emanuelsson.

"Time passes," he said. "Any news?"

For a brief moment she was afraid that Lars Emanuelsson had somehow found out that Birgitta Roslin was the intended victim in the London hotel.

"Nothing at all," she said. "I don't suppose the police in Hudiksvall have changed their minds, have they?"

"About the dead man being the murderer? An insignificant, unimportant, presumably mentally defective man who commits the most brutal mass murder in Swedish criminal history? It might just be true, of course. But I know that many people wonder. Such as me. And you."

"I don't think about it. I've put it behind me."

"I don't think that's quite true."

"You can think whatever you like. What do you want? I'm busy."

"How are things with your contacts in Hudiksvall? Are you still talking to Vivi Sundberg?"

"No. Will you please go away now?"

"Obviously I want you to get in touch with me when you do have something to report. My experience tells me that there are still an awful lot of surprises concealed behind those terrible goings-on in that little village up north."

"I'm hanging up now."

She wondered how much longer Lars Emanuelsson would continue pestering her. But perhaps she would miss his persistence when it finally stopped.

That morning shortly before Midsummer she came to her office, gathered together all the documents relating to the case, spoke to one of the court secretaries about a date in the fall for sentencing, then headed for the courtroom. The moment she entered it she noticed Ho sitting in the back row of the public gallery, in the same seat as the last time she'd been in Helsingborg.

She raised a hand in greeting and could see that Ho smiled back at her. She scribbled a couple of lines on a scrap of paper, explaining to Ho that there would be an adjournment for lunch at noon. She beckoned to one of the ushers and pointed out Ho. He took her the note; Ho read it and nodded to Birgitta.

Then Birgitta turned her attention to the sorry-looking rabble in the dock. When it was time to pause for lunch, they had reached a stage in the proceedings that indicated there would be no problem in concluding matters the following day.

She met Ho in the street, where she was waiting under a tree in full blossom.

"I take it something's happened and that's why you're here?" she said.

"No."

"I can meet you this evening. Where are you staying?"

"In Copenhagen. With friends."

"Am I wrong in thinking you've got something important to tell me?"

"Everything is clearer now. That's why I'm here. And I've brought something for you."

"What?"

Ho shook her head. "We can talk about that this evening. What have they done? The gang on trial?"

"Robbery. Violent assault. But not murder."

"I've been observing them. They're all frightened of you."

"I don't think so. But they know that I'm the one who's going to decide their sentences. Given all the trouble they've caused, that probably feels pretty scary."

Birgitta suggested they should have lunch, but Ho declined, saying she had other things to do. Afterward Birgitta wondered what Ho could have to do in a town like Helsingborg that was totally unknown to her.

The trial continued slowly but relentlessly, and

when Birgitta closed proceedings for the day, they had progressed as far as she had hoped.

Ho was waiting outside the courthouse. As Staffan was on a train to Gothenburg, Birgitta suggested that Ho should come home with her. She could see that Ho was hesitant.

"I'm on my own. My husband's away. My children live in other towns. So you needn't be afraid of meeting anybody."

"But I'm not alone. I have San with me."

"Where is he?"

Ho pointed to the other side of the street. San was leaning against a wall.

"Call him over here," said Birgitta. "Then all three of us can go to my house."

San seemed to be less disturbed now than he had been in the chaotic circumstances of their first meeting. Birgitta could see that he took after his mother: he had Hong Qiu's face, and something of her smile.

"How old are you?" she asked him.

"Twenty-two."

His English was just as perfect as Hong Qiu's and Ho's.

They sat in the living room. San wanted coffee, while Ho drank tea. Set up on the table was the board game Birgitta had bought while in Beijing. In addition to her purse, Ho was holding a paper bag. She produced from it several pages of handwritten Chinese. And she also took out a notepad with an English translation.

"Ya Ru had an apartment in London. One of my friends knew Lang, who was his housekeeper. She prepared his meals and surrounded him with the silence he craved. She let us into the apartment, and we found a diary, which is where these extracts come from. I've translated part of what he wrote, which explains why most of this business took place. Not everything, but all the aspects we can understand. There were some motives that only Ya Ru could explain."

"He was a powerful man, according to what you've told me. That must mean that his death has attracted a lot of attention in China?"

San, who had said nothing so far, was the one who responded.

"Nothing. No attention at all, just silence—the kind of silence Shakespeare writes about. 'The rest is silence.' Ya Ru was so powerful that others who were just as powerful have succeeded in hushing up what happened. It's as if Ya Ru never existed. We think that a lot of people were pleased or relieved when he died, even among those regarded as his friends. Ya Ru was dangerous. He collected knowledge that he used to destroy his enemies, or those he regarded as dangerous competitors. Now all his companies are being wound down, silence is being bought, everything is stiffening up and turning into a concrete wall separating him and his fate from both official history and those of us who are still alive."

Birgitta leafed through the papers lying on her table. "Shall I read them now?"

"No. Later, when you're alone."

"And I don't need to be afraid?"

"No."

"Will I understand what happened to Hong Qiu?"

"He killed her. Not with his own hands; somebody else did it for him. And was killed in turn by Ya Ru. One death covered up for the other. Nobody could believe that Ya Ru had killed his sister—apart from the most astute observers, who knew how Ya Ru thought about himself and others. But what's remarkable and something incomprehensible is how he could kill his sister and yet at the same time value his family, his forefathers, above all else. There's something contradictory there, a riddle we'll never be able to solve. Ya Ru was powerful. He was feared for his intelligence and his ruthlessness. But perhaps he was also ill."

"In what way?"

"He was possessed by a hatred that corroded his personality. Perhaps he really was out of his mind."

"There's one thing that has puzzled me. What were they actually doing in Africa?"

"There's a plan that involves China sending millions of its poor peasants to various African countries. Political and economic structures are currently being put in place that make some of these poor African countries dependent on China. For Ya Ru this was a cynical repetition of the colonialism practiced earlier by the Western world. For him this was a farsighted solution. But for Hong Qiu, and for me and Ma Li and lots of others, this is an attack on the very foundations of the China we have helped to build up."

"I don't understand," said Birgitta. "China is a dictatorship. Freedom is limited at every turn; justice is weak. What exactly are you trying to defend?"

"China is a poor country. The economic development everybody talks about has only benefited a limited part of the population. If this way of leading China into the future continues, with a gap between the rich and the poor growing wider all the time, it will end up in catastrophe. China will be thrust back once more into hopeless chaos. Or fascist structures will become dominant. We are defending the hundreds of millions of peasants who, when all's said and done, are the ones whose labor is producing the wealth on which developments are based. Developments they are benefiting from less and less."

"But I still don't understand. Ya Ru on one side, Hong Qiu on the other? Suddenly discussion is cut short, and he kills his own sister?"

"The battle of wills currently taking place in China is about life and death. The poor versus the rich, those without power versus those with it all. It's about people who are growing more and more angry as they see everything they have fought for being destroyed, and those who see opportunities to make their own fortunes and achieve positions of power they could previously never dream of. That is when people die."

Birgitta turned to look at San. "Tell me about your mother."

"Didn't you know her?"

"I met her, but I can't say that I knew her."

"It wasn't easy to be her child. She was strong, determined, often considerate; but she could also be angry and spiteful. I freely admit that I was scared of her. But I loved her, because she tried to see herself as a part of something bigger. To her it was just as natural to help a drunken man onto his feet when he falls over in the street as it was to conduct intensive discussions about politics. For me she was more of a person to look up to than somebody who was simply my mother. Nothing was easy. But I miss her and know that I now have to live with that sense of loss."

"What are you going to do?"

"I'm going to be a doctor. But I'm taking a year off. To mourn. To try to understand what it involves, living without her."

"Who is your father?"

"He died a long time ago. He wrote poetry. All I know about him is that he died shortly after I was born. My mother never said much about him, only that he was a good man and a revolutionary. The only part of him left in my life is a photograph of him holding a puppy in his arms."

They spoke at length that night about China. Birgitta admitted that as a young woman she had wanted to be a Red Guard in Sweden. But the whole time she was waiting impatiently for the moment when she could read the papers Ho had brought with her.

At about ten she called a taxi to take Ho and San to the railroad station.

"When you've finished reading," said Ho, "get in touch."

"Is there an end to this story?"

Ho thought for a moment before answering.

"There's always an end," she said. "Even in this case. But the end is always the beginning of something else. The periods we write into our lives are always provisional, in one way or another."

Birgitta watched the taxi drive away, then sat down with the translation of Ya Ru's diary. Staffan wasn't due back home until the following day. She hoped she'd have finished reading by then. It was no more than twenty pages, but Ho's handwriting was hard to decipher because the letters were so small.

What exactly was it, this diary she was reading? Afterward, when she looked back on that evening alone in the house, with traces of Ho's perfume still in the room, she knew she should have been able to work out for herself most of what had happened. Or, rather, she should have understood, but refused to accept what she really did understand.

Naturally, all the time she was wondering about what Ho had left out. She could have asked, but knew that she wouldn't get an answer. There were traces of secrets that she would never understand, locks she would never be able to open. There were references to people in the past, another diary that seemed to have been written as a sort of counter to the one JA had written, the man who became a foreman on the building sites of the American cross-continental railroad.

Over and over again Ya Ru returned in his diary to his frustration at Hong Qiu's failure to understand that the path China was now following was the only right possibility, and that people like Ya Ru must be the controlling influences. Birgitta began to realize that Ya Ru had many psychopathic traits that, reading between the lines, he even seemed to be aware of himself.

Nowhere could she find any redeeming features in his character. No expression of doubt, of a guilty conscience with regard to the death of Hong Qiu, who after all was his own sister. She wondered if Ho had edited the text in order to depict Ya Ru as a brutal man. She even wondered if Ho had invented the whole diary herself. But she couldn't really believe that. San had committed murder. Just as in the Icelandic sagas, he had taken bloody revenge for the death of his mother.

By the time she had read through Ho's translation twice, it was almost midnight. There were many obscurities in what Ho had written, many details that still weren't explained. The red ribbon—what was its significance? Only Liu Xin could have explained that, if he had still been alive. There were threads that would continue to hang loose, perhaps forever.

But what still needed to be done? What could or must she do on the basis of the insight she now had? She would spend part of her vacation thinking about it. When Staffan was fishing, for instance—an activity she found deadly boring. And early in the mornings, when he was reading his historical novels or biographies of jazz musicians and she went for walks on her own. There would be time for her to formulate the letter she would send to the police in Hudiksvall. Once she'd done that she'd be able to put away the box containing memories of her parents. It would all be over as far as she was concerned. Hesjövallen would fade slowly out of her consciousness, be transformed into a pale memory. Even though she would never forget what had happened, of course.

They went to Bornholm, had changeable weather, and enjoyed living in the cottage they had rented. The children came and went, days passed by in an atmosphere generally characterized by drowsy well-being. To their surprise Anna turned up, having completed her long Asian journey, and astonished them even more by announcing that she would be embarking on a political science degree in Lund in the fall.

On several occasions Birgitta decided that the time had come to tell Staffan what had happened, both in Beijing and then later in London. But she didn't—

there was no point in telling him if he would never be able to get over that she'd kept it from him. It would hurt him and be interpreted as a lack of confidence and understanding. It wasn't worth the risk, so she continued to say nothing.

She did not say anything to Karin Wiman either about her visit to London and the happenings there.

It all stayed bottled up inside her, a scar that nobody else could see.

On Monday, August 7, both she and Staffan went back to work. The previous evening they had sat down at long last and discussed their life together. It was as if both of them, without having mentioned it in advance, realized that they couldn't start another working year without at least beginning to talk about the decline of their marriage. What Birgitta regarded as the major breakthrough was that her husband raised the question of their almost nonexistent sex life of his own accord, without her having put the idea into his head. He regretted the situation and was horrified not to have the desire or the ability. In response to her direct question he said that no one else attracted him. It was simply a matter of a lack of desire, which worried him but was something he usually preferred not to think about.

"What are you going to do about it?" she asked. "We can't live another year without touching each other. I simply couldn't take it."

"I'll try to get help. I don't find it any easier than you do. But I also find it difficult to talk about."

"You're talking about it now."

"Because I realize that I have to."

"I hardly know what you're thinking anymore. I sometimes look at you in the morning and think that you're a stranger."

"You express yourself better than I ever could. But I sometimes feel exactly the same thing. Perhaps not as strongly."

"Have you really accepted that we could live the rest of our lives like this?"

"No. But I've avoided thinking about it. I promise to call a therapist."

"Do you want me to come with you?"

He shook his head. "Not the first time. Later, if necessary."

"Do you understand what this means to me?"

"I hope so."

"It's not going to be easy. But with luck we'll be able to get past this. It's been a bit like wandering through a desert."

He started his day on August 7 by climbing aboard a train to Stockholm at 8:12 in the morning. She didn't arrive in her office until about ten o'clock. As Hans Mattsson was still on vacation, she had responsibility for all the district court's activities and began with a meeting for the legal and secretarial staff. Once she was convinced that everything was under control, she withdrew to her office and wrote the long letter to

Vivi Sundberg that she had spent the summer composing in her head.

She had obviously asked herself what she wanted or at least hoped to achieve. The truth, naturally; the hope that all the happenings in Hesjövallen would be explained, including the murder of the old hotel owner. But was she also looking for some kind of redress for the distrust shown her by the police in Hudiksvall? How much was personal vanity, and how much was a genuine attempt to persuade the investigation team that the man who had committed suicide, despite his confession, had nothing to do with it?

In a way it also had to do with her mother. In searching for the truth Birgitta wanted to pay tribute to her mother's foster parents, who had met such a grisly end.

It took her two hours to write the letter. She reread it several times before putting it in an envelope and addressing it to the police in Hudiksvall, attention Vivi Sundberg. Then she put it in the tray for outgoing mail in the reception area downstairs and opened the windows in her office wide in the hope of blowing out all thought of the victims in those isolated houses up in Hesjövallen.

She spent the rest of the day reading a consultative document from the Department of Justice regarding what seemed to be a never-ending process of reorganization affecting all aspects of the Swedish judiciary.

But she also made time to dig out one of her unfinished pop songs and attempted to write a couple more lines.

The idea had come to her during the summer. It would be called "A Walk on the Beach." But she found it hard going, today especially. She crumpled up her failed attempts and tossed them into the trash before locking the unfinished text in one of her desk drawers. Nevertheless, she was determined not to give up.

At six o'clock she switched off her computer and left her office.

On the way out, she noticed that the mail out-box was now empty.

37

Liu Xin hid among the trees on the edge of the forest: he had arrived at last. He had not forgotten that Ya Ru had told him this was the most important mission he would ever be given. It was his task to bring matters to a conclusion, all the shocking events that had started more than one hundred years ago.

As he stood there Liu Xin thought about Ya Ru, who had given him the job he was about to perform, given him the necessary equipment, and exhorted him to be efficient. Ya Ru had explained everything that had happened in the past. The journey had continued for many years, back and forth over oceans and continents, travels filled with fear and death, unbearable persecution—and now came the necessary ending, the revenge.

Those who had made the journey had passed on a long time ago. One lay dead at the bottom of the sea; others lay in unmarked graves. During all these years a constant lament had risen up from those resting places. He had now been given the task of putting an end to that painful dirge.

Liu Xin had snow under his feet, and was surrounded by freezing-cold air. It was January 12, 2006. Earlier in the day he had noticed a thermometer saying it was negative nine degrees Celsius. He kept shuffling his feet in an attempt to keep them warm. It was still early in the evening. In several of the houses he could see from where he was standing that the lights were on, or in some windows the bluish glow from television screens. He strained his ears but couldn't hear a single sound. Not even dogs. Liu Xin thought that people in this part of the world kept dogs to guard them during the night. He had seen tracks in the snow, but gathered that they were being kept indoors.

He had wondered if the dogs inside the houses would cause him problems, but he'd dismissed the thought. Nobody suspected what was going to happen; no dogs would be able to stop him.

He took off a glove and checked the time. A quar-

THE MAN FROM BEIJING

ter to nine. There was still time before the lights went out. He put the glove back on and thought about Ya Ru and all his stories about the dead people who had traveled so far. Every member of Ya Ru's family had been involved in part of the journey. By a strange coincidence the one who was destined to put an end to it was Liu Xin, who was not a relation. It filled him with deep thoughts. Ya Ru trusted him as if he were his brother.

He heard a car in the distance, but it was not approaching. It was on the main road. In this country, he thought, during the silent winter nights, sound travels a very long way—as if over water.

He continued shuffling his feet. How would he react when it was all over? Despite everything, was there a tiny part of his consciousness, his conscience, that he was not familiar with? Everything had gone according to plan in Nevada. But you could never know, especially as this task was so much bigger.

His thoughts wandered. He suddenly remembered his own father, who had been a low-ranking party official, and how he had been taunted and mistreated during the Cultural Revolution. His father had told him how he and the other "capitalist swine" had had their faces painted white by the Red Guards. Because evil was always white in color.

Now he tried to think of the people in the silent houses that way. They all had white faces; they were the demons of evil.

The lights gradually went out. Two of the houses were now in darkness. He waited. The dead had been waiting for more than a century, he only needed to cope with a few hours.

He took off his right glove and felt with his fingers the sword hanging at his side. The steel was cold; the sharp edge could easily cut through his skin. It was a Japanese sword he had come across by chance on a visit to Shanghai. Somebody had told him about an old collector who still had a few of these much-prized swords left after the Japanese occupation in the 1930s. He had found his way to the unremarkable little shop and not hesitated once he had held the sword in his hand. He had bought it on the spot and taken it to a blacksmith, who had repaired the handle and sharpened the blade until it cut like a razor.

He gave a start. The door of one of the houses opened. He drew back farther into the trees. A man came out onto the steps with a dog. A lamp over the door illuminated the snow-covered yard. Liu Xin gripped the sword tightly, screwed up his eyes, and carefully observed the dog's movements. What would happen if it picked up his scent? That would ruin all his plans. If he was forced to kill the dog he wouldn't hesitate. But what would the man do, the man standing in the doorway smoking?

The dog suddenly stopped and sniffed the air. For a brief moment Liu Xin thought it had detected him. But then it started running around the yard once more.

The man shouted to the dog, which ran inside immediately. The door closed. Shortly afterward the light went out.

He continued waiting. At midnight, when the only light came from a television screen, he noticed that it had started snowing. Flakes fell onto his outstretched hand like feathers. Like plum blossoms, he thought. But snow doesn't smell; it doesn't breathe like flowers breathe.

Twenty minutes later the television was switched off. It was still snowing. He took out from his anorak pocket a small pair of binoculars fitted with a night-vision device and slowly scanned all the houses in the village. He couldn't see any lights. He put the binoculars away and took a deep breath. In his mind's eye he envisaged the picture that Ya Ru had described to him so many times.

A ship. People on the deck like ants, eagerly waving with handkerchiefs and hats. But he couldn't see any faces.

No faces, only arms and hands, waving.

He waited a bit longer. Then he walked slowly over the road. He was carrying a little flashlight in one hand and his sword in the other.

He approached the house on the very edge of the village, heading west. He stopped to listen one last time.

Then he went inside.

Vivi,

This narrative is in a diary written by a man called Ya Ru. He had been given an oral report by the person who first went to Nevada, where he killed several people, and then continued to Hesjövallen. I want you to read it so that you can understand all the other things I've written in this letter.

None of these people are still alive. But the truth of what happened in Hesjövallen was bigger, far different from what we all thought. I'm not sure that everything I've written can be proved. It's probably not possible. Just as, for instance, I can't explain why the red ribbon ended up in the snow at Hesjövallen. We know who took it there, but that's all.

Lars-Erik Valfridsson, who hanged himself in a police cell, was not guilty. At least his relatives ought to be told that. We can only speculate about why he took the blame on himself.

I understand that this letter will wreak havoc with your investigation. But what we are all searching for, of course, is clarity. I hope that what I have written can contribute to that.

I have tried to include everything I know about the case in this letter. The day we stop searching for the truth, which is never objective but under the best circumstances built on facts, is the day on which our system of justice collapses completely.

I'm back at work again now. I'm in Helsingborg and will expect you to be in touch, as there are a lot of questions, many of them difficult.

With best wishes,
Birgitta Roslin
August 7, 2006

Epilogue

Birgitta Roslin did some shopping in her usual store on the way home from work that same day in August. While standing in line at the checkout, she took one of the evening papers from its stand and leafed through it. On one page she read in passing that a lone wolf had been shot in a village north of Gävle.

Neither she nor anybody else knew that the same wolf had crossed into Sweden from Norway through Vauldalen one day in January. It had been hungry and not had anything to eat since finding the remains of a dead moose in Österdalarna.

The wolf had continued eastward, passed Nävjarna, crossed over the frozen Ljusnan River at Kårböle, and then vanished again into the vast forests.

Now it was lying dead on a farm near Gävle.

Nobody knew that on the morning of January 13 it had come to a remote village in Hälsingland by the name of Hesjövallen.

Everything had been covered in snow then. Now summer would soon be over.

The hamlet of Hesjövallen was empty. Nobody lived there anymore. In some of the gardens rowanberries were already glowing red, with nobody to admire the splendid show of color.

Fall was closing in on Norrland. People were beginning to prepare themselves for another long winter.

Author's Note

This is a novel. That means that what I have written has a background in reality, but not all parts are a realistic reproduction of events that took place. I don't think there is anywhere by the name of Hesjövallen—I hope my scrutiny of maps was sufficiently meticulous. But that the president of Zimbabwe is Robert Mugabe at the time of writing is an indisputable fact.

In other words, I have written about what could have happened, not necessarily what actually did happen. In the world of fiction that is not only a possibility, but the basic prerequisite.

But even in a novel, the most important details ought to be correctly presented, whether they refer to the presence of birds in present-day Beijing or whether or not a judge has a sofa provided by the National Judiciary Administration in his or her office.

Many people have assisted me in my work on this book. First and foremost, of course, Robert Johnson, who once again has worked persistently and meticulously with regard to establishing facts. But there are many more who, if named, would make this list very long. Not least many people in Africa with whom I have discussed the book.

I am not going to mention anybody else by name but hereby express my sincere gratitude to everybody concerned. The story itself is naturally my own responsibility and nobody else's.

Henning Mankell
Maputo, Mozambique,
January 2008

A NOTE ABOUT THE AUTHOR

Internationally best-selling novelist and
playwright Henning Mankell has received
the German Tolerance Prize and the U.K.'s
Golden Dagger Award and has been nomi-
nated for a **Los Angeles Times** Book Prize
three times. His Kurt Wallander mysteries
have been published in thirty-three countries and consistently top the best-seller
lists in Europe. He divides his time
between Sweden and Maputo, Mozambique, where he has worked as the director
of Teatro Avenida since 1985.

www.henningmankell.com